KU-283-672

GIFTED

DONALD HOUNAM

CORGI BOOKS

GIFTED
A CORGI BOOK 978 0 552 57187 6

Published in Great Britain by Corgi Books,
an imprint of Random House Children's Publishers UK
A Penguin Random House Company

This edition published 2015

1 3 5 7 9 10 8 6 4 2

Copyright © Donald Hounam, 2015
Cover artwork © Sean Freeman, 2015

The right of Donald Hounam to be identified as the author of this work has been
asserted in accordance with the Copyright, Designs and Patents Act 1988.

All rights reserved. No part of this publication may be reproduced, stored in a
retrieval system, or transmitted in any form or by any means, electronic, mechanical,
photocopying, recording or otherwise, without the prior permission of the publishers.

Penguin Random House is committed to a sustainable future for
our business, our readers and our planet. This book is made from
Forest Stewardship Council® certified paper.

Set in Baskerville MT 12/16.5pt by Falcon Oast Graphic Art Ltd.

RANDOM HOUSE CHILDREN'S PUBLISHERS UK
61–63 Uxbridge Road, London W5 5SA

www.**randomhousechildrens**.co.uk
www.**totallyrandombooks**.co.uk
www.**randomhouse**.co.uk

Addresses for companies within The Random House Group Limited can be found
at: www.randomhouse.co.uk/offices.htm

THE RANDOM HOUSE GROUP Limited Reg. No. 954009

A CIP catalogue record for this book is available from the British Library.

Printed and bound by CPI Group (UK) Ltd, Croydon, CR0 4YY

For Cecily

CHAPTER ONE
Fortitude

I've been up all night, while the cat's still fresh.

And I'm wrecked. I've washed the dead animal in exorcised water, fumigated it in rosemary smoke, held it up to the four points of the compass and rattled through all the formulae of purification. I've got the whiskers in a bowl, and the skin neatly folded up in a bucket on the floor.

I hinge back the ribcage and gaze down at the liver, lungs, heart and the rest, all stuffed in like dirty laundry in a bag. I feel queasy and kind of guilty . . .

But dead is dead, and I need the parts. I can use the teeth for a couple of defensive spells; the eyes and whiskers will cook up for elementals; and a few rather unpleasant Presences of my acquaintance are partial to dried cat's liver.

Time flies when you're having fun. My studio used to be a chapel and it's got these thick stone walls, so it's like the outside world doesn't exist. The fire up at the east end, where the altar used to be, has burned down

1

to a dull glow. I've got all sorts of muck all over my gloves and the side of my nose is itching like mad. As I rub my cheek against my shoulder, the lamps flicker spookily, like something is passing through . . .

I play around with dead people all the time, up at the mortuary, so the cat really shouldn't bother me. But it's creeping me out, just lying there with its mouth open, its eyes closed and its guts glistening. It doesn't look at all happy and I feel like I ought to apologise. I glance up at my magic watch, hanging from a hook out of harm's way. Nearly four thirty. Just get it done, Frank. I fumble for my tweezers . . .

And there's this sharp click behind me.

I nearly jump out of my skin. I look round, heart pounding, and see that my door has locked itself and the inside surface is rippling like the wind churning up the surface of a lake.

Which means trouble.

I can hear voices coming through this hole I've hacked in the wall between my studio and the corridor. Call me paranoid, but I don't like surprises. The termites – they're these monks who feed me and keep an eye on me and beat me up when they're stuck for entertainment – well, I don't trust them. And this is a particularly toxic termite: a voice I've come to know and love.

'Have you ever met a sorcerer before?'

'Oh yeah.' A girl's voice. What's going on?

'They're difficult.' Brother Thomas: my least favourite termite. Always manages to wind me up. The door doesn't think much of him either. I can see the wood bristling now, like the hairs along a dog's back.

'Personally, I'd burn the lot of them.' He knocks hard on the door. It makes this low, dangerous growling noise.

It's not just the five quid – the going rate for a dead moggy round the back streets of Doughnut City – it's the hours I spent purifying and dismantling the corpse. And now I'll just have to dump it along with all the bits I wanted.

I slam a cover over it: disassembled animals can create a bad first impression. I drape a cloth over the bucket containing the skin. I look around. The place niffs a bit, so I throw a few sprigs of rosemary into the brazier. I chuck a couple of books into the safety of the cabinet and run around turning down the lamps. I grab a pair of underpants hanging over the back of a chair. If they weren't dirty before, they're dirty now: I wipe the blood off my hands and toss the pants in the laundry basket. I pull on a shirt. I'm neat and presentable. Maybe they'll go away.

'Brother Tobias!'

'Get lost, parrot-face!' I yell.

The door handle rattles.

Just so you know to avoid them, the termites are

3

Agrippine monks, a small order established in 1747 to keep a lid on sorcerers like me, living out in the big bad world. I've been with them for more than a year but they're still a mystery to me. This arse knows about the door – he's got the scars to prove it. Like, maybe he's stupid, but is he deaf too? Can't he hear it growling? He starts hammering. There's a vicious snarling noise. Even on this side, the surface of the door bulges and twists.

A long, gratifying silence. Then his voice, a trembling whisper: 'You talk to him.'

Hers: 'This is Detective Constable Marvell an' I don't need this shit!'

Oh hell, not her again! Shouldn't have ignored the scryer. I tell the door to open. Which it does, with all the trimmings: sinister creak, flickering lamps and an icy draught across the floor.

She's come dressed as a deckchair. Red duffel coat with one toggle missing, blue jeans, a yellow bag over her shoulder. She's about my age: dead skinny, with curly black hair and pale skin and that weird darting gaze that all tatties have.

While her eyes flicker round the studio, Brother Thomas's fat, self-satisfied gob looms over her shoulder, his bald skull shining greasily in the gaslight. He's sucking one finger, so the door must have taken a chunk out of him.

She steps inside, still checking the joint out. It's not

what you'd call homely. Grey stone. No windows, unless you count a tiny circle of stained glass high on the west wall, above the stove.

She cranes her neck to stare up at the stone ribbing across the ceiling. Her gaze flashes over my stuff: shelves of books, cabinets of metal and glass instruments, a wire cage with a couple of white rats scuffling around inside it. Brother Thomas tries to follow her in. Shifty little weasel: he's never actually got inside and it bugs the hell out of him. He manages one step before the door slams in his face.

She jumps, but she doesn't turn to look. She stands there, working hard at staying cool, looks me up and down. 'You're up early.'

'What do you want?' I'm not going to pretend I'm pleased to see her.

'A bit of light wouldn't hurt.'

'I like it like this. Helps me think.'

'Dark teenage thoughts, I bet.' She sniffs. 'What died?' She pulls a flat, round silver case out of her bag and waves it at me. 'I scried you. Why didn't you answer?'

'Coz I saw it was you.' Her face twitches and I realise I've upset her, which is good. 'Never even heard it, if you really wanna know. I was busy.'

Her name's Magdalena Marvell. Really. We've never actually worked together; but I did something incredibly stupid a few weeks back – took an eyeball

5

from a corpse in the mortuary, if you must know. It was for a good cause, OK? And nobody would have cared, if she hadn't gone and shopped me.

She's staring up at a tinted photograph of an elderly Japanese gent dressed like a Christmas tree: his holiness Pope Innocent XVII. Finally she mumbles, 'Wasn't my fault.'

'Ah. I thought maybe you'd come to apologise. You got me in a load of shit.'

She just looks at me. After a bit I start to think, are my flies open? Is there toothpaste round my mouth?

'So, what *are* you doing here?' I ask.

She's gazing down at the floor, at the smeared remains of a chalk circle scattered with symbols. The smoke from the rosemary in the brazier wafts around her as she turns and walks her fingertips along the bench that runs down the centre of the nave: over charts, around glass jars, flasks and phials, paper packets, bunches of herbs, balances, knives, a mortar and pestle – your standard Junior Sorcerer's kit. She peers across at the blackboard behind the door, covered with scrawled code that even I can't make sense of any more, but which could still get me roasted in front of a large, appreciative crowd.

'Clue,' she says. 'It's not a social visit.'

Like I said, it's been a long night and I'm slow to catch on. I just stand there with my mouth open until she folds her arms and says:

6

'You're still the junior forensic sorcerer, yeah?'

'Far as I know.'

'So are you coming?'

'Where?'

'You'll find out when we get there.'

I duck into what used to be the south transept, and dive under the bed.

'What are you looking for?'

'My boots.'

'There's a pair by the door.'

I know there is, but I need a few moments to get my thoughts straight. It's like this every time a new job comes up. I love the buzz, but I'm already making this list in my head of all the things that can go wrong . . .

I crawl out and see that she's found something new to stare at: a charred book lying on a red velvet cushion, under a glass dome. 'What's this?'

'You're the tatty.'

I get what I'm trying to provoke: her angry look. She lifts the dome and picks up the book. Blackened fragments of paper fall away as she turns it to examine the lettering down what's left of the spine.

'*In Defence of Sorcery.*' She looks up at me. 'Does sorcery need defending?'

'That didn't set fire to itself.'

'Author's name's been scratched out before it was set alight. Title page burned away . . .' She lifts the book to her nose and sniffs at it. 'Published here, though – that's the glue the cathedral press uses.' Another sniff: tatties stick their noses in things a lot. 'Set alight with consecrated oil – the stuff they use in churches—'

'And termite nests.'

'Huh?'

'I found it outside my door.' I'm lying back on my bed, one foot in the air, tying my bootlaces.

She sniffs again and pulls a face. 'Did *you* pee on it?'

'No, that was the generous donor.'

She drops the book on the cushion and goes across to wash her hands at the sink in the corner.

'What d'you keep it for?'

'A reminder that I, too, am combustible.' I roll forwards, onto my feet. 'Come on then.'

But she's back at the bench, turning up the lamp. Will we ever get out of here? She picks up a notebook that I forgot to hide. I grab it and toss it into a corner. That's the trouble with tatties; they can't leave anything alone. She's reaching for the cover over the cat . . .

'Pick a card.' I grab a pack of Tarot cards and shuffle them. 'Any card.'

I fan them out. She hesitates, then takes one.

'Remember it.'

She's peering at the design on the face. 'What is it?'

Unless my card-sharping skills have deserted me, it's *La Force* – Strength or Fortitude – a woman holding a lion's jaws open.

'Just remember what it looks like. You can do that,

8

can't you? Put it back.' I shuffle the cards, riffle them dramatically . . . and chuck them in the fire. 'So let's go.' I grab a woollen hat from the antlers of a stag's skull.

'Why'd he call you "Brother Tobias"? The monk—'

'The termites use my stage name. You can call me Frank.'

'How old are you, Frank? Fifteen?'

'Nearly sixteen. And you, Magdalena?'

'Sixteen.' That's peak for a tatty. She's got ten years or so before she burns out. 'An' if you call me that again, I'll kill you.'

I pull on my black leather jerkin and pick up my case. The door opens.

'What about my card?' she says, looking back at the fire. I just shrug and wave her out into the corridor. No sign of the wounded termite; just the gaslight flickering in the draught.

'Don't you want a coat?'

I ignore her. She mutters, 'Your funeral.' The door closes. She watches me set it: a touch, a couple of words. When I turn away, she can't resist stepping back to push it. A section of the door transforms itself into the head of a wolf, snapping and snarling at her. She jumps away, shaking. The wood settles back.

'Simplest spell in the world,' I say. 'I could give you one for your place.'

'Yeah, my mum'd love that. A key's fine. You gotta tell anyone you're going out?'

Bloody cheek! I'm not a prisoner.

I open the outside door and stand at the top of the steps. It's cold and pitch-black. The moon set exactly fifty-seven minutes ago.

How do I know that? I'm a sorcerer, OK? I just know stuff like that. So anyway, there's no sign of dawn yet. I close my eyes and take a deep breath. The termites were out late last night throwing manure around the vegetable garden and it's pretty ripe – but it makes a welcome change from decomposing cat.

I gasp as a sharp elbow digs into my side. Marvell barges past and heads off along the path.

'So where are we going?' I call as she disappears into the darkness.

'Osney. The Bishop's Palace.'

'Who's dead?' I can't see her. I just follow the sound of her feet crunching on the gravel. I hear the whisper of her coat brushing against the hedge; the smell of lavender fills the air.

'Who says anyone's dead?'

'They don't drag me out for stolen bicycles.'

'Prob'ly coz they know you stole 'em.'

I can just make out the monastery chapel now, silhouetted against the dirty brown glow of Doughnut City. Marvell is just this dark shape, bobbing up and down ahead of me. I'm waiting for her to crash into the low wall, just ahead where the path twists. But she makes the turn like she's lived here all her life and whizzes off up a flight of steps.

'All they told me, someone's dead,' she says. 'At the Bishop's Palace. Dunno who.'

She's struggling with a heavy door. I step up to help her, but she pushes me away and throws herself at the black wood. The door bangs back and our feet echo on the stone floor of a corridor that brings us out into the cloister running round the front quadrangle. Water splashes in the fountain.

'Are you spotting it?' I ask.

That's what tatties do: they spot stuff that the rest of the CID are too blind, stupid or lazy to notice. Until they go blind themselves.

'What do you think?'

'Who's the grown-up?'

'Caxton.'

'Oh, great!'

We're at the porter's lodge. 'Shop!' I call. A hatch opens. This kid a couple of years older than me, with buck teeth and tonsured, carroty red hair, stares suspiciously out.

'Brother Andrew! Unleash me on an unsuspecting world.'

He's not blessed with a sense of humour. 'Where are you going?' he whines.

'None of your business.'

'Who's she?'

'None of your business,' Marvell says. Against my better judgement, I'm in danger of beginning to dislike her less than I probably should. 'Open the door, you little squirt.'

Andrew whizzes out and fumbles with a ring of heavy iron keys. The locks scrape. The door creaks open. Marvell steps out into the big wide world.

I put one foot over the threshold . . . and freeze.

There's a single lamp post almost opposite, and a van, painted in blue city police livery, standing beneath it. One of the horses shifts in its harness and I hear a series of soft, splattering thuds. Steam rises from a small pile of dung.

I peer into the shadows along the narrow street. Yesterday was the feast day of Saint Cyprian of Antioch, and since he's the patron saint of sorcerers there was a crowd of protesters out here, yelling for me to come outside and face the music.

I didn't let them bother me, just climbed in and out over the back wall. They seem to have gone, anyway, leaving just a scrawled message on the wall opposite: 'Rot in hell!'

'You comin' or not?' Marvell hisses back at me.

Course I'm coming. It's only a matter of time before I get bored with harming domestic animals and start in on myself again.

Final look up and down the street. All quiet. I step out and as the door slams behind me I realise that although a leather jerkin makes an effective style statement, it won't keep out the arctic wind.

'Told you!' Marvell crows as I pull my hat down over my ears.

As we cross the road, the driver, perched on the box in front of the van, extends his hand towards me, the middle and ring fingers tucked under the thumb, the index and little fingers pointing towards my eyes.

I'm used to ignoring superstitious crap like this. I mean, it's not like it works or anything—

Except that this time he's got lucky because there's the thunder of hoofbeats behind me and a hansom cab comes screaming round the corner.

Unbelievably, Marvell stops dead in the middle of the road and sticks her hand up like a traffic jack. The cabbie hauls on his reins, but can't stop the horse. I take a run and knock her out of the way, just in time. We go flying under the police van's team and her elbow hits the cobbles with a crack.

As I stagger to my feet, spitting out horse shit, the cab door flies open and this guy throws himself out at me.

I grab my case and hit him with it.

Not hard enough. He pulls a knife.

I wonder if, in the interests of fair play, he'd be

prepared to give me a moment to put my case down, open it, and find my own knife.

Guess not.

I'm stumbling backwards, holding the case defensively in front of me. In a situation like this, you get a kind of blinkered vision of the world you're about to leave. I've no idea where Marvell's got to. All I see is a sudden flash of reflected light as the knife slices through the air . . .

There's a loud bang. Me and the guy both look round.

Marvell's holding a pistol, pointed into the sky. As she lowers it threateningly, I notice that my attacker's wearing an armband with an emblem: a burning five-pointed star.

He throws himself back into the cab. The whip cracks. The cab thunders off, the door still flapping.

CHAPTER TWO
Style Counts

'Who the hell was that?' says Marvell.

'Why didn't you shoot him and find out?'

We pile into the van. Marvell falls back into the seat opposite me, clutching her left elbow in her other hand.

'Let me see that,' I offer. But she shoves me away and pulls her elbow closer to her chest.

I hate jack vans. The dirty yellow panelling. The overflowing ashtrays and the stink of stale tobacco. The driver's had enough excitement for one night and isn't taking any more chances; so rather than risk going through the Hole, he takes us the long way round, through Iffley and across the bridges to the Grandpont.

The sleeve of Marvell's coat has a gaping tear in it and she's dripping blood onto the leather seat.

'Christ, I can't go to casualty,' she groans. 'Caxton'll kill me!'

'The hell with Caxton.' That's Marvell's boss. Mine too, sort of. 'I can fix it.'

I knock on the roof and yell at the driver to stop under one of the lamps. I can see Marvell doesn't trust me; she pulls faces and makes hissing noises while I help her out of her coat and sweater. I tear the sleeve of her shirt up to the shoulder.

She's got these scrawny little arms, like she's never lifted anything in her life, and I can see she's self-conscious about them. Her elbow is split open, right on the joint. I can see the bone.

I open my case.

'Bloody hell!' she mutters.

As well she might. One of the customs of the Craft is that your Master presents you with a case when you get your licence. My Master is a big noise in the Society of Sorcerers and a very rich bunny indeed.

The Society, by the way, is big on chastity and massive on obedience, but crap at poverty.

Anyway, my case is crocodile with silver fittings outside, and snakeskin and ivory inside. It's divided into compartments with black silk linings for all the instruments, herbs and other gear I need in the field. There are good thaumaturgic arguments for all this, but frankly other sorcerers seem to get by on calfskin and brass. In short, my case is pretty tacky – and I love it.

I squeeze a few drops of aloe into my palm – I always carry a couple of leaves because I've a tendency to set fire to things, including myself. I sprinkle in comfrey, add a few drops of exorcised water and mix it all together with the tip of a small silver knife.

'In the name of Adonai the most high. In the name of Jehovah the most holy!'

Marvell's eyes go wide with shock as I slap the goo over the wound. I clamp my hand round her elbow, so she can't wriggle loose. It's a simple spell and it works fast, or not at all. I make a shape in the air with the first two fingers of my free hand.

'In the name of the Lord who maketh all things whole. In the name of the Lord who is blessed. In the name of the Lord who healeth the sick.' I do a lot of stuff in threes. I take my hand away. 'You can give it a wipe now.'

She's twisting her arm, staring at her elbow in disbelief. 'That's amazing!'

'It's routine.'

She stares at me for a moment, then she says, 'Suit yourself.' She's prodding her elbow, where the wound has vanished completely. She won't even have a scar. 'That lunatic.' She pulls down her sleeve. 'Who was he, anyway?'

'Didn't you see the badge?' I point to my arm, where he was wearing the burning pentagram emblem, but she just shakes her head. 'He was ASB.'

'Anti-Sorcery . . . Brigade?'

'Brotherhood.'

The protesters I get outside the termite nest are just

17

a nuisance, but the ASB are genuine nutters. I close my case and knock on the roof of the van.

' "Does sorcery need defending?" Huh!'

We pass warehouses and a stockyard, with mad-eyed cattle staring out at us between the bars. Then we're rattling over the main bridge across the Isis. Through the crumbling stone pillars of the balustrade, I can see the wharves along the riverside. The gaslight gleams on the bodies of a couple of big guys, stripped to the waist, stretching up like lost souls in hell to steady a pallet swinging from a crane. And there's a boy, aged maybe eight or nine, perched on a seat at the top of a ladder, checking off a manifest and screaming at dozens more guys chucking stuff into a boat.

Enjoy it while it lasts, kid!

Out in the darkness of midstream, the lights of a chain of barges drift slowly past. Even with the van windows closed, the sinus-clenching stench of rotting rubbish makes the horse shit smeared across my face smell like roses.

Marvell has fastened the torn remains of her shirt-sleeve at the cuff. She looks round for her sweater, sees that I'm wiping my hands on it and grabs it.

'You don't look too hot,' she says.

'I'm fine.' But I'm not. I feel sick and I'm sweating – nervous about what's waiting for me at the palace. Despite all the practice with cats, I've never really got used to seeing people mangled up and spread around the place. With my right index finger, I draw a protective pentagram in the condensation on each window.

'What's that for?' Marvell says.

I shake my head. Without an incantation and some more symbols, the pentagrams have no real power, but they make me feel better.

Marvell leans forward. I slap her hand away before she can draw in the condensation.

'You don't know what it is,' I mutter. 'So don't fiddle.'

She frowns and looks round the van, obviously wondering what to fiddle with next. She makes a grab for my case.

'Leave that alone!' I snap. 'It could have your hand off.'

There's this flicker of anger across her face. She pulls her sweater on and says, 'Never really worked with a sorcerer.'

'Don't worry about me. Just keep Caxton off my back.'

'You've still got horse shit on your face.'

'I may need you to help me with some stuff.' I wipe my shirtsleeve across my face. 'Just here and there. I'll ask.'

'Whatever.'

'Never do more than I ask. Things bite – like my door.'

She nods, but she doesn't like being told what to do.

19

I add insult to injury: 'You'll get the hang of it.' I'm dangerously close to patting her on the knee.

Amazingly, we get there without her strangling me.

From the Oxpens I can see the silhouette of the cathedral looming over the gasworks, the spire still shattered at the top and shrouded in scaffolding after the Montgolfier raids twenty years back.

As we pass under the railway bridge, the early train to London rumbles overhead, spitting out cinders and leaving a plume of steam. We turn left down the Palace Road. In the greengrocer's on the corner, the shop-keeper is holding up a lantern for this kid to write out price tags. The boy turns to stare at us, and the shop-keeper clips him one round the ear.

We rattle along a terrace of crumbling houses to the palace lodge, a dingy Gothic heap of stones with a hole through the middle for carriages to go in and out, and deep ruts worn into the pavement by centuries of metal-bound wheels. There's no security elemental here, just a uniformed jack and a knock-kneed old geezer in tights – some sort of gatekeeper, I suppose. They wave us straight through.

The van drives around some sort of lawn and stops on a paved area in front of a red brick building that's far too big for one bloke, however holy, and must be murder to heat. A couple of torches are burning in brackets hanging out of the wall.

In the middle of the lawn, two uniformed jacks are bent over in an ornamental pond, their trousers rolled up above their knees, fishing around with their hands. And beyond them I can see another jack holding up a lantern while a young guy with white hair pokes around in the bushes.

I let Marvell get down from the van first. I stretch back to wipe away the pentagram from the far window: it's dangerous to leave any sort of trace behind you. I grab my case and I'm just stepping out, erasing the second pentagram with my sleeve, when I hear Marvell mutter:

'Oh hell! Can't stand them things.'

I look round. There's a lion prowling towards us, its mane fluorescent in the flickering torchlight. It stops a couple of yards away, its eyes burning. Marvell's hand trembles as she holds it out. The lion advances, lowering its head and giving out a deep growl like machinery turning underground.

It's not a machine, though; it's an elemental. It sniffs at the small ruby set in the ring on her little finger, and licks the back of her hand. She nearly faints with relief.

My turn. Style counts. I hold out my hand, palm up. The lion watches with interest as I make a fist. Abracadabra! When I open my hand again there's a white mouse running round it. I toss the mouse into the air. The lion opens its mouth and swallows it whole.

Bit rough on the mouse, but Marvell's impressed.

21

The lion too – it turns and pads away. The front door of the palace swings open.

'Show-off!' Marvell mutters, just a whisker too late.

Inside there's an entrance hall, with black-and-white chessboard tiling and a giddying stench of furniture polish.

It's pretty dark, but through an open door to the left I can see people sitting round a table. There's a kid my age, and a middle-aged woman with dyed red hair, who looks up at me, crosses herself and fumbles with a couple of chains hanging round her neck. It takes her a few seconds to disentangle a pair of spectacles from a silver amulet, which she raises to her lips.

Household staff, I guess. Bishops, in my admittedly limited experience, don't make their own beds.

Peering round the hall, I can see half a dozen portraits hanging high on the walls, above the wainscoting: dead bishops keeping an eye on the visitors. They don't like the look of me; I don't like the look of them.

To my right, there's a wide staircase. The light is coming from a chandelier hung high in the stairwell. And as the candles flicker in the draught, I glimpse someone leaning over the banister two floors up.

She's got blonde hair, cropped dead short. It's hard to tell at this distance, and it could be just wishful thinking, but it looks like she's staring at me. Maybe that's encouraging. Maybe she's thinking, who's the twerp? Me and girls – there's not much to say; I'm too busy dismantling domestic animals.

'Through here,' says Marvell, pointing to a heavy door.

How does she know? Coz she's a tatty and sometimes . . . OK, it *is* kind of weird, but it's like sometimes tatties just know stuff without being told. The uniformed jack slumped in the chair in the corner looks like he's happy to know nothing. He gets up and pushes the door open. I take a moment to peer up the stairwell.

'Don't get your hopes up,' Marvell mutters.

The girl has gone.

We stumble down a long dark corridor with a single candle glowing in the distance. The floor is stone, uneven and slippery. We pass the outlines of doorways, heavy furniture and dark, indecipherable paintings. More dead bishops, I guess. This isn't a murder, it's a suicide brought on by the interior decorating.

Halfway along, Marvell jumps as a dark shape looms up from a chair. I can't see his face, but I've been waiting for him to pop out.

'Nice lion, Charlie!'

The candlelight gleams on his teeth as he grins. My old pal Charlie Burgess has great choppers; otherwise he's this wispy little bloke with curly hair bleached white, like most of the CID wear it.

He whispers, 'Best behaviour, Frank. It's Caxton.'

'Yeah, I know. My cup runneth over.'

We've reached the candle, stuck in a bracket screwed to the rough stone wall at the end of the corridor. On our left there's a doorway. Marvell reaches for the handle—

'Hang on!'

I've got this sudden attack of stage fright. My stomach's doing cartwheels and I'm shaking like a monkey on a barrel organ. I'll admit it, OK? I'm wound up about what's waiting for me behind the door. Not just the corpse, either. Beryl Caxton is like every jack I've ever met: aggressive around sorcerers. And me, it's like I've got this special talent for getting right up her nose.

Fact is, I lack a good corpse-side manner. And when I get twitchy I act like an arsehole.

'Mr Memory?' I croak.

'Inside with Caxton.' Charlie doesn't look too hot either: it's not difficult, instantiating elementals, but it takes it out of you. 'Wound up and ready to go.'

Marvell opens the door. As I pass Charlie, he whispers, 'Deep slow breaths.'

Good advice. Caxton's a pain, just in case you weren't getting the picture.

Charlie closes the door behind us.

CHAPTER THREE
A Dead Gent

The first thing I see is the reason we're all here so early in the morning. There's a massive wooden desk in the middle of the room, and a man wearing a blue silk dressing gown and clutching an open book, sitting motionless in the chair behind it.

'Wow!'

Detective Chief Inspector Beryl Caxton glares at me. 'Behave yourself, Sampson, or clear out now.'

I *am* behaving myself. I've managed not to throw up. This guy has no head.

I catch a glint of silver as Caxton sticks the inevitable amulet back in her coat pocket. Damned if I know what she's afraid of; she's twice my size with hands like shovels. I checked her file once so I know she's thirty-five, but she's got this permanently sour expression that makes her look even older. Like Charlie, she's bleached her hair snow white. On her, it doesn't look even remotely cool.

She takes off her glasses to stare at the damage to Marvell's coat. 'What happened to you?'

'Nothing, Chief. I'm fine.'

Yeah, right. Her boss might not have clocked her hands trembling before she stuffed them in her pockets, but I did. Now Marvell's just standing there, face blank, sniffing the air and looking round the rest of the room.

On with the show. I put my case down on the floor and dig in my pocket. I pull out a couple of tiny silver pentagrams and look round for the best place to put them.

We're in some sort of library. From behind the door, the shelves, crammed with dark, leather-bound books, run unbroken along two walls. The first hints of dawn seep in through open French windows that stretch from the high, painted ceiling – all curly clouds and pink cherubs – to the wooden floor.

'That's where they got in,' says Caxton. The gaslight is reflected in splinters of scattered glass where one pane has been smashed.

Marvell stoops to peer at a silver candlestick lying on the floor. It's ornately worked, about fifteen inches long, heavy enough to do serious damage.

'It's from the cathedral. One of a pair.' Caxton sticks her specs back on and squints down at her notebook. 'From the Lady Chapel, apparently.'

'And who's the stiff?' I ask as I place the pentagrams at each end of the mantelpiece. I'm getting a faint tingle of residual magic off everything, but I'd expect that in a building this age.

'Show some respect, will you?' Caxton growls. 'It's the bishop.'

'Sez who?'

There's a typewriter on the desk, and an electric lamp that must have been on all night, because the battery's nearly flat and it casts only the faintest glimmer over the piles of books and documents. I take a deep breath and stoop to examine the body. Whoever he is, he's incredibly dead. There's a fair amount of gore where the neck has been severed.

'Clean job,' I say, just managing to keep my voice steady. 'One blow, maybe two. An axe or a cleaver – a guillotine if you had one to hand.'

'A sword?' says Marvell.

'Who the hell drags a sword around with them these days?'

'You do, Sampson.' Caxton has taken her spectacles off and is polishing them furiously. She sticks them back on her face and screws up her eyes as she goes round the desk to peer at the book the stiff is clutching. 'Marvell, what *is* this?'

But before Marvell can get there, a voice pipes up from a chair beside the ornate marble fireplace. '*In Defence of Sorcery,* by Henry Wallace, MD, Bishop of Oxford.'

Mr Memory looks strikingly like Charlie. Not really surprising: Charlie instantiated him. He's the data elemental for the case, who gets to remember everything then spit it out later; and since Charlie has a sense of humour he's wearing a baggy, slightly threadbare dinner suit over a crumpled white dress shirt and a black bow tie with a food stain on it. His eyes are closed. He looks tired. But then Charlie's elementals always look tired.

Marvell looks round at me. 'That's that book you've got back at your place . . .'

'Clever of you to remember. The termites loved it.'

'Termites?'

I mime hands clasped in prayer and a haircut with a hole in it. 'Obviously they're blind as bats' – Caxton glares at me – 'so they had to get someone to read it to them. Turns out they loved it so much, they burned a copy and left it outside my studio, like I told you.'

'So what's it about?' says Caxton.

'Basically Wallace doesn't understand what the Church has got against sorcerers.'

Caxton pulls a face.

'He thinks all this stuff about rounding us up and barbecuing us for playing with demons is a distraction from the Church's true mission, whatever that may be. In particular, he defends local boy made good, Oswald Devereaux—'

'That's . . . *Saint* Oswald?' says Marvell.

'One and the same.'

'My mum's always goin' on about him. He was beheaded, right?'

28

Mr Memory starts up. 'During the great witch panic of 1493, Saint Oswald refused to leave Oxford. He was dragged from the altar and beheaded on the cathedral green.'

Marvell gestures towards the headless corpse behind the desk. 'Coincidence?'

Caxton tosses her a pair of silk gloves. 'See if he'll let go of it.'

Marvell pulls them on and turns to the corpse.

There's something fundamentally wrong about a headless body. I saw one when I was a student at Saint Cyprian's and I remember thinking: if I look away, by the time I turn back someone will've fixed it.

Careful to avoid looking at the bloody stump, Marvell takes the book in one hand and the dead fingers in the other, and pulls gently. The book moves . . . and the entire left arm with it. The chair creaks. She grabs the thumb lying on top of the book and levers it upwards. It straightens reluctantly, releasing the book. She leaves the left hand resting against the edge of the desk and leans across, still trying to ignore the disgusting mess next to her face.

'Rigor mortis?' I ask.

'Some. Want a go?'

She pulls at the book again. It slips easily out of the fingers of the right hand.

'There's a thumbprint here, Chief.' She's pointing to a brown smudge on the page.

Caxton nods indifferently, probably to cover the fact that she can't see it.

The technical name for the condition is presbyopia, by the way, but that's a right mouthful, so everyone just calls it the Blur. What happens is, after you're twenty your eyes start to go. You can't read in a poor light; things in the distance are still clear, but your close vision goes all fuzzy and you get these blinding headaches. There's nothing healers can do about it and by the time they're twenty-five most people have gone Blurry and need thick glasses to see anything less than a couple of yards away. By the time you're thirty, you're in big trouble. Like I said, Caxton's well past that, and she'd be helpless without Marvell to see things up close for her.

'Blood on the left palm – he was stabbed there.' Marvell raises her own hand defensively, in front of her chest, to demonstrate. 'He couldn't've been holding the book in that hand when it happened. An' I'd be dead surprised if he picked it up afterwards . . .'

I peer over her shoulder as she pulls the dressing gown open. No Adonis, whoever he was. Broken veins. Liver spots. Black body hair turning grey across the sagging chest . . .

And Caxton may be half blind – even with her glasses on – but if she'd not let the absence of a head mislead her and taken the trouble to open the dressing gown, there's something else she might have noticed.

'He wasn't killed here,' Marvell says. 'No blood anywhere in the room.'

Caxton nods. 'Killed somewhere else, brought here, sat at his desk, the book stuck in his hands—'

'Cause of death?' I ask.

'Are you stupid?'

'He was stabbed first.' I'm pointing at a black crust of dried blood over the heart. Caxton slaps my hand aside and leans in to stare, eyes screwed up, mouth open.

I'd probably feel sorry for her if she wasn't such a total pain and if the sharp corner of her security ring hadn't scratched the back of my hand. Like I said, I just seem to get up her nose.

'How old was the bishop?' Marvell asks.

'Henry Alfred Wallace,' says Mr Memory. 'Born 13th August, 1958—'

'Fifty-five then.' Caxton cuts the elemental off as she closes over the dressing gown.

'Anyway,' I suggest. 'Shall we see if it really *is* Wallace?' I've dragged a small table out from the wall and I've got my case open on it. I don't feel sick any more and this is beginning to look like it might be fun. I'm unwrapping a small brass brazier when the door opens behind me and a familiar voice whines:

'What's *he* doing here?'

Won't you give a big Doughnut City welcome, please, to Ferdia McKittrick! He's tall. He's handsome – at least, Marvell is giving him a sort of glassy stare. His tonsure is so immaculately shaped that I'm convinced a personal demon flies in every day to touch it up.

There's a lot of money in Doughnut City, which means a lot of sorcerers – maybe a dozen or so. I don't have anything to do with them, but I know there's one at the big Ghost factory out at Cowley and a couple more coming up with Bright Ideas around the industrial estates. The corporation has one, even if he's rubbish, and there's another who wanders round the hospitals, trying to prevent the healers killing too many patients.

There's a few vanity sorcerers, working for rich bunnies. Then licensed cosmetic sorcerers, private detectives, and treasure-hunters taking money off idiots who ought to know better.

The jacks use two of us, mostly for forensic work: me and Ferdia. He's an arsehole. He's twenty-one . . . and he's post-peak. Past it. Over the hill. A waste of space.

'I told Marvell to bring Sampson,' says Caxton. 'I don't want any mistakes on this one.'

'I can manage.' Ferdia gives Marvell the once-over as he swaggers over to the table and puts his case down beside mine. He sweeps up all the sachets of herbs I've laid out, and dumps them back in my case.

'Hey!' I squeal. It's against Society protocol to handle another sorcerer's gear.

Oh, the laughs we had with that one back at Saint Cyprian's: '*Sir, Jenkins is handling my gear again!*'

Anyway, Ferdia ignores me. He sticks my brazier back

inside my case, slams the lid – and jumps back as it growls at him.

I'm pissed off, but I don't need a fight and the cat back in my studio is missing me. I'm just reaching for my case when Ferdia grabs my pentagrams from the mantelpiece.

'Fat lot of good these'll do you!' He tosses them at me. I catch one, but have to chase the other across the floor.

'And you can stick that outside while you're about it.' Ferdia's pointing at a small round mirror hanging on the wall to the right of the door.

My instinct is to suggest somewhere else to stick it, but my better nature prevails. I pocket the pentagrams and park the mirror in the corridor, and I'm just stepping back into the library when the young guy with the bleached hair – the one we saw poking around in the bushes outside – wanders in through the French windows. He's Gerry Ormerod, one of Caxton's sergeants.

'There's a gate open.' He's got this high, squeaky voice.

'Where?' says Caxton.

'Down by the river.'

Caxton turns to Marvell. 'Do you want to check that out for me?' She nods in my direction. 'Take Sampson.'

'I've got stuff to do.' I grab my case and head for the door.

'Get back here, you little creep!'

'You've got the boy genius.' I nod towards Ferdia. 'How much magic do you need?'

'That's for me to decide.'

I point at Marvell. 'Look, you send her to drag me out when I'm in the middle of something important—'

'Such as what?' Caxton looms over me like a building.

I prefer not to admit what I'm up to, so I stare down at the floor like I've seen something important there.

'Just shut up and do what you're told!' Caxton jabs a forefinger the size of a bread roll into my chest and nearly knocks me over. 'If I get any more lip from you I'll put in a complaint to the Society – and I think you're in enough hot water already. Am I right?'

Marvell's standing there with her mouth open.

Another jab. 'I said, am I right?'

I nod reluctantly. There's stuff I could do – make Caxton's nose bleed, bring her out in spots – but she'd know it was me. 'Yeah, OK.' I put my case down.

Caxton turns to Marvell. 'So what are you waiting for?'

Marvell's eyes flicker towards me, then to Ferdia. He gives her – well, I think it's supposed to be his sympathetic look, but it's more like bad constipation.

'Yes, Chief.'

'And try to keep the skinny little freak out of my hair.'

'That's not my job.'

'Do it anyway.'

As I step past him, through the French windows, Gerry murmurs, 'Wish I had a fan club like yours.'

* * *

Out on the terrace, I button up my jerkin and jam on my hat.

'Told you it was cold,' Marvell reminds me.

As we stumble down the brick steps on to the lawn, a couple of sheep run off. The rich have elementals to keep the grass down; the merely prosperous make do with sheep. The poor don't have lawns.

There's a cold glow in the eastern sky. Despite rumour to the contrary, I don't shrivel up and crumble into a tiny pile of dust at the first glimpse of the sun; but I never feel quite safe in daylight. From the other side of the lawn, I look back at the palace. The brightening sky is reflected in the French windows, the broken pane black like a missing tooth. When I glance up at the second floor, I can see a face staring down at me. Blonde hair, cropped dead short.

The face disappears after a moment. As I follow Ormerod into an alley between yew hedges, hugging myself to stay warm, there's the sound of running feet.

This bloke is scurrying across the lawn after us. I put him in his early twenties, wearing ecclesiastical gear – nice if you like purple – and with a pair of rimless spectacles bouncing on a cord round his neck. 'Edward Akinbiyi,' he pants. 'I'm Bishop Wallace's secretary.' A big ring glistens on his middle finger as he sticks out his hand.

I step away. 'Not while I'm working.'

Akinbiyi pulls a face. But so what? Let him think I'm being obnoxious. In this line of work, you don't shake hands with possible witnesses or suspects; it can mess up the magic.

'Do you need any assistance?'

'Nope.' Marvell heads off after Ormerod.

'I left the bishop downstairs in the library around ten thirty,' Akinbiyi says as he follows her. 'He had some personal letters to write.'

'Did you tell DCI Caxton that?' Marvell asks.

'Of course.'

She catches my eye. I guess we're both asking ourselves the same thing: if he told Caxton, why's he telling us? And Marvell has another question:

'Isn't that what he hired *you* for? Letters and stuff.'

'No, I just do official correspondence and administration. Bishop Wallace had perfect close vision.'

'How come?'

'I suppose he was one of the lucky ones.'

Luck has nothing to do with it, but I decide to keep my mouth shut. 'How long have you been here?' I ask.

'Just over a year. Before that I held a curacy in Nigeria.'

I nod. 'I wrote an essay once on *egba ogwu*—'

'I'm Yoruba and I disapprove of witchcraft.'

I could explain that sorcery is different from witchcraft, but he's too busy rabbiting on about how he found the body and called the jacks. Maybe he wants a medal.

We do another set of steps and a gravel path. The palace grounds end at a line of spiked iron railings, about six feet high and set in a low brick wall. A couple of uniformed jacks are standing around beside an open gate that leads to the towpath, overhung by trees. Beyond them I can see half a dozen red and white lights and the dark outlines of a tug and a string of barges heading downstream.

Just inside the gate, Charlie is on his knees with his arm round a figure sitting on the grass: a young guy wearing a blue anorak and trousers, his head buried in his hands, sobbing fit to die.

'Security elemental,' I whisper to Marvell.

They do what it says on the tin. They can work twenty-four hours, seven days a week. They can see in the dark and hear a flea fart. They don't need to be fed or watered, although I think they appreciate a pat on the back every now and then. They never get bored and they don't need to be paid or pensioned. You just pay a rental to the supplier, to cover instantiation and maintenance. When the job's done, he dismisses them. Poof!

Charlie gets to his feet. 'I can't get any sense out of him.'

'Any ideas?' says Marvell.

'Someone got in.'

'How? I mean, if he's a security elemental . . .'

If you really want to know about elementals, Charlie's your man. A lot of sorcerers go into elemental work when their Gift is taken away and they can't control full Presences any more. Basically it's repetitive work with the occasional laugh and no personal risk.

But Charlie just shrugs hopelessly. I stroll over for a closer look. I like elementals. You give them something to do and they just get on with it, no fuss. You ask them a question and they give you a straight answer. They don't whisper stuff behind your back or try to make you look like a fool.

The trouble is, they're emotionally insecure. If anything goes wrong they fall totally to pieces. I kneel beside him and put my hand over his. Like all elementals, he's stone cold. He looks up at me, his face wet with tears.

'It's just an elemental,' Ormerod mutters, pinching the bridge of his nose hard between two fingers.

The guard buries his face in his hands and sobs helplessly. I pat him on the shoulder because I can't think of anything better to do.

'It's all right,' I say. An obvious lie.

Marvell has wandered out through the gate to the towpath, but the ground is bone dry so there's no chance of footprints. Akinbiyi is just standing there, watching her. Charlie is rolling a cigarette. There's no point in asking if the guard will calm down enough to make sense. They never do. He'll just have to be put down.

I turn to Akinbiyi. 'Who has clearance?'

'All the staff.' There's a tiny flash of red as he holds

out his right hand to show the security ring on his middle finger.

'The body in the library didn't have one of them,' Marvell calls.

'The spell would be in the stone of his episcopal ring.' I glance down at my own ring, a gold band etched with symbols and set with a small sapphire. When I'm not trying to impress tatties that's my preferred way of getting through police lines.

'He wasn't wearing any sort of ring.'

'I'm sure he was wearing it when I left him.' Akinbiyi is looking deeply perplexed. He jumps as Charlie strikes a match.

'What if someone was carrying the bishop's body?' I ask Charlie. 'Would the elemental let them through?'

He shakes his head. The wind snatches a cloud of smoke from his mouth as he takes my arm and leads me away. He whispers, 'What about sorcery?'

Akinbiyi heard that. His eyes are like saucers.

'What about a stolen ring?' I suggest.

Charlie shakes his head. 'A ring's only effective if the right person's wearing it. Like I said: sorcery.'

'OK, but don't say anything to—'

'What are you two muttering about?' Marvell's down at the river's edge, clutching a tree branch with one hand while she leans out over the river to peer along the bank. Behind her, the gas lamps are still glowing where Seven

Bridges Road crosses the river just west of the railway station.

I turn my back on her and whisper to Charlie. 'Not till I've spoken to the Society.'

Akinbiyi has wandered through the gate to join Marvell. 'What are you looking for?'

'A boat.'

'Bit cold for a pleasure trip,' I suggest.

Nobody laughs. The branch creaks ominously as Marvell leans out over the rolling brown water. She catches my eye: 'I know what you're hoping.' She pulls herself back to safety.

'Never even crossed my mind.'

Honest.

CHAPTER FOUR
Love

Back in the library, there's the smell of herbs burning on cedarwood. Caxton is standing in front of the fireplace, treating the world to her thoughtful look as she squints up at an oil portrait of a middle-aged, self-satisfied-looking bloke in episcopal robes.

'That's him, right?' Marvell turns to Akinbiyi. 'How long ago?'

'Two years. It was painted just after his appointment.'

If that *is* him in the chair, he's put on weight since then. The figure in the portrait has black hair, worn quite long, and a hint of a smile, like he knows it's all a joke – or maybe he's just remembered something nobody else knows. Like where the money's stashed.

Mr Memory is standing beside the stiff, lifting documents from the desk one by one and reading them. He'll remember the position and contents of everything; he can even re-materialise stuff for you to examine yourself. I give him a big smile, but he doesn't respond. He pulls the sheet of paper out of the type-writer, pores over it, then puts it aside to hang in mid air. A nice little touch of Charlie's.

'All right,' Ferdia announces. 'I'm ready.'

He's wearing a white linen apron, embroidered with symbols, and a square paper hat with the word 'EL' written on it. He's got a small brass brazier burning on the table, beside a couple of knives, a hazel wand, and various porcelain dishes and paper sachets. The painted cherubs on the ceiling stare down appre-hensively at the wisp of smoke spiralling towards them.

'I'm about to test for contiguity.' Ferdia turns the dazzling light of his personality on to Marvell. 'If any two objects ever touch each other, they retain an affinity that a sorcerer can detect. I can tell you if a knife inflicted a wound, or if a bullet was fired from a particular gun.' He gestures at the table, apparently for her benefit alone. 'I have two samples of hair – one from the body and the other from a brush in Bishop Wallace's bedroom . . .'

Marvell manages to look interested. Akinbiyi looks unhappy.

Caxton mutters, 'Just get on with it.'

Ferdia raises his wand theatrically. 'In the name of Adonai the most high—'

Akinbiyi frowns. 'I'm not comfortable with this.'

'Tough,' I say. 'Second Council of Trent, 1907. The

42

Church officially recognises sorcery as a legitimate field of research, a valuable tool of social order and an expression of the omnipotence of the divine will.'

Caxton's glaring at me. 'How'd you get to be such a precocious little brat?'

'I'm a sorcerer. What d'you expect?'

'In the name of Jehovah the most holy,' Ferdia chants in this strange, high-pitched voice. He was always a desperate show-off and now that he's post-peak it's getting worse.

I turn to Marvell. 'Did you know the present pope had the Gift?'

'He was only at Saint Cyprian's for a year,' Akinbiyi protests.

'Some people say that's how he wound up being pope. A couple of other candidates died unexpectedly.'

'Those were just malicious rumours.'

'Is there such a thing as a non-malicious rumour?' Caxton seems to be having one of her rare moments of lucidity. 'What'd be the point?'

We all take a few seconds to puzzle over that.

'It's just a routine contiguity test,' I reassure Akinbiyi. 'No animals will be harmed, or supernatural beings invoked. Anyway, you don't have to watch.'

'This is consecrated ground. And under the terms of the Concordat, the Society of Sorcerers is obliged to seek the diocesan authorities' consent before any thaumaturgic procedure can be carried out.'

'Thaumaturgic?' Marvell whispers.

'Magical,' I whisper back.

'That could take weeks,' Caxton says.

'I'll take responsibility for formally identifying the body,' says Akinbiyi. 'I've worked for Bishop Wallace for more than a year and I'm one hundred per cent certain it's him.'

'So the rumours are true,' I say. 'The clergy *do* sauna together.'

Caxton covers a smile by turning to Ferdia. 'I suppose we can do it back at the lab.'

'Great,' Ferdia mutters. 'Fine!' And starts throwing stuff back into his case.

Mr Memory has finished sifting through the documents and is putting them back exactly as he originally found them on the desk.

'Well?' says Caxton.

'There's correspondence about a boundary dispute between the diocese and a Thomas Stevens.' Mr Memory passes his hand across the desk, palm down. Half a dozen papers, scattered around, glow briefly. 'Stevens claims—'

'What else?'

'A letter of resignation from James Groce, rector of Saint Ebbe's.' Another document flickers. 'A request from the Warden—'

'Anything that isn't diocesan business?'

'Sermon notes—'

44

'Give me strength!'

Mr Memory looks at her, dead puzzled.

'Anything personal?' says Caxton.

'Several anonymous letters.'

A sheaf of papers rises from the desk. Caxton's glasses go on. Akinbiyi's too, as he pushes in beside her.

'Did he get a lot of these?' Caxton asks.

'Quite a few, since his book was published.' Akinbiyi reaches for a loosely wrapped silk bundle on the desk. 'Is that it?'

Like he doesn't know. 'Don't touch!' I say. 'Contiguity—'

'Thank you, Sampson.' Caxton turns back to Akinbiyi. 'Was he reading it when you left him last night?'

'Not that I recall.' Akinbiyi takes off his glasses and looks round the room. 'But he was holding it when I found him.' His eyes widen. 'So whoever murdered him—'

'Apparently.' Caxton opens her notebook.

Akinbiyi watches her write laboriously in block capitals. His voice sinks to a dramatic whisper. 'They're trying to tell us something!'

We all stand around watching Caxton print away, until a uniformed jack strolls in to announce that the meat wagon has arrived. Caxton turns to Mr Memory. 'Got everything you need?'

He nods. She turns to me. 'Your turn, then. And

please, Sampson.' Heavy pause. '*Try* not to mess it up.'

I'm still doing my offended look when this shiny metal trolley comes crashing through the door with two big, pissed-off-looking blokes in black silk overalls pushing it. I call them dieners, which is just a fancy word for mortuary attendants. Anyway, they barge past Marvell and stop the trolley beside the desk. She nudges me and hisses, 'Are they elementals too?'

One of the dieners looks up from putting on a pair of black silk gloves and snarls, 'You think we'd be farting around with all this crap if we were elementals?'

Marvell watches them pull silk bags out of a compartment underneath the trolley. I explain, 'They're flesh and blood, so if they touched the body they'd create a new contiguity. Silk's a magical insulator and black is the densest colour.'

'That's a bit—'

'Literal? Yeah, magic's dead literal when it puts its mind to it.'

One of the dieners whistles through his teeth as they pull the bags over the dead man's hands. They lever him out of the chair and onto the trolley, where they cover him with more black silk.

'I have to do time of death now,' I tell Marvell. 'You can watch some of it.'

'Doesn't *he* do that?' She glances at Ferdia. He goes bright red.

'I'll explain later!' I whisper.

'How long does it take?'

'Three or four hours.'

'So you'd better stop wasting my time and get on with it,' says Caxton.

We follow the trolley back along the corridor to the entrance hall. The staff are still sitting round their table in the side room, playing with crosses and amulets.

And the girl is standing at the bottom of the staircase. Before anyone can stop her, she darts forward and pulls back the sheet covering the body.

She screams – more like a bird than a human being. The dieners stop dead, unsure what to do. She seems to have frozen there, clutching the sheet to her breast. Her eyes are wide, like she can't believe what she's seeing.

Charlie's beside her. He takes her arm and says, 'Come on, love. You shouldn't see this.'

But she won't move – maybe she can't. She's trembling and her face is white and there's tears running down her cheeks. She's pulling her elbows in to her sides, tighter and tighter like she can't make herself small enough.

Akinbiyi wades in. Barges past Charlie, grabs her by the shoulders, shakes her. 'Kazia!'

For a moment I think he's going to slap her. She's staring into his face and it's like she's going to fall into his arms. But then she drops the sheet and buries her face in Charlie's shoulder. He blinks in surprise, then puts his arm round her, and as he leads her into the room where the staff are still staring like owls, I can't help thinking, why couldn't *I* have been that side of the trolley?

The woman with the red hair whispers to the young kid. He gets up and comes round the table. He looks straight at me as he closes the door. The dieners rearrange the sheet over the body.

'Who was that?' I ask, since nobody else has.

'The bishop's niece,' says Akinbiyi.

I'm in love.

CHAPTER FIVE

Dead Pigs

Imagine, if you can be bothered, a circular, domed room about twenty yards across. Dark wood panelling. Cedarwood floor . . .

And electric lights. Probably the only thing Ferdia and I have ever agreed on. The lighting in the mortuary amphitheatres used to be gas, but you have to burn candles for the actual rituals and turning a couple of dozen gas fixtures off and on was always a pain. Modernising was Ferdia's idea – he's always had this delusional image of himself as a go-ahead, cutting-edge sorcerer – and I was tempted to fight it just for the sake of being difficult. But darkness and light at the flick of a switch is pretty cool.

Except for the poor sod who has to change the batteries.

The outer circle is a yard or so inside the perimeter: two concentric copper rings set into the floor, about two feet apart. The dieners are carrying in small round tables and fumbling around with them until the legs engage with notches in the floor around the circle.

Further in, there's another double circle, about twelve feet across. Fixed circles can be inflexible; but they save a lot of time messing about with string and chalk.

The service doors swing open for a couple of dieners to wheel in the plinth: brass, with a cluster of dials set into a panel on one side. The silk-shrouded body is already lying on it.

They trundle it across to the centre of the inner circle. One of them is in his mid-twenties and still has some close vision: he goes down on his hands and knees and, with a bit of squinting, engages the bolts with more notches in the floor. The dieners' breath hangs in the cold air as they unwrap the body, naked now. He's got quite a gut, which moves around like it doesn't know it's dead yet.

I give him the once-over, front and back. Marvell is beginning to look queasy; in contrast to the wine-red stains down the back of the body, her face has gone deathly white.

So let's give her something constructive to think about. 'OK, what do you see?'

'Livor mortis. The heart stops beating, so the blood stops circulating and sinks towards the lowest parts of the body.'

She looks round at the sound of footsteps. Mr Memory has come in and slides along a bench in the gallery. I raise a hand. He gives no sign that he's seen me, but I know he sees everything; like God, only without the flaky track record.

'But livor starts anything from a few minutes to several hours after death, so that's not much use.' I can see she's trying to impress me, and she's not doing badly. 'Was he killed standing up?'

'Ferdia can check the angle of entry tomorrow. The wound to his hand was made trying to defend himself. Let's say he falls over—'

She grins. 'Dead people usually do.'

'His heart stops beating – within seconds if the knife penetrated it. Ferdia can check that tomorrow too.'

'How long before they cut his head off?'

'Can't tell, but apart from the chest wound the only blood I can see is around his shoulder blades, so he must've been lying on his back when they did it. Blood starts tipping out—'

'Not much, though. They must've sat him up almost immediately' – Marvell turns to the dieners – 'Where's the dressing gown?'

'Behind you.' One of the dieners nods towards a silk bundle on a bench. She hesitates, waiting for him to bring it. When he just stands there, she goes red and walks over and unwraps it herself.

'Can you see a hole?' she asks, spreading the gown out, like a matador with a cape.

I shake my head.

'No blood down the front. All on the back.' She turns the dressing gown inside out and back again. 'Not much, though . . . smears, really, and all on the inside . . . didn't even soak through. Was he naked when he died?'

'Looks like it.'

'Dirty old bleeder!'

Look, I don't like her: she got me in a lot of trouble. But it's fun having someone sharp to bounce stuff around with.

'OK then,' I say. 'They put the gown on him, carry him . . . well, it's easiest under the knees and armpits . . . sit him up in the library—'

'No trail of blood. No footprints. Nothing at the gate.'

'Once the heart's stopped pumping, the body's like a badly designed vase. If you carry it upright and steadily, it won't spill.'

I can see where she's heading, and sure enough . . .

'Could it have been moved . . . you know, by magic?'

'Easier to carry it.'

'Could it, though?'

I look her in the eye. 'Do you have any idea how much hard work magic is? That trick with the cards – it was just sleight of hand.'

'What trick? You just chucked them in the fire!'

'Oh, didn't I finish that?' I make a shape with my fingers. 'Hocus-pocus!'

She jumps like she's been stung in the arse. She sticks her hand in the back pocket of her jeans and pulls out the tarot card I forced on her back in my studio.

La Force. Strength or Fortitude.

'Post-hypnotic suggestion,' I explain. 'Every time I say the cue you'll feel something in your back pocket.'

'For ever?'

'Till I get bored.' Actually, the effect wears off after a week or so. 'Akinbiyi says he left him at ten thirty.'

'If you believe him. He scried emergency a few minutes after three.'

I take our friend's hand. Several deep gashes in the palm. I try to raise his arm, but he's having none of it.

'That's the trouble with rigor. This soon after death, all it really tells you is what you know already: that he's dead.'

'What about body temperature?'

'I'm happy to let you stick a thermometer up his bum if it turns you on, but different people cool at different speeds under different conditions.' I turn to the dieners. 'Let's try between nine last night and three this morning. Six hours . . .'

'What about the tattoo?' Marvell's leaning over the corpse, pointing to a tiny triangular mark above the right nipple.

'It's not a tattoo. It's the Society's mark.'

She stares at me. 'He was a sorcerer?'

53

'According to that, he was. A novice, anyway. There's a lot of kids who have the Gift when they're young, but it never really develops. So they drop out after a year or so and usually move over to the mainstream Church.'

'Why didn't you tell Caxton?'

'He studied magic, that's all. Never graduated.'

Saint Cyprian's started out as part of a secret society in All Souls' College, back in the sixteenth century. Ever since then, most bishops of Oxford have been former students. The fact that our friend's got the mark . . . well, it's a strong indication that this really is Wallace. But my first loyalty is to the Society and, like I said to Charlie, I need to talk to them before I decide how much to tell Caxton.

Marvell's still leaning over the corpse. 'What d'you mean, a mark?'

'You can remove a tattoo. Take off the skin there – even bite a lump out of him – the mark'll just pop up somewhere else.'

'So it's a spell?'

'Nope, it's an attribute, like hair colour. Magically induced. It changes as the novice progresses through his training. See?'

I pull up my shirt so she can see the complex pattern of circles and symbols across my chest. 'That's a full licence.'

She peers at me. 'You don't eat enough.'

'You can talk!'

She blinks, and I realise it's dead easy to hurt her. 'The work kind of feeds off you, that's all.' I pull down my shirt and say, 'Right, time for you to go.'

'Sorry?'

'This is what that business with Ferdia was all about. I'm about to invoke a Presence.'

'Huh?'

'An angel. That's why Ferdia can't do time of death. He's post-peak, so he can't control a Presence any more.'

'But he can do contiguity.'

'Coz it doesn't require a Presence. Anyway, you can't stay.'

'Why not?'

'You don't have a licence.'

'How do I get one?'

'By being Gifted and getting kidnapped by the Society when you were six. This is a secret procedure.'

'What about him?' She's pointing at Mr Memory, gazing benignly back at us from the gallery.

'He's an elemental, instantiated according to Society specifications. Look, thanks to you I'm in enough trouble already—'

There's clanking noises from underneath. She steps back as a trap door opens in the floor. 'I'm not leaving unless Caxton gives me a direct order.'

Plan B, then: right on cue, a platform rises from the

basement. There are two dieners on board, steadying a metal trolley. It has four shelves, each packed with severed pigs' heads, their snouts and ears glistening with ice crystals.

'Bloody hell,' Marvell mutters.

'If you don't like the smell, get out of the kitchen.'

'No way.'

So on to Plan C: bore her to death. I plant her in the gallery with Mr Memory and take my time getting tooled up.

There are three forensic amphitheatres in the city mortuary. Ferdia uses the two in the east wing; I get the smaller one in the west wing to run amok. You can't be forever dragging instruments and materials in and out, so I've got a robing room sealed by a spell like the one on my studio door, but without the amateur dramatics.

The door here knows me, so all I have to do is touch it and it swings open. Inside, there's a teak wardrobe, lined in black silk, containing several complete party outfits: white linen coats, belts, slippers, and paper hats folded and ready to go. Everything's spattered with symbols embroidered in silk thread, or drawn with ink or blood – mostly mine.

I drop my ring into a drawer, where it won't interfere with the ritual. I pour exorcised water into the basin and recite the prayers as I wash and dry my face and hands. I scrawl more symbols on the coat and slippers and struggle into them.

Candles. Braziers. Herbs and spices. Two silk-wrapped wands from a box. Cutlery from the array of knives, sickles, lancets, burins and swords in the cabinet. A silver bowl. Goat's milk . . .

It's over an hour before I rattle my way back into the amphitheatre. The last of the dieners puts a bird-cage down on the floor. As he disappears through the service door he switches off the electric lights, leaving four tall white candles flickering: north, south, east and west.

Disappointingly, Plan C has failed: Marvell is still sitting beside Mr Memory in the gallery, one knee bouncing dementedly up and down.

'Cool outfit,' she says. 'Ever thought of joining a circus?'

I award that a bleak smile. The official line – that there are significant thaumaturgic reasons for having no mirrors in any room where a ritual is performed – is contradicted by the fact that we use mirrors for scrying. The real reason, of course, is that no sorcerer wants to be reminded that, dolled up in his party outfit, he looks less like a highly trained, massively talented professional wielding supernatural powers than a total prat in a paper hat.

'What's the sword for, anyway?'

'Shut up!'

Around the outer circle, twenty-four pigs' heads rest on their tables, all gazing blankly in towards the plinth. I'm wearing my coat and slippers, with the paper hat poised at a rakish angle. I've got a couple of wands – straight hazel twigs exactly nineteen and a half inches long, cut with a single stroke on the day and in the hour of Mercury – stuck through a red silk scarf tied round my waist.

Inside the inner circle, I have a brazier on a stand beside each shoulder of the body on the plinth. I strike sparks from a flint and steel.

A voice from the audience again. 'What's wrong with matches?'

'The fire has to originate in the brazier.'

I light both braziers and sprinkle in chips of agarwood. That's what the grimoires specify; it's hideously expensive and not strictly essential, but I adore the smell.

'I exorcise thee, O creature of fire, by him by whom all things are made, that forthwith thou castest away every phantasm from thee, that it shall not be able to do any hurt in any thing.'

Flames flicker. Smoke begins to rise.

'No interruptions.'

I've got my instruments and materials lined up on a silk square on the floor. A white dove flutters in the cage. I chalk the last symbols into the inner ring.

I close my eyes and take a series of deep, slow

breaths. Every time I start a ritual, it's like there's this voice in my head telling me I'm going to mess up. I asked my Master about it when I was at Saint Cyprian's. He said it would go away.

It never has.

I look round the space. There's only one shot at this. I open the cage and take out the dove. I secure it, wings pinned, in one hand, while I stretch for my white-handled knife with the other.

'In the name of Adonai the most high. In the name of Jehovah the most holy.'

And I cut off the dove's head.

'Jesus Christ!' Marvell bolts for the door with her hand to her mouth.

So Plan D worked.

Now that I've got the place to myself, I let the blood spurt into a bowl, then stick the twitching corpse back in the cage. The head's rolled off across the floor. I pick up the bowl and kneel beside the plinth. A lot of what you learn, training as a sorcerer, is simple physical dexterity, like juggling. You can't afford to spill or break things. I dip my fingertips into the blood and write the word 'Tetragrammaton' along one edge of the plinth.

I shuffle round the plinth and smear more words round the edge. 'Adonai'. 'Tetragrammaton' again, because it's a big enough word not to look lost along the long side of the plinth. 'Jehovah'.

I rinse my fingers in a basin of exorcised water. I formally seal the inner circle by drawing a line round it with my black-handled knife – there's a lot of cutlery involved in sorcery – and sprinkle herbs and spices into the braziers.

'In the name of the Lord, Amen. In the name of the Lord who is blessed. In the name of the Lord, Amen.'

The smoke from the braziers rises vertically then folds out into a flat cloud suspended just above my head. The candles are still burning, but the light seems to hang heavy in the room. It is reflected red in the forty-eight eyes watching me unblinkingly from the outer ring.

I start in on the names of God: 'Adonai, Tetragrammaton, Jehovah, Tetragrammaton, Adonai, Jehovah, Otheos . . .'

Stuff happens because I want it to. These names, the books say they're magical; but I think they're just sounds, and remembering them and pronouncing them correctly – in the right sequence and with the right cadence – concentrates my mind.

Why do I need to concentrate my mind? Because I'm distracted. I'm thinking about the girl – what was her name? Kazia. I remember her horrified expression as she stared at the body on the trolley, but apart from the blonde hair, I can't really remember what she looked like. I wonder what she thought of me – probably reckons I'm an arsehole, most people do. But suppose she doesn't; how do I get to meet her again?

I'm thinking about the cat, decomposing back in the studio. I can salvage the skin, claws and whiskers, but the heart and liver will be unusable.

Then there's Marvell. I don't think she trusts me any more than I trust her, but at least she isn't waving amulets and making protective signs in my face.

And I really ought to visit my mum.

The smells and symbols concentrate my mind. Magic is all in the detail. Picking a herb at a certain time, under a particular conjunction of planets; cutting, shaping and purifying a wand; making a knife myself – forging, quenching, tempering, setting, attaching the handle . . .

My Gift is focused by the instruments I wield, the space I occupy and the words I say. What I want to happen, happens.

I stoop to pick up two lengths of thick silk thread – one black, one white. Draping one over each shoulder, I move round to the head of the plinth. Below me, the stump of the dead man's neck. Above me, just visible through the cloud of smoke, crystals set into the domed ceiling in the form of the major constellations. No expense spared, folks!

I sprinkle saffron into each brazier. The cloud of smoke thickens.

'In this, by this, and with this, which I pour out before thy face—'

The bowl of milk spatters across the floor. On top of everything else, from now on I have to watch my step: it's a death trap in here.

I raise my arms.

'Oh Eternal! Oh King Eternal! Deign to look upon thy most unworthy servant and upon this my intention. Vouchsafe to me thine angel Anäel, that in thy name he may judge and act justly in all that I shall require of him.'

More names. More smells and smoke. Finally I come to the point.

'Make manifest unto my eyes the things that are hidden from me.'

I pull out the two wands and use them to lift the silk threads from my shoulders. I stretch out my arms and let the white thread fall into one brazier; the black into the other.

I feel a faint tingling through my slippers and just for a moment time seems to stop. The silk threads drop vertically, as straight as arrows, until their bottom ends touch the glowing charcoal. For a second they stand there like charmed snakes. Then flames flicker up from bottom to top, completely consuming them.

There's a sound like rushing air. The candles flutter and go out. The amphitheatre is in darkness. It's freezing cold.

I cross the wands over my head. 'Come, great Lord, come, according to thy good pleasure!'

There's this loud rumbling sound. I feel the floor tremble beneath my feet as the plinth shakes. And I get this sudden sharp pain in my chest, like someone's poked a sword through me and they're wiggling it about. I hold my breath – and the Presence passes, leaving only a dull ache.

Silence.

'I thank thee, because thou hast appeared and satisfied my demands.' I pick up my sword and make a single sweep with it, narrowly avoiding taking my toes off. 'Do thou therefore depart in peace, and return when I shall call thee.'

The candles are burning strongly again. I cover the braziers. I grab the black-handled knife and formally cut the inner ring. Mr Memory slides out of the gallery and comes to kneel beside me as I examine the readings from the instruments on the plinth.

The dieners slouch in again. The electric light goes on. The trap door in the floor opens for the pigs' heads to go straight back to the cold store.

CHAPTER SIX
White Mouse

Marvell's waiting for me outside the amphitheatre, still white as a sheet.

'Why didn't you warn me?'

'I told you to get out. Anyway, he died within a few minutes of midnight.'

'How do you know?'

'Simultaneity.'

'What's that?'

I sigh. According to my magic watch it's nearly three. I've drunk more than a pint of water since the ritual, but I'm still thirsty – magic dehydrates you like hell – and I haven't eaten anything since the plate of cold shepherd's pie the termites left outside my studio eighteen hours ago.

I stumble off along the corridor. Marvell trails after me.

'I said, what's simultaneity?'

Why fight it? 'Say a butterfly flaps its wings in China and *at that very same moment*, a man falls off his horse in

Oxford. There's a relation of simultaneity between the two events.'

'What's that got to do with pigs?'

'Will you shut up and listen? The reason they built the mortuary here . . . the city abattoir's just round the corner and we've got this deal. Every fifteen minutes, they pick one of the pigs they slaughter, label the head with the time of death and send it over to us – there's a tunnel under the houses. Then they're kept for six months in a cold store in the basement.'

We've reached the lobby. The receptionist frowns as I turn the logbook and grab his pen.

'That's a hell of a lot of heads,' says Marvell.

'Nearly twenty thousand at any one time. So if there's a murder within fifty miles, say, and we need to establish time of death, they bring the body in—'

'But how do you know which particular heads?'

'You've usually got a rough idea when someone was killed – like I was pretty sure our guy died after nine last night and before three this morning. That's six hours. I got them to bring up the heads of pigs killed at nine, nine-fifteen, nine-thirty . . . every fifteen minutes until two forty-five.'

'And what if the pig wasn't killed dead on time?'

'There's a chronometer. And the Society does regular inspections.' I push the logbook back across the desk. The receptionist pushes his glasses up his nose and squints suspiciously at my scrawl. I turn back to

Marvell. 'Look, can we just get out of here? I'm starving.'

After the gloom of the mortuary the real world is alarmingly bright. I stand at the top of the steps, blinking in the autumn sunlight as I look out over a small herb garden.

'So you've got this body—'

'Don't you ever shut up?'

'Just wanna know what's goin' on.'

I lead her down the paved walk, between two laurel hedges, towards the street.

'The body's got all sorts of potential affinities with the pigs' heads. Like, he could've walked in the field where one of the pigs foraged, or once eaten meat from one of its parents. The purpose of the ritual is to exclude all those possibilities and isolate the relation of simultaneity between his death and that of whichever pig was slaughtered closest to the same moment. And that was at midnight.'

'Caxton'll want to know.' Marvell stops dead and hauls her scryer out of her pocket.

I say, 'You know the Society can listen in to those things.'

She stares at me. She really doesn't know whether to believe me or not.

'I'm not saying don't use it. Just telling you, that's all.'

Her scryer is this flat, round case, about five inches in diameter, made of silver, with an enamel eye set into the lid and symbols engraved round the rim. When she opens it, there's a diagram etched inside the base: a man inside a circle, his head, hands and feet touching the points of a five-tipped star. She touches the five tips, then blows on the surface of the mirror inside the lid.

I leave her to it and wander away to lean over the gate to the street and gaze out at a normal day in Doughnut City. Vans and horses, a few idiots on bicycles trying to weave their way through the mountains of dung, pedestrians scuttling for their lives . . .

But here's something to brighten everyone's day: a line of maybe a couple of hundred men shuffling up the road in single file. It's freezing cold for late September, but they're all stripped to the waist; and each one of them is holding a sword, resting across the nape of the neck of the man in front of him.

I can only pray that the idiot leading them doesn't trip. He's cross-eyed with concentration, clutching a heavy wooden cross.

Marvell's beside me, stuffing her scryer back in her pocket. 'It's his Mass.'

'Huh?'

'Saint Oswald . . . you know, to commemorate his death. Tomorrow night.' She nods towards the line of penitents. 'Stupid bloody prats! My dad used to do that lark – nearly got his ear cut off one year. I'm telling you, this whole case, it's no coincidence—'

'How's Caxton?'

'She's got a job for us.'

'Us? Look, we can get a sandwich round the corner.' I often go to this scruffy dive, the Russian Tea Room, with Charlie.

'There's a housemaid at the palace – doesn't live there, comes in every day. Only she didn't turn up this morning and the Chief wants to talk to her.'

'You know where she lives?'

'Eynsham.'

'So you don't need me.'

The line of penitents is still passing. People on the pavement cross themselves and haul out rosary beads. Behind them, on the window of an empty shop, there's a poster. It shows a screaming face surrounded by red and yellow flames. Big letters: 'Thou shalt not suffer a witch to live.' And an emblem in the top right-hand corner: a burning pentagram.

Ring any bells?

'Her name's Alice Constant.' Marvell smiles. Not at me, but sort of down into herself. 'I used to know her.'

'That's useful. You won't need a photograph either, then.'

'So are you coming?'

I'm about to say no, when I notice a man standing beside the poster, staring fiercely back at me.

68

I know that stare. The first time ever I ever saw it, I'd been at Saint Cyprian's for about a year and I'd decided the rule forbidding novices to leave the seminary was stupid, so I jumped out of a window into a tree, climbed down and scuttled off into the town, looking for adventure.

I found it, all right. I was going past a pub when I spotted these four blokes giving me the look. I knew at once what it meant and I turned and ran for it, but I was too slow. They got bored with kicking me quite quickly, and it was getting late; so they stripped me naked, tied me to the railings outside Saint Cyprian's and rubbed nettle leaves into my eyes.

This time it's not just the stare that I know, it's the man doing the staring. I recognise him from earlier this morning when he tried to stick a knife in me.

So we're miles out of town, rattling up a grubby street in Eynsham, when Marvell says, 'That's all very clever. The thing with the pigs.'

'We think so.'

'In a demented sort of way. It's like a religious order, right? The Society?'

'Founded by Johannes Trithemius in 1513. Approved by the papal bull *Regimini artis magicae ecclesiae*, 1563.'

And pretty much a law unto itself. It doesn't actually take over small countries, but it knows people who do

69

and it's always happy to supply the necessary resources. At a price, of course.

'This is a waste of time,' I say.

'Yeah, it's what I told Caxton: we find Wallace sitting there with his head cut off, holding this book he wrote about this saint what got his head cut off and who's got this big Mass comin' up in the cathedral tomorrow night.' She stops to breathe. 'Not a coincidence.' She folds her arms. 'And Alice wouldn't hurt a fly.'

I'm about to point out firstly that we don't know for certain that it *is* Wallace and secondly that there's got to be sorcery because of the elemental on the gate, when the van stops dead and I remind myself to keep my mouth shut until I get a chance to speak to the Society. Marvell gets out and starts arguing about over-time with the driver. I step down and look around . . .

The way my life works, I don't see much of the big wide world. Most days I scurry round my studio like a hamster in a wheel. Every now and then I get tossed into a van and hauled across to the mortuary to wave wands and watch Ferdia turn dead people inside out. The plan is that I'll be this expert forensic sorcerer by the time he's gone hopelessly post-peak. Sometimes I get driven out to crime scenes all on my own to pretend I know what I'm doing. And there's the occasional midnight flit out into the back-end of nowhere to gather wild herbs or trap animals.

'You OK?' Marvell's staring at me.

My point is, I don't do normal stuff – so-called. I've never been to the kinema. My dad took me to the Vaudeville when I was a nipper and there was a stage magician who made a little boy disappear. Later I realised it was mirrors, not real magic, but at the time I was so scared that I set the theatre on fire.

If only my dad had understood then that he had a paying proposition on his hands.

'I'm fine,' I say. But I'm not: I'm dead nervous. I really don't like being out in the open like this. And I'm not sure that I like the look of the cab that's just pulled in, a hundred yards back along the street.

'That one, right?' I'm pointing at a crumbling terraced house. But Marvell's still busy swapping pieces of paper with the driver.

There's a dozen kids slumped on a step outside a small factory on the corner. One by one they look up and stare at my case.

'Hey Marvo,' I hiss. 'Hurry it up!'

The kids haven't quite worked out what I am, but they know I'm not right and they're whispering intently to each other about it. And there's this old bloke staring out at me from the front window of the house with an amulet to his lips.

'Marvo!'

'What did you call me?'

'Marvo. You know, coz of Marvell.'

She grins. 'Yeah, I can live with that.'

There's this narrow staircase going up, floor after floor, with no light and just a rickety banister to cling on to. My case weighs a ton and I'm sweating like a pig. One false move and I'm a pancake in the cellar.

'When I was really small,' I pant, 'you know, before they discovered I was Gifted – I had this fantasy of going on the stage and doing tricks. I was going to call myself Marvo the Boy Wonder.'

'Thank God I missed that!' I know Marvo's stopped dead because I've crashed into her. 'Watch it!' She sniffs. 'Room on the left – and let me do the talking.'

She knocks.

'Alice?' she calls. 'It's Magdalena Marvell.' She punches me. 'Shut up, Frank.'

'What did I say?'

Another punch. She calls, 'Do you remember me?'

I pull off my jerkin while she knocks again. 'Alice, are you there?'

Still no answer. 'Wait here, Frank.' The handle turns. She pushes the door open.

As I step silently back into the shadows at the top of the stairs, I glimpse a pale-faced young woman with greasy, mouse-coloured hair sitting on a bed in the small room. She looks up at Marvo.

'Magdalena?'

'Yeah. Are you all right?'

'What are you doing here?'

'I'm with the police now.'

'You're a jack?'

'Can I sit down?' Marvo drops on to the side of the bed next to Alice. 'You work at the Bishop's Palace, yeah? Why aren't you at work today?'

'I didn't feel well.'

Marvo puts her hand to Alice's forehead. 'Do you want a doctor?'

I hear the front door bang downstairs. I step across to peer down into the darkness, and see movement on the stairs a couple of floors down. The banister creaks under my weight.

'Who's that?' says Alice.

I can see them now: three men. I step into the room and close the door behind me. No window, just a skylight in the sloping ceiling, the glass spattered with bird shit.

'Someone's coming,' I say.

'Who's he?' Alice is on her feet, staring at me with pale grey eyes. She must be a lot younger than she looks because she doesn't have the small red marks each side of the bridge of her nose where a pair of spectacles would press in. Mind you, if she's a domestic servant she doesn't need to read anything . . . just so long as she doesn't confuse butter with furniture polish.

'Frank's a friend.'

'Are you a jack too?'

'Nope,' I say. 'A sorcerer.'

I don't know why I think it's a good idea, but I lean forward and pull a white mouse out of her ear.

OK, I'd better explain: this is partly just sleight of hand again, but the mouse isn't something I keep up my sleeve, it's a crude form of elemental – like the one I fed to the lion – and it's only actually good for a few minutes. So it's kind of magic . . . and kind of a bit of a cheat.

Anyway, Alice twitches like she's been struck by lightning, and I'm just thinking that maybe it wasn't such a clever idea, when there's the sound of heavy boots on the stairs outside.

Marvo pulls her gun. Maybe that, rather than the mouse, is the last straw. Alice shoves me out of the way, yanks the door open and dashes out of the room. She reaches the top of the stairs at the same time as the three men. I can't see them clearly in the gloom of the landing, but they stand aside to let her pass. As her feet rattle on the steps, they close ranks and move forward.

'Stop right there.' Marvo levels her pistol.

As they step into the light I recognise one of them: it's that bloke again – the one who tried to kill me. He's taller than I realised, in his twenties, with curly fair hair like a Greek god and one of those open faces that make you want him as your friend.

Obviously he doesn't feel the same way about me.

He's got his Anti-Sorcery Brotherhood emblem round his arm, an amulet round his neck and his knife in his fist.

His pals are a long-haired bloke with a droopy moustache and a pickaxe handle. And this dark, over-weight priest with a birthmark that looks like a tuft of hair growing in the middle of his forehead. He's wearing a black cassock, dog-collar and all, with a dozen crucifixes hung round his neck and both hands wrapped round a long pole with a heavy metal cross at the dangerous end.

The Greek god is first into the room.

'I'll shoot!' says Marvo. But any fool can see she won't.

So it's up to me and my secret weapon. I chuck the mouse at him.

I'd love to pretend that this was all part of a clever plan, but actually it's pure panic. I can't think of anything better to do.

The mouse lands on the Greek god's shoulder and quacks, like a duck. His eyes nearly pop out of his head. 'Get it off me!' he yells.

The priest shoves the cross at the mouse. It quacks again and jumps onto the cross. As it scuttles down the shaft towards his hands, it's the priest's turn to panic. He's waving the cross around, trying to shake the mouse loose.

He gets the worst possible result. A split second

before the cross hits the Greek god bang between the eyes, the mouse goes airborne again and crash-lands on Droopy.

The Greek god is sitting on the floor, blinking and bleeding from a hole in his forehead. Droopy vanishes down the stairs, waving his arms and screaming, with the mouse clinging on for dear life.

The priest takes a moment to assess the situation. Marvo's hands are steady now as she turns the gun towards him.

He smiles. 'Come to God, my child. Destroy the evil one.'

I think he means me.

'The Lord is merciful—'

'An' you're a birdbrain an' you're under arrest.'

He's still smiling. He mutters a couple of words under his breath. The room fills with black smoke and by the time I've got the skylight open and worked out how to breathe again, it's just me and Marvo.

Outside in the street there's no sign of Alice; just the mouse, chasing round after its own tail on the front step. I scoop it up.

'Damn it, Frank,' says Marvo. 'How did you get to be such a prat?'

'Hey, it was me who got us out of trouble.' When I open my hand, I can see my palm through the mouse. I blow. It quacks and vanishes, leaving a wet patch on my skin.

'Ugh!' Marvo pulls a face.

I put my hand to her nose. Her eyes widen as she catches the smell of roses.

'What's with those guys, anyway?'

'What it says on the tin. They're a brotherhood and they don't like sorcerers.'

'So do they trail around after every sorcerer in town, or is it just you that gets up their nose?'

'Must be my charm and charisma.'

'Yeah, right. What about the priest?'

'They've got a lot of support in the Church, but I've never seen a priest, you know, out in the front line.'

'But he did magic . . .'

'Baby stuff. Must've been a novice sorcerer before he was ordained – like the dead bloke in the palace.' I'm cold now, so I'm fighting my way back into my jerkin. 'Quite a few of the ASB are dropouts from Saint Cyprian's who want to get back at the Society for messing with their heads. Some of them can still do a bit of magic, but mostly they lurk round corners trying to look dangerous. They killed a sorcerer in London, about two years ago.'

'Can I join?'

'Brotherhood: what does that tell you?'

Marvo pulls out her scryer.

'Don't tell Caxton,' I say.

'I have to tell her about Alice.'

'You could just say she wasn't there.'

'Them idiots attacked a police officer in the execution of her duties.'

'It was me they were after. Look, Caxton's got enough against me already. I don't want her thinking I'm a liability.'

'Yeah, but you are.'

'Then whatever.'

So we're back in the van and Marvo's still thinking. Finally she raises her scryer. Touch. Blow . . .

'No sign of her,' she says into the mirror. 'Unless she's at the palace, nobody knows where she could be.' She looks round. 'Yes, he's here.'

I lean across. All I can see in the mirror is the reflection of Marvo's face, but I know Caxton can see me. I grin and wave.

Marvo pushes me away and listens. I can't hear a thing, but finally she says, 'So what'm I supposed to do now?' She nods. 'OK. What time's Ferdia doing the autopsy?' She catches my eye and whispers, 'Ten.'

'Am I invited?' I ask.

But Marvo's closing the scryer. 'She says, piss off home and stay out of her way.' She frowns. 'She really doesn't like you, does she?'

CHAPTER SEVEN
The Boss

It's dark by the time we hit the outskirts of town. The driver's mission is to get me back to the termite nest, preferably alive. He has a choice between the scenic route – through Summertown and over the Ferry Bridge – or the white-knuckle ride through the Hole.

Either he feels he's got something to prove, or he's been sniffing something stimulating, because five minutes later we're in the heart of the Hole, banging through piles of rubble and the sawn-off stumps of street lamps. The van lurches dangerously as the wheels crash into a pothole. I grab Marvo's arm to stop her getting thrown off the seat. She pulls away, the van bounces over a pile of shattered masonry or something and her elbow catches me right on the ear.

'Hey!' I mutter.

'Just stay out the way!' She gives me a shove and my head hits the woodwork.

We're on smoother ground. Marvo shifts away

along the seat and folds her arms, staring intently at the empty seat opposite.

'This isn't going to work,' I say. 'Is it?'

'What isn't going to work?'

'You and me.' I draw another pentagram on the window and gaze blankly past it, trying to pull up the image of the blonde girl at the palace. Kazia. I can see the haircut, but her face won't come.

'It's not like we're partners or anything,' Marvo says. 'We're just on the same case.'

'I don't need any help.'

'I know, Frank. You don't need anybody.'

We're passing a gang of kids, rooting in a pile of rubbish by the side of the street. One of them turns to stare back at me. He's probably only eight or nine, but he's got this thin, pinched face like an old man, with one cheek sunk in where he's lost some teeth.

The thought is racing across my mind, that it's only having the Gift that saved me from winding up like this kid, when he jumps up and comes chasing after us. As he catches up and scuttles alongside, he pulls off his cap and holds it out. I dig a few coins out of my pocket and I've just grabbed the strap to lower the window when the driver cracks his whip and the horses speed up.

'Who the hell do you think you are anyway?' the kid screeches. He trips and goes sprawling.

I turn to peer through the rear window. He's grabbed a cobblestone and throws himself into the air to chuck it after us. I duck as it bangs off the woodwork.

There's a fire raging through the wooden shacks packed into the shell of one of the old colleges. People are screaming and throwing buckets of water around.

I'm taking another crack at trying to remember what Kazia looked like when I notice Marvo looking at me funny.

'She's not really his niece,' she says. 'The girl. She's his daughter.'

'How do you know?'

'Don't be stupid.' She's right, of course. There's guys in the Church who've been going on for years about letting priests marry, but it hasn't happened; meanwhile rather a lot of them seem to have orphaned nephews and nieces living with them. Draw your own conclusion.

'Wouldn't want you to make a mistake,' Marvo mutters. 'That's all.'

We cross the Cherwell Bridge and the gaslights start working again. It's Marvo's turn to gaze out of the window, her right elbow on the sill, her cheek resting on her hand. Her face is round, but it comes to sharp points. From where I'm looking, the tip of her nose projects beyond her cheek like someone's pinched it out of clay.

Maybe it works for Ferdia. Not for me, though. My

heart belongs to a dead bishop's illegitimate daughter. If it's the bishop that's dead.

Anyway, I'm still dreaming up ways to see Kazia again when Marvo says, 'Are you an only child?'

I nod. Why do I suddenly get the feeling that I'm being set up for something?

'I had a kid brother. He died just over a year ago.'

'I'm sorry.' I think that's what I'm supposed to say.

'He was run over by a Ghost.'

'That's impossible—'

'Bastard didn't even stop.'

'Marvo, that can't happen.'

'It did, though. Sean died. There were witnesses an' all – saw it drive right over him. But no investigation.'

I'm not surprised there wasn't. This makes no sense at all.

'What do your parents think?' Unlike sorcerers, tatties aren't actually whipped away from their families at a tender age.

'My dad's dead.' Then, before I can say I'm sorry again: 'Cancer. From working in the paint shop at the Ghost factory.'

OK, that I'm prepared to believe. They took us round the works out at Cowley when I was in my first year at Saint Cyprian's, just to show us how Ghosts are made. I don't remember any magic, just noise and thick fumes.

'I just want to know what happened to Sean an' I figured, coz you're a sorcerer—'

'Frank,' says a voice out of nowhere. Thanking my lucky stars, I drag my scryer out and open it to find myself looking into the pale eyes of a thin-faced, middle-aged man with tonsured grey hair and a neatly trimmed beard. My Master: Matthew Le Geyt.

'Are you at home, Frank?'

Home? Why would anyone call it that? 'I'm on my way.'

'Are you alone?'

'No, I'm with Detective Constable Marvell.'

I turn the scryer to point at Marvo. But she can't see him, of course, and just waves it away.

'How long will you be?' Matthew asks.

'Fifteen minutes.'

'I'll see you in half an hour.'

The mirror mists over and a moment later I'm looking at my own reflection, wondering what's going on. It's not like Matthew never visits me, but there's always more to it than just the pleasure of my company.

I'm still wondering what I could've done wrong when the van jerks to a halt outside my luxury residence and Marvo asks, 'Will you think about it?'

'Think about what?'

'Sean. You know, whose Ghost it was. Who got paid to stop the investigation. Whatever.'

No way! None of this adds up. A Ghost has a top

speed of more than fifty miles an hour, but it's driven by an elemental that's incapable of harming a human being. I assume Marvo did have a brother and he died; but that's not how it happened.

'Sure.'

I climb down. I stand beside the van, waiting to see if anyone wants to take a run at me. All clear. I lean back to grab my case. The monastery door opens behind me.

'Where've you been, anyway?' Brother Andrew's got this wheedling voice, like wet fingers on a windowpane.

'Visiting the Bishop of Oxford.'

'That shit.'

'That dead shit now,' says Marvo, from inside the van. 'What did he ever do to you, anyway?'

'He's a schismatic.' I doubt if Andrew even knows what the word means. He chuckles, like loose teeth rattling in a skull.

'That a reason to cut his head off?'

Andrew's eyes widen. 'Murder's wrong.' He's read his Bible and actually remembered one of the important bits. 'But it was a divine punishment.'

'Tell Caxton. God dunnit.' I'm about to close the van door on Marvo when she says:

'Look, I know I got you into a lot of trouble – reporting you for that stunt with the eye an' all that. But it was your own fault.'

'No problem.' Actually I'm due up in front of a Society board of discipline next week.

She bangs on the roof and the driver flicks the reins. As the horses pull away, she leans out of the window and yells, 'I like Marvo.'

At least my door's pleased to see me. Safely inside, I park my case on the bench and check my magic watch. I've got ten minutes at most.

The first thing to do is to get rid of all the code on the blackboard. I turn on all my lamps and move them up close. I step back and just stand there, staring and scanning, while I count down from three hundred to zero. Then I rub it all out, praying that Matthew doesn't stay so long that I forget it.

I'm still dithering over how much of the cat I can salvage, when I hear a voice through the hole in the wall.

'Frank.'

I tell the door to open and the Boss steps in.

He's tall – well over six foot. When I was still his student, I used to think that if his beard was longer, that's what God would look like. He takes off this expensive-looking grey coat and he's wearing this even more expensive-looking suit underneath it. He's about to drape the coat over the back of a chair when he hesitates, runs one finger along the wood and peers distastefully at a smear of chalk dust. He sniffs the air suspiciously and looks round.

'My God, this place is a mess!'

'I've been busy.'

'So I see.' He doesn't sound angry, just amused in a despairing sort of way. He's at the bench, with the coat over his arm, staring down at the cat. Interesting detail: he's middle-aged, like I said, but he doesn't need glasses. 'Sometimes,' he says, 'I'm relieved that I don't have to deal with this sort of business any more.'

Me, I'd rather get my hands dirty. I dread going post-peak.

Matthew sighs. 'I never understood how you could be so disorganised, Frank, yet such a brilliant sorcerer.' He's staring at the blackboard now. 'Did you just clean that?' He smiles. 'Something you didn't want me to see?'

'Only because it's rubbish.'

'None of your work has ever been rubbish. Ill-advised, maybe, but never rubbish. Anyway, the reason I'm here . . . I was supposed to be having dinner with Henry Wallace this evening.' He crosses himself: his piety always comes as a bit of a surprise to me. 'I can't be bothered requesting a formal briefing from the police and since I knew you had been called in . . .'

OK, that's a relief: I know why he's here now, and for once I haven't screwed up.

He listens patiently as I run quickly through the facts. When I get to the sorcerer's mark on Wallace's chest, he says:

'Yes, that's how we met, as novices at Saint Cyprian's. But Henry was only marginally Gifted. He left after a year and transferred to Douai to train for the mainstream priesthood.'

'His book—'

'I heard he was found holding a copy.' The Boss smiles sadly. 'He'd have appreciated that, he was very proud of it. Didn't make him any friends in the Church, of course, but that doesn't seem like a reason to kill him.'

'Was it a coincidence, though?'

'Was what a coincidence?'

'Half of the book's about Saint Oswald, who got his head cut off five hundred years ago. And here we are now, running around like chickens, trying to work out who left a decapitated corpse—'

'You sound like you're not sure the body *is* Henry.'

'There's no proof yet.'

'Who else could it be? And Henry *is* missing . . .'

'What I'm trying to say . . . whoever he is, he's lost his head and he's sitting in Wallace's library, clutching a copy of this book. And they've got this big Mass tomorrow night and they're gonna pull out Saint Oswald's head and make everybody come over all queasy.'

Matthew sits down, his coat draped over his knees. 'Do the police have any thoughts?'

I roll my eyes.

'Yes, I can imagine it would be a little esoteric for them. They'd probably prefer a burglar.'

'Or the ASB.'

Matthew looks at me keenly. 'Would the Brotherhood go that far?'

'They had two goes at me today.'

He smiles. 'That's understandable, though, isn't it?'

I pretend to think that's funny.

'They're the most likely suspects, I suppose.' He stares down at the chalk marks on the tiles. I'm just beginning to wonder if there's more trouble that I've forgotten I'm in, when he looks up. 'Since it might concern the Society, can I ask you to keep me informed? Obviously you don't work for me, strictly speaking . . .'

I like to think of myself as a sort of hostage, handed over to the jacks in return for an unspoken promise not to look too closely at what the Society's getting up to.

'I'll do my best,' I say.

'Good boy. I don't want you to withhold any information from the police, just let me know what develops.' He gets to his feet. 'Is there anything else?'

I describe the confused security elemental at the river gate, but the Boss holds up his left hand, the one missing the little finger. 'I'd look for an instantiation error before jumping to conclusions.' He checks his watch. 'Frank, I have to rush. Call me if you need to.'

I nod.

He pulls on his coat and says, 'You haven't forgotten the disciplinary committee hearing next week?'

'Certainly not.' Thanks, Marvo. Matthew is looking down at me like he's waiting for something, so I mumble, 'I'm sorry. I know it was stupid, the business with the eye.'

'And then you go and pick the wrong people to be rude to.'

In this case, a Society investigatory committee. I do my apologetic face. 'I usually do.'

'I've noticed.' The smile flickers and dies. 'But maybe it's time you learned that you can't just charge around leaving a trail of destruction behind you.'

He's right, of course. Pity I can't get the hang of it.

'Anyway, I'm not going to preach.'

My door opens. I watch Matthew walk away along the corridor. The outer door closes behind him.

When I'm sure he's gone, I sit down and close my eyes. I don't move for twenty minutes. Then I grab a stick of chalk and step up to my blackboard. I give myself another minute to wonder whether this is such a good idea; then I write all my code out again from memory.

After that it's routine. Up at the fireplace I crumple a few sheets of newspaper in the grate and lay twigs across them. As the flames flare up I kneel and hold out the two wands I used in the amphitheatre. 'In the name of he who died on the tree.' I break each of them into three, and drop the fragments into the fire. The bark curls and darkens . . .

And I get this sharp pain again, where my heart would be, if I had one.

Sympathy.

And that's only the start of a very long night, tidying, replenishing and re-purifying. I'm sure I reconstructed the code on the blackboard correctly, but it makes less sense than ever. Still, there's Kazia to dream about . . .

Except that I can't help wondering about Marvo's brother. Far as I'm aware, nobody's *ever* been killed by a Ghost – with an elemental at the wheel, it's just not supposed to happen.

Sure, I know I told her I'd think about it; but I was just trying to shut her up. Even to ask anybody about it . . . I'd sound like an idiot.

My mum never gave my dad a second thought – just glad to see the back of him. It's a year since Marvo's brother died, and it still bothers her enough for her to ask somebody she doesn't even like to help her out.

The hell with it. Back to Kazia. I can picture the haircut, and something about her eyes. But that's as far as I can get . . .

Even so, I can't get her out of my mind. My heart's banging away. Can this be love? Unfortunately it's not a subject we covered at Saint Cyprian's.

There's a ritual in one of the old grimoires to cause

maidens to dance naked before you, and there's all sorts of spells to make a woman fall in love with a client. Which tells you a lot about the sort of clients private sorcerers get.

But what do I know about it? Somewhere along the line I signed up to a vow of chastity. I was six at the time and didn't even know what the word meant.

Change the subject, Sampson! I feel bad about spooking Alice Constant, but it wasn't really my fault—

Damn! I need to bury that bloody cat before it totally stinks the place out.

CHAPTER EIGHT
Autopsy

The time by my magic watch, when I manage to get my eyes open, is eight o'clock. Brush teeth. Shave face and head. Examine result. Smile. Not a pretty sight. And I've spotted a mistake in my reconstructed code that I'd better fix while I remember . . .

So it's after ten when I slip into the autopsy room. No sign of Caxton, but Marvo's there. She's abandoned the deckchair look and come dressed as a funeral director: black trousers and shoes and a dark grey coat, missing a button.

The main attraction is the body, laid out naked on a solid silver slab under a bank of electric lights. The entire ribcage has been lifted away and Ferdia – smartly turned out in a pale blue rubber apron over black silk overalls and exorcised latex gloves – is leaning over the glistening stew of internal organs, hacking away with a scalpel.

I put my case on the bench and hang up my jerkin. 'Have I missed anything?'

Ferdia straightens up and stretches. 'He was stand-ing when he was stabbed. He went down, first on his knees' – he points to bruises on both kneecaps, then to more on the left arm and shoulder – 'then on his left side, with his arm caught under him. The little finger of the left hand is broken.'

'Well, I don't suppose that bothered him too much.' I pick up the silver dish containing Wallace's heart.

'Blood in the pericardial sac,' says Ferdia. 'Moderate hypertrophy—'

'He liked his food,' says Marvo.

'Puncture in the right ventricle.' Ferdia points with his scalpel in case I've missed it. 'Definitely the stab wound that killed him. Narrow, unserrated blade. Triangular cross-section. Fruit knife. Penknife . . .'

No argument from me. Ferdia may not be able to control anything more demanding than a contiguity test these days, but he's dissected a lot more corpses than I have. I put down the heart in time to catch him staring intently at Marvo.

The door opens. 'I thought I told you to wait for me!'

Caxton is looking her usual cheerful self as she kisses and pockets her amulet. She's brought a friend: a small dog, wearing a pink flea collar. Not a real dog, of course; a search elemental built to bark and wag his tail if his twin, who's sniffing around out there somewhere, turns up the missing head.

She plonks her spectacles on her nose and pulls out

a notebook. She blinks and runs the point of a pencil down a list. 'Contiguity?' she says.

Ferdia turns to the bench and opens a silk bundle to reveal a small brush. 'From Bishop Wallace's bedroom.' He picks up a pair of tweezers and teases out a few hairs. 'I'll run them against hairs from the body this afternoon.'

'Good.' Caxton ticks something off. The notebook and pencil go back in her pocket. She puts on a pair of silk gloves, pulls out an evidence sachet and tips a small sheet of paper into her palm. 'We found this in the pocket of one of Wallace's jackets.'

The note is short, simple and to the point. I can read it upside down, but even with her goggles on, Caxton can't. Sometimes I'm dangerously close to feeling sorry for her. Luckily Marvo knows what she's here for. ' "Leave her alone," ' she reads, and looks up at Caxton. 'No signature.'

'*Cherchez la femme!*' Caxton mutters.

Ferdia smirks. 'The husband, more like!'

'What about Alice?' Marvo glances at me. 'Has anyone seen her?'

'Not yet.' Caxton nudges the dog out of the way and squints distastefully down at the body. 'Could a woman have done that?'

'Sure,' I say, stepping back out of whacking distance. 'My mum did it to my dad.'

The dog stares up at me in surprise.

'Stupid nekkers!' Caxton stuffs the note back into the sachet and drops it on the bench.

While Caxton gets Ferdia to run through everything again, Marvo whispers to me. 'What was that about your dad?'

'Just kidding. He did for himself. Fell asleep with a lighted cigarette.'

That was before my mum won the lottery. She blew the money and now she's living in this wreck of a place just outside town, up on Boar's Lump. Unlike my dad, she wouldn't hurt a fly.

Ferdia is pointing at bits of the body like the true professional that he is. Caxton has her notebook and pencil out again and is printing away laboriously. Her eyes swim dizzyingly behind her glasses as she struggles to focus.

Finally she turns to Mr Memory, sitting patiently in the corner in his baggy suit. He's changed his bow tie, but carried the food stain across.

'Knives from the palace,' she says. 'Anything sharp . . .'

The elemental raises his hand and an array of cutlery manifests in mid-air. There's various carving and bread knives; and a dozen more, too small to have severed the head and too big to have inflicted the chest wound. Plus a potato peeler. Also a meat cleaver.

'Show me that.'

Tell Mr Memory what you want and he'll give it to

you. He exists to oblige. He hands Caxton the cleaver. No risk of creating a contiguity, by the way: the real cleaver is safe in a drawer, wrapped in silk.

She peers at the blade, then holds it up for Marvo to examine. 'Blood?'

'Can't see any, but it could've been washed.' Marvo looks up at Ferdia. 'Better test it.'

Caxton runs a finger along the edge. 'Waste of time. Too blunt. What do you think we used to pay executioners for? You've got to be strong and the blade's got to be razor sharp.' I don't like the way she's looking at me. 'Even professionals sometimes took four or five swipes to finish the job.' She hands the cleaver back to Mr Memory.

'One good blow in this case,' says Ferdia. 'Chipped the fifth vertebra and severed the spinal cord. A sharp weapon rather than a heavy one.'

'How d'you know?'

'The second blow was accurate, right into the existing cut.'

'OK,' says Caxton. 'Suppose the bishop's being unbishoply—'

'Suppose it's not the bishop,' I suggest, just for the hell of it.

'If you've nothing useful to say, don't say it!' Caxton's giving me what's meant to be a blank stare, but with her prescription it actually looks like a couple of angry jellyfish trapped in goldfish bowls. 'The husband's sent him that note. Lures him out, say to the river bank, kills him, brings the body back—'

'But that doesn't makes sense, Chief,' Marvo objects. 'You'd need two people to move the body – three, with a loose head—'

This is the bit I love: when nobody actually knows anything, so they just make up stories and try to fit the facts around them.

'Have you got a better idea?' says Caxton.

'Not yet.'

'Well let me know when you do.'

That's the other thing tatties are for: coming up with bright ideas out of nowhere. They call them insights.

'The beheading could've been done back inside the palace,' says Ferdia.

'No blood,' says Marvo.

Caxton's turn. 'But if he was already dead . . .'

'There's still got to be two weapons.' Marvo turns to Mr Memory. 'And what about the book?'

'In his new book, the Bishop of Oxford turns his formidable analytic intelligence to one of the great controversies of Western Christendom, the acceptance of sorcery as an article of faith. In particular he re-examines the martyrdom and subsequent canonisation of Saint Oswald of Oxford—'

'All right,' says Caxton. But the elemental is on a roll.

'The bishop concludes that the cult of Saint Oswald has the potential to heal the current rift between the Society of Sorcerers and the mainstream Church. This is a provocative and insightful book by one of—'

'That's enough!' Caxton glares at me. 'You told Marvell that Wallace was a sorcerer.'

'No, I said he was a novice.' I give Marvo my withering look. She sticks her tongue out at me. 'Most bishops of Oxford are former members of the Society.'

Ferdia nods. 'It's a tradition.'

'You nekkers,' Caxton mutters, 'you're all in it together.'

'Wallace gets beheaded, just like Saint Oswald, forty-eight hours before this big Mass in Oswald's memory – it's gotta be something to do with that.' Marvo's frowning like her head hurts. 'Makes more sense than a jealous husband with a dagger in one hand and a cleaver in the other.'

'Where *is* that bloody head, anyway?' says Caxton. The dog looks up at her apologetically.

'I know!' says Marvo.

'Yes?' Caxton's pencil is twitching to go.

'The beheading and the book, it's like . . .' Marvo's face is all screwed up. 'You know what I mean, Frank . . .'

I raise my hands. 'I don't know anything.'

We wait. 'Sorry, it's gone.' Marvo's face is white. 'Maybe it'll come back.'

'I hope so,' says Caxton.

Marvo blinks. 'But this isn't some burglary gone wrong, where the killer could be any creep in the city.'

'Maybe it's a burglary trying to pretend it's not a burglary,' says Ferdia helpfully.

'Maybe it was an accident.' I pull on my jerkin.

'Did I say you could go?' Caxton turns to Mr Memory. 'Any other knives?'

He shakes his head.

'Garden tools?'

He makes a pass in the air. The array of kitchen cutlery evaporates, to be replaced by a pair of secateurs.

'Sure,' I say. 'He was snipped to death.'

'The cathedral,' Marvo says quickly. 'P'raps we should search it again.'

It's the first intelligent suggestion anyone's made, but Caxton just peers cross-eyed at her watch, gives up and turns to the clock on the wall. 'They'll be setting up for tonight. And we've been right through the place, anyway.'

I've got this picture in my head: a line of jacks, all wearing glasses, down on their hands and knees, feeling their way up the nave of the cathedral.

Caxton turns a page in her notebook. 'I don't get it;

they come in through the gate from the river and go all the way round to the cathedral, just to steal a candlestick to break a window? Because there's nothing missing . . .'

'Apart from the obvious,' I point out.

We all stare down at the empty space, just north of the corpse, where there ought to be a head.

'But who'd want to decapitate a bishop?' Caxton's razor-sharp brain has registered this crucial detail and she isn't letting go of it. She's got it written down in large capital letters: 'DECAPITATE A BISHOP?'

'Someone with a grudge against bishops?' I suggest, bending down to scratch the dog's ears. 'Another bishop, who fancies this bishop's palace?'

'At midnight.'

'*Around* midnight.' I've got a nasty feeling about where she's going with this.

'What the hell would anyone want with a bishop's head?'

The question seems to be directed at me, so I put the noose round my own neck. 'D'you mean, what would a *sorcerer* want with a bishop's head? We don't use human body parts.'

Everyone just looks at me, including the dog. I can feel my face going red.

That stupid thing I said I'd done – the thing Marvo shopped me for . . . Look, the reason I've been scrawling all that stuff on the blackboard back at my studio is because I've been trying to decode an old incantation and I'd tried just about everything and it still wasn't working, and I had this wild idea that a human eye might do the trick. So a few weeks back, there was this body we'd finished with in the mortuary . . . I mean, I didn't think anybody would notice, you know, once the eyelids were closed.

But of course bloody Marvo noticed.

I don't think the jacks cared much, one way or the other. It's the sort of thing they expect – the sort of thing they wave amulets around to protect themselves from. But the Society took a Very Dim View of it.

'Shut up, Frank,' says Ferdia.

Caxton's busy in her notebook again, drawing something vaguely resembling a human hand. 'What about the hand of glory?' She looks up at Marvo. 'You get the hand of an executed criminal and dry and pickle it. When you go to burgle a house you set up the hand as a holder for a candle made of human fat and it puts everyone in the house to sleep.'

She draws round the outline of the hand again and looks up at me triumphantly. 'If a hand of glory, why not a head of glory?'

'Why not an arsehole of glory?' I say. 'Stick your corpse face down—'

'Don't try to be clever with me.'

'Then don't talk crap!' I pick up my case. 'There's no such thing. It's a myth.'

I'm heading for the door.

'Who said you could go?'

'I've got stuff to do.'

And I'm gone.

CHAPTER NINE
Holy Matter

I've got a choice. I can spend a long and boring day running routine contiguity tests between a bullet I pulled out of an unidentified body and a cupboardful of loose guns, on the off-chance of getting a match. Or I can check out a dead saint.

Time for a history lesson. Saint Oswald of Oxford. Born 1445. Died, rather unpleasantly, 1493. Alchemist, theologian and the first important cleric to propose bringing sorcery out of the cellars into the heart of the Church. Appointed Bishop of Oxford just in time to find himself on the sharp end of a witch panic. Defied a lynch mob at the altar of the cathedral. Lost his head. Literally.

You know what they say: history gets written by the winners. The Society of Sorcerers was founded twenty years later and the surviving witch-finders came to a significantly stickier and longer drawn-out end than Oswald.

He was declared a martyr. But, somewhere in the

confusion surrounding his death, his head had got lost . . . only to turn up sixty years later – miraculously preserved!

That's what saved the cathedral. It had cost a fortune to build – and it was costing an even bigger fortune to stop it falling down again. It's no use littering the joint with collection boxes unless you've got something to pull in the punters. And for some reason people will shell out good money to pray to bits that fell off dead saints: fragments of bone, clumps of hair, loose teeth. They're called relics, and my personal favourite is the Holy Prepuce, Christ's foreskin, which you can still pay to admire in several different cities across Europe.

Anyway, they gave Oswald's head a wash, pickled it, and stuck it in this flashy reliquary in the crypt of the cathedral – where I vaguely remember seeing it as a kid. I still think there has to be sorcery involved in Wallace's murder, and if Marvo's right and it's got something to do with his book . . . well, maybe I should drop in on Oswald and get reacquainted. It's right next to the palace, so maybe I'll get to see Kazia too . . .

It's uncomfortably bright and sunny, and I'm standing on Seven Bridges Road, clutching my case and staring across at the cathedral: a massive pile of marble, dirty white with bands of red and green, like a shop-soiled wedding cake. The wind isn't much warmer than it was yesterday, but for once I had the sense to wear a sweater. I button up my jerkin, pull my hat down over my ears and look up and down the road.

It's busy. A queue at an omnibus stop. Kids on lunch break, huddled on benches around the green.

A voice behind me: 'I know you.'

I look round. Yeah, he knows me because I know him: Norrie Padstowe. Ugly gorilla with a beer belly and curly hair that used to be bright red but has gone grey now, leaving just his nose to shine like a shipping beacon.

'Don't think so.'

'Yeah, you're Joe Sampson's nipper.' He pulls out a string of beads. 'The nekker—'

There are words that work . . . well, like magic. Shout 'fire!' in a crowded theatre and everybody'll bolt for the exit. Yell 'nekker' on a busy road and it's the opposite, like a magnet.

The effect is slow at first. An old priest stops in his tracks and sticks one hand up in the air, index and little fingers raised like horns.

'Yeah, the nekker!'

Who could forget Norrie? Once an idea wormed its way into his thick head, it took explosives to shift it. Or industrial quantities of alcohol. He used to prop up the bar at the Brazen Head with my dad. I thought he'd drunk himself into a hole in the ground years ago, but here he is, large as life and dead set on being a pain.

'Nekker!' His voice rings across the cathedral green.

It may not be real magic, but it sure works like it is. A couple of kids have stopped to stare. One puts her hand to the other's ear and whispers something. A bus has pulled up at the stop, clouds of steam rising from the horses' flanks, but the dummies in the queue are too busy whispering and staring to get on board. The driver turns and the sun glints on silver as he raises a charm to his lips.

Along the green, there's a row of almshouses built recently to show that somebody cares. Despite the cold, a middle-aged woman is sitting on her door-step, her hand shading her eyes as she stares back at me.

And suddenly the tide's crashing in, lifting me off my feet and carrying me out into the road. Someone's grabbed my case and I'm hugging it for dear life, trying to prevent it making things worse.

'You're making a mistake. He's a drunk, for Christ's sake—'

'No I ain't!' Norrie's waving his beads frantically. 'He's a nekker, I tell you – look for the mark!'

They're all over me, yelling and screaming and elbowing each other out of the way. My hat's gone. They've got my jerkin up at the back and they're tear-ing at my sweater. Someone's tugging at my belt. Fingernails digging into my skin.

'It's on his back,' someone yells.

'No it's not.' There's always got to be a perv, right? 'It's on his arse!'

Back, chest, scalp, groin – they've all heard of this mythical sorcerer's mark, but they can't agree where it is. The good news is that now we're all close up in one big heap, the grown-ups can't tell one kid from another and everyone's just throwing punches at random. I let my legs buckle and try to slide to the ground. Someone lets go of my ear and I slam down hard on my case, narrowly missing the broken fragments of some idiot's glasses. I get kicked in the stomach. Someone falls on top of me and someone on top of them.

My case is whimpering. Norrie's beads roll past me. Through the dancing forest of legs I glimpse a burly, middle-aged man in round sunglasses, watching from the edge of the scrum. There's something about the way he just stands there, arms folded, legs astride, like he's weighing up what he sees . . . I dunno, it kind of spooks me.

One thing at a time. I kick and roll. I see blood running down a screaming face. I'm free – on my feet – case clutched under my arm – running like hell.

Down an alley between the almshouses, over a fence – trampling someone's vegetable patch – jumping another fence. Through the railings along the gardens of the Bishop's Palace, I can see Charlie's lion basking on the lawn in the sunshine. It's going transparent; it's done what it was built for and in a day or so it will just fade away.

I stop, panting for breath. There's nobody on my tail. Beyond the railings, a uniformed jack is watching a small dog snuffle around in the palace flowerbeds. It could just be some stray mutt, but the pink flea-collar is kind of a giveaway. Charlie's work: the active half of the search elemental, still trying to sniff out the missing head.

A bit of trespassing will get me into the cathedral, without having to go back round by the green. I grab one of the railings. There's a low, warning growl. I haul myself up. The growl is louder, more threatening and the railings start curling over at the top to stop me climbing over. Charlie's lion has lifted its head.

I'm hanging there, trying to figure out how to get over in one piece, when I spot something else: the kid from inside the palace yesterday, standing in the shrubbery with a spade. He's got his hand over his eyes and he's staring at someone coming out of the back door of the palace.

I jump as a hand clamps on to my shoulder. The woman from the almshouse doorstep is gazing into my face, her eyes screwed up. 'You ain't no policeman.'

I can't stop her dragging me down. She stinks of alcohol and it's a miracle she can stand, even with one talon clamped to my shoulder.

'Do I look like a policeman?'

She hauls out the inevitable amulet. 'You're a sorcerer.'

'So what?'

I'm wondering if I can offer to turn her into anything, when I see what's fascinating the kid with the spade: Kazia is kneeling on the grass, tickling the dog's nose. Another reason to go over the railings – if I can get away.

'You look like my son, when he was your age.' The woman has jammed a pair of cracked glasses on her face and is still peering up at me, squinting against the sun.

'Some guys have all the luck.' How do I get out of this?

'He's a manager at the works out in Cowley. Don't come to see me no more. Better things to do.'

'That's kids for you. No gratitude.'

The bloke with the sunglasses – the one who was watching me get pulled apart – he's appeared out of nowhere and now he's just standing there, fifty yards off, watching us. He folds his arms slowly. It seems like a good point to end this conversation and make myself scarce. I pull away from the woman and try to massage some life back into my shoulder.

'There was a demon.'

OK, she has my attention again.

'Last night, round midnight.' She points across the palace gardens, where Kazia is staring back at us. 'Down by the river.'

'What did it look like?'

'Like a dog.'

'Maybe it *was* a dog.'

For a moment, that seems to shut her up. But then: 'That's what the detective said. Stupid woman. Full of herself.'

'That'd be Beryl.'

'Who's Beryl? Do I know her?'

'No.'

'Well I ain't blind and I knows a demon when I sees one.'

'What was it doing?'

'Your friend Beryl says she was just taking it for a walk.'

'Who?'

'Beryl.'

'No, who was taking it for a walk?'

'This woman in a nightdress. But it weren't on a lead, it were in front, leading her. And there was this man following her . . .'

'Where was it leading her, the dog?'

'Told you: not a dog – a demon. Didn't stay to find out. Ask him.' She points to where Sunglasses was standing a moment ago. Her voice softens to a sinister whisper. 'He's gone now, but he were there last night, too. Didn't have them dark glasses on, though. He'd have walked straight into the river if he had.'

Inside the palace garden, Kazia is just standing there, staring at me.

What the hell? I point towards the cathedral.

It's cold inside and almost pitch-dark. During the Channel Islands War, they bricked up all the cathedral windows to save the stained glass from the Montgolfier raids and never got around to knocking them out again. The scrape of my boots on the stone floor echoes up into the roof as I scuttle behind a pillar and scry Caxton.

I've got halfway through the woman's story about the people with the dog when Caxton says, 'Stop wasting my time.'

'But I'm not. I mean, just before midnight – and she says it was a demon.'

'Rubbish! I've interviewed her.' Caxton's face jumps around in the scryer as the glasses go on and the corner of her notebook wobbles into view. 'Her name's Amber Trickle.'

'I'm sorry?'

Caxton frowns down at her note. She raises it for me to read. Trickle it is.

'She's a drunk.'

'I'm not surprised.'

'Thank you, Sampson. A drunk and an attention-seeker, and she's as blind as a bloody bat!'

I could make the obvious cheap crack, but I say,

'Something spooked the elemental on the gate. OK, I'd be dead surprised if it was a demon, but you've got a witness who says she saw a man, a woman in a night-dress, and a dog. Nothing about anyone carrying a body. And she said there was this other bloke—'

'Haven't you got something useful to get on with?'

The mirror mists up and I'm staring at myself. Still not a pretty sight.

I put my scryer away and follow the line of candles up the nave. Tonight's the night, all right. Clergy scuttle around like black beetles. And I can see crews setting up these whopping big scryers in the side-chapels. Like elemental work, it's the sort of thing you can do when the Gift is taken away. A single sorcerer can instantiate a dozen scryers in an hour; then, once they've been set up and pointed in the right direction, any old post-peaker can stagger in and put down his beer long enough to say the right words at the right moment.

I avoid a bright pool of light at the top of the nave and turn right into the south transept, where I remem-ber there's a door leading through the cathedral cloister to the Bishop's Palace. But I don't get far.

'Brother Tobias!' My stage name, remember.

Stay cool, Frank. 'Who let you out?'

Brother Andrew pulls a face. 'They're making me do the Mass tonight, for Saint Oswald . . .'

He's still droning on about how fed up he is and

how it's all, like, totally unfair, when, to my amazement, Kazia appears out of the darkness behind him.

Her haircut is extreme, but it works for me. I've got the same buzz I get before doing magic – and the same giddy feeling. My legs are trembling. I may fall over.

'Are you listening?' Andrew whines. 'I said to them, I want nothing to do with it.'

Any chance of a thunderbolt, Lord? I'd promise to be good. 'With what?'

'The Mass. What's your problem, Brother?'

'Forgive me, Brother, it's these bloody demons!'

That works. He jumps back, crossing himself. Right into Kazia. 'Hey, watch where you're going!' he snaps.

'Watch yourself!' She shoves him away and turns to me with this sort of forlorn smile. 'You were there yesterday.'

'Yes. I'm sorry about . . .'

What am I sorry about? Was Wallace really her father? Looking at her – and I'm dead happy to look at her – I don't see any resemblance to the portrait in the library.

Andrew hasn't finished yet. 'Can't anyone see? Oswald was one of the false prophets foretold—'

She steps in front of him and holds out her hand to me. 'My name is Kazia.'

'Frank,' I croak.

I don't know whether it's because I'm a sorcerer, or just because I'm me . . . Anyway, people usually avoid touching me, so any hand is a novelty. Hers is soft – well, what did you expect? She's trembling . . .

'Are you all right?' I ask.

I can feel my pulse racing and think maybe she can feel it too. I'm wondering how long before I'm supposed to let go . . .

'You are the other sorcerer,' she says. Her hand slips away like a wraith.

In the candlelight, her eyes are so blue that I could just dive into them . . . if there wasn't this weird thing, like a film across them, hiding whatever's swimming around beneath the surface . . .

'The junior forcer, yes.' Why did I have to say that?

'Sorry?'

'It's what people call us. Forensic sorcerer.'

I'm struggling to prioritise. I mean, I'm with this girl who's turned my knees to jelly, only I'm really nervous about talking to her in case I say something truly stupid. I just want her to stand there so I can stare at her – like, fix her in my memory. But I still need to go down and take a peep at what's left of Saint Oswald.

I turn to Andrew. 'Can we get into the crypt?'

'Why?'

'I want to see the reliquary.'

I'm already sorry I asked because Kazia's got this unhappy look on her face. Too late, though.

'Just curious,' I hear myself say. 'They opened it at the Mass when I took my vows but I've kind of forgotten.'

'I suppose so,' Andrew groans. Oh dear, I've upset him too.

And he's not alone. 'I wanted to talk to you,' Kazia whispers. For a split second I think she's angry with me. Then I realise she's disappointed. Which can't be right.

My sense of duty is a fatal flaw in an otherwise exemplary personality. 'I'm sorry, I kinda need to see this . . .'

'But—'

'You can come too,' says Andrew. Obviously she works for him, as well. He grabs a lantern and takes off down a flight of wide, shallow steps into the darkness beneath the cathedral floor. I follow him, then turn. Kazia hasn't moved. To my own amazement, I hold out my hand.

OK, she doesn't take it. But a sad sort of smile – maybe it's just pity – flickers across her face. She slips past me and follows Andrew.

It's years since I've been in the crypt. It's a deathtrap, scattered with tools and materials from the restoration work that's been sucking up money ever since they built the joint. A couple of workmen are playing cards by candlelight on the flat top of a tomb. They grin as I duck just in time to avoid braining myself on a low arch.

Looking around the walls I can see enough spare parts down here to build an army of saints. They've got the forearm and left index finger of Saint Thomas Becket; a lock of Mary Magdalene's hair; the skulls of Saint James the Lesser and Saint Michael of Abingdon; various ribs belonging to Saint Paul, Saint Peter, Saint John of Patmos and a dozen more besides. All in caskets and jars, some made of gold, some encrusted with rubies and emeralds, glistening resentfully in the flicker of Andrew's lantern and surrounded by thousands of glass and metal charms nailed to wooden panels.

Down at the back there's second class: the ossuary is a maze of shelf-lined corridors, stacked with the skulls and bones of hundreds of years' worth of dead termites that nobody's willing to pay to see. Let's not go in there – it's spooky and claustrophobic. Let's concentrate on the girl just ahead of me.

'It's cold!' she says, wrapping her arms round herself before I can offer to do it for her.

'Where are you from?' She's not English. There's a precision about the way she speaks, as if she has to think about what she says. But it's a bit weird: like running your fingers across velvet when you're not sure which way the nap goes.

'Lithuania.'

'Where in Lithuania?'

'Kernave. You have heard of it?'

It rings a bell, but who cares? Here and now, Frank. Here and now . . .

We follow Andrew under more head-crunchingly low arches to a side chapel caged behind elaborate wrought-iron railings. Inside, I can just make out an altar with two candlesticks, a simple brass cross and a curious object like the helmet and shoulders of a suit of medieval armour.

Andrew takes a heavy key from a nail in the wall. 'They should burn all this.' One day, I realise, he'll run amok. He hands me the lantern and stoops to unlock the gate. 'Superstitious rubbish!'

'What about the miracles?' There are always miracles – like the one I did with Marvo's tarot card.

'Huh!' He pushes the gate open.

I stand aside to let Kazia pass. The floor is thick with dust, the walls stained by damp. I hold up the lantern.

After they found Oswald's head, back in 1553, the party went on for weeks, and by the time everybody had got over their hangovers, Doughnut City was on its way to being one of the most popular shrines in Christendom. People came flooding in from all over, to kiss the head – gross or what? – and be cured of all sorts of diseases that you really don't want to know about. The Church had to find some way of protecting it from the wear and tear – and building the brand, of course – so they stuck it inside this reliquary.

'Wow!'

OK, I've seen it before, but I'd forgotten how fabulous it is. I catch Kazia's eye and I'm relieved to see that she's staring intently at it too.

The real miracle here is that the reliquary has never been stolen. It stands on a white altar cloth. It's made of pure gold, encrusted with jewels that gleam in the lamplight, and has been sculpted to resemble Oswald: the head and shoulders of a man, slightly over life size, wearing a monk's cowl. On the wall above hangs a painting of him looking remarkably relaxed about the sword sweeping towards his neck.

Kazia looks round nervously at the sound of somebody knocking something over, out in the crypt. I'm too fascinated to pay any attention. This thing is beautiful.

And inside . . . well, probably not so beautiful: what's left of the thing I came here to see: the head of Saint Oswald. Holy matter, the most precious and magical substance there is. A sorcerer can have a lot of fun with a relic. Thank God the Society's here to protect the world.

'He's still in there,' Andrew giggles. 'He's lost a few teeth.'

He's still rattling on when I hear Marvo's voice say, 'Frank.' I hand the lantern to Andrew and pull out my scryer.

'What d'you want?'

She's got her coat on and I can see sunlight

splattered across the mortuary building behind her. 'Ferdia's finished.'

'Did I miss anything?'

'I thought you'd help me look for Alice. Hey, it's your fault she's missing.'

'Well I'm busy.'

'Doing what? Where are you?'

'Guess.'

I turn the scryer towards the reliquary. Andrew and Kazia can't hear Marvo's end of the conversation and he's complaining that he's been roped in to carry the reliquary up to the altar at the Mass tonight. He sounds pretty narked off. Kazia looks pretty bored.

'That's the cathedral crypt, right?' says Marvo. 'Saint Oswald—'

'Yeah, just wondered how he was getting on.' I turn the scryer back, so that I can see her in the mirror. 'Happy now?'

But it's like she's been turned to stone. Her mouth is open and she's got this weird, lost expression plastered across her face. Her eyes close. She's as white as a sheet.

'Marvo?'

She looks like she's going to fall over.

'Hello?'

Still nothing. Andrew is looking at me, dead puzzled. I blow on the mirror so it mists up for a moment. When it clears, Marvo's eyes have opened, round and blank like the moon, and she's staring out at me like she's never seen me before.

'Marvo!'

She twitches like a rag doll that's been shaken. 'It's in the reliquary . . .'

'What?'

'Wallace's head. It's inside the reliquary.'

Insight.

That's what all the play-acting's about. Tatties – the good ones, anyway – they don't just have great eyesight, they get this . . . I dunno, some people say it's magical, or a trance or something. But it looks to me like they've got all this information coming at them and they're concentrating so hard on making sense of it that everything else sort of shuts down.

Whatever you like. All I know is, it's spookier than a lot of Presences I've met.

And for once in my life I'm actually speechless, because I realise she's right: it isn't Oswald's skull in the reliquary, is it? I mean, I don't know about you, but it's suddenly, blindingly obvious to me that Marvo's bang on the nail and what's inside is . . .

Ta-dah! The missing head.

'It's like Akinbiyi said, back in the library yesterday.' Marvo's voice is shaking. 'Someone's trying to tell us something. Don't you get it, Frank? This isn't just a murder, it's a *message.*'

'OK, leave it to me.'

I hear Marvo say, 'I'm on my way,' as I snap the scryer shut.

'Sorry about that.' I step up to the reliquary. At the side, where a tiny catch opens the faceplate, there are clear trails through the film of dust covering the gold surface. I pull a pair of silk gloves out of my case – hopefully there's contiguity between the reliquary and whoever opened it and I don't want to mess that up. I reach for the catch.

'You can't!' Andrew slaps my hand away. 'It's a sacred relic, even if it shouldn't be.'

I'm about to explain that I think it's a missing bishop rather than a sacred relic. But I glance up at Kazia. She's watching me keenly, and I remember the expression of sheer horror on her face when she pulled the sheet off the body on the trolley. I want to impress her; not send her screaming up the walls.

'Sorry.' I step back and take my gloves off.

Another bang from outside. Kazia clutches the wrought-ironwork and peers out into the darkness of the crypt.

'You can come to the Mass tonight if you want to see it,' Andrew says. 'I've got to help carry it up to the high altar. It'll be opened then for the ignorant to venerate.'

Of course. That's when the message is supposed to get delivered.

He turns to Kazia. 'You'll be there, won't you?'

But she's vanished. I dart to the chapel entrance and see her silhouette disappearing up the steps to the nave.

'Sorry. Gotta go.' I grab my case. 'Thank you.' It's not Andrew's fault his parents tried to secure their places in heaven by handing him over to the termites.

By the time I get upstairs, there's no sign of Kazia except a streak of light across the floor of the south transept, narrowing to nothing as the door to the cloister closes.

I hear footsteps and turn, expecting to see Andrew coming up from the crypt. But it isn't him, it's the stocky bloke who was watching me earlier – the one the unfortunately-named Amber Trickle spotted down by the river. If he can see anything, it's another miracle because he's still wearing his sunglasses. Maybe he's a tourist, blinded by the splendour of the architecture. On the other hand, maybe he's the Anti-Sorcery Brotherhood with something unpleasant on his mind. I decide to wait for Marvo outside, and make a dash for the west door.

CHAPTER TEN
Alchemy

So I get to skulk on the bridge, looking out for trouble. After five minutes there's no sign of Sunglasses and I relax a bit and watch a gang of uniformed jacks poking around the reeds in waders. Through the trees, I can see the famous gate to the palace gardens, with a shiny new elemental on patrol in a dark suit and blue shirt.

Before I can get too bored with it all, there's a yell behind me and Marvo's hanging out of a van. She looks wrecked: pale as a ghost, dark rings under her eyes, the works.

Insight. You don't get something for nothing.

Back inside the cathedral, still no Sunglasses, but things are really hotting up for the Mass tonight. People are swarming all over the place, fiddling with the scryers, brushing between the pews, throwing hymn books around, jamming new candles into holders, hanging banners.

Down in the crypt, the workmen are too busy

clearing up to pay us any attention. But when we get to the back, there's this mob of clergy packed into the side chapel watching an old woman in a ragged grey coat, as she polishes up the reliquary.

'Why didn't you open it?' Marvo hisses.

My pal Andrew's lurking at the back of the chapel with his arms folded and a disapproving look on his gob.

Marvo ploughs on: 'It was coz the girl was there, right?'

'What girl?' Hey, it's worth a try.

'The girl from the palace.' Marvo pulls out her scryer. 'Don't mess me about, Frank – I saw her.'

I could make up a story, but what's the point? 'I didn't want to gross her out, OK? I mean, if you're right—'

'I *am* right.'

'Then that's her uncle's head inside the reliquary.'

'I told you, Wallace was her dad—'

'Was Wallace Lithuanian? Coz she is.'

'So you had a good chat.'

'The point is, she knows the guy and I'd be surprised if he's looking his best. I didn't want to upset her.'

'Didn't want to hurt your chances, more like.' Marvo looks round. 'Anyway, she's gone now—'

'Wait.' I grab her arm and I'm amazed again how scrawny it is. 'The guy in the corner, next to Andrew.'

124

Marvo's eyes widen. He's only got one crucifix hanging round his neck and he's lost the cross on the pole, but it's unmistakably the fat priest with the birthmark from Alice Constant's lodgings.

'I'll scry Caxton,' Marvo says, and tries to wrench her arm away.

'No.' And before anyone sees us, I drag Marvo back across the crypt towards the steps.

It's a struggle, but I manage to get Marvo out of the cathedral and into the van, where I tell the driver to take us to my place. According to my magic watch, it's just after five. I've drawn my pentagrams in the dirt on the windows on each side of the van, but even if they succeed in keeping evil forces at bay, they can't shut Marvo up.

'Frank, we gotta call Caxton. Get back in, open that thing up.'

'No, leave it alone. Let it play out.'

Marvo stares at me. 'What's the point of that?'

'For a start, if you're wrong we don't get into trouble for prising open a saint on his big day.'

'But I'm not wrong.'

'Then it's what you said: a message. Listen, Marvo—'

'Marvell's fine. You can call me Magdalena, for all I care.'

I can see she's dead set on feeling pissed off and the

more I try to explain, the more she's going to hang on to the wrong end of the stick like her life depends on it.

'Fine,' I say. 'So listen, Magdalena. They'll open the reliquary at the Mass tonight. So we can be there, and we can see how people react and maybe that'll give us some idea what this is all about.'

'Maybe the girl will be there.'

'Look, the reason I went to the cathedral was because I wanted to see the reliquary. You know, get a fix on all this crap about Saint Oswald.' OK, I can't put my hand on my heart and say it never occurred to me that Kazia would be around, but still . . .

'Honest.'

So we both sit there sulking and staring out of the windows until we're halfway up the hill to the termite nest and Marvell starts up again.

Apparently Caxton's a pain. As if we didn't know that. But somehow Marvo gets on to how unfair *everything* is, just because we're kids and we can do stuff that grown-ups can't do . . . like actually see objects smaller than a building.

I'm about to point out that she gets a pretty easy ride off Caxton compared with me; but she's already switched to how it wasn't her fault that her and me got off to a bad start, because nobody explained things to her and this is typical of how they treat tatties and nekkers. So I take a couple of minutes to explain that nekker is short for necromancer; and that necromancy is raising the dead to predict the future and is a toastable offence and I'd prefer it if she stuck to 'sorcerer' – or 'freak', if she must.

She goes all quiet then and we both sit there staring out of opposite sides of the van until she says, 'But it's still not fair. I got Caxton on my back, goin' on at me to get an insight and solve the case for her. And then when I do get one, you tell me to keep my mouth shut.'

'I'm sorry.' I can't believe I said that. 'Look, the fat priest – we know he's ASB. And there was this other bloke—'

'What other bloke?'

I tell her about Sunglasses following me round by the river and into the cathedral, and how the woman from the almshouse said she'd seen him outside the palace the night Wallace was murdered.

'So you think he's ASB too, yeah? An' it was them that done Wallace.'

'Well, we still don't know that it was Wallace.'

'Oh, come on, Frank!'

'OK, obviously the ASB didn't like his book. I thought it was pretty damn boring myself. But this whole circus . . . it's all too *complicated* for them. I mean, they shout and scream and come at sorcerers with knives—'

'Can't say I blame them.'

So we don't say anything for a bit, and we're just

coming up to the termite nest when she cracks and says, 'What *is* contiguity, anyway?'

'Didn't they teach you it?'

'Just that it's a force. Like gravity, only magic.'

I'll take that as a no. Still at least we're talking again, so pay attention at the back . . .

'Sympathetic magic. First law: the Law of Similarity. A sorcerer can produce an effect by imitating it. That's how most curses work. You make a wax doll to look like somebody; then when you stick pins in the doll, the victim feels the pain.'

'That don't work though.'

'Done right, you can kill somebody.'

'Have you?'

I do my enigmatic smile and put my fists together, knuckles touching.

'Second law: the Law of Contiguity. When any object comes into contact with another, they establish a physical affinity – they remember each other.'

I move my fists apart. 'When they're separated, the contiguity weakens over time, but never completely disappears. If you pick up a pebble on a beach, that creates a contiguity. You can throw it out to sea, but the affinity between you and that pebble persists.'

'What's the difference between contiguity an' affinity?'

'No difference. Contiguity's the technical term. I use "affinity" sometimes to avoid tiresome repetition.

So that pebble you threw away, right? I could identify it eventually, by picking up every pebble in reach and testing it.'

'That'd take for ever!'

'More usefully, if someone gives me a pebble I can tell if you've ever handled it.'

She nods and says, 'Coz Ferdia did the contiguity test with hairs from the body and from the hairbrush they found in Bishop Wallace's bedroom. He said it was absolute.'

'But he's post-peak. And the brush could've been planted.'

'That's what I said. But Akinbiyi identified it.'

'And he's clergy so he must be telling the truth.'

The termites, right: they don't like me any more than I like them, but at least they're used to me. The evidence is in the kitchen: two plates of cold ham. I hand Marvo the one from the icebox. The cook's pet dog hasn't got to the one on the floor yet, so I grab it for myself.

'You sure it's not poisoned?' she says, sniffing suspiciously.

'Here.' I swap with her. 'They wouldn't hurt the dog.'

It's getting dark as we hike across the vegetable garden to my studio. It's beginning to look like maybe we're friends again, when she starts up. 'And why'd you have to be such a prat with Alice?'

'How was I to know she was scared of mice?'

'She wasn't.' Marvo frowns. 'Not when I knew her, anyway. She had a pet rat at training college – I told you she had the Tats . . .'

'No you didn't.'

'Do you know how I was spotted? As a tatty, I mean.'

'No. But I'll bet you're going to tell me.'

'I was twelve, yeah? I was in town with my mum and I saw this old guy doing that trick with the three shells.'

I know the scam. He's got three walnut shells, or whatever, on a flat surface. He puts a dried pea under one of them and shuffles them around, dead fast.

'It was obvious,' says Marvo. 'Sleight of hand, like your trick with the card. He slipped the pea out before he moved the shells, then after this prat bet ten quid on where it was, he stuck it under a different one. So I'm about to call the jacks but this guy grabs my arm and shoves a badge in Mum's face and says he's from your lot . . .'

Yeah, that's another job you can do when you're post-peak: hang around doing stunts on street corners to winkle out tatties.

'So they drag me in for these tests – games with playing cards and stuff like that – and that's where I bumped into Alice.' Her voice has gone a bit funny. 'Coz I sort of remembered her from primary school.'

130

'Small world.' We're going up the steps to my luxury residence. I open the outside door for Marvell to go in ahead of me, still rabbiting on.

'I passed, obviously, but Alice didn't make it. I always thought she should've, coz I could see she was good, but she got nervous when it was, you know, a proper test . . .'

I'm not really listening. I'm thinking, we'll get the head out of the reliquary soon and we can do contiguity with the body and maybe we'll have some idea what's going on.

Marvell stops outside my inner door. 'So I think you should help me find her. There's something funny goin' on and I don't want her gettin' hurt just coz you're a prat.'

I whistle and my door opens. Thank God something likes me. Inside, as I light the gas, there's still a distinct whiff of a cat that'll never eat fish again.

Marvo wrinkles her nose. 'Jesus, do you ever air this place?'

I'm more worried about the code staring down at us from on my blackboard – the stuff that could get me barbecued.

'Anyway, is that all right?' Marvell asks. 'You can do a spell or something that'll find her.'

'Thanks to you I'm up in front of the board of discipline next week. Serious misconduct.'

'How serious?'

'Seriously serious. I could lose my licence.'

'Maybe you'd be better off without it.'

'Maybe you'll enjoy being blind.'

That shuts her up. The downside of being a tatty: you can see razor-sharp till you're nearly thirty. Then, just like that, you go stone blind.

Look, I know I'm giving her a hard time, but she's been on my case and I'm dead tired and wound up about stuff and it's like she just won't let go. That's the trouble with tatties – I mean, it's what makes them so useful, but it's a pain in the neck.

'So what about Alice?' she says.

'Ask Ferdia.'

'Yeah, but he's post-peak, right? I mean, he's nice – an' that's not how I mean it!'

She's stuffing ham into her mouth with her fingers. I've spotted another error in my code. I put down my plate and grab a stick of chalk. I rub out a couple of symbols with my finger and rewrite them.

'What's that?'

'Magic.'

'What's it do?'

'Raise the dead. It's John Dee's last incantation.'

John Dee was Queen Elizabeth I's tame astrologer. He talked to angels and claimed to have raised the dead using a spell he devised, the legendary last incantation. Over the four centuries since his death, sorcerers have devoted entire careers to trying to make it work.

'Oh yeah, I read about him. And there was a picture of him in a graveyard with this dead bloke just standin' there, all wrapped up in a shroud. Sort of creepy stuff you'd be into.'

'That's right.'

She watches me scrawl away, then she says, 'Do you want me to go?'

'I got stuff to do. I'll see you at the cathedral.'

But she doesn't move. I'm doing my best to ignore her but finally she says, 'Frank, I've seen the way people act around you . . .'

'Yeah, well it's not just me. Most sorcerers get that.'

'But that amulet Caxton messes about with—'

'Fat lot of good it'll do her.'

'What's she so scared of?'

'Being turned into a toad.'

'No, seriously. I mean, she's OK with me, but it's like she's really got it in for you. So you're a sorcerer, so what? It's not illegal and you're doin' useful stuff.'

'Don't you get it?' I drop the chalk in the box. 'If we didn't have sorcerers the whole world would fall apart. People like Caxton, they depend on sorcerers and tatties.'

'Yeah, I get that.'

'But with sorcerers there's that extra thing. We pretty much made the world the way it is. And we can mess it all up.'

I check my watch: I've got time for this. I pull the

chain to open the window. I turn on a Bunsen burner and stick a small crucible over it.

'Here's your chance,' I say. 'Something to really shop me for.'

It's an absolutely basic . . . no, it's *the* basic spell. I don't even need a wand. Marvell just stands there with this narked-off look on her face while I ransack my cupboards and finally come up with a jar of tin filings.

'Lead is traditional,' I explain as I tip the filings into the crucible. 'But tin has a lower melting point. You'd better wear this.'

I toss her a face mask and start pulverising a few fragments of oak bark.

'Ever hear of Aleister Crowley? He defined magic as the science and art of causing change to occur in conformity with will. In other words, you don't need to be Gifted to do magic – you can do it by sheer force of will.'

'Did it work for him?'

'He said it did. Nobody really knows, so they burned him anyway. Keep back, this is poisonous.'

The tin has melted. I toss in an ounce of verdigris, five drachms of arsenic and some other stuff I'm not going to tell you about, then a few drops of nitric acid. I jump back as the crucible hisses viciously, drowning out the sound of my incantations. The stink is awful – although at least it blots out the lingering smell of cat. I make the final shapes with my hands, then turn off the Bunsen and beckon her over.

'Don't breathe the fumes.'

She peers into the vessel. The molten metal running around the bottom has turned bright yellow.

'Is that gold?' she whispers.

'Tell Caxton, if you like. Should get a promotion . . .'

'What about you?'

'I'd lose my licence.' I waggle my fingers. 'Probably these too.' I begin packing the gear away. 'Sorcery started with alchemy. All sorts of idiots spent centuries trying to turn base metal into gold. By the time they figured it out, they'd learned how to conjure up demons, turn princes into frogs – the whole circus. But making gold was always the thing.'

'Is it real? I mean, could I—?'

'Middle of the eighteenth century, the Spanish got kicked out of the Americas. No silver, no sugar. Mainly no gold. They were going bankrupt. So they called in every sorcerer in the kingdom. They cracked the last few problems in alchemy – you can see it's dead easy once you know how – and started manufacturing huge quantities of gold. They melted down weapons, stripped the lead off church roofs . . .'

Marvell's still staring into the crucible. I take down a pair of tongs from a hook on the wall.

'There was a panic. Every country in Europe had every available sorcerer hard at work. The world's awash in gold, so its value drops like a stone. Before long it's worth less than the lead and iron that were melted down to make it. Took a century to turn all the gold back and straighten everybody out.'

I pick up the crucible and tip the molten gold into a basin of water, where it fizzes and bubbles.

'You want to know what everyone's so afraid of? A few sorcerers can do a lot of damage. First Geneva Convention, 1864: every country agrees not to use sorcerers for military or economic purposes. Of course that's all fine while the number of sorcerers is limited by the need to have the Gift – and the fact that it gets taken away. But what if Crowley was right? What if anyone can do it? That's a lot of people out in the garden shed, melting down saucepans and drainpipes.'

Marvell smiles bleakly. 'So we'd be better off without magic.'

'Maybe your brother would still be alive.'

'That's not funny, Frank.'

'I'm sorry.' Why do I keep narking her off? 'Twenty-four carat gold is ninety-nine point nine per cent pure. This is alchemist's gold: one hundred per cent. If you tried to sell it you'd be arrested.' That's why I alloy it with copper before I sell it for pocket money. I fish out the misshapen yellow lump with a spoon and tip it on to the bench. 'Like I said, turn me in. Stop me before I do real damage.'

'You need to get some sleep.'

And out of nowhere she reaches out and runs the back of her fingers down my cheek. It makes me shiver – actually, for a second I'm afraid I'm going to cry. I jump back.

'Sorry,' she says, and blushes.

'I just don't like being touched.'

'What if it was the girl?'

'What girl?'

'Shut up, Frank.' She grabs her coat. I raise my hand and the door opens. She takes one step . . . then stops dead and hauls her scryer out. She waves me away angrily and stamps out into the corridor. I hear her say, 'Are you sure? Where?' She reappears in the doorway and hisses, 'Wallace's head.'

'What about it?'

'They found it.'

'That's a shame.' I was quite looking forward to see-ing the reliquary opened in front of an unsuspecting congregation.

She's flapping her hand to shut me up. 'I'm on my way.' She closes the scryer. 'Sandford Lock. Washed up on the bank.'

'Then it's not Wallace.'

'Don't be stupid.'

'Hey, you're the one who had the insight. Marvo—'

'I told you not to call me that!'

'Why fight it? You know it suits you.'

* * *

I toss the plates back in the kitchen – there's a few lumps of gristle left and with luck the dog'll choke on them and I can grab the spare parts – and five minutes later I'm out in the street and the driver's pointing fingers at me.

Marvo's already sitting inside the van. 'Caxton's gonna kill me.'

'So play safe,' I say. 'Go to Sandford.'

While she struggles to make up her mind, a solitary firework splutters up into the sky and bursts in a white star. One of its five points is badly malformed, but the colour work is good: it turns red, then blue, darkening and fading. A long, sad sigh is followed by a deafening bang as hundreds of tiny gold and silver bomblets whizz and explode. There's a smell of spices.

'Nah, I'll go with the insight. Get in.'

I toss my case onto the seat opposite her. She bangs on the roof and as we lurch forward I'm thrown across the van, into the seat beside her. She pushes me back and screams at the driver. By the time I've opened my case and checked that nothing's broken, we're charging down towards the bridges and she's sitting there with her head buried in her hands.

'You OK?'

'My head's killing me.' She's grinding the palms of her hands into her eyes.

I don't really understand tatties. I mean, I get the general idea, but it's not magic. Not consciously, anyway. They just . . . see things. And it seems to cost them like hell. Not just the fact that they go completely blind in the end, but the headaches and stuff along the way.

'I can fix it,' I say. 'Your head.'

'I'm fine.'

She doesn't look fine. She leans back in her seat and massages her temples with her fingertips. She looks up at me. 'An' don't get keen on that girl.'

'I'm not . . .'

'She's not right.'

'Who sez?'

'I sez. The body, the book, the head . . . it's like bits out of a puzzle.' She mimes moving them around.

'Yeah, I get that.'

'The girl, though . . . I can't read her. I dunno what it is.'

'Maybe you're jealous.'

'As if!'

'Can you read me?'

'Like a book.'

Time to change the subject. 'That note Caxton found—'

'Like an open book.' Marvell's got this superior look on her mug.

'"Leave her alone . . ." D'you think it meant your friend Alice?'

We've come round the Oxpens and under the

railway bridge. There's the sound of people yelling and screaming.

'No, prob'ly nothing to do with her. Dunno, but I can't imagine her with Wallace. Gives me the creeps!' Marvo shudders.

I can see several hundred people milling around outside the cathedral under a full moon. Some are holding flaming torches and lanterns that cast a flickering light over the placards waving above their heads:

Burn the lot of them!

Sorsery = Satan!

Thou shalt not suffer a witch to live!

A sorserer and a witch are two totally different things. But I don't think I'll risk going among them to explain that.

There are two police lines holding the mob back. People going in for the Mass scurry nervously along the clear path to the west door of the cathedral.

'Look, you better go in on your own,' I say.

'It's just a few idiots—'

'All I need is one idiot who realises I'm a sorcerer. Or that nutter with the knife from yesterday. And this is a bit of a giveaway.' I put my hand on my case.

'Leave it in the van.'

'No way!'

So she has a word with one of the jacks and I crouch down on the floor while we drive on.

'You're gutless, Frank.'

'Better gutless than headless.'

The van stops and I kick the door open. As I dash for the west door, waving my ring at security, a stone rattles along the pavement at my feet.

Inside the cathedral, the dancing flames of thousands of candles throw only the faintest glimmer of light up into the vaulted ceiling, high overhead. At the top of the nave, they've set up a temporary altar, covered with a crimson cloth. White-robed acolytes flit around making final adjustments.

Marvo and me, we've found a spot beside a pillar. Censers swing, emitting toxic clouds of incense. And I'm still scanning the first few rows of pews, looking for the Boss among the People Who Matter, when a mob of overdressed clerics, enough to invade a small country, converge on the altar.

There's this rumbling and scraping, echoing round the building, as everyone scrambles to their feet. And now I spot Matthew, towering over his neighbours as he turns to inspect the congregation . . .

And sees me. He smiles and raises one hand, then turns back to the front. He crosses himself as a procession emerges from the crypt. I never could get my head round how seriously he manages to take all this stuff.

I spot Andrew towards the back of the procession,

purple with concentration and bottled-up resentment, sharing the weight of an elaborately carved oak litter.

This is it: the relic that made Doughnut City's fortune.

The procession fans out along the steps that separate the nave from the choir. And I recognise the guy helping Andrew carry the litter: the fat priest with the birthmark. Arms shaking with the weight, sweat pouring down their faces, they lower the litter onto the altar.

The precious stones gleam in the flickering candle-light. The gold face of the reliquary stares impassively out over the breathless congregation.

The racket from the choir smacks off the walls like the crack of doom. And now the first twitch of un-certainty. An old priest steps forward. He trips and almost goes flying.

I dunno why, but this seems to spook everybody. The choir falters and goes quiet. The congregation just stand there blinking. A collective whisper of doubt comes rustling up the nave and flutters away into the darkness of the roof, where it finds a perch and settles to await a revelation.

The west door bangs open. There is a shrill, spine-chilling scream: a woman's voice, from outside.

I shiver as a cold wind blows through the building. Marvo clutches my arm. When I turn, her face is white and bathed in sweat. All around me, people are looking at each other like they know what's coming . . .

The old priest steps up to the altar. He frowns angrily behind his glasses as he struggles to locate the tiny catch at the side of the reliquary. His arthritic fingers fumble hopelessly until Andrew twitches like a rabbit and hops forwards to do it for him. The click of the mechanism echoes unnaturally through the silent building. The faceplate swings open –

Bingo!

Mouth gaping. Eyes staring. That's no fifteenth-century skull inside the reliquary.

I grin at Marvo. 'The Bishop of Oxford, I presume.'

But I can't help noticing that the fat priest is looking as astonished as anyone.

CHAPTER ELEVEN
An Unfortunate Business

An hour later, I'm the star of the show.

All the candles have been moved up to create this pool of light round me. I'm kneeling with my elbows resting on the altar, examining the main exhibit. I see spatters of dried blood, and bruises and contusions down one side of his face. Otherwise he's as grey as a ghoul, his lips blue, his eyes clouded over. He smells . . . well, dead.

Trouble is, the head's so like a waxwork that I can't help wondering, did some smartarse have it knocked up to see if they could spook me? But when I glance over my shoulder, nobody's giggling or nudging each other. There's just a ring of jacks standing there staring at me like owls; and flocks of clergy, decked out in black and purple, fluttering round in confused circles.

Can't see the fat priest anywhere. Never even saw him go.

'Any sign of the previous occupant?' I ask.

'Yeah,' says Marvo, putting away her scryer. 'That

head they found down the river – well, the idiot I spoke to had it all wrong. It was a skull.'

'What the hell are *you* doing here?' Caxton has finally rolled up and is standing over me, hands on hips. Her faithful dog has gone.

Credit where credit is due. I nod towards Marvo. 'She had a sneaking feeling.'

'Well, you can get lost now.'

Caxton puts one foot up on the altar step and goes into her detecting pose: leaning forward, one hand still on her hip, the other forefinger to her lips. I suspect she practises in a mirror. After a while she realises that she can't see anything, so she fishes out her glasses and plonks them on her face.

'Has anyone actually identified it as the bishop?' she asks.

'I can identify him.' The Boss has appeared beside her. He smiles at me. 'You look tired, Frank.'

'And who the hell are you?' Caxton frowns as she registers the flash coat and dark suit.

'Matthew Le Geyt, from the Society of Sorcerers.'

Caxton takes an unrehearsed step backwards and nearly goes flat on her arse. Matthew manages not to smile. He turns. 'And you're Detective Constable Marvell.'

She smiles nervously and lets him shake her hand. She realises who he is: he's not just my Master, he's the Superior General of the English branch of the

Society of Sorcerers and a very powerful bunny indeed.

Matthew puts his hand on my shoulder. 'Frank and I are old friends so I know he can be difficult—'

'Difficult?' Caxton splutters. 'He's a liability!'

'But he's also the most brilliant sorcerer I ever taught and if you're not prepared to listen to him, you're the liability.'

I get this warm glow and just for a second it's like the candles have blazed up and all the light in the universe is shining on me. It's an uncomfortable feeling: too much exposure. I'm pleased to see that Caxton has gone red in the face; but the thing is, I believe Matthew and I don't believe him, both at the same time. I know he's right. I was streets ahead of anybody else in my year. I could do stuff that all the other kids struggled with. But it's like there's this parrot on my shoulder, nibbling my ear and whispering that Matthew's taking the mickey.

Charlie is sitting in one of the choir stalls, reading his newspaper, with Mr Memory beside him. Beyond the candles, in the darkness of the nave, the scrying crews are packing up their gear. I can see a group of people talking in the gloom of a side-chapel. There's Akinbiyi and a couple of other clerics. And there's someone else with them – a jack, I guess, judging by the bleached hair.

'Can I ask you something?' Marvo has turned to Matthew. 'How many sorcerers are there in this country?'

'There are five hundred and thirty-seven active, licensed members of the Society. Plus one hundred and twenty-one novices at Saint Cyprian's; several thousand post-peak adepts doing elemental work; and an unknown number of unlicensed practitioners.'

'That's illegal, though.'

'Punishable by death.'

They burned one poor sod at the stake a few years back. Mind you, he had summoned up Beelzebub to get a two-bedroom flat in Woodstock, so he kind of had it coming.

'Where do you find an unlicensed sorcerer?' she asks.

'On the black market. I believe most of them come in from Scandinavia and the Middle East.'

I pipe up, 'I got an offer. Just before I graduated. I don't know who they were.'

Matthew looks at me for a moment. 'You should have told me.'

'I wasn't tempted.' If I need a few quid extra I can make it myself, back at the studio.

He smiles and turns back to Marvo. 'Is he behaving?'

'Up to a point.'

'Thanks a lot,' I mutter.

Matthew smiles. 'This is an unfortunate business.' He crosses himself and turns to the unfortunate business on the altar. 'He was a close friend . . .'

'Did you read his book?' Caxton asks.

'Is this a formal interview?'

'I just want an informed opinion. Save me having to read it myself.'

Yeah, right. Even if Caxton wanted to read the book, she'd have a struggle.

'It's a good book,' says Matthew. 'It needed saying.' He pulls out a small notebook and a pencil. 'Henry sent a short *précis* of his argument to me, while he was still writing it.' He makes a note. 'I'll have it copied and sent over to you.'

Caxton is staring at him. It's not the missing finger; it's the fact that the one thing Matthew *hasn't* pulled out is a pair of spectacles.

'It's easy to dismiss sorcery as cheap effects and superstition, but it offers ordinary men and women a glimpse of the divine.' Matthew puts everything away and turns back to the reliquary. 'We had three thousand people in here tonight—'

'As well as the scrying audience.' Akinbiyi steps up behind him.

'So call it three thousand and one,' I say. Large public displays have to be empowered by an elemental, so outside the magic game only the very rich can afford them. Actually I'm being mean: streets club together to fund a receiver. And for gigs like this they'll set them up in kinemas and churches. And take a collection.

'So.' Caxton glances at Marvo. 'Could the bishop's murder have been, I don't know . . . political?'

'Political in what sense?' Matthew checks his watch. 'Frank, I need a word with you.'

'Well, the book didn't make him many friends in the Church.'

'He wasn't the only member of the hierarchy who took that point of view. You'll excuse us . . .'

Caxton doesn't like it, but she can't stop it. Matthew leads me out of earshot. He glances round at Marvo. 'Isn't she the girl who informed on you?'

'It was my own fault.'

'I'm glad you're prepared to admit that.'

We both know that every sorcerer lifts a few human body parts from time to time, when there's no alternative. The trick is not to get caught at it.

'I'll have a quiet word with the board of discipline.'

OK, that's a relief. I mean, I thought he would. Well, hoped, anyway. And I'm still thinking about all the times he got me out of trouble at Saint Cyprian's, when I realise he's peering over my shoulder. As I turn to look . . .

'Frank?'

I go red and mumble, 'Thank you.'

'You'll be fine so long as you keep your head.' He beckons . . .

And she's here – Kazia! What I thought was a jack talking to Akinbiyi and the other priests . . . it was the blonde hair that confused me.

So what's going on? Is she with Matthew? You know what I mean. Because he's not that old and I know some teenage girls have a thing about old guys. Especially when they've got his power and his seriously cool Ghost.

Matthew smiles, like he's read my thoughts. 'You've met Henry's niece, Kazimíera. I'm trying to contact her family in Lithuania.' He turns to her. 'Do you need anything?'

She shakes her head.

'All right, I won't be long.' He turns back to me. 'Where's Caxton going with this?'

'For a while she thought the head had been taken for black magic.'

'Oh, you're joking!'

'Then she thought it was a jealous husband. But obviously it's all too . . .' I gesture at Wallace's head, which isn't looking any happier than it was when Andrew opened the faceplate.

Matthew nods. 'Too baroque for a crime of passion.'

'Marvell thought it was the ASB.'

'I hear the police are rounding them up. But what do you think?'

I shake my head. 'There was one of their guys here tonight – he was actually carrying the relic—'

'The young monk?'

'No, the fat priest. But he looked as surprised as anyone when it was opened. So I dunno.'

Matthew peers searchingly into my face for a moment. 'Anyway, keep me informed. And behave yourself.'

Kazia is still standing there. And Marvo is just a few yards away, staring at her . . . well, kind of fiercely.

'I meant what I said,' Matthew continues, loud enough for both of them to hear. 'About you being a brilliant sorcerer – you might even be a great one.' I can dream. He drops his voice to a whisper. 'But you're not invulnerable.'

He pats my shoulder and he's off towards the door leading through to the cloister and the palace, with Akinbiyi chasing after him. Kazia has to pass close to me as she follows, but when I try to catch her eye she gives me this blank, closed-up look.

'Sampson!' Caxton is standing at the altar, pointing to the reliquary. 'Do you want to wrap that and get it over to the lab?'

I turn back to Kazia, but before I can even open my mouth, Caxton yells, 'And don't start anything. Ferdia can pick up in the morning.' She turns to Marvo. 'Go with him. Make sure he doesn't do anything stupid.'

'Too late,' Marvo mutters.

And the last I see of Kazia, she's disappearing out of the cloister door after Matthew and Akinbiyi.

'Your boss bigged you up.' The road is pretty rough and we're being bounced from side to side in the van.

151

Marvo has to shout over the racket of the wheels.

I yell back, 'What's wrong with that?'

'What happened to his finger?'

'Demon got it, years ago. Anyway, you were right about the reliquary.'

'Tell Caxton that.'

She doesn't seem to be getting her hopes up, just turns away and stares out of the window. So just to be sociable I say, 'What about the priest?'

'The fat bloke? Totally gobsmacked.' At least she turns back to face me. 'So it can't have been the ASB.'

'Doesn't follow. They could have, you know, separate cells. One lot to kill Wallace. Another crowd chasing round after me.'

'You know your trouble? You think the world revolves around you.'

'Yeah, but it kind of does, doesn't it? Sorcerer, and that.' I feel the scrape of the bristles as I run my hand over my head, which I shave completely clean most mornings. 'Isn't that what bugs you?'

And after that she doesn't open her gob again till we bounce over the cobbles into the mortuary courtyard.

'Your boss,' she says. 'He's not what I expected.'

'What do you want? Silk robes and a tiara? The Society doesn't do fancy dress any more.'

'What about the haircuts?'

'The tonsure? You can't afford to give demons anything to grab hold of.'

'But he's too old to summon demons, right, so why bother?'

'It's still customary.'

'So what about you?'

I run my hand across my skull again. 'Style counts.'

It's pitch-dark and I can't see her face properly. I just hear her laugh.

'Caxton doesn't like me,' I say.

'You spook her, Frank.' She's first out of the van and turns to watch me dismount with my case. 'Damn it, you spook us all!'

'Just trying to do my job.'

'Well p'raps part of your job is realising you're working with people who aren't sorcerers and find it all . . .' She follows me round to watch the dieners unload the silk-wrapped reliquary. 'I mean, s'pose it's true?'

I'm too far gone for this. Two nights ago I was up late, wrestling with a dead cat. I'd just about pinned it to the canvas when I got dragged off to admire the lifestyle of the rich and holy and determine when he went to meet his maker. I didn't get much sleep the next night; then there was another busy day and now it's two o'clock in the morning and I'm still running around juggling heads. My world is doing backflips.

'Suppose what's true?' I groan.

'My uncle: he's a priest.'

'Good for him.'

'But I never really thought about it before.' She's looking almost as knackered as I feel. 'Spirits, demons . . .'

'Don't be stupid. It's just a metaphor – a way of talking about natural forces.'

'It don't look like natural forces.'

'If you don't like it, ask to be reassigned.'

I turn and walk off, into the building. By the time she catches up with me, I'm at reception, shuffling forms.

'That what you want?' she says.

I push the paperwork back across the desk. 'What I want is someone to keep Caxton off my back and not screw up the contiguity. Doesn't seem like much to ask, but what do I know?'

'You don't seem to know very much, Frank. You're certainly crap with people.'

'I don't like people.'

'Make you feel better, does it, sayin' that?'

The security elemental outside the lab looks up. The doors open. The delivery is here ahead of us.

'Don't unwrap anything,' Marvell tells the dieners. 'Ferdia's starting fresh in the morning.'

They give me their disappointed look, then shuffle off.

'An' it's true what Caxton says . . .'

Will she never shut up?

'Your job is just to look at the evidence an' interpret

it for us. It's not up to you to solve the case. Just tell us what you know an' let us get on with it.'

'That's what I'm trying to do.'

We stand there, glaring at each other. Over her shoulder I can see the dieners hesitating in the doorway, hoping for a fight.

'But I *was* right, wasn't I?' she says, and turns and follows the dieners out. Their footsteps fade, there's the final bang of a door and I've got the place to myself.

Yeah, I know what she said. But I grab a pair of gloves, untie the silk cords around the reliquary and pull the cloth away. I release the catch and flip the faceplate open. The bishop's eyes stare blearily back at me.

Funnily enough, I remember Henry Wallace. Matthew used to bring him round Saint Cyprian's now and then. I think he patted me on the head when I was seven or eight. And he gave a lecture on the nature of demons – eternal, cunning, smelly, vindictive – and the fundamental paradox of sorcery: that we summon them from hell in the name of God.

As I recall, he didn't have an answer to that. Just rambled on about faith until it was time for lunch.

So where is Wallace now? With the angels or the demons? Maybe he's nowhere. Maybe he just isn't.

A couple of years ago, some American sorcerer claimed that when someone dies, there's this sort of psychic trace left on the retina of the last thing they saw. And he said he had composed a spell to develop the image – sort of like a photograph – and display it.

The whole thing was a con, of course. The only thing that was magical was how quickly he pocketed several large development grants and vanished.

But examining the head I wonder, what was the last thing Wallace saw? The stab wound probably didn't kill him instantly. So what went through his mind in those final seconds? Was he aware of what was happening? Was he still conscious of the world spinning as his head rolled away from his shoulders, across the floor? And is he maybe still in there, peering desperately back at me through lenses that have almost completely clouded over?

Why is it such a struggle for me just to congratulate Marvell for spotting the trick with the reliquary?

And it's true, what I said to Matthew: there's something about this case that we're all missing.

We can do this the Ferdia way, and mess it up. Or we can do it the Frank way.

CHAPTER TWELVE
The Frank Way

The faceplate hinges off a ring of metal, secured to the main body of the reliquary. I undo a few screws and lift the assembly away.

Confession: this is my first solo beheading. I observed that demonstration I told you about at Saint Cyprian's, but since I started at the mortuary all I've done is shootings, stabbings, drownings and bludgeon-ings. I've played marbles with eyeballs and skidded across a room on a loose kidney, but I've never actually had to wrestle with a detached human head.

Still, I'm on a roll – and I'm wearing gloves, so it's not like I've really got to touch this thing. I tip the reliquary so that the head falls out on to a silk square. I take a deep breath, grab it and turn it face up.

It looks . . . well, totally not right.

I wheel the body in from the ice room, fold a silk square and drape it over the neck, covering the wound. I put the head down carefully, just half an inch from the body: the silk prevents any new contiguity being created. I drape another large silk square over the neck and torso, covering the autopsy damage. I stand back and squint.

They look happy together. But when I pull the silk away and take a closer look I see a problem.

I spend an hour playing around with the head and getting stuff ready. I make a final trip across to the small basin in the corner to wash my hands and face in exorcised water and I turn round to find Marvell standing beside the trolley.

'What are you playin' at?' she says.

'Contiguity. I want to know if Exhibit A, one head, was ever happy to be seen out and about with Exhibit B—'

'I told you, Ferdia found contiguity.'

'With a hairbrush.'

'Obvious though, isn't it? Hair colour, for a start. And you can match the wounds.'

'Not if the neck's been hacked about.' Marvell looks away as I poke at the back of the neck with a scalpel. 'He's missing a vertebra. There should be twenty-four. There's nineteen on the body – that's in Ferdia's report. Four here. Making only twenty-three. They hacked out one vertebra. Here—'

I turn to point at a crust of blood and a few shreds of tissue, clinging to the lower rim of the reliquary's faceplate.

'They had to do it to squeeze him into the reliquary.'

She points at the head. 'We know that's Wallace, yeah?' Can't argue with that. She turns to the body. 'And that's gotta be him—'

'It was found behind his desk. Didn't have a label on it, though.'

'Who else could it be, apart from Wallace?'

I grab a scalpel and stoop over the body to cut fragments of flesh and dried blood away from the stump of the neck. I drop them into a blue porcelain dish.

Marvo stands there watching me, tapping her teeth with her fingernails.

I put the blue dish aside. I find another scalpel and scrape samples from the head into a yellow dish.

'Please, Frank. Why can't you just leave everything for Ferdia like Caxton told you?'

'Because he'll skip this and it's bugging me. Don't worry, I can do it with my fingers up my nose.'

Her voice goes hard. 'I'll leave you to it then.'

'You know your problem, you let Caxton scare you. It's just contiguity – no Presence. Stay and learn.'

The door slams.

'I exorcise thee, O creature of fire, in the name of he by whom all things are made, that forthwith thou castest away every phantasm from thee, that it shall not be able to do any hurt in any thing.'

The body is back in the ice room. My ring is in my case, where it can't mess anything up. The head is watching suspiciously from a silk square on the bench. I've chalked a square on the tiles round a small table, leaving myself enough room to light a couple of braziers and hop around inside without falling over my own feet. I've done the symbols, put on my paper hat and pinned a sheet of paper to my chest. The grimoires specify that the operator should wear a linen coat with various symbols embroidered across the breast in red silk, but I can't be bothered dragging one across from the amphitheatre. So I use a sheet of paper with a complicated symbol representing the coat – complete with its symbols – drawn in my own blood. It's all in the maths.

'In the name of Adonai the most high. In the name of Jehovah the most holy.'

I take a paper sachet from the table and sprinkle the herbs into both braziers. Flames crackle and dance. An almost invisible mist rises to fill the magic space inside the square. I pick up my wand and draw the signs in the air.

'Adonai, Tetragrammaton, Jehovah, Tetragrammaton . . .'

I pick up the blue dish and tip out the scrapings of blood from the stump of the neck into one of the braziers. They spit momentarily on the hot charcoal. I hold my wand out horizontally and watch as a thin plume of powder-blue smoke drifts up and wraps itself in a spiral round the wand. The colour's a bit flashy, but I like to keep myself on my toes . . .

This is delicate work. They'll tell you that sorcerers abstain from alcohol and all that stuff to keep their bodies pure, but that's bollocks: we're working with all sorts of poisons all the time. The reason we don't drink or do drugs is because if your hands aren't steady, at best you have to start again. And at worst you're dead – and dragged off to God knows where by God knows what.

I have to keep the wand absolutely motionless while I put down the blue dish and pick up the yellow one. I tip out the blood scrapings from the head. A plume of smoke rises from the second brazier, cowslip yellow this time.

'Adonai, Jehovah, Otheos . . .'

I clear my mind and focus on the two plumes of smoke, coiled round the wand. Carefully I pull it back, leaving them suspended in mid air, still entwined.

'Athenatos, Aschyros, Agla, Pentagrammaton . . .'

What's supposed to happen, right – the blue and yellow plumes should blur and drift together into a pure green, proving contiguity.

Except that nothing happens.

I wait. Ten seconds. Twenty . . .

I hear the door open. I figure it's Marvo and I raise my free hand to shut her up before she distracts me.

'What the hell are you playing at?'

Oh Christ, it's bloody Ferdia!

Concentrate, Frank. One yellow plume. One blue. What's going on here?

'Sampson!'

Ferdia has walked across to face me. I try to ignore him, but he plants himself in front of me.

I shake the wand, grab my black-handled knife and stoop to cut the square. The two plumes of smoke drift out, one yellow, one blue, maintaining their distinct identities until they finally disperse into the air of the laboratory.

Ferdia puts a silk-wrapped package on the bench. 'The skull from the river.' He turns to Marvo, who's standing just inside the door. 'Are you going to scry Caxton, or do I have to?'

She just stands there looking down at the floor.

'Suit yourself.' He pushes past her. His footsteps recede along the corridor.

'Told you not to do it.' Marvo puts a plate on the bench. 'Sandwich. Ham and pickle all right?'

'What do I owe you?'

'Don't be a prat, Frank.'

'Sorry.'

Well, I am. Sorry. And a prat. My trouble is, I want people to like me, but don't trust them when they give any sign of it. Most of the time, I find Caxton's hostility easier to deal with. I guess that's why I keep winding her up.

I'm starving. I grab the plate.

'I gave them all a lick, so I'd be sure I was getting you the best one.'

'Don't hang around for my sake.' I don't know why I'm saying this, but I can't stop myself. 'Stick with lover boy.'

She pulls her scryer out of her pocket and stabs at it with her fingertips. 'Damn!' She snaps it shut and opens it again. More wild stabbing. She glares up at me. 'Can't have a sensible conversation on these bloody things anyway. I'm going over to wait for Caxton.' The scryer's back in her pocket. 'You coming?' She grabs the plate from me and she's gone.

A relic's a relic; I unwrap the skull and pocket a loose tooth. I realise, as I scoot after Marvo, that the result of the ritual was no surprise: I was expecting something like this. I just thought everybody would be telling me how clever I am.

Heading into the jack shack we pass Charlie, sitting on the steps outside the main door, smoking a cigarette. He gives me this look, like, what's going on? But Marvo's already got the door open and steam coming out of her ears.

Inside, up a dingy flight of stairs and along a sad

corridor, it turns out that the grown-ups have got more important stuff to do than talk to us kids. Marvo throws herself into a chair outside Caxton's office and starts rapping her heel on the green linoleum. I don't want to talk to her, but I don't want her to think I'm ignoring her, so I tell her I need some fresh air and wander back outside.

Charlie's tipping tobacco into a fresh cigarette paper. I park my case and sit down beside him. Daylight, ouch! I pick up a sharp pebble and scratch a pentagram on a paving stone.

Sorcerers. We're an insecure bunch. We've been handed this Gift that everyone's jealous and scared of, only it doesn't last. With luck you get five years, maybe seven, at the peak of your powers. After that it's down-hill. And what are you when you're not a sorcerer any more? Just some sad bastard with a set of skills you can't do anything with. Except teach, or mess around with elementals.

'Charlie, can I ask you a question?'

He grins. 'Can I stop you?'

'When you lost it, what did it feel like? I mean, how did you know?'

The grin has disappeared. He runs the tip of his tongue along the gummed edge of the paper and rolls the snout between his fingers. He picks away a loose strand of tobacco from the end. He holds it out to me. I shake my head.

'Never tempted?' he says.

'If I want to damage myself, I've got a studio full of cutlery.'

'Are you still at that lark?' He sticks the snout in his gob and sets fire to it.

'Nah, got bored. You don't have to answer the question if you don't want to.'

Smoke drifts off up the street. Finally he says, 'I think it's different for everyone. I mean, you were pals with Dinny Saint-Gilles, weren't you?'

Dinny was in the year ahead of me at Saint Cyprian's. He was an OK guy, even if he *was* French. He graduated and got a job with Research and Development at the Ghost works out in Cowley. Golden future, the world his oyster . . .

Until his Gift was taken away. Like, overnight. He went to bed a sorcerer and woke up . . . well, not a sorcerer. He took the train into work, hung up his coat, walked down to the body shop and fed both hands into the machinery.

'Me,' says Charlie, 'it was just getting more and more like hard work. So you're tired and you convince yourself that's the problem and you just need to try harder – you know, get the symbols spot-on, and all that. You spend hours setting up, so now you're whacked before you even start to make magic—'

The door opens behind us and Caxton's sergeant, Gerry Ormerod, steps out. He's followed by this sad-looking middle-aged bloke wearing a grubby dog-collar and struggling to poke a spindly pair of horn-rimmed glasses into the top pocket of a shiny black suit.

Gerry looks down at Charlie. 'Caxton wants an elemental if you've got a minute,' he squeaks. I have to struggle to keep a straight face. Charlie nudges me in the ribs. We watch Gerry lead the cleric across the street to a van.

'Go easy on him,' says Charlie.

'Why?'

Charlie points to his eyes. 'Just starting to go.'

'It's not the same as losing the Gift, though.'

'Isn't it?' Charlie takes a long drag at his roll-up. 'I was nearly twenty-two.'

'That's late.'

'Yeah, I'd even begun to think I was the exception – you know, the guy who never loses it.' He turns away from me as he puts the snout up to his mouth again, but he makes this weird movement with his hand and I realise he's wiping away tears.

'Then one day, it's not like you're getting funny results or anything. You're just standing there with all the gear on and, I dunno . . . it just isn't happening. You look round and everything's right – the geometry, the symbols, the smells . . .'

Gerry slams the van door on the bloke in the

166

dog-collar. The driver flicks the reins, and the horses twitch resentfully and move off.

'I was afraid, Frank. That was it.'

'But everyone's afraid.'

'Nah, this was different. I wasn't afraid of looking a fool or of what could go wrong. I was afraid of myself. I knew I couldn't be trusted any more.' He throws away the fag-end and pulls out his tin again. 'I did consider topping myself.'

'Nobody does, though, do they? Funny, that.'

'Not being a sorcerer's better than being dead and not a sorcerer.' Charlie shrugs. 'You get used to elementals.'

Gerry is coming back across the street towards us.

'So what about me?' I ask.

'Sorry, can't help you. Law of averages says you should be good for another few years . . . maybe longer – you're the best sorcerer I ever saw.'

I blush. I mean, Matthew says that but he's kind of got this interest, you know? Because he's my Master.

When Charlie says it, it's like it really counts.

He frowns. 'Who knows, though. It's a bugger.'

Gerry arrives. 'Who was that?' I say, nodding towards the van as it disappears round the corner.

'James Groce. Rector of Saint Ebbe's church. There was a letter from him on Wallace's desk, remember?'

'Not really.'

'What about the note we found in Wallace's jacket pocket? Remember that?'

'Sure I do. It said, "Leave her alone", right?'

Gerry nods. 'The handwriting on Groce's letter matches the note. Get it?'

'What's Groce's story?'

'He admits to writing the note, but he says he only did it to give Wallace a scare.' Gerry's squeak sharpens. 'Apparently there's a whole gang of clergy who don't like nekkers and resented Wallace's book, and they were planning to resign their livings together in protest. Groce is one of them. He says he'd heard rumours that Wallace had an eye for the ladies, so he sent the note out of malice, just to put the wind up him.' He glares at Charlie. 'Didn't I tell you—?'

'That Caxton wants an elemental. Sure,' says Charlie. 'What's it for?'

'The missing housemaid, Alice Constant.' Gerry turns to me. 'Nobody's seen her since you and Marvell lost her.'

I say, 'I thought you were trying to fit the ASB up for Wallace.'

'We're open-minded. Seems like Groce was playing around with the housemaid. We figure—'

'We?'

'Me and Caxton.' Gerry blinks and moves his hand towards his eyes. But he catches me watching him and jams it in his pocket. 'We figure maybe Wallace stuck his oar in and Groce murdered him. But Groce says he's never even heard of Alice Constant.'

'He doesn't really look bright enough to juggle a book, a head and a reliquary,' I point out. 'I mean, have you got anything specific that ties him to the murder?'

'No.' He glares at Charlie. 'So are you coming or not?'

Charlie sighs as he puts his tin away and climbs to his feet. He's almost back inside the jack shack when he turns back to me and says, 'The ritual this morning – yeah, news gets around. But how did it feel?'

'OK, I guess. It felt right.'

'There you go, then.'

The door closes behind him. I sit there watching one of the police drivers set his horse up with a nose-bag. Finally the door opens again and Marvo yells, 'Caxton says, where the hell have you got to?'

The more energy someone wastes yelling at you, the less likely they are to hit you. About the only useful thing I learned from my dad.

Caxton finally gets bored of hammering on about stupid teenage sorcerers making a mess of everything. Hanging on the wall behind her is a curious silver object: a circular plaque, about ten inches across. Engraved in the centre is an open human eye, with an owl perched on top. An amulet against the evil eye. Ironic, really. I nudge Marvo and nod in its direction, but she ignores me.

'OK,' I say. 'But there's still no contiguity between the head and the body.' And in case I'm being too technical for Caxton: 'They've never been in contact with each other.'

I'm sitting beside Marvo beneath row after row of framed prints of women's football teams, most faded to a uniform grey by exposure to the sheer tedium of Caxton's company. Marvo's knee is bounding up and down. Ferdia is perched seductively on a filing cabinet wearing his 'I'd never do anything that stupid in a million years' look.

I'm definitely the centre of attention. Caxton has gone red in the face. Even the football teams in the pictures look narked off with me.

Marvo just looks . . . disappointed.

'That's impossible,' says Ferdia. 'There's got to be contiguity.'

'Sez you.'

'You're this close!' Caxton has got hold of a penknife and waves it in my face. She's in a crap mood again. Maybe she's missing the dog.

'The head,' says Marvo. 'Definitely Wallace, right? So the body has to be him too.'

'Does it?' I ask.

Caxton has abandoned the idea of cutting my

cheek open – for now at least – and is hacking away at a pencil. 'Who else could it be?'

'You're the detective.'

Before she can fly across the desk at me, Marvo says, 'Frank, you didn't sleep last night . . .'

Is that meant to help? 'I'm fine.'

'But you could've made a mistake.'

'I don't make mistakes.' I turn to Caxton. 'Do you want me to do it again?'

'What's the point if you don't make mistakes? Or are you losing it?'

I catch Ferdia's eye. He doesn't exactly shrug – in fact, he hardly moves. Just for a second, though, it's like we're both staring down the same hole.

'I'll do it,' he says.

'No way!' I'm on my feet.

'What's your problem?'

'You're crap, for a start.'

'You mean, I'm taller than you.' Ferdia smirks at Marvo. The ghost of a smile flickers across her face before she manages to set it straight.

Just what the world needed: more magic.

We're in the east wing of the mortuary, in one of Ferdia's luxury arenas, complete with the major constellations inlaid in real diamonds across the dome. The electric lights are switched off and the man himself is standing in the middle, winding himself up.

171

There was this weird moment, though, two hours ago outside Caxton's office, where he caught my arm and whispered, 'I'm sorry, Frank – I didn't mean for it to go this far.' I could see he meant well and I figured he was thinking of the moment when it all started to go downhill for him. But what I said was, 'Just get on with it.'

So he did.

He looks the very model of the fashionably attired sorcerer. He has the hat. He has the gown and slippers. He has the wand and knife. He looks like something out of a pantomime. Also present: one headless corpse and one head, allegedly the property of said corpse. Ferdia's perfumes and fumigations can't cover up the fact that they're both getting just the tiniest bit high.

The audience are taking their seats in the gallery: me; Marvo; Caxton, tapping her pencil on an open notebook; and Mr Memory, still in the same grubby suit and bow tie.

'This is a waste of time,' I mutter.

'In which case you'll be proved right,' says Caxton. She catches Ferdia's eye and nods. He glances at me uncertainly for a split second . . .

And the herbs start flying.

He's going the tried-and-tested route: two samples of hair, one shaved from the head and the other from the body's forearm. Wisps of smoke drift up from two separate braziers, side by side.

It's not like he can turn up anything different from my results. He can't rearrange the universe.

'In the name of Adonai the most high. In the name of Jehovah the most holy.'

The candles flicker. Not a dramatic touch, just a draught that he hasn't suppressed. He wouldn't have let that happen eighteen months ago. I give him another year before he's trying to steal elemental work off Charlie . . .

He tips hairs from a dish into the left-hand brazier. Some of it falls to the floor but enough crackles and hisses on the glowing charcoal. A plume of black smoke rises into the air. He tips hairs from another dish into the right-hand brazier. A plume of white smoke rises. It's a mess – all tiny eddies twitched this way and that by the draught. If this was a paying audience, they'd be hissing and booing and throwing things by now.

'Adonai, Tetragrammaton, Jehovah . . .'

This isn't right. The two columns of smoke are already drifting into each other and he hasn't even started the punchline.

'Otheos, Athenatos, Aschyros, Agla, Penta-grammaton . . .'

He's wasting his breath. Invisible hands have already crushed the smoke into a compact grey cloud. No untidy wisps. No loose eddies. Ferdia looks round at me and leers triumphantly.

'I'm convinced,' says Caxton. She puts on her

173

glasses and prints 'CONTIGUITY' in her notebook. She looks down proudly and ticks it.

'Yeah, but you're easily pleased.' I turn to Ferdia: 'The smoke was merging before you even started the final incantation.'

Marvo's nodding, but Ferdia ignores her. 'That's a sign how intense the contiguity was,' he says.

'That's a sign that you'd presupposed the result. That wasn't a valid test. You just got what you expected to find.'

'What's wrong with you, Sampson?' says Caxton. 'Why can't you admit you messed up?'

'Because I didn't.' I hope I sound confident, but what I'm actually thinking is: I can't have got it wrong, can I?

Marvo must realise I'm about to get up and walk out. Her hand is on my arm.

'No,' she whispers.

But I've lost this battle; now it's just a question of what sort of exit I make. I can go gracefully. I can crawl out with my tail between my legs. I can slam out in a shower of sparks and a cloud of green smoke.

No contest really. I've got my case. The door's open. I'm in the corridor . . .

Caxton's voice: 'I'm not finished with you yet.'

I'm trembling like a leaf. 'Well I'm finished with you.' With an effort I bring my voice down an octave. Can't keep it steady though. 'Solve your own stupid murder.'

So far, not so bad. I'm almost at the stairs and I'm thinking I've made it. I can stop pushing my luck and get out of here and we can all calm down.

But then I have to go and be an arsehole. 'Fat cow!' I mutter.

Caxton's paw's on my shoulder. My head slams into the wall. I think she kicks my legs out from under me.

You want to know what this is all about? OK, I wind her up, but what it's really about is the fact that she's gone Blurry and even with lenses so thick you could use them as paperweights, she's helpless without Marvo to make out anything less than a mile away. It's about the fact that if it really comes down to it, she's the one who's dispensable.

But mainly it's about what I told Marvo: Caxton's scared of sorcery. And of me.

She's got me on the floor, where she wants me; but she isn't quite sure what to do with me. She's afraid to hurt me, so she decides to take it out on my case.

She stoops and grabs it and fumbles with the catch, but she can't get it open. That makes her even angrier, because she knows she's starting to look like a fool. She bangs it on the floor.

My case *really* doesn't like anybody touching it, except me. The catches click. It opens wide. I don't know what it shows Caxton, but her eyes light up and she makes a grab for something inside, and the lid slams shut on her hand.

175

'Get it off me!'

'Say you're sorry.'

'Come on, Frank.' Ferdia wants to help Caxton – bloody arse-licker! – but he can't get near because she's hopping around trying to shake her hand free.

'Not me – the case. Tell it you're sorry. There's a spell on it – an elemental. It won't let go till it thinks you're sorry.'

I can see Marvo struggling to keep a straight face. Caxton falls back against the wall, locks the case between her feet and tries to pull her hand free, but the case is having none of it. Obviously she's damaging stuff inside, but it's worth it.

'Stop fighting it,' I tell her.

And fair play to her, she does. Nobody moves. Ferdia and Marvo are just standing there with their mouths open. Mr Memory watches with his usual bland smile.

The case relaxes. We all take a deep breath.

'Now will you get it off?' Caxton's red in the face, sweat pouring down her forehead.

'I can't.' I'm lying, obviously. I could talk the case out of it if I wanted, but Caxton can't be sure of that. 'It's between you and the case. Say you're sorry.'

'Sod it, I'm sorry.'

'Politely.'

'I'm sorry.'

To my relief, the case lets go. Caxton stumbles away. There's blood on her wrist and she's as pale as a ghost. Ferdia picks up her glasses from the floor. She snatches them from him and digs for her handkerchief.

The case closes. 'Good boy.' I pick it up. 'I'll invoice the department for any damage.'

And I sweep out, leaving Caxton to crawl back and polish her goggles.

CHAPTER THIRTEEN

Dee's Last Incantation

Marvo's chasing after me. 'That was stupid, Frank!'

'I don't make mistakes.' I stop to wait for her. 'Not with magic.'

'So what are you saying? Is Wallace's body still rattlin' around out there somewhere? There'd have to be a loose head too—'

'Maybe he had a twin brother.'

'He was an only child.'

'I'm just pointing out, there's other possibilities besides me being wrong. Maybe it's a double. Maybe he'd had a head transplant.'

'Is that possible?'

'Christ, no. Maybe he was a man so tortured by self-loathing—'

'All right, I get the picture.'

'No you don't. Damn! Why did I do that stupid test in the first place?'

'Yeah, Frank, why did you? If you'd done what Caxton told you—'

'Arsehole!' I mean me. I ought to shut up, but I can't let go of it. 'Have you got any idea what it's like having to deal with idiots like Caxton?'

'How d'you think I feel? At least you've got the Society to look after you.'

'On my back, you mean. Thanks to you.'

'It was your own bloody fault. An' if you'd just stop being such a prat—'

'I could lose my licence.'

'What does that mean?'

'That I'm not allowed to do magic.'

'Well, so what? Is it the end of the world? I mean, at least you can still see!'

Fair point. I take a couple of deep slow breaths. My heart stops racing. 'How *are* your eyes?' I ask.

'Good. I had my check-up the other week and they're fine.'

'How many fingers am I holding up?'

'It's not funny, Frank. I don't just lose the ability to do stupid stuff with twigs – I go stone blind!'

'But that's years.'

'Ten years. Max.'

'And it's not like they don't pay you well, so you can afford a guide.' Even while I'm saying it, I know that's a crap thing to say. I mumble, 'I'm sorry.'

'Never even thought about it, have you? It's all poor little Frank, going post-peak.'

'I said I'm sorry.'

'Don't apologise. Fix it.'

I just stand there blinking like an idiot. I know what she's asking, but I just don't know what to say.

'Come on, you're the boy genius. Can you help me?'

Actually I can, but I'm not allowed to. I can't even tell Marvo that it *could* be done.

'I'm sorry.'

'You keep saying that.'

I manage not to say it again. 'OK,' I mutter at last. 'I'll try not to get up Caxton's nose.'

'Well, that makes me feel a whole lot better.' Marvo sighs. 'Look, forget it.' She takes my wrist and turns it so that she can see my watch. 'You must be starving.'

We're out the back of the building, in the courtyard where all the bodies come in and out. And yes, my gut's screaming at me for food.

I don't know what to say about Marvo. What we've got here, right, is a world where kids do all the seeing. It wasn't always like that. I mean, it stands to reason, things must've been different once upon a time, otherwise the world wouldn't be so impossible for grown-ups to deal with when they go Blurry: we'd have organised things so they could get by, even half blind. Instead we've got this situation where people need to read and do stuff . . . and most of them can't.

Who dreamed up this stupid mess?

There are several versions knocking about. One

story says it goes right back to ancient Greece when some idiot let a whole bunch of demons loose. The ASB don't buy that; they insist everyone could see perfectly fine up until about 1550 . . . not long after the Society of Sorcerers was founded. They say it was a conspiracy: a way for the Society to get control of everything.

I don't know.

There's another thing, though. Like I say, there's nothing I can do to help Marvo, but ever since those two columns of smoke merged into each other inside Ferdia's circle I've realised there's something I *can* do to settle this business about the contiguity once and for all. It's not a good idea. In fact it's dead stupid, and even thinking about it brings me out in a cold sweat.

'Frank, you OK?'

What I ought to do, of course, is apologise to Caxton and say I made a mistake – a bit of arse-licking and everybody's friends again. But it'd still be hanging over me: the fear that it's happened once, and it can happen again.

I mean, we all know Ferdia's post-peak. But what about me?

Either I can work magic, or I can't. And this wheeze that I've dreamed up, it'll sort out who's right – me or him. Or it could just get me killed . . . which is kind of a neat way out.

Marvo's still staring at me. 'So do you want to get something to eat?'

I shake my head. This bright idea, if I decide to go through with it . . . and if I had any sense I wouldn't go through with it . . . well, one way to guarantee that I'll wind up splattered across the floor in tiny charred pieces is to have anything to eat in the next twenty-four hours.

I'm standing there, feeling very cold inside and wondering if there's any way I can explain to Marvo without sounding rude or giving the game away . . . when I see a let-out. He's about my height, and looks dead smart in a peaked cap, black belted jacket and jodhpurs with shiny boots. He's Matthew's driver.

'The Superior General would like to know if he can offer you a lift.'

'What about—'

'I have no further instructions.'

I turn to Marvo. 'I'm sorry.' I point towards the silver Ghost parked across the courtyard.

'Frank . . .'

I realise she can't look at a Ghost without thinking about her brother and I feel bad, but I say, 'Matthew's my Master. I'll see you tomorrow.'

'Whatever.' She glances at the driver and whispers, 'How come he don't need specs, your Boss?'

'The Superior General is waiting,' says the driver.

As I follow him, I turn back to Marvo and waggle my fingers. Her eyes widen.

'Magic?'

I nod.

'Frank, if they fixed *his* eyes—'

I jump into the Ghost before I have to say no again.

Listen, the rich have got it made. There's four white calfskin armchairs in the back of the Ghost. As I put my case on the floor and lean back, there's a faint perfume – musky, like soft hands round my thoughts – and gentle music playing . . .

'I won't pretend I was just passing,' says Matthew, with a smile. 'I was worried about you.'

'Why?'

'The disciplinary hearing . . .'

'Oh, that.'

'Friday afternoon at three. And it's not a joke, Frank. Most of the board want your licence suspended or revoked entirely.'

'That's not going to happen, though.'

'Ignacio Gresh wants the death penalty.'

Crunch. My thoughts go flying around. I see flames and smoke and a screaming face, the skin blistering and peeling.

I see a man in a black suit, silhouetted against the fire. I see Ignacio Gresh.

He's the Society's Grand Inquisitor. Yes, we have

our own Inquisition: thirteen former sorcerers, each with a bigger chip on his shoulder than the next. Anyway, there's nothing grand about him, he's a complete knob and he's never liked me.

I shake my head violently. Gresh and the fire vanish. I'm still safe in Matthew's Ghost. His hand is on my arm.

'Are you all right?'

'Will you be there?' I manage to whisper.

'Of course I will.' He takes his hand away. 'But it wouldn't hurt your case if this investigation was successfully concluded.'

The ride round the scenic route, over Ferry Bridge, is utterly smooth. Not a tremor of vibration. I know Matthew is watching me closely.

'I'm sorry, Frank. I just need you to understand how serious this is.'

I manage to nod. Death? Can't happen.

Finally he says, 'So can you explain the discrepancy between your result and Ferdia's?'

'Who told you?'

He just smiles.

'Ferdia's post-peak,' I say. 'He expected a certain result. He got it.'

He sits in silence for a while. Finally: 'There's no question about the head. And it's the only body you've got . . .'

'The wounds on the body,' I say. 'The knife he was

stabbed with . . . narrow blade, triangular cross-section, probably about four or five inches long. Then he could have been beheaded with a sword.'

'I'm not quite with you, Frank.'

'I've got a knife that could've done the job. And a sword . . .'

He smiles. 'Are you confessing?'

The driver has always known that we were going to the termite nest. The Ghost doesn't exactly stop. There's no sense of braking. It simply ceases to move.

Do you have any idea what a Ghost costs? More than Caxton could earn in a lifetime, that's how much. The coachwork, the fittings – it's all the best money can buy. But that's just a drop in the ocean compared with the price of the driver.

He's an elemental. An elemental with the Knowledge of every road in the country. An elemental who can create a contiguity between the Ghost and wherever the owner wants to go, and can get there without driving over small boys. An elemental who takes a lot of skilled, highly-paid work to build and maintain. Charlie missed a trick there.

I know what you're thinking: a Ghost is magically powered anyway, so why bother with a separate driver? Why not build the ability to navigate into the structure of the vehicle? Well, it could be done, in theory at least. But someone has to open the doors.

'Thank you,' I say to the driver as I step out. He doesn't care, but I do.

A solitary protester pushes himself off the wall and holds up a placard: 'Go to hell!'

Matthew is beside me. 'I'll walk you in.'

I'd rather he didn't. Dee's last incantation is up on my blackboard, itching to get me into trouble.

'It's still a mess,' I say.

But he takes my arm and walks straight at the protester, who jumps aside.

The monastery door opens. It's my favourite termite, Brother Thomas.

'Where've you been?' he grumbles. 'You were supposed to—'

Matthew may be thirty years post-peak, but it's like he just walks through him. The door closes.

Sometimes, when all the termites have stopped howling in the chapel and retired to their lairs, this place really is the oasis of tranquillity it's supposed to be. The sun has almost disappeared behind the roof and its last light is shining across the cloister, casting a tiny, perfect rainbow through the fountain. A goldfinch speeds past in a flutter of yellow and red.

There's only one blot on the landscape: Brother Thomas, glowering suspiciously at us as he finishes locking the main door. Finally he gives up and scuttles back into the lodge.

Matthew smiles. 'You're saying it could have been a sorcerer who killed Henry.'

'I'm just speculating about the weapons.'

'Have you mentioned this to DCI Caxton?'

'No.'

'I appreciate you talking to me first.' He gestures me to lead the way.

'But she must be aware there's a problem with the security elemental in the palace grounds,' I say.

'Does she still think they brought the body in through the gate by the river?'

'There's not a drop of blood anywhere in the palace or the cathedral.'

'Did anybody talk to the elemental's operator?'

'Nothing. They had to put it down. But Caxton knows Wallace was at Saint Cyprian's . . .'

Matthew nods. 'If there *were* a sorcerer implicated in the crime, the Society wouldn't protect him. But maybe you should be . . . economical with any ideas you pass on to the police, at least until it becomes necessary.'

We're in the passage leading to the garden. Matthew chuckles: 'Henry struggled with sorcery. He could achieve the basic magical effects, but he didn't really believe in them – he seemed to regard them as some form of self-hypnosis or mass hysteria. In the end it was demonology that did for him. It was rather amusing, actually. The Master Thaumaturge performed a demonstration ritual to call up . . . oh, some minor demon or other . . .'

There are three Institutes of Sorcery in western Europe: Saint Cyprian's outside Doughnut City, Saint Martin's at Würzburg in Germany, and Saint Eugenio's at Salamanca in Spain. Most novices start at the age of seven. I was six when I went to Saint Cyprian's. The course lasts seven years, if you're lucky. There's a lot to learn.

At the end of your first year you attend your first demonstration summoning. It's impressive. Look, I'll come clean for once: it's scary – literally as scary as hell.

'Henry simply denied having seen anything. The supervisor accused him of falling asleep, but Henry described the ritual in exact detail, right up to the point of manifestation. Except that he insisted that nothing had manifested. Of course there was a huge row. Henry didn't say much, but he managed to imply that the ritual had simply induced a mass hallucination to which only he was immune. Several of the novices bought it. One tried to commit suicide. Obviously Henry was kicked out. There was some talk of hauling him in front of the Inquisition. This is all in confidence, by the way.'

I nod. 'Yes.'

'I lost touch with him for several years. I worked for the intelligence services, as you know. Then a couple of years after I came here as Superior General of the Society, he was appointed Bishop . . .'

We're in my corridor. My door barks. Matthew smiles. 'May I try?'

There's nothing I can do to stop him. And if I'm honest I have to admit that I'm curious to see what happens. He stops dead, a couple of feet from the door. He closes his eyes. After a couple of seconds there's a disturbance across the surface of the door. For a split second the wood liquefies to form the head of a wolf . . .

Then it relaxes and goes smooth. The door swings back. Matthew opens his eyes and smiles.

Peak Gift is seventeen to eighteen. You're OK for a year or so after that. By twenty-one you're struggling, like Ferdia. By twenty-five all you're good for is elemental work. There are about a dozen documented cases of sorcerers hanging on to their Gift into their thirties: there was one Master at Saint Cyprian's who was said to have summoned a demon at forty-five. Maybe that's why he was in a wheelchair.

So Matthew is one of the unusual ones. It's faded, but he hasn't entirely lost it. I never saw him in action: by the time he supervised me he was way post-peak. Technically I suspect I'm better than he ever was, but I'll never be Superior General of the Society – you can bet on that. I'm just a junior forcer hauling lumps of meat in and out of the mortuary ice room. The magic's the easy bit; it's staying awake through it that's the challenge.

Matthew steps into the studio ahead of me and lights the gas. And of course the first thing he sees is the code on the blackboard.

I put my case on the bench. It's cold, so I open the draught on the stove and go up to the other end to light the fire. 'Let's say I *did* make a mistake . . .'

I glance round and Matthew is smiling. 'That must hurt, Frank.'

It does, like hell. 'So if the body *is* Wallace—'

'Which I think you have to assume—'

'—could it have anything to do with what happened at Saint Cyprian's?'

'It's an interesting thought.'

'Should I mention it to Caxton?'

'Leave that to me, if you don't mind. I need to think about it.'

I watch him think about it, and I'm just beginning to believe that I've steered myself out of trouble when he points to my code and says, 'So what's this all about?'

'John Dee's last incantation.'

He stares at it for a long time. 'You're on dangerous ground.'

'I know. I was going to bring it to you. I'm working from the 1687 Bulwer edition – I found a copy in a junk shop – but it's a mess.'

I make a few shapes and the cabinet swings open with a contented sigh. I hand Matthew a ragged book, coming apart at the spine. As Marvo noticed, he doesn't need spectacles to read; the Society has a procedure – dead expensive and very exclusive – to reverse the Blur. If you're over twenty-five and can still see things close up, either you were a sorcerer, or you can afford to pay one . . . or you're a tatty and you'd better enjoy it for the few years you still can.

Matthew opens the book carefully at a paper marker. 'You know this is worth a fortune in the wrong hands.'

'That's what I was going to ask you: does the Society have Dee's original manuscript?'

'It's in the Closed Archive.' Matthew gives the blackboard another long, hard look. Then he says, 'I think you'd better rub that out. I'm sorry . . .'

I hesitate. I take the duster and count to five. I wipe the blackboard clean. Hell, it's not like I can't remember it.

'And on second thoughts . . .' He strides across and tosses the book into the fire.

'That's not fair!'

Matthew stares at me for a moment in surprise. 'I'm sorry, Frank, but in the present climate the last thing the Society needs is you dragging people back from the other side.'

What the hell: it's too late anyway. The book is

already blazing happily away. Matthew examines his watch.

'Don't go looking for trouble. Behave yourself. Let me find a place for you. You've got to think ahead: what will you be doing ten years from now? You know, after . . .'

The great unspeakable thought.

Unspoken thoughts go unanswered. 'Anyway, I must get on. I'm glad we had this chance to talk.'

'I'm better than Ferdia,' I say.

'That goes without saying. But there's something not working for you. Some sort of resistance, maybe.'

His fingers tap on the door. I've got my work cut out stopping it from turning on him.

'It happens,' he says. 'To all of us. I told you, you've put a lot of people's backs up, but if you can just step back from all this, trust your own abilities, stop over-compensating . . .'

'I'm trying,' I say, too loudly.

He smiles. 'See what I mean? Working for the police—'

'That wasn't my idea.'

'It's a waste of your Gift.'

'But you're always saying that!'

The first time he said it was after I finished at Saint Cyprian's, when I didn't get the exam results I expected and I thought Matthew would step in and fix it, but he said he couldn't. Just gave me this sad smile, agreed that the examiners had had it in for me and told me not to worry, he'd find something for me.

'And I'm always telling you that I'm going to get you back at Saint Cyprian's doing work like that.' He points at the smudges on the blackboard. 'Legitimately. It's just a question of finding the right time.'

And me staying out of trouble. So it's in the bag.

'Trust me,' says Matthew. 'It'll all work out. I've every faith in you.'

After he's gone, I grab the tongs and try to pull the remains of the book out of the fire; but it just disintegrates into a pile of glowing ashes.

I drag out a chair, sit down and close my eyes. I settle my breathing and clear my mind. It takes longer this time because I didn't have a chance to scan the blackboard properly. It's nearly an hour before I step forward and write all my code out again.

CHAPTER FOURTEEN
Demonology

There are these things out there called demons. They'll drag me off to the hell I refuse to believe in, if they get half a chance. They'll eat me alive, starting with my fingers and toes. They'll twist me in a knot and use me as a firelighter. They'll cut off my head for a bowling ball. They'll make me eat my own intestines for all eternity.

Different grimoires, different threats. But they all agree on one point: demons are a Bad Thing.

According to the *Popular Grimoire*, to control a Bad Thing you must be free from common weakness and common vice, and you must be fortified by divine grace and favour.

According to the *Grand Grimoire*, you must arm yourself with prudence, wisdom and virtue.

I meet all these requirements.

But there's one thing everyone agrees on: you must prepare . . . well, like hell. There's your basic chastity – generally defined as abstaining from the company of females, which leaves several loopholes I can think of. You have to fast. You're supposed to meditate upon the forthcoming task. And pray a lot.

Some of the grimoires say you must prepare for three days. Some of them say three months . . .

I have twenty-four hours, so I cut quite a few corners. And by the way, none of the published or pirated grimoires are accurate or complete. The Society is dead protective and anything I describe is edited down. So don't bother trying any of this at home.

I spend four of those precious twenty-four hours asleep. My chances of surviving this are zero if I'm totally wrecked. Then I devote three hours to lying flat on my face in front of the altar in the monastery chapel.

I know what you're thinking. Three hours is a long time – what's going through my head? If anything . . .

Well, what's supposed to be going through it is a whole bunch of stuff about what a wretched little worm I am and how, through the grace of God, this miraculous Gift was bestowed upon me. And how the purpose of this Gift is not to make me look clever, but to shed the light of truth over all humankind . . .

Then I'm supposed to pray for steadfastness and purity – no sniggering at the back. And so on, and so on. Actually, my mind's pretty much a blank. The floor is cold and hard. If I had any sense I'd be tucked up in bed.

But I've got to know.

I hear the termites shuffle in and there's a lot of whispering – and a couple of sly kicks – before they step over me and get on with their wailing.

Back in the studio, I disable my scryer and petrify my door behind me: if I get any visitors, they'll just see a blank wall. I consider going back to bed and hiding under the covers. Finally I dive into my cabinet and haul out a thick, battered book, bound in black leather: the 1863 edition of Jacques Auguste Simon Collin de Plancy's *Dictionnaire infernal*. After leafing through it for an hour, I've decided who – well what, really – to invoke. I dig out a dozen detailed demonologies and settle down to work out all the smells and symbols.

I cut a new goose quill – the third feather from the right wing, if you're interested – and write out all the conjurations I'll need on virgin parchment.

I sharpen, purify and mark up the cutlery. For a procedure like this, the proportions of the herbs and spices for the incense have to be precise; I weigh out an ounce of rosemary, seven drachms of frankincense, twenty scruples of myrrh, nine scruples of cinnamon and three ground-up cat's whiskers. While I grind and mix, I alternate the set prayers with rehearsing everything over and over again in my head.

Around four o'clock in the afternoon I hear Marvo yelling in the corridor. She goes away after a while.

As the sun sets, I'm back in the chapel, with my

forehead against the cold slabs of the floor, wondering who I'm trying to impress and reminding myself that I'm supposed to get authorisation from the Society for something like this.

You don't need me to tell you that demons are dangerous. The Society doesn't want to spend years training sorcerers just for them to blow themselves up, so it usually appoints a supervisor, partly to oversee the summoning and make sure that whatever gets called up gets put back down again, and partly because if two different sorcerers invoke the same demon at the same time . . . well, it can only end in tears. So even if I survive the night, I'm in a heap of trouble if anybody finds out.

But I've got to know. Remember that guy I told you about, Dinny? It was about a week before his sixteenth birthday that his Gift disappeared. That's just a couple of months older than I am now. I mean, it's rare for it to go just like that, but it can happen. And if the reason I failed to detect contiguity between the head and body is that I'm losing it . . . then best to get it over with.

Make or break.

I check and pack all the gear I could possibly need. I drink off a concoction of my own invention that'll keep me bouncing like a kangaroo for hours. My head hurts. The room's folding in and out around me . . .

But I am steadfast. I shave. Then I strip and wash myself from head to foot with exorcised water.

Shivering with cold, on top of sheer terror, I mumble the final prayers and struggle into clean silk socks and underwear.

It's two o'clock. There's always a few termites awake, counting their blessings in the chapel. So I creep across the garden, pausing briefly to throw up in one of the herb beds, and sneak into the stable. I harness a horse and muffle its hooves, then lead it out through the back gate to the street.

Maybe I'm deliberately trying to sabotage myself, because I take the direct route over the Cherwell Bridge and through the Hole. There's the usual fires burning – the Hole never seems to run out of stuff to burn – but I'm too busy with the pictures in my head to pay any attention . . .

I imagine the chapel at Saint Cyprian's. It's night and the light of the candles barely penetrates the heavy clouds of incense. The pews are crammed with sorcerers, their faces invisible in the black shadows cast by their cowls. There's a coffin in front of the altar – not very big, they didn't find much of me – and Matthew's standing there with one hand on it and he's saying what a tragedy it all was, such an amazing Gift.

It's great. Watching it play in my head, I'm nearly in tears myself.

The crack of gunfire snaps me out of it. I pull at the reins, but the horse is already aware that it's in danger of finding itself on the menu tomorrow and swerves to a halt in the shadows beneath an overhanging wall. Two men run into sight, chased by four uniformed jacks on horseback. Several shots; one of the runners drops to the ground. His companion scuttles off into the darkness, with the riders on his tail.

I figure the grown-ups are checking if anybody in the ASB is in the mood to confess.

At the mortuary, half a dozen men in identical baggy suits are sitting side by side on a bench. They're all data elementals for different cases; they've all got their eyes closed and they're all snoring gently. As I tiptoe past, one of them gets up and follows me into the autopsy room.

I close the door behind us. 'Stay!' I say. Mr Memory drops into a chair and goes back to sleep.

Inside the cold room, I have this sudden wild hope that in my absence somebody will have got me off the hook by taking the head and body away. But no such luck. I waste ten minutes leaning on the trolley, trying to persuade myself not to go ahead with this. Finally I wheel the body out into the main lab and give it a wash. Nothing very thorough; it's just a symbolic procedure. Then I tell the lift to take us down to the sub-basement.

I push the trolley along a short corridor, past a deep alcove lined with cupboards and sinks, towards a set of double doors that glow with a faint blue light. I wriggle round the trolley and hold my ring up. The light flickers. The doors – solid cedarwood, ten inches thick – rumble back. I push the trolley through into the summoning room.

This is just an empty square space, about thirty yards across, with black marble walls, floor and ceiling . . . and one hell of an echo. The walls are oriented to the four points of the compass. The ceiling is heavily soundproofed: things can get a little out of hand sometimes. There are no fittings, apart from a few brass studs sunk into the floor. No furniture: it'd only get wrecked.

I park the body in the corner and start by washing the floor. Partly symbolic, mainly practical: I don't want any left-over chalk marks. And a distraction from the fact that I'm shaking with nerves.

While the floor dries out, I take the lift back upstairs and get the head.

After that I sit on the floor of the summoning room for ten minutes. Eyes closed. Breathing slowly. I can take everything back upstairs and nobody need be any the wiser. When I open my eyes, the wrapping has fallen open and Wallace's head seems to be looking at me reproachfully.

I purify a brazier and set it up. Once the charcoal is glowing, I throw in cloves and cinnamon, praying as I go. I trot back to the alcove and dig out a cedarwood box containing various lengths of cord. I select one and fumigate it in the smoke rising from the brazier. I loop one end round the stud at the exact centre of the room and, with a piece of chalk, trace out the first circle.

The grimoires are packed with designs for magic circles and squares, all different; even successive editions of the same book will have dramatically different floor plans. The Society codified them during the nineteenth century, but I don't think it got them right.

That's where it all went wrong at Saint Cyprian's. In my final year I worked out some improved designs and a couple of the examiners wanted to fail me on those – except that my outcomes were near perfect. So they gave me a Second instead of a First and I wound up working for Caxton instead of doing what I wanted to do: theoretical thaumaturgy.

Anyway. Two hours later the floor is covered in a network of circles, squares and symbols. I'm standing in the middle, scratching my head and wondering if I've missed anything, when I hear the lift doors rattle.

'Don't come in!'

Too late. The doors from the corridor rumble open and Marvo steps right out into the summoning room. She looks round. 'Now what are you playin' at?'

'Watch it!' I fish the chalk out of my pocket and repair the outer circle where she's scuffed the line. 'How did you get down here?'

'Your pal—'

Mr Memory is standing just behind her, fiddling with his bow tie. I've never actually seen an elemental look sheepish before. I beckon him in and point to an empty corner.

'Stand there. Don't move.' I turn to Marvo. 'You too.'

'You had anything to eat?' she asks.

'Not allowed to.' I pull the sleeve of my sweater up. 'Now the time by my magic watch—'

She's staring at the face. 'What's magic about it?'

'Absolutely nothing; it's just what I call it. What the hell are you doing here?'

'I was going out to look for Alice an' I went to the studio to ask if you wanted to help me, coz it was your fault an' all for being an idiot . . . Only your door wasn't there.'

'That was a hint. So did you find her?'

'No, I looked all over, but nothing. Anyway, I'm on my way home an' I realise you're up to something stupid.'

'And you're here to save me from myself.'

At four o'clock in the morning. Dressed as a deckchair again.

She smiles. 'Someone's got to.' She's spotted the head and body. The smile has gone. 'Frank?'

'Get out of here, will you?'

She's staring round at all the circles and symbols and the penny drops: 'This isn't a contiguity test. What's goin' on?'

'You don't want to know.'

'Why can't you just let it go? Yeah, I know, stupid question.' She leans over a small wooden cage and recoils as a black rat scuttles up to the bars. 'This amount of work . . . You gotta be up to something really stupid.' She looks up at me. 'Something that could get you killed.'

'Hey, I'm fine.'

'You're gonna prove you're right – no, it's more'n that . . .'

She's got that glazed look again. For a moment it looks like we've lost her and I'm just hoping she'll keel over and I can drag her out and lock her up somewhere until I've finished . . . when she blinks and says, 'You haven't lost it, Frank.'

'You know that for a fact?'

'Enough to stay and watch.' She takes off her bag and drops it in the corner. 'I know what you're thinking: you've got this picture in your head of being found dead an' there'll be all these people – Caxton, Ferdia, your boss – saying what a tragedy, the way your Gift just disappeared, and what a great sorcerer you were – how brave an' all that crap.'

I'm desperately trying to look like she hasn't got me bang to rights.

'If you go into this, you know, thinking like that . . . well, that's what'll happen an' I'm not letting you get away with it.' She drags off her red duffel coat and tosses it after the bag. 'If you go down, I'm going down with you.' She pokes her finger hard into my chest. 'So you better get it right, yeah?'

'It's illegal. I haven't got authorisation from the Society.'

'You didn't have to get it before.'

'This is different. I'm going to summon a demon.'

Marvo's staring at me. 'Won't you go to hell?'

'Not if I'm careful.'

She hesitates, just for a moment. 'Better get on with it then.'

'Right, there's four censers in the second cupboard along the alcove outside. You'll find silk gloves in the drawer under the bench.'

Hell, I need all the help I can get.

One good thing about Marvo: she's quick to catch on. I show her where to hang the censers, and get her to fill them with laurel charcoal and start it burning, while I unpack all the cutlery from my case. We set up four candles and light them. I pull a linen surcoat out of one of the cupboards and tell her to put it on.

I'm rushing because the dieners come in at seven and even though they're half blind they may just notice that the body and head have disappeared from the ice room. But at last I've got everything set up. I close the doors. I jab a finger towards Mr Memory, still standing in his corner, looking mildly interested.

'Don't move.'

Right. Starting from the centre and working out,

I've got a circle just large enough for me to stand in and wave my arms about without knocking over a small copper brazier and the cage containing the rat. Another concentric circle outside that, making a ring with symbols scrawled round it.

That's all inside a square with its sides parallel to the walls of the room. Then another larger square, rotated through 45 degrees so that its corners point north, south, east and west. Inside each of its angles there's a small pentagram: a five-pointed star drawn with five single strokes. Plus a small cross extending from each corner. Pay attention at the back . . .

Further out, I've got four circles, each containing a hexagram – a six-pointed star constructed from two interlocking equilateral triangles. Marvo, in her linen coat, is standing in the western star with a brazier at her feet. She's clutching a silver shaker and a glass bottle and looks justifiably scared.

Not half as scared as I am. But then I know what's coming.

Surrounding all this I've drawn an outer ring: two more concentric circles, a couple of yards apart. Between these I've drawn the outline of a snake. Starting from the head, at the north, it spirals inwards through two and a half loops so that the tail ends at the south. Along the entire length of its body I've drawn almost a hundred symbols.

This ring isn't closed. There's a gap of about ten

inches in the outer circle, to the north, beside the snake's head. And there's a similar gap at the southernmost point of the inner circle, by the snake's tail.

Another yard outside the outer ring, at the northeast, south-east, south-west and north-west, four pentagrams, each with a blue candle burning at its centre.

And finally – no, really! To the east, there's a large equilateral triangle. Along its sides I've written TETRAGRAMMATON, PRIMEUMATON and ANAPHAXETON. Inside the angles, the word MI CHA EL, split into three. The triangle encloses three circles. One contains the body and another the head, both lying on silk cloths on the floor.

The third circle is empty. So far.

I'm wearing a white linen robe with symbols embroidered over my heart in red silk; white silk slippers; and a paper crown with 'EL' written on it. I've got a lionskin belt tied tight round my waist, with a wand and a sword stuck through it. I'm clutching a handful of white ash and a black-handled knife.

A silver disk hangs from my neck by a silver chain.

Moving dead carefully – I can't afford to drop anything – I enter the outermost circle through the gap at the north, by the snake's head. I turn to let a trickle of ashes fall through my fingers, sealing the boundary behind me.

Then I move sideways along the body of the snake,

running the tip of the knife along the circumference of the outer circle. I lift and place my feet carefully, so as not to smudge any of the symbols. I recite the prayers as I go . . .

When I reach the snake's tail, I step back through the gap in the inner circle and seal it with more ashes.

One final look round – and yeah, I've remembered to take off my ring. I step into the central circle. Blue flames flicker in the brazier. The rat peers up at me from its cage.

I turn to Marvo. I want to tell her how grateful I am. If it wasn't for her I'd've charged into this and got myself blown up, just to prove a point.

'Whatever happens,' I say, 'don't step off the star.'

CHAPTER FIFTEEN
Naturally Blond

I pull my ceremonial sword out of my belt. White bone handle. Steel blade, razor sharp, polished like a mirror and etched with divine names.

The sword has only one application. A summoning creates an affinity. So when you dismiss a demon at the end of the ceremony, you use the sword to sever the link and prevent the Presence coming back to bother you. Every year or so a sorcerer – not the same one, obviously – simply disappears after failing to sever the affinity with a demon.

The sword goes across the toes of my slippers. With shaking hands I pull a paper sachet from my pocket and sprinkle my prepared incense into the brazier. The heavy smell fills the room and I begin the conjuration.

'O Lord God Almighty, full of compassion, aid us in this work which we are about to perform.'

I raise one hand and hear a sizzle as Marvo, behind me, sprinkles spices and brandy into her brazier.

'I conjure thee, O Spirit Cimerez, by the living and

true God. I invoke thee by all the names of God: Adonai, El, Elohim, Elohi, Ehyeh, Asher, Zabaoth, Elion, Iah, Tetragrammaton . . .'

This goes on for quite a while. I become aware of a faint tapping noise. I glance round and see that Marvo's left heel is rapping on the floor. I give her my fiercest frown.

'Sorry.' She tosses more spices into the brazier.

I put a warning finger to my lips and get back to work. 'I exorcise thee and do powerfully command thee, that thou dost forthwith appear before me in a fair human shape, without noise, deformity or any companion. Come hither, come hither, come hither.'

My voice no longer echoes off the walls and floor; the room has gone dead.

'Come forthwith, and without delay, from any part of the world wherever thou mayest be, and make rational answers unto all the things that I shall demand of thee. Come thou peaceably, visibly, affably and without delay, manifesting that which I shall desire. Thou art conjured by the name of the living and true God . . .'

The rat has stopped moving and sits at the centre of its cage, its front paws to its mouth, glancing nervously around.

More names. The candles are still burning steadily, but the air inside the room seems to have thickened, blotting out their light.

I raise my hand. Hearing nothing – not even tapping – I glance over my shoulder. Through the gloom, Marvo is just visible enough for me to see that she has gone deathly white and is staring back at me, mouth open.

I wave frantically. She jerks into life and tips brandy into the brazier. A blue flame leaps up but casts no light.

I turn back to the east, facing the triangle where the head and body lie. I take the silver disk between two fingers and put it to my lips, then hold it up.

'Behold the pentacle of Solomon which I have brought into thy presence. I compel thee by order of the great God, Adonai, Tetragrammaton, Jehovah. Come at once, without wile or falsehood, in the name of our Saviour Jesus Christ!'

We're making progress. There is the sound of falling rain. A vibration through the floor. The rumble of thunder in the distance.

'Why tarriest thou? Obey in the name of the Lord—'

I thrust the tip of my wand into the brazier. As flames flicker into life, there is the sound of a crashing wave.

'Don't move!' I call to Marvo, and push the wand in deeper.

A blinding flash of lightning. A deafening detonation.

Silence. I withdraw the wand and blow out the flames.

A sudden foul stench, like an entire chapelful of termites farting in unison. As if a door has opened, a figure appears in the empty circle in the eastern triangle.

He looks about my age, maybe a couple of inches taller, with shoulder-length blond hair and piercing blue eyes. His skin is golden, and glitters. He's wearing smart blue trousers and leather shoes whiter than the souls of the blessed. The silver vest that strains across the muscles of his chest and upper arms has a message stitched in gold thread: 'Naturally blond – please speak slowly.'

Also, he has golden wings, about ten feet across. I'm not quite sure how that works with the vest at the back. But then it doesn't have to.

He says, 'Hey Frank. How are you doing?'

I hear a sharp intake of breath from Marvo. He sounds exactly like me. You get used to it.

'I was talking to your old man. He's fine, you know? Bored as hell though.' He smirks. 'Says he misses you.'

This is standard stuff, just trying to wind me up, so I ignore it. I indicate the body in the circle beside him. 'Lord Cimerez—'

'Why so formal, Frank? We're old pals, aren't we?'

I'm formal because I'm playing with fire. 'Lord Cimerez, I charge thee in the name of—'

211

Well, to cut a long story short, and to preserve at least some of the secrets of the Society, I charge him in a lot of names – I need all the muscle I can muster. Eventually, before we all nod off, I come to the point.

'By the pentacle of Solomon have I summoned thee. Reveal unto me that which I seek.'

He stares at me for a moment, then turns to the body. He puts his hands on his knees and leans across for a closer examination. OK, he's taking the mickey. He scratches his head, breaks wind, and turns to give me this puzzled look.

'If I've got the right end of the stick here, Frank, what you're after is this guy's head. Am I right?'

'Thou divinest correctly.'

Why the archaic lingo? Partly custom: the English branch of the Society codified the incantations in this sort of mock-medieval language and it tends to infect everything sorcerers say in the circle. But it's also a sort of defence: a way of saying, 'Listen, chum, we're not friends', and keeping it all . . . well, like Cimerez said, formal. This thing comes on like it's my best mate. What it wants, if the books are to be believed, is my living soul.

He looks round at the head and sighs. 'Well, that's not it for a start.'

I catch Marvo's eye and leer triumphantly. She just pulls this 'Huh?' sort of face and I realise: where does that leave us? Cimerez is standing there grinning all over his gob and I'm still trying to figure out what he could mean and what my next question should be when he turns to Marvo:

'Hey sweetheart, saw your little brother. Y'know' – he jabs his thumb towards the floor – 'down there.'

The brandy bottle shatters on the floor.

'Kinda depressed, but that's kids for you.'

I've got to stop this right now. I thrust my wand right into the heart of the brazier. The entire room crashes and shakes like a car on a fairground ride. The wand bursts into flame and Cimerez's hair is transformed into a nest of writhing, hissing yellow snakes.

'Marvo!'

She isn't listening. One pace backwards has already taken her to the edge of the star. Another will take her out of its protection. Cimerez gazes greedily, fire burning in his eyes.

'Marvo!'

She still doesn't hear me. Flames flicker across the floor towards her . . .

Last shot: 'Hocus pocus!'

She spins round and makes a grab for her back pocket. She pulls out the tarot card and stares at me. Cimerez snarls with frustrated rage as I gesture her back into the safety of the star.

My wand still protrudes from the glowing charcoal, but it's burning fiercely and my power only lasts as long as it survives. I've got quite a few names to get through.

'Aglon, Tetragrammaton . . .'

I'm screaming over what sounds like the entire building falling in on us. Cimerez is doubled over, clutching his stomach, the snakes writhing and spitting around his head. The wand is burning right along its length. I stoop to fumble for the sword across my toes.

'Adonai, Eloim, Ariel, Jehovah! I charge thee to return whence thou camest, without noise or disturbance—'

Who am I kidding?

'Begone in the names of Adonai and Eloim. Begone in the names of Ariel and Jehovah—'

I wrench the cage open and grab the rat. I toss it across . . .

Cimerez opens his mouth wide and swallows it whole.

Marvo screams. The wand collapses in a shower of glowing ashes. I raise the sword.

Cimerez belches. 'Fact is, Frank—'

I sweep the sword down. 'Begone!'

Whatever he was saying, I didn't hear it. As the tip of the sword touches the floor there's a final, deafening crash like a huge door slamming shut.

And he's gone, in a final, sickening blast of sulphur. The candles flare up, illuminating the room.

I let the sword fall to the floor. My hands are trembling so badly that I can barely get the cover over the brazier. Rubber-kneed, I shamble across to cut

214

the outer circle with my knife. I turn to Marvo. 'It's safe now.'

She's on her hands and knees, being sick. She croaks, 'Who was that?'

'Cimerez. He's a night demon with the rank of marquis, ruling twenty legions of spirits. He teaches grammar, logic and rhetoric, and he reveals things lost and hidden.'

She clambers unsteadily to her feet. 'So what did he reveal?'

'What I already knew: that there's no contiguity between the body and the head. They don't match.'

'He said it *had* no head.'

'Huh?'

'Just as he was disappearing. He said, "Fact is, Frank, this guy *has* no head."'

I stand there, watching the smoke clear from the room. 'That doesn't make sense.'

'So what went wrong?'

Did anything go wrong? The summoning was correct.

'Cimerez is a pain in the arse,' I say. 'But he gives good answers.'

'But you can't have a body without a head. It's—'

'A logical impossibility. Yes.'

CHAPTER SIXTEEN
Smart Aleck

What I need is somewhere quiet to sit down and get my head round all this. But first I've got to hide the incriminating evidence. Marvo is just about strong enough to push the trolley. I carry the head. Riding up in the lift, she's as white as the silk sheet covering the body.

'Was that really a demon?'

'What d'you think it was?'

'I thought black magic was illegal.'

'Black magic, white magic . . .' I haul my shirt up and point to the mark on my chest. 'There's just licensed and unlicensed. Suppose I'm . . . I dunno, commissioned to find a piece of lost jewellery. The client's so excited to get it back, he has a heart attack and pegs out. Does that make the magic black?'

'But if you call up a demon . . .'

'There's three kinds of entity I deal with: elementals, angels and demons. You can try to fit them into some sort of cosmic scheme . . . Like elementals

216

are natural forces that sorcerers can tap into – they have purpose, but no consciousness. Angels are conscious, beneficent beings. Demons are fallen angels—'

'From hell?'

'I don't believe in hell. I don't know what happens to us, but Sean isn't there.'

We step out of the lift. All quiet, thank God. The last thing I need is the dieners reporting that I've been playing fast and loose with the Dear Departed again. We move the remains through to the ice room.

'I think angels feel sorry for us,' I say. 'But demons want to do damage. They pick up on stuff – pull it out of your mind. They want to hurt you.'

'Why?'

'Maybe they feed off your pain. It's not good or evil; it's just in their natures.'

'So he was lying.'

'About Sean, yeah.'

'And the head?'

'The ritual compels him to respect my intention. He has to give a truthful answer to the specific question.'

'Says who?'

Good question. 'All the books. If he was lying about that, the entire edifice of ceremonial magic collapses.'

'Well, we can't have that.' She parks the trolley. After a moment's hesitation, she lifts the sheet. 'You didn't ask a specific question, though.'

'You don't. You formulate it in your head. It's safer that way. The demon can't trip you up.'

But he did. Cimerez is a nasty piece of work, but all the grimoires say he gives good answers. The whole point about demons is that despite the fancy dress and antisocial behaviour they're boringly predictable, eternally unchanging . . .

Human beings change. We grow up and get old. The Gift matures and dies. I have this sudden sense of panic, a boulder on my chest.

I turn to Marvo. 'You won't tell anyone about this, will you? Like I said, it could get me in a lot of trouble.'

'Whatever. I'm going home.'

Back down in the summoning room, it's just me and the echo. Mr Memory has disappeared.

I take all the gear through to the alcove and drink three glasses of water. Then I sweep up the broken glass and mop up the pool of vomit. I wash all the chalk lines away.

While I clean and re-purify the instruments, I think about Albert Einstein, another of those sorcerers who just didn't know when to stop. He was twenty-five, way past peak, when he made his last attempt to summon up Lucifer, in 1904. Judging by the mess they found afterwards, he succeeded. But as well as a pile of ashes he left behind his three laws of contiguity . . .

One: contiguity fades over time to the point

of undetectability, but never absolutely disappears.

Two: it cannot be destroyed by magical means.

Three: it cannot be magically induced between two remote objects.

Anyway, I'm starving. And I still can't figure it out: Cimerez was supposed to prove that I was right and that I could still hack it. The summoning was perfectly OK and I was able to control him, even when Marvo nearly came unstuck. But the answer I got makes no sense whatsoever.

I kind of wish I had no head – or I could get a new one. This one hurts.

Upstairs again, I step out of the lift to find a couple of the dieners washing a new arrival. One of them glances at me, then turns and whispers something to his mate. Before I can get into a fight with them, I hear Caxton's voice. I dig out my scryer. She wants to see me over at the jack shack.

Hell, that was fast.

I get over there, feeling increasingly ill, and find myself in a queue outside Caxton's office. Ferdia greets me with the air of a man who knows more than I do. Marvo's there too.

'I thought you were going home.'

'I did,' she says. 'I got a call.'

I reckon she's lying, but before I can pin her down there's a yell from Caxton's office: 'Are you just going to sit around out there all morning?'

We troop in. Mr Memory is parked in the corner, looking surprisingly alert. And Caxton has found a new friend to play with: a sad-looking guy in a grubby raincoat, turning his hat nervously in his hands.

'Who are you?' Marvo says, sitting down in the chair next to him.

'Buzz off.'

Definitely Charlie's work. This must be one end of a search elemental; his twin's out there somewhere—

Marvo's got there. 'You're looking for Alice Constant, right?'

'I said, buzz off!'

Marvo blinks. 'You're wasting your time.' Suddenly tears are rolling down her cheeks. She turns to Caxton. 'She's dead.'

'Someone tell me,' Caxton sighs. 'What's the difference between an insight and a wild guess?'

'I just know, that's all.' Marvo wipes her sleeve across her face and turns to me. 'Frank, d'you remember when we were at her place—'

I mouth, 'Shut up!' Luckily, Caxton's distracted, holding her glasses up to the window and blinking at them suspiciously.

Marvo hisses, 'Yeah, but why did she run *out* of the room, *into* trouble? What was she so scared of?'

I kick her foot. While she's still glaring at me, Caxton's glasses go on and the notebook comes out.

'You're the smart aleck, Frank.' I hate it when she calls me by my Christian name; it always means trouble. 'Maybe you can explain something.' She finds her page and peers at it. 'It seems you were at the mortuary this morning—'

And right on cue the door opens and Matthew walks in.

There's a split second where I'm tempted to make a run for it, but the room is crawling with people and elementals. I drop my case on the floor and fall into a chair.

Matthew's voice is weary. 'So, Frank. What is it this time?'

Everyone is looking at me, except Marvo. She's just staring at the floor.

Ten minutes later, she still hasn't looked at me. I've told them all about Cimerez. Caxton has printed 'SIMAREZ' in her notebook; and 'HAS NO HEAD', which she promptly crosses out.

'So you summoned a demon without authorisation.' She turns to Matthew. 'Is that right? He didn't inform the Society.'

'I didn't have time,' I mumble.

'And as if that wasn't bad enough, you didn't even get an intelligent answer.'

'That's a matter of opinion.'

Caxton snorts. 'You're stupid and incompetent. You've turned this entire investigation into a farce.'

Normally I'd feel obliged to point out that all her investigations are a farce. But she's still rolling. She nods in Ferdia's direction. 'I've got enough problems with him. The last thing I need is a second post-peaker on my team.' She turns to Matthew. 'I'll be putting in a formal request for a new sorcerer.'

I have to mumble, to conceal the fact that my voice is shaking. 'You can't ignore the result of the summoning.'

'Even when it's an unauthorised summoning, and it doesn't make sense?'

I turn to Matthew. 'Magical logic trumps all other forms of logic. You taught me that.'

'I know I did, but . . .'

I can see how disappointed he is. The miracle is that he's not even more narked off.

'Frank, you have to explore other avenues. You can't simply say, "It's magic!" just because things don't come out the way you want them to.' He smiles sadly. 'And maybe you do have to consider the possibility . . . well, that some of us have the Gift taken away sooner than others.'

My heart goes cold.

Marvo is still fascinated by the floor. I owe her for sticking with me through that business with Cimerez, especially since it nearly got her fried. I thought we'd progressed to her not minding me, but I guess I've freaked her more than I realised. Enough for her to shop me . . .

Well, someone grassed me up to Caxton . . .

Here's a question, maybe you can answer: what's the point of being a sorcerer if you can't undo stuff – make it like it never happened?

'Do you want me to do it again?' I ask.

'Are you out of your mind?' Caxton splutters. She turns to Matthew. 'I assume the Society will deal with him.'

The Society has several ways of getting at a rogue sorcerer. They can beat you up; they can suspend or revoke your licence . . .

Or they can set you on fire. But there's no way that's going to happen.

Look, I realise there's something wrong with me. My mum always used to say, 'Your trouble is, you've got no sense of responsibility.'

Magic does cause and effect. You make the right smells and say the right words and *tontus-talontus*! – the right stuff happens. In the circle, that works for me; but outside in the real world . . .

Hell, what's so real about it anyway? Sometimes it just feels like a dream, like I'm stuck out in the middle of nowhere with this vast army of demons all headed in my direction.

I pick up my case. Matthew nods. 'I'll talk to you later, Frank.'

Marvell still hasn't had the guts to look at me.

It's quiet in the corridor. Just the sound of my own footsteps.

When I was a kid – before they realised I was Gifted and took me away from my parents – sometimes when my dad was sober he used to stick me on the back of his bike and take me up to the Downs. We'd climb a hill and follow this track until we came to a small wood. Among the trees there were these two lines of standing stones leading up to a sort of tunnel into the earth where my dad said a great sorcerer lived, long long ago. That was the first thing I remember hearing about magic.

Anyway, in the summer we'd go round the back of the wood and pick cowslips, for Dad to take home and make wine.

That's why I've always done that stuff with the coloured smoke. Yellow like the cowslips, blue like the sky . . . green like the grass, if the spell works.

My dad always told me I'd never amount to anything – never have any friends . . .

So here's a touching scene. I'm back in my studio. I've put all my gear away and there's stuff I ought to be doing, like checking the code on the blackboard in case I misremembered any of it, or looking for another dead cat to dismantle . . .

Instead I'm sitting at my bench. I know I try to make out that stuff just bounces off me, but of course it doesn't. It sticks into me, like the tip of the knife I've got pressed into my inner arm, making this indentation in my skin . . .

Self-harming: one of the useful skills they taught me at Saint Cyprian's.

I overreact, OK? What Marvo said about me, that I don't need anybody . . . that's not exactly right. Truth is, I'm kind of scared of people.

Ever since I was six I've lived and breathed magic. I realise that if you're not a sorcerer it looks like it's all weird stuff flying in and out of nowhere; but if you're in control you know what's going to happen. You get the words out of the books. Maybe you tweak them a bit, but when you say them – if you say them right, with all the right smells and other stuff – you get pretty much what you expect.

You say to a Presence, 'I command thee by order of the great God, Adonai, Tetragrammaton . . .' and all the rest. And it does what it's supposed to. People – you say words to them, they hear something different.

Caxton, the Society . . . it's 'Do this, Frank', 'Do that, Frank', but it's never clear what they mean and when it doesn't work out the way they want, then it's all my fault.

There's a bead of blood oozing out through my skin. I press harder – I like the pain, it feels more real than anything else that's going on in my life. I twist the tip of the knife.

The thing about doing this is, it's all mine: nobody else can mess about with it. While it lasts, all the crap rushes away, out of my body. I'm not thinking about anything or anybody. No worries. No pain inside, because it's all there, on my skin where the tip of the knife is pushing harder and harder. It's great to have it, that tiny spot that I'm staring at, where there's this bead of blood and nothing else. A bead of blood that wells up, runs down my arm and drips on to the bench top.

There's a noise behind me.

I look round. It's like the inside surface of my door has turned into a sheet of brown cloth and there's a wolf trapped behind it, chewing and scratching at it, trying to get out. The creature's teeth and claws scrabble desperately. It's making these pathetic whimpering noises.

I put down the knife. After a minute the door is still.

There's a trick to self-harming: know how to take care of yourself afterwards. The knife is cleaner than a soul in heaven. A couple of passes and a few words, and it's like the incision in my arm was never there.

It's just an elemental, my door. OK, it's a bit bonkers, but it's right: there's no point in poking holes in myself. It doesn't even make me feel better; just like I'm a bit of a fraud because it's so easy to fix the damage.

I can do depression, no bother. I can walk off the case – OK, Caxton's pretty much ordered me off, but you know what I mean. In the end, though, either I'm still the best sorcerer in Doughnut City, or I'm nothing, in which case I need to do something far more drastic than just leave a few bloodstains on the benchtop.

Remember what I told Cimerez? 'I compel thee.' He can't lie: the rules say so. But he can twist things a little. What he said – that the body had no head – there has to be some way that's true.

Is there a hole in Einstein's laws? Like I said, there were three of them originally. But ten years after his death, this clever bloke called William Morris knocked a hole in the third law – that contiguity cannot be magically induced between two remote objects – by inventing the Ghost. That left two laws.

Contiguity fades over time but never absolutely disappears.

It can't be destroyed by magical means.

Hours later I've read through all my books on contiguity and I'm none the wiser.

I know I'm right: I'm just not sure what I'm right about. One thing's for sure, smells and spells won't get me out of this one, so it's back to the simple question: on the night of the murder . . . *who saw what*?

Akinbiyi, well I doubt if he'll talk to me and I don't trust him anyway.

But Kazia . . . what can she tell me about what was going on in the palace . . . ?

CHAPTER SEVENTEEN

First Date

By the time I've talked my way past the knock-kneed old geezer at the lodge, the sun is going down. So I'm standing on the steps of the Bishop's Palace, trying not to shiver.

Obviously I'm wearing my leather jerkin; it's the nearest thing I've got to a coat. And a new woollen hat because people stare at the top of my head if I don't wear one. I've polished my boots and found a pair of grey trousers and a white shirt that's been ironed within living memory.

I'm cold, but smart.

Once a year, my mother remembers that I still exist and sends me a birthday present. As a mother, she seems to feel that she should express her love through an item of clothing. And since she has only a vague idea what size I am, that item of clothing is always a tie. I am the proud owner of eight ties. All blue. In an attempt to make the best possible impression this evening, I'm wearing the bluest.

I ring the bell. The front door opens. The red-haired housekeeper takes one look at me, whips out an amulet and waves it in my face.

Ten seconds later we're both amazed to see that I haven't vanished in a puff of smoke.

I smile politely. 'Can Kazimíera come out to play?'

The door slams in my face.

I guess we'll have to do it the hard way, then. I chalk symbols on the wall each side of the door. The pockets of my coat aren't big enough for a brazier, so I pull out a paper cone, a couple of inches tall, and put it on the top step.

I make a shape with my fingers. 'Melchidael, Baresches, Zazel, Firiel.' I light the blue touchpaper and jump back. The firework emits a fountain of sparks and a cloud of red smoke that smells of roses, cinnamon and rosemary. Then it goes off with a bang.

There's the sound of screaming from inside. I step up and touch the door. It swings back enthusiastically. I'm crap with people, but doors seem to like me.

The housekeeper's in the middle of the entrance hall, dancing like a dervish, beating frantically at her clothes with her hands and screaming, 'Get them off me! Get them off me!'

Her son tries to get her in a sort of bear hug, but she fetches him a whack, bang on the nose. He staggers back, streaming blood. Akinbiyi charges in, but his legs turn to rubber and he has to grab the back of a chair.

229

Only one person is immune: Kazia is halfway down the stairs, staring at me. I beckon frantically.

There's no magic to help me now. It's up to her. Can she resist my natural charm? She's just standing there, her knuckles white where she's clutching the banister like she's glued to it. I beckon again.

She runs down the steps, ducks round the housekeeper and grabs a brown coat.

'Kazimíera!'

Damn! Akinbiyi's got her by the arm. But she pulls free and darts past me, through the open door and down the stone steps to the pavement. Akinbiyi tries to stumble after her, but goes flat on his face. The door slams shut, nearly knocking me down the steps after her.

She's already running off towards the lodge. As I catch up with her, out on the street, she stoops to tie her shoelaces. Her hair is cut incredibly short and I can see her scalp through it. I'm itching to find out how it feels and I'm dangerously close to running the palm of my hand over her head when she turns to look up at me . . .

The coat she grabbed, it's a man's; it's swimming on her and falls in folds onto the cobbles. I mean, it looks great on her, but when I pictured this, on the way over, for some reason I imagined a red duffel coat like Marvo's.

'I don't want to talk about my uncle,' Kazia says, standing up and rolling back the sleeves of her coat.

Amazingly, I've got enough money for the tickets and although I've never been to the kinema before, I manage to find my way inside without making a complete fool of myself.

It's this barn of a place, lit by gas, with murals along the sides showing Montgolfiers sailing serenely across blue skies stained brown by leaking rainwater. We've got seats down the front, near the scryer, and while we wait for the show to start we can see ourselves reflected in the glass. An attractive couple, if you can ignore my woolly hat. I pull it off and stuff it in my pocket. My heart sinks as I catch Kazia staring at my clean-shaven head.

She looks away quickly. Now what do I say?

I remember a couple of weeks after they first tossed me in through the front door of the termite nest, all shiny and new, one of the old monks took me aside and put me straight about chatting up girls. Basically, he said, make it sound like you're interested in them. There were two things I didn't get: how he knew, and why you'd want to talk to girls if you weren't interested in them in the first place. He confused me even more by telling me that they were snares of the devil and if I had anything to do with them I'd burn in hell for all eternity, next to Judas Iscariot and Attila the Hun.

Kazia watches me chalk a pentagram on the wooden back of the seat in front of me. The chat-up line I'd planned was, 'OK, so tell me about your uncle.' Yeah, I know: not very romantic, but straightforward and to the point. If she doesn't want to talk about him, I'm stuck.

I say, 'So have you been to the kinema before?'

'Not much.'

'Did your uncle disapprove?' Clever, eh?

'I told you, I don't want to talk about him.'

Not clever enough. And I'm still wondering what to try next when she says, 'How long have you worked for the police?'

'The jacks? About a year.'

And now it's her asking me questions, it seems to go easier. Of course I have to be careful: I don't want to tell her how I pissed everyone at Saint Cyprian's off so much, they gave me a crap degree and lumbered me with the job at the mortuary.

Which doesn't pay, by the way. Like I said, I'm basically the Society's property on loan to the jacks.

Anyway, I make it up. I tell her I was always fascinated by all the exciting things you can discover when you take a dead body to pieces and Kazia gives me this funny look. So I change the subject and we talk about several more things that aren't her uncle but finally there's no escaping him any more. I know nothing about Henry Wallace, apart from the fact that he's dead and may have had a thing about housemaids, but

I'm getting this feeling that maybe he wasn't that nice to be around.

I'm probably imagining this, but despite the dead bodies I get the impression that maybe Kazia likes me. Time to put an end to that.

'Before your uncle was killed—'

'I told you—'

'But was there anything – I don't know . . . Was there anything that happened . . . ?'

Her face has gone hard. 'Many things.'

If you're in a hole, keep digging. 'Something that didn't make sense. Something . . .'

The auditorium is nearly empty. A couple of families with kids; a gang of cool-looking guys about my age, with their legs over the seats in front; old blokes sitting on their own; three men coming in at the back. I want to explain to Kazia why I'm doing this, but I know if I try I'll make a mess of it—

'Could he have been using an unlicensed sorcerer?' She's on her feet. I say, 'Please, don't go. Do you know what I'm talking about?'

'Have you ever met an unlicensed sorcerer?'

'Once. He was just this kid, about twelve. Small-time stuff – you know, buried treasure, love potions . . .'

She's staring down at me so intently it's actually kind of scary. God, she's beautiful!

'Did you tell anyone?'

'No. He wasn't doing any harm and I didn't want to see him wind up on a bonfire.'

A couple of ushers are going round turning down the gas; the fading light dances across her cheek and for a second I imagine it's my lips and I come over all giddy.

'Akinbiyi,' I manage to say. 'How old is he?'

'Twenty-one . . . twenty-two. Why?'

'Too old. The kid who works in the gardens – he's the housekeeper's son, or something – anyway, he's the right age.'

'For what?'

'To be Gifted. There has to be sorcery. Too many things don't make sense.'

She settles back into her seat. 'Your friend the monk . . .'

'Andrew?'

'He has – what do you call it?' She gestures. 'On his shoulder.'

'A chip on his shoulder?'

'Yes. And he knows the cathedral.'

I shake my head. 'But there has to be someone under twenty . . .'

She leans closer to me and whispers, 'What about me?'

'Huh?'

Only the emergency lights are still glowing. I can't see her face any more, just this tiny sharp gleam in her eyes.

'If you suspect anyone who's under twenty . . .'

'Yeah, right.' Do I have to explain this? 'You're a girl. Women can do witchcraft, but they never get the Gift.'

'What's the difference?'

'Witches serve demons. Sorcerers command them.'

The audience starts clapping as a spotlight comes on and a bloke in a dinner jacket and a bow tie walks out on to the stage below the mirror. He bows and sits down with his hands resting on his knees.

'And women never have the Gift?' she whispers as everyone goes quiet.

'Never. Count yourself lucky.'

The guy on stage is an elemental. His eyes close. The scryer glows . . .

And we're in Mexico, flying down the Grand Canyon. I suppose they've stuck a scryer in a Montgolfier and it's all dead impressive if you like rocks, but I'm finding it hard to pay attention. My elbow is touching Kazia's, on the rest between the seats. I can sort of feel her breathing and I want to concentrate on that . . .

Except that I'm still running through names in my head, trying to come up with a likely sorcerer. And Einstein's Laws have crept back to haunt me. Contiguity fades over time, but never absolutely disappears. It cannot be destroyed by magical means . . .

I found no contiguity between the head and body. Ferdia found lots, but he's an idiot. Cimerez told me . . . what did Marvo say? 'Fact is, Frank, this guy *has* no head.' Now what the hell did *that* mean?

I realise that Kazia has stopped breathing. When I look round, she's staring past me.

Next thing, she's on her feet, stumbling away along the row and dashing for the exit. I jump up and chase after her. As I run up the aisle I hear scuffling behind me. I chase her along passages, down stairs . . .

It's dark outside. When I catch up and grab her arm, she looks scared.

'Kazia?'

It's like she's trying to hide behind me, and when I look round I see three men coming down the steps from the kinema.

One of them's the size of a building. Number two is this skinny little runt – the top of his head's so flat, if it rained it'd form a puddle. Light flickers across the pock-marked face of the third as he stops for a moment to light a cigarette.

Kazia jerks her arm free and she's off like a hare, her coat billowing behind her. I give chase and when I look round the three men are charging after us. I follow her round the side of the kinema – my God, she can move! – across the road and down a high-walled, narrow alley between two derelict buildings. I realise she doesn't know where she's going.

'Kazia!'

She scorches down a flight of rough stone steps, like all the hounds of hell are on her tail. I can hear the thunder of boots behind me and I'm getting a stitch. She's through an archway, across a wooden footbridge over a stagnant stream, and we're struggling across a rubbish dump. Rags. Rotting food. Rats squealing in the darkness. The stink is ghastly and I'm up to my knees in crap; but I'm doing better than her and even if I can't see where I'm going, at least I know where I am.

I grab her hand. There's an iron rail, muddy ground, a row of derelict warehouses . . . and the lights of a busy street market that stinks of rotting vegetables and ragged lumps of meat, buzzing with flies. There's two blokes – one on an accordion, the other on bagpipes – glaring across the street at each other and hacking out different tunes. A solid mob of people is shuffling, pawing and haggling in the light of lanterns and torches. I look back and see the Building peering over the crowd at us. I duck low, drag Kazia down the side of one of the stalls and double back.

Peering through a rack of dried fish, I see the Building ploughing through the crowd with Flathead on his heels. After a few seconds there's no sign of the bloke with the cigarette. I turn to Kazia . . .

Oh God! She's pulled her coat open and she's panting for breath, and I can see her breasts rising and falling beneath her sweater. Inappropriate thoughts! Where are the termites when you need them? I turn quickly and lead the way over a pile of rubble between two collapsed buildings . . .

Into the heart of the Hole.

CHAPTER EIGHTEEN
The Hole

History lesson. They used to have this real hot-shot university here, until they got bored of rugby and cricket and decided that real weapons and live ammunition would liven things up a bit. By the time the fun stopped, about eighty years back, most of the real estate had been burned and looted.

A few of the old colleges survived by bringing in sorcerers. They still take in students and hand out degrees, but mostly they deal in conventional weapons and the occasional freelance sorcerer. And according to Gerry Ormerod more than half the drugs that come into the country are shifted by Christ Church or Keble.

Most of the old city centre was flattened during the fighting. When things quietened down it sort of grew back, from the outside in, like new grass round the ashes of a fire. There's the cathedral at Osney and the municipal offices on reclaimed ground across the river, out to the west; the rich – like my mum, before she blew it all and had to start taking in lodgers – up on

Boar's Lump; the middle classes out in Summertown, Marston and Headington; the poor around the factories in Cowley, Littlemore and Kennington and down the river to Abingdon, where the Society turned the old abbey into a headquarters.

That's why they call it Doughnut City: there's nothing in the middle apart from burned-out buildings, tin shacks and a population of thugs, maniacs and witch doctors.

Why have they never sent in the army? At first because the army had its hands full, fighting off the French. Later they said there was no future in trying to recapture a square mile that had been packed with enough explosives to turn most of Oxfordshire into a crater. But now there's another story: that there's a renegade sorcerer in the Hole, so powerful that even the Society is scared to take him on.

I can see problems with both stories, but either way it's a standoff. There's talk of a deal to re-house the riffraff in a huge new town out the other side of Otmoor. Or the corporation may just call their bluff and finally send in the cavalry.

Anyway, not quite what I anticipated on what was, if you look at it the right way, a first date.

Apart from a few bonfires and braziers I can't see much. I'm dragging Kazia along a ragged line of wood and tin shacks, built into the shell of one of the old colleges. Basically we're back in the Middle Ages. There's guys struggling with crutches and rolling themselves around on little wooden trolleys. A boy with only one arm, lying on his side squeezing howls of agony out of a set of bagpipes held between his legs.

A man struggles out of a torch-lit doorway. Both eyes are bandaged and his hand clutches the shoulder of a child, maybe five or six and covered in filth and sores. The man stumbles over a loose plank in the crumbling walkway and almost falls. He lashes out with a stick. The kid howls, pulling at the chain that keeps her from running away.

The pole to which the torch is attached has a mouldy-looking stuffed snake wound round it, indicating some sort of healer. Another satisfied customer: the blind man's hand clamps down again on the kid's shoulder.

Kazia pulls away. 'I want to go home.'

I'm too busy trying to catch my breath to speak. We're near what's left of the old museum, so the palace is, let me see . . . that way. Kazia, unfortunately, is walking determinedly off in the opposite direction. My turn to trail after her again, deeper into the Hole. There's the sound of shouting not far away. The crack of gunfire . . .

There's this fountain. Well, sort of. The basin's taken a bashing so the water spurts out of a ragged hole and makes a scummy pool an inch or so deep around a

241

stone figure with no arms or head, then trickles out through a crack and into a ditch. Drinking water and a place for the locals to get their annual wash.

I lean over the spout and splash water into my face. We're in a kind of square – except it's not really square, just an irregular open space surrounded by wooden shacks shoved one on top of another three, even four storeys high. They fall down regularly. The locals clear the bodies away then rebuild, just as dangerously.

I shake my head wildly, to throw the water off and clear my thoughts.

'Frank, do you like me?'

I don't think I really have to answer that question. I wet my finger and draw a pentagram on the stone rim of the fountain. It won't last long, but I don't think we're hanging around here . . .

'Will you help me? I'm in a lot of trouble.'

Do you know what I see here? I see an *opportunity*. I can't imagine why she'd like me, but maybe she'd feel grateful to a boy who helped her.

'What sort of trouble? Who were those guys?'

'I don't know.'

I'm making a list in my head of all the reasons why this is a lie, when she puts her hand on my arm.

'Can you take me away from here?'

'Yeah, this way—'

'No, *right* away – I want to go home . . .'

I'm slow sometimes. Even while I'm standing there

staring at her, it's like I can hear this clock ticking down and I know I'm blowing it. She's peering into my face:

'Frank?'

And suddenly it's too late. Her gaze flickers to the side, over my shoulder. Her eyes widen with fear . . .

We've got four friends now. OK, Flathead is even more of a runt than I am, so I figure I can take him . . . until the Building hands him a knife. As the third guy lights another cigarette, the flame is reflected in the lenses of a pair of round sunglasses that hide the eyes of the thick-set bloke I saw in the cathedral the morning I met Kazia there . . .

Seconds later I'm haring off down an alley, dragging Kazia after me. The goons are right behind us . . .

It's pitch-dark, but I know my way around here. Two corners. Up some steps between a couple of battered stone heads on pillars. Into a sea of rubbish: broken glass, scrap metal, rags and bones, bits of old carriages and bicycles.

There's even the burnt-out remains of a Ghost with half a dozen yelping, skeletal dogs tied to it.

The building I'm making for, it must've been nice till somebody took explosives to it. We race inside and stumble up a flight of stairs. The banisters have all been hacked out for firewood. There's holes in the walls and lumps of charred stone and plaster all over the place.

243

First floor, three men come out of a doorway. My heart does a somersault, but then I recognise one of them. Dinny. The French guy I told you about: the one who lost both hands at the Ghost plant.

'Ah, Fronk.' He's swinging a couple of dead puppies from one hook. 'You can use them, maybe?'

I cast a professional eye over them. One's a beagle and fresh enough, but the other's been run over or something; it's basically soup held together by the skin.

'Are you kidding, Dinny?' His face falls. 'Look, what I need is a shark. Can you get me one of those.'

There's a lot I can do with a dead shark.

Kazia is looking out of a window. 'Frank!'

Priorities, priorities.

'Sorry, Dinny. Another time, yeah?'

And we're off again. This was a library once, but the books were sold or burned for fuel long ago and now the empty bays between the stacks of shelves have been turned into tiny dwellings. We fight our way through a line of washing and dodge through a hole in a wall, across a smoke-filled room where someone's set up a still, down two staircases, along a basement corridor, then up and out into a courtyard where chickens squawk and scatter.

'Hey!' A kid with yellow teeth like a hamster heaves a half brick at us.

I drag Kazia over a pile of rubble and through a gateway – and we're back in the street market, where the accordion and the bagpipes are still struggling to drown each other out.

Within seconds the crowd has swallowed us up. We struggle past a fight going on around a stall piled with crude chinaware. I get over to a wall and stop, gasping for breath. I feel dizzy, like the world keeps falling away beneath my feet and coming up in a different place.

But the fun's only just begun. I don't know which is the bigger shock, the crash as the crockery stall topples over . . .

Or the gentle feeling of Kazia's fingers brushing down my cheek. I'm still blinking when she kisses me.

As she pulls away, the world isn't bouncing any more. It isn't even turning. Everything has stopped dead, including the fight around the broken crockery. Even the buskers have shut up.

The only thing moving is me. Slowly. Towards her. Her lips are open, ever so slightly. A moment's warmth, then she pulls back again. She looks at me. In the dim lamplight, her pupils are huge and for a moment I feel myself falling into them . . .

I'm asking myself, what's her game? – when I see that our four friends have caught up with us. It's turned into this dead social evening.

'Who are you guys? ASB?' I step in front of Kazia. 'She's got nothing to do with this.'

Apparently they don't see it that way. The Building swipes at me with a broken shaft from the crockery stall. As I jump aside, the goon with the cigarette stubs it out on the back of my neck. And by the time I've stopped yelling, he's holding Kazia from behind for Sunglasses to whack her across the face. He's screaming at her – something I can't hear, because the bloody music has started up again . . .

I dodge another swing from the Building and make a lunge in Kazia's direction. I've got Flathead riding on my back and we get tangled up in a gang of kids, fighting over scattered crockery.

It gets really messy now. Kazia wriggles out of her coat and manages to kick Cigarette in the pills. He staggers back, clutching himself. I crash into him and we both fall down. The Building should have looked where he was waving his knife, coz he's stuck it into one of the kids and they're swarming all over him.

Sunglasses has got Kazia round the neck and is trying to drag her away. I roll over and manage to grab her foot.

Her shoe comes off.

A kid comes flying out of nowhere and shoves a burning torch at the Building. Sunglasses has still got Kazia in a stranglehold. Flathead jumps over me, grabs her round the knees and lifts her off the ground. The Building is stumbling around, flapping away at the flames rising from his coat . . .

There's a shadow like a tombstone beside me.

Cigarette is just kneeling there with a knife sticking out of his back.

I grab his shoulder to haul myself up. As he goes face down in the mud, I throw myself into the scrum. The Building is right behind me, trailing smoke. We all stumble around like a drunken spider then fall down in a heap. I hear something snap, and when I try to get up I realise it was my leg.

A moment later, somebody kicks me in the head. I'm seeing stars. My leg is agony and when I grab it I feel the bone sticking out of it. Blood is pouring down my face. Kazia is screaming.

This has been a memorable first date, but I'm losing it fast now. I can't see properly but there seem to be more and more people piling in. There's a blinding flash and a bang, right in front of my face.

There were some questions I needed answered. Somebody wanted to go somewhere . . .

Maybe it was me. Goodbye, cruel world. Tell everybody I forgive them . . .

CHAPTER NINETEEN
Not Heaven

To my surprise I wake up. Everything's white and clean. There's one angel leaning over my leg and a second, with curly black hair, smiling down at me. So this must be heaven.

'Where's Kazia?' I ask.

The second angel stops smiling and I recognise Marvo. The brightness isn't divine radiance, but the sun streaming through high windows and bouncing off white walls. With a wave of relief, I realise that I'm in hospital and that the angel fondling my leg is Reg Garston.

Reg is an old pal of Charlie's. They smashed windows and made cats and dogs fly when they were kids together; but when Charlie went to Saint Cyprian's, Reg went to Saint Thomas's in Lambeth to study healing. It's less fun than sorcery, but a longer career.

'Bend your knee,' he says.

Contiguity again, innit? The fragments of the broken bone remember what it was like to be whole, so the healer just has to talk them back into shape. A good one can reattach amputated limbs. There's some maniac in America who claims he has transplanted organs – hearts, kidneys – from one person to another, but nobody believes him.

'You weren't at the convention,' Reg says.

'Sorry. Busy.'

'You're always busy.'

I shrug. 'Victim of my own success.'

Reg frowns as he pushes my knee around. 'How's it feel?'

'Pretty good.'

'So what happened?' says Marvo.

I start to tell her, but she holds up her hand and wanders off into a corner with her scryer. So I ask Reg how long I've been unconscious and he says thirty-six hours.

Bloody hell! Healers put their patients into a sort of coma while the cure's working. It's partly to keep you still, partly because it's kind of unsettling to be awake while the bones in your leg are moving around of their own accord.

Marvo's got several calls to make, but finally she closes her scryer. Reg is saying. 'You ought to make an effort, Frank – muck in more. You're missing out on a lot of stuff.'

'Such as?'

'There's talk of . . .' He looks round. 'Well, sort of a

strike. If the Church wants to get rid of us, let's show people what it'd be like without us. No healers, no scryers, no Ghosts—'

'Yeah,' says Marvo. 'The world'd be a poorer place without Ghosts.' She's looking straight at me. I'm still feeling a bit fuzzy and it takes me a moment to realise that this is one of her hints about her brother. I'm still trying to decide how guilty to feel about it, when she frowns impatiently and turns to Reg. 'Can he walk?'

'No problem.'

'Then I'll let you get dressed, Frank. I'll be in the corridor.'

'What's going on?' I ask, but she isn't listening.

The door closes behind her and Reg says, 'You know your trouble, Frank?'

'I'm a smartarse.'

'We're all smartarses.'

'Except Ferdia.'

'C'mon, he's not a bad bloke. Nah, your trouble is, you think you can do it all on your own – like, you don't need the rest of us. Here . . .'

He opens the locker beside the bed and tosses me out my clothes, tied up in a neat bundle.

'I mean, have you got any friends?'

'I told you, I got a lot to do.'

'You should ask Marvell out.'

'You gotta be joking!'

'Why not? She's pretty.'

'You reckon?'

'She's another smartarse.'

I nod. That's true.

'And she fancies you.'

Reg has given me lots to think about, so natch I decide not to think about it. It's not like there isn't a queue in my brain. Let's start with how I wound up in hospital.

The jacks tend to steer clear of the Hole unless there are bodies to tidy away. Apparently they were disappointed to find that only one of them was actually dead. Even more disappointed, according to Marvell, when they realised it wasn't me. They hauled me across to the hospital and tossed me out of the back of the wagon, then took Cigarette on to the mortuary where they pulled the knife out of his back . . .

'So you want me to take a look at him?'

Marvell just shrugs.

'Then what are you dragging me out for?'

She's sitting hunched up in her corner of the van in her red coat, with her knee going and this tight look on her face. 'Dunno,' she mutters. 'Caxton told me to get Ferdia, but he's been called in by the Society an' nobody there'll talk to me. Any ideas?'

'Maybe they want him to dish the dirt on me.'

'Anyway, I figured you'd do instead.'

'Doubt if Caxton'll see it that way.'

'Who cares?'

'I'll need my case.'

So she bangs on the roof and barks at the driver to go round by the termite nest. Then she leans her elbow on the windowsill and stares out, her chin cupped in her hand. Her hair's all tangled, like she hasn't washed it for ages; and I can see dirt under her fingernails.

Gerry told me she lives out in Littlemore, with her mother. He didn't know anything about her dad. When I asked him about what happened to her brother, he shrugged and asked why was I interested anyway? And I said I wasn't really, just curious . . .

'You know where we're going, though,' I say.

'Saint Ebbe's. The rectory.'

'What's his name – that guy Caxton had in . . . the one who sent the spoof note.'

'Yeah, James Groce. His place. Now shut up and let me think.'

We're rattling out towards Summertown and the Ferry Bridge. The sun is still beaming out of the sky and if she wants to sulk that's fine by me. I realise she's taking a chance, dragging me in. Caxton really doesn't want me, but maybe Marvell sees this as some chance to make us all friends again . . .

Reg is right. Her forehead slopes back and her nose comes to a sharp point, and overall her face makes me think of the aerodynamic locomotives they use on the main line up to Scotland. But once you get used to it, she is . . . maybe not pretty, but kind of cute.

Not my type, though.

She says something, but she's talking into her hand. 'What?'

She turns to me. 'The bloke they took the knife out of – they found a Lithuanian newspaper in his pocket.' She gives that a moment to stick to the woodwork. 'Told you she wasn't right.'

'Maybe it's just another coincidence.'

'Yeah, sure.'

'So where is she now? At the palace?'

'Don't know. Don't care.'

'C'mon, Marvo—'

'Don't call me that! Marvell is good.'

'Whatever. Just make up your mind.'

Cigarette was Lithuanian, then. OK, maybe the ASB have a Lithuanian chapter, but I can't imagine what they'd be doing chasing round Doughnut City after me.

So chances are that Sunglasses has got nothing to do with the ASB. If it was him that poor Amber Trickle saw on the riverbank behind the palace, the night of the murder, then it must have been something to do with Kazia. It was her, not me, that he was on the look-out for that afternoon in the cathedral. And it was her again that he was after in the Hole . . .

Maybe he's her dad, or something, in which case God knows where Wallace fits in; although there must

253

be documents and no better person to winkle them out than Marvell . . . except that she's totally narked off with me and anything I ask her will find its way back to Caxton . . .

I'm still trying to untangle it all when the van pulls up outside the termite nest. My least favourite reception committee is waiting for me: a dozen scruffy-looking priests, waving crucifixes and amulets.

'Hurry it up,' says Marvell.

One advantage of being a sorcerer: you get the best private medical care. I feel a slight stiffness in the leg, that's all. But I'm not as fast as I'd like when I dash out again with my case. As I throw myself back into the van, a paper bomb hits my head and showers me with what I assume is holy water. The priests cheer, then look disappointed when I don't go up in a fizz of sparks.

Marvell just watches with her knee bouncing up and down. She bangs on the roof and as the van pulls away, she says, 'It wasn't me who told Caxton about Cimerez.'

'Whatever.'

I want to believe her.

The rectory of Saint Ebbe's church is a crumbling modern building jammed up an alleyway, backing on to a high wall that seals off the Hole. Another of Charlie's lions is on patrol outside and the man himself is lurking behind a cloud of cigarette smoke.

I've got my usual attack of stage fright, but I take a deep breath and follow Marvell up the narrow staircase to a tiny landing, where Gerry Ormerod is squinting at an old engraving, in a black frame, hanging on the wall. It shows a teenage boy, tied to a ladder, being lowered by ropes on to a bonfire. We admire it together for a moment and as we turn away I spot the telltale signs that he's going Blurry: two faint red marks each side of the bridge of his nose.

He realises I've noticed. 'Don't tell the chief,' he whispers.

I nod. He pushes a door open.

It's a small bedroom, and it's a tight fit.

Let's start with the woman lying on the floor beside the narrow bed.

'Alice Constant,' says a voice.

He's this miserable-looking little guy in a raincoat, standing by the fireplace, clutching his hat. Remember the elemental Caxton commissioned to find Alice? This is the active twin, who did all the legwork. He's found what he was looking for, but he doesn't look very happy about it. I can see the pattern on the wallpaper through him.

I hear someone gasp behind me and when I look round at Marvo, tears are pouring down her face.

'I should've seen it,' she sobs. 'The note an' everything.'

Oh yes, Groce's note: 'Leave her alone'. Not a wind-up after all.

'It's not your fault,' I say.

She shakes her head and smears snot across her face with her coat sleeve.

Tatties. They're great for spotting things. Trouble is, they don't always spot everything and, a bit like elementals, when they miss something they can't handle it.

I put a couple of my silver pentagrams on the mantelpiece, then open my case and pull on a pair of gloves. I kneel beside Alice.

'If it's anyone's fault,' I whisper, 'it's mine.'

Alice's grey eyes are wide open, staring back up at me like she agrees.

'The chief's on her way,' says Gerry. 'Don't move anything.'

Arsehole.

You know what'd be good? If I could tell Caxton that I realise I've messed up and then if she'd just step back and let me pick up the pieces and examine them and see where I went wrong . . . You know, maybe I'd be able to figure it all out.

But people like Caxton, they never give me that chance. They just come at me like the ASB or those goons in the Hole, knives flashing.

I don't need other people poking sharp objects into me. I can do that myself, in the privacy of my own studio, and get some sense that I can control this and stop it before it all hurts too much.

Marvo's turned off the waterworks and is just sniffing and wiping. I guess she feels sorry for Alice. Me, I'm not sure who I really feel sorry for. Probably just myself.

But Alice is the one who's dead, still staring emptily upwards like the answer's written on a sheet of paper nailed to the ceiling. I pull her pale green cardigan open and count seven stab wounds to her chest and abdomen. I'd need some pigs' heads to be precise, but at first glance I'd say she's been dead for two or three days.

'And here,' says Gerry. 'Careful.'

A dark-haired man is slumped in an armchair in the corner behind the door. He's wearing a black clerical vestment, a white dog-collar and a pair of spindly horn-rimmed spectacles with one lens cracked.

'James Alfred Groce,' says the elemental. 'Rector of Saint Ebbe's church. Born on the fourteenth of May . . .'

Groce's right arm hangs over the side of the armchair. His left arm is across his lap and still holds a kitchen knife. Both wrists have spilt blood everywhere.

'Why's he wearing his glasses?' I ask.

Marvo leans past me and pulls a small envelope out of the breast pocket of Groce's jacket. She draws out a letter—

'It's to the Most Reverend and Right Honourable

Dr Nicholas Thackeray, Archbishop of Canterbury . . .'

'He was wearing them to write that,' Ormerod sneers. He stares down at Groce's wrists. 'And to do the job right: a coward's way out.' He turns back to Marvo. 'Well?'

Marvo reads:

'*Your Grace,*

'*My name is James Groce and I am the rector of Saint Ebbe's parish church in the city of Oxford. And I wish to confess to the murder of Henry Wallace, Bishop of Oxford.*

'*In Exodus chapter 22, verse 18, the Lord instructed the children of Israel: "Thou shalt not suffer a witch to live."*

'*Bishop Wallace's heretical defence of sorcery*——'

Footsteps bang on the stairs and Caxton walks in. She takes one look at me. Her amulet flashes . . .

'What's he doing here? I told you to get Ferdia.'

'The Society called him in about something. Frank was available . . . I left a message.'

'Well I didn't get it.' She's noticed Groce's letter. 'What's that?'

'Looks like a suicide note.'

'So read it.'

Actually it's not very exciting. Groce says he dunnit and he knows he's going to hell, but that's OK because he deserves it. He sounds pretty depressed.

'That doesn't make sense,' I say.

Caxton is leaning over Alice, doing her detecting pose; she doesn't even look round. 'Are you still here?'

So I guess it's time to go – except that the doorway's blocked by this little guy in a raincoat, clutching his hat. I can see the stairs through him. He's the double of the character in the corner, who pushes past me and takes his twin's hand.

There's a change in the light, like the momentary shadow you get when a Montgolfier passes across the sun. I've seen this a hundred times, but I'll never get used to it. Marvo's staring.

'Who are you looking at?' the elementals say simultaneously. And a moment later they've simply vanished, leaving a faint musky smell. Job done.

Marvo's standing there with her mouth open. 'Where do they go?' She turns to me. 'I mean, you said they were some natural force or something.'

'That's right.'

'So do they . . . what d'you call it, revert? Or just . . .'

'Evaporate? Dunno. But no elemental's ever claimed to have come back from anywhere, or given any sign of knowing about events that took place before they were instantiated.'

She's shaking her head. 'But they're so like real people . . .'

Well, yes.

Caxton's got the letter and she's going through this pantomime of checking it. 'Right,' she says at last. 'I guess that wraps it up.'

259

'You can't be serious,' I splutter.

'Sampson, you've been a pain in the neck since the first day you came to work for me—'

'Yeah, but I *don't* work for you.'

'That's exactly what I mean!' She points at the door.

'You never liked me,' I say. 'Did you?'

'Didn't I just say that?' She takes off her glasses. 'But for what it's worth – and this is just between you and me and your girlfriend' – Marvo turns bright red. Wow! – 'I dislike you less than I do Ferdia. You're sharp – you can be quite funny. But you're a nekker . . . and nekkers screw up everything they touch.'

Without her glasses, her eyes are pathetically small, with red rims. She looks, I dunno . . . defenceless and bewildered. Like she's scared of all the stuff that she can't see properly.

She's right up close to me and even if she can't focus, she's staring straight at me. She points at her eyes. 'I've got nekkers to thank for this.'

OK, here's the story. Well, myth actually. I mean, it's bollocks but people swallow it . . .

A couple of thousand years back – long before the Society of Sorcerers was there to stop silly things happening – there's this Greek magician called Empedocles. Basically he's just some nutter farting about in a cave halfway up a mountain or something. And he doesn't really know what he's doing.

Just a myth, right? But the way it goes, one night he's bored or he's had too much to drink and he starts summoning up demons.

All of them.

It's a messy few days. Falling stars, thunderbolts, rivers of blood, plagues of frogs. Maybe there's some other magicians who come round and sober him up, and eventually he gets the stopper back in the bottle.

But a hell of lot of people have died, or just vanished. And almost all the survivors are stone blind. So they stumble around for a while tripping over each other, but gradually they find a way to survive. Obviously there's a lot of things they used to do to pass the time that they can't do any more, so they have to find what amusement they can . . . And a year or so down the line there's kids being born, and they can see.

Except they've got the Blur. They don't go blind; but once they hit twenty or so, they can't make out anything close up.

And that's how it all started. Sez the myth. Which I don't buy for a second.

Still, if Caxton wants to believe it, this isn't the time to talk her round.

'I'm sorry, Beryl,' I say.

I'm not sure whether she's more astonished by the

apology or by me using her Christian name. Anyway, she blinks at me. And I realise that because she's half blind and needs Marvo to see anything this close, I always treat her like she's stupid. And that's unfair because she's good at what she does, she's not on the take and she usually treats Marvo OK. She's not that bad with Ferdia either, even if he is a nekker too, as well as an arsehole.

So it's just me, really. Maybe I'm the problem. But I'm just trying to help, you know. I do my best . . .

Is that it? What Marvo said: 'It's always about you, Frank, isn't it?'

Caxton puts her glasses on again. She steps back and I can see her eyes sharpen as she gets me in focus.

'You mess up everything you touch.' She glances at Marvo. 'Every*one*, too.'

She's hunting through her pockets. 'Anyway, you're no damn use to me.' She pulls out her notebook and opens a clean page. 'And if you don't go now I'll have you arrested for obstruction.'

I'm halfway down the stairs when she calls after me, 'And I've written to the Society.'

I'm kicking myself. Not just because I've got myself thrown out and I'm in even more shit with the Society, but because I meant to ask Caxton if anyone knew where Kazia was, and I didn't. So I decide to play Boy Detective again.

It's getting dark when I finally roll up at the palace lodge, and a uniformed jack is standing in the way. To my relief, my security ring works for him. I ask him where Knock-knees is and he tells me, in hospital. Apparently there's been a break-in. Just after lunch, a couple of vans came charging through, knocking the porter for six. Up at the palace, ten or twelve armed men piled out, ran inside, beat the staff up and ransacked the place . . .

I trot up the drive and find more jacks standing around.

Who am I? OK, I remember the answer to that one.

What am I doing here?

'I wanted to talk to Kazimíera.'

'I don't know where she is,' mumbles the house-keeper, keeping a safe distance and fingering her amulet furiously. The left side of her face is swollen up like a football.

'When did you see her last?'

'Yesterday afternoon,' she says after a moment.

OK, if I was unconscious for thirty-six hours that means Kazia got home safely from the Hole. But what's happened to her now?

The housekeeper turns to the jacks. 'Can I go?' She kisses her amulet and turns away.

'Wait,' I say. 'Your face – I can fix it.'

Terror struggles with pain. Terror wins. She moans and runs off up the stairs.

According to the jacks, the invading army burst into the house, waving guns, and ran through all the rooms, rounding up the staff and dragging them downstairs. Their leader was a thick-set middle-aged man in sun-glasses – I just nod at this point – who pushed the staff around a bit, then barked orders at his men in some foreign language. Russian or Polish or something. Anyway, they charged round the palace for fifteen minutes or so, throwing furniture about like they were looking for something. They got into the attic, the cellars and the outbuildings. They grabbed a few bits of jewellery and silver, jumped into the vans and galloped off down the drive.

'So it looked like a burglary,' I say.

The jacks look at me. 'Don't be stupid, it *was* a burglary. Now get lost.'

Over at the mortuary I show my ring to the security elemental outside the autopsy room. The door doesn't open.

'What's going on?'

He just stands there like a statue.

The door opens. Marvo steps out. Inside, I can see Ferdia bent over the slab.

'How's it going?'

'None of your business.' Ferdia doesn't look up from Alice's body.

'C'mon, let me have a look.'

264

'You should be worrying about that hearing tomorrow,' says Marvo.

'Piece of cake.'

Ferdia makes this sort of snarking noise. 'Doesn't sound like a piece of cake. From what I hear, you could be in real trouble.'

'What do you care?'

'Just don't want to see you on a bonfire.'

'I'll be fine.'

'Like I said, not what I hear.'

'Did they ask you about me?'

He finally looks up at me and nods.

'So what did you tell them?'

'I told them you're an idiot. They said they knew that.' He goes back to work.

'So what you gonna tell them?' says Marvo.

'I'll think of something. And Matthew will be there.'

'Don't count on it,' says Ferdia.

But I know Matthew's the one person I *can* count on. And maybe Marvo . . .

'It's not your fault,' I say. 'I mean Alice. She chose to hide out—'

'Maybe I could've looked harder.'

'Don't beat yourself up.' Behind her, Ferdia's still doing his best to pretend I'm not here. 'Look, you gotta let me in.'

She shakes her head.

'What is it with you two, anyway?' I say.
'Love?'

She looks at me for a moment, then she says quietly,
'Get lost, Frank.'

The door closes.

CHAPTER TWENTY

Doctor Death

'Hang on, Charlie, let me get this straight. Alice Constant was sleeping with Groce, but she was having it off with Wallace . . . ?'

'At the same time. Right.'

Charlie's sitting opposite me in his favourite dive: the Russian Tea Room, just across the road from the mortuary. It's this windowless maze of booths and staircases, lit by black candles. There's nothing even remotely Russian about it, apart from a framed, yellowing page from a newspaper, reporting the Tsar's state visit to London a few years back. I don't know where the tea's from, but if it's from Russia no wonder they're rioting there all the time.

Mr Memory's here too: the makings of a conspiracy.

I'm struggling to make everything stack up. 'So Caxton reckons Groce found out about the affair. He's got it in for Wallace anyway, because of the book, so he kills him . . .'

Charlie nods. 'Amber Trickle – you know, the drunk—'

'How could I forget her?'

'Anyway, she identified the bodies as the man and woman she saw entering the palace on the night of the murder.'

'And the guy in sunglasses?'

Charlie shrugs. Mr Memory just looks blank.

'Did Groce or Alice have a dog? And why was she just wearing a nightdress?'

Charlie turns to the elemental, who shakes his head.

'Caxton can't have it both ways. If Trickle's a drunk, nothing she says is reliable and we can't be sure it was Groce and Alice outside the palace. If we believe her—'

'We?'

'All right, if Caxton believes her, she has to explain the rest of what Trickle says she saw.'

'Well, the way Caxton sees it,' Charlie says, 'Groce follows Alice inside, interrupts a bit of how's-yer-father, sees red, and kills Wallace. Alice panics and makes herself scarce . . .'

Yeah, I remember when me and Marvo caught up with her: she was certainly jumpy about something.

'Groce tracks her down and kills her,' Charlie says. 'Then he tops himself.'

The candles gutter as the café door opens. I look up to see a chubby, rosy-cheeked little man heading for our table. He grins and raises his hand, like I'm his best friend and he's delighted to see me again.

I know him. He doesn't have a name, but I gave him one anyway: Doctor Death.

'You don't think Groce killed Alice?' Charlie hasn't noticed that we've got company yet. 'Ferdia's got contiguity between her and Groce's knife. OK, so he doesn't have an exact time of death—'

I move my pentagrams along the table as Doctor Death sits down beside Mr Memory. Charlie stares across the table at him. 'Already?'

Doctor Death smiles. 'Case closed.' He lays his hand on Mr Memory's shoulder. When I grab it and pull it away, it's as cold as ice.

'Is there contiguity between Groce's knife and Wallace?' I ask.

Mr Memory's face has gone grey. He shakes his head.

'Groce and the book? The candlestick used to break the window?'

This time Doctor Death shakes his head in unison with Mr Memory.

'I need to see the bodies again.'

'And prove what?'

'I dunno. Maybe that Groce didn't kill himself.'

'Too late.' Charlie checks his watch. 'He's on his way to the suicides' plot right now.'

That's an area of unconsecrated ground just over

the wall from the cemetery out at Wytham. No markers, just coarse grass with mounds over the city's suicides and the occasional excommunicant.

'That's fast,' I say.

Charlie pulls a face. 'The Church doesn't like suicides. It really doesn't like suicidal clerics.'

'What about Alice?'

'Alice Constant is on the 3.45 train . . .'

Mr Memory's voice tails off as Doctor Death puts his hand back on his shoulder and finishes the sentence: '. . . on the 3.45 train to Southampton for her funeral.'

'I didn't ask you!'

He just smiles.

I've found yet another losing battle to fight. A basic data elemental like Mr Memory is instantiated for a single case. If the country isn't to be overrun by well-behaved little men in baggy suits they have to be . . . well, terminated when the case is solved. So we've got characters like Doctor Death, who's lived – sort of – in an office on the top floor of the jack shack ever since it was built, and retains all the data for long-term archiving. If you want to know about any crime committed in Doughnut City over the last fifty years, talk to him.

'Charlie,' I whisper, 'none of this makes sense. If Groce killed Alice because she was sleeping with Wallace, why all the business with the head?'

'Trying to muddy his tracks?' Charlie's voice is

unsteady as he watches Mr Memory.

'Then *where* did he kill him? We never found any blood. And what about the security elemental at the back gate? You said it yourself, it looked like sorcery—'

'Mad rector. Theological bone to pick. Finds his girlfriend sleeping with the enemy. Sees red—'

'Case closed,' say Mr Memory and Doctor Death in unison.

'Frank, the real reason you won't accept that Groce killed Wallace . . . Isn't it because that makes it all dead stupid and simple, and it means your contiguity test had to be wrong?'

'That doesn't follow.' It's true though.

'Caxton's not unreasonable. Go home, stay out of trouble. Go and see her in a week or so.'

That's good advice.

'And stay away from the blonde bit.'

That's more good advice. I put my hand on Mr Memory's sleeve.

'Kazimíera Siménas. Tell me about her.'

Mr Memory looks back at me with an expression of infinite sadness. There is already a hint of transparency about him.

I yell at him, 'Stick up for yourself, damn it!' But Mr Memory just closes his eyes.

Doctor Death smiles. 'Kazimíera Siménas. Age seventeen. Daughter of Vitas and Maria Siménas . . .'

I'm angry. I hate what he's doing to Mr Memory and I want to punch and bite. But I listen . . .

It seems the trouble started ten years back, in a farming district just outside Kernave, in southeast Lithuania. Bad weather. Disastrous harvests. People borrowing cash from a local money-lender who wound up dead under mysterious circumstances. The police said it looked like an accident. The widow said it was murder and started naming names. There were a couple of arrests. Animals were found dead. Barns burned down. More human deaths . . .

And people started accusing each other of witch-craft. The government rounded up everybody in sight and handed them over to the Inquisition.

Doctor Death reaches into his pocket and pulls out a black leather wallet. He takes out a newspaper clipping and places it on the table. I can't read the story; it's in Lithuanian or whatever. But I can make out the date, ten years ago, and there's a picture of a man, probably in his late thirties although the police mug shot makes him look older.

Charlie turns the clipping so he can peer at it. 'Recognise him?'

'Dunno.'

He isn't wearing his sunglasses.

His name, according to Doctor Death, is Vitas Siménas. At the time the story was written, he was married, with a daughter. The newspaper describes how he and his wife are accused of being the leaders of the coven of witches and sorcerers currently on trial.

He has confessed. Not to sorcery, but to being aware that his wife was practising witchcraft. He describes how she killed two neighbours who she thought had cheated her out of money.

Doctor Death describes the spell that Vitas claims his wife used and I recognise it as one I came across in a sixteenth-century Polish grimoire while I was at Saint Cyprian's. I had a go at it myself – I was nine years old and totally narked off with one of the other novices. It doesn't work.

Mr Memory is fading away like a dream. Charlie wipes his sleeve across his face.

Doctor Death pulls another newspaper clipping out of his pocket. It's in English, thank God: an interview with the British Society of Sorcerers' official representative at the trials. He says the proceedings have been conducted in an exemplary fashion and that the outbreak of witchcraft has been contained. He welcomes Vitas Siménas's confession, but regrets the fact that seven people – two men and five women, including Siménas's wife – have been found guilty of unlicensed sorcery and witchcraft and condemned to be burned at the stake.

His name is Matthew Le Geyt.

Before Charlie can open his mouth, I turn to Doctor Death. 'So what happened to Vitas?'

The elemental just shakes his head as he gathers up his clippings.

'And the girl, Kazimíera?'

Doctor Death smiles and produces another piece of paper. 'Matthew Le Geyt adopted her and brought her back to England with him.'

I grab the paper: some sort of official document, in Lithuanian, but I can make out the names and dates. How do I feel about this? If she's Matthew's daughter – OK, just adopted, but even so . . . Well, that idea I had about them . . . it must've been wrong, I guess. Even so, why didn't Matthew tell me? Because this is, you know, quite a big thing.

I hand the document back to Doctor Death. 'Long night ahead?' I ask.

He nods and smiles.

'Coz you look pretty whacked to me. Like you need a rest.'

I raise my hand, palm open, and move it down in front of his face. His smile softens. As his eyes close, Charlie says:

'Le Geyt was your Master.'

'It makes sense. Matthew probably couldn't save her mother, but he could keep her out of her dad's hands . . .'

'You recognised him, didn't you? The picture in the newspaper.'

'He was leading the gang who beat me up in the Hole. He wants his daughter back.'

I'm putting this together in my head. For me, Matthew has always been this sort of symbolic figure: my Master. It's like every time I pick up my instruments I can feel him watching me: approving . . . shaking his head . . .

But I've never really thought about what goes through his mind when I'm not there – unless it's to do with me, of course. I've got this sudden sense that he was a kid like me once, with parents who didn't make much sense to him, and maybe sorcery wasn't what he wanted. Maybe what he really dreamed of was to get married, have kids . . .

To struggle to see clearly, like any normal person. Like Caxton or Ormerod. I shudder.

I've got this picture in my head of Matthew looking across a Lithuanian courtroom at a little girl whose parents are on trial for their lives. It's not the Matthew I know; it's this more complicated person who decides to save somebody from the wreckage . . .

Matthew was a member of a religious order living under monastic discipline. There's no way he could have looked after Kazia. He must have persuaded his old pal Henry Wallace to pass her off as his orphaned niece and keep her safe as a member of his household . . .

And now the past has come for her. I get up. 'I'll talk to Matthew.'

'One thing, Frank.' Charlie hesitates for a moment.

'Your pal Marvell . . . She's asked to be transferred to another division.'

Doctor Death is just sitting there, eyes closed, the beatific smile still blanketing his face. Beside him, Mr Memory – no more than a ghost now – stares blankly down at the top of the table.

I don't feel so real myself. I mean, I don't know why I should feel so upset. Marvo and me . . . we just worked together and most of the time she's been more trouble than she's worth. I don't want to think about her going blind.

I can take this lying down, like Mr Memory. Or I can kick and scream. I've got that bloody disciplinary hearing tomorrow and the subject of Cimerez is bound to come up. Which kind of means I've got nothing to lose . . .

'Charlie, could you round up a couple of resurrection men for me? I feel an exhumation coming on . . .'

When I slip out, a few minutes later, there's just Charlie and Doctor Death sitting there.

CHAPTER TWENTY-ONE
Discipline

The important thing about power is, who's got it?

Exercise books out for another history lesson. It's 1555 and anybody who's anybody – the French, the Turks, the Germans, the Spanish – has got an army on the rampage in Italy. There's this huge Spanish army camped outside the city of Siena, lobbing explosives over the walls. The situation inside is desperate... until someone manages to come up with a couple of sorcerers. Just kids, but keen to do some damage. Next thing you know, there's this huge bloody storm – thunder, lightning, a mighty flood and a great wind from heaven – and ninety per cent of the Spanish army is lying on its back with its feet in the air.

A catastrophe like this concentrates minds wonderfully. Everyone's standing there with their mouths open thinking, who's next? And the pope has this brilliant idea: I'll make sorcery legal ... and the Church will run it. There's a bit of jostling – goodbye Milan, goodbye Venice – but everyone very quickly realises that it's safest for all concerned if *someone* takes charge.

Obviously there's this massive contradiction. If the Church really believes that demons are fallen angels who rebelled against God and were cast out of heaven, what's it doing letting teenage boys summon them up from hell? The answer was a papal bull of 1601, *Deo ipso annuente*: on God's nod, sorcerers can legitimately use the power of divine language to compel the obedience of demons.

Are *you* convinced?

Anyway, with the pope's blessing the Society organises itself and sets up national branches all over Europe. In England, they start out in Oxford, in the basement of All Souls' College where nobody can hear the screaming. That works fine for over three hundred years, until the college wars kick off and the Society declares itself neutral and ships itself seven miles downstream to Abingdon, where it knocks down the ruins of the old abbey and builds itself this swanky Gothic heap with offices in one wing and Saint Cyprian's, where I learned how to be so clever, in the other.

Let's jump ahead another seventy years. I'm six years old and I'm standing in the kitchen watching my dad open an envelope and pull out a fistful of banknotes. I stare up at the light shining through the paper: yellow like cowslips, blue like the sky . . .

I say, 'Dad, it's my money.'

I stretch out my hand, but he laughs and dangles a couple of banknotes just out of my reach. I'm part of the deal, not one of the dealers. And next day I'm sitting on my own in the back of a Ghost, staring at the back of the driver's neck and wondering what I've done wrong and what's going to happen to me.

As we swish through the town, people actually cross themselves and dash indoors. We turn into the driveway of Saint Cyprian's and I stare up at this massive pile of mad brickwork – all spikes and gargoyles, with thousands of tiny pointed windows.

There's this older kid waiting for me on the gravel: Charlie Burgess, dressed all in white, like an angel from a nativity play. It isn't raining, but as I step out of the Ghost, shaking like a leaf, he opens this huge white umbrella and holds it over me as we walk between two lines of black ash, up to the main door.

Inside, it's all black and white. Chessboard tiles. White walls and ceiling covered with black symbols. There's an arched double door opposite us: one half black, the other white. Two men waiting for me, one wearing black robes, the other white.

They lead me up a flight of stone stairs, across a tiled landing and through another door into the library. Stacks of books. Reading desks. The hiss of gas and the dark, heavy smell of magic. At the far end, a man in black robes, his hair tonsured, reading.

The door clicks shut behind me. I stand there

waiting for someone to tell me what to do. When no one does, I walk nervously towards him. Despite my best efforts, a floorboard creaks, but he doesn't look up until I'm just a couple of yards away.

'Sit down, Sampson.'

I've seen demons of all shapes and sizes. I've seen things appear and disappear and explode into a thousand fragments. But this was the biggest shock of my life: to be addressed for the first time ever by my surname, by this tall, thin-faced man with his beard and his ice-grey eyes.

For years I was terrified of Matthew.

Today I'm counting on him.

The reception committee is different, for a start. Instead of Charlie, a platoon of Knights of Saint Cyprian carrying swords and dressed in full protective livery: white shoes with magical symbols tattooed into the leather; white linen coats and trousers with symbols embroidered in red silk thread; bronze helmets.

I know what you're going to say: this is all symbolic. But even if the Society of Sorcerers isn't a private army, it sure acts like one. The Knights of Saint Cyprian are its disciplinary branch, recruited from its most antisocial dropouts: thugs with a pathetically weak Gift and no table manners who feel flattered at being allowed to hang around and do the Society's dirty work. They're crap with rabbits, but they can make a disobedient sorcerer disappear at the drop of a hat.

I'm expecting them. I manage not to faint.

I'm also expecting a windowless, candlelit room with a gang of middle-aged men in fancy dress and silly haircuts sitting round a long table. And that's what I get. No sign of Matthew, and everybody looking at me like I'm something that crawled out from under a stone.

I'm expecting them to give me a hard time for waltzing off with human body parts. And that's what I get. I point out that most of them must've done much the same in their time, which doesn't go down very well.

After that it's all downhill. The name Cimerez comes up. There's no point pretending that I didn't know what I was doing: demons don't just turn up by accident. I explain that I was under a lot of pressure and struggling to get my head around the fact that I didn't find contiguity and then Ferdia did . . .

'Look, I panicked,' I say at last, wondering where Matthew's got to.

The committee just sit there like mangy, stuffed parrots. These guys, they're all has-beens and I despise them. None of them are under fifty so they haven't done a spark of magic for thirty years. What right have they got to sit in judgement on me? I could take them all out with one flick of my wrist . . .

If it wasn't for the four magic circles, one in each

corner of the room, and the four kids in full regalia, wands at the ready. I suppose I should feel flattered that they think I could be that dangerous.

I decide to play for sympathy. 'I thought my Gift was being taken away,' I whisper.

My heart skips a beat at the sound of the door creaking open behind me. I look round, expecting Matthew. I shiver as a silky voice says:

'And has it?'

Ignacio Gresh, the Grand Inquisitor, wears a black suit over a grey shirt and a black tie with the Society crest embroidered on it. He has a fringe of tonsured silver hair over a dark, heavily scarred face. It looks like he was in a fire, or something, but nobody ever seemed to know for sure.

'Has the Lord taken back your Gift?'

'No,' I stammer. 'At least, I don't think so. I mean—'

'Which makes you the luckiest person in this room.'

'Not luck, just—'

'Tell me one thing, Sampson: what makes you so special? Every member of this board has had to face up to going post-peak, and we've managed it without resorting to cannibalism or unauthorised summonings—'

'Yeah, well that's what *you* say.'

Not very clever. Gresh steps forward to pick up a small silver handbell from the centre of the table. 'I think we can proceed to the vote now.'

He rings the bell.

Chairs scrape back. Where's Matthew? He *promised* he'd be here . . .

There's a small altar at one end of the room. Just a metal box on legs with enamel images of Saint Cyprian summoning demons and being cooked in a cauldron of boiling water. One after another the committee walk across to take a small ivory marble from a dish on top of the altar.

Along the wall at the other end of the room is an oak shelf supporting five wooden boxes, each about a foot square and six inches tall, and with a round hole in the top. The committee vote by dropping a marble into one of the boxes. It's a simple count: the box with the most marbles wins.

Innocent: I walk away without a stain on my character.

Reprimand: I get torn off a strip in front of as many members of the Society as feel the need for a laugh.

Suspend: I lose my licence for up to a year.

Revoke: I look for a new line of work altogether.

Death.

The vote is in no particular order; they just stand around waiting for the mood to take them. Three of them are whispering to each other. One is kneeling at the altar, eyes closed and hands clasped, praying for divine guidance . . . or waiting for someone to slip him fifty quid and tell him which way to vote.

There is still a single marble left in the dish on the altar. Gresh hasn't moved.

His eyes follow the first member of the committee to step up to the shelf and cast his vote. The marble rattles in one of the middle boxes – I can't see which. Not innocent, anyway. Not dead.

The bloke kneeling at the altar clambers to his feet. 'As God is my judge,' he says, and walks across to vote to suspend me.

Three more of them are on the move, but they stop dead as the table creaks and Gresh takes his marble from the dish. He looks at me. Dead eyes, like a shark.

Nobody moves as he walks across to the shelf. He turns, with his arm extended, to make sure that everyone can see what he's doing. His marble rattles in the box. Death.

I feel sick.

Yeah, something wrong with me – something missing. Every time the shit hits the fan I think, oh right, that's how it feels. Then more shit flies and I feel even worse and I think this is it, this is as bad as it gets . . .

But this time it's different.

I could say it's like the rug being pulled out from under my feet. I could say it's like falling into the abyss. I could say it's like someone's reached in and grabbed my guts and pulled them out.

But it's not 'like' anything. I mean, I'm trying to

think. I feel cold. But it's no good – this isn't happening to me. I'm not dreaming, so they must've got the wrong bloke.

Yeah, this is about somebody else.

Whispering. Shuffling. The rattle of the marbles in the boxes. I'm trying to keep count. I see a couple of suspensions, maybe one revocation. But nobody's said I'm innocent, or thinks a reprimand will do it.

And I've counted at least five votes for death.

Oh dear God.

The last marble rattles. Gresh and a couple of the committee members huddle round the shelf. The door creaks. Everyone looks round—

'Sorry I'm late.'

Matthew steps into the candlelight. He's wearing the formal costume of the Superior General: a plain black cassock. My head's spinning. My heart is banging away. Saved! I grab the back of a chair to stop myself falling over.

'We have finished the vote,' says Gresh. He walks over to the table, holding one of the boxes. He slides it open. The marbles clatter out.

He smiles. 'Death.'

Maybe not saved.

I've got this picture in my head: Matthew's study, the day I got my final results at Saint Cyprian's. He's standing at the window, a black silhouette against the blazing sunshine. He turns with a sad smile and tells me that even though he is Superior General, there is nothing he can do.

I blink. I'm back in a room lit only by candles with everyone staring at me solemn-faced – except Gresh. You know that expression: 'unholy glee'? Well that's what's plastered all over his face. I've really made his day.

Nobody speaks. Nobody moves. That feeling again: this is nothing to do with me – they're talking about somebody else.

I feel like I'm going to crap myself.

Matthew says, 'As Superior General, I am exercising my veto.'

This seems like a good moment to pass out.

I'm sitting on a stone bench in a windowless cell, with my feet fettered to the wall. The key scrapes in the lock. The door opens.

'Take those off.' Matthew stands aside so that the warder can kneel to remove the legcuffs.

'Thank you,' I say.

He holds up his hand and says to the warder, 'That's all.'

I hear the door close. I'm staring at the tiny stump where Matthew's missing the finger. I was twelve when he fed it to a Presence to get me out of a hole.

'You're a fool, Frank.'

'So why did you stop them?'

He takes a minute to think about that. 'In the first place, because you were my pupil and I'm supposed to look after you. But mainly because it's nothing to do with you: Gresh is just trying to use your stupidity to undermine my position as Superior General.'

I can't think of anything better to do than hang my head.

Matthew explains the deal. My licence is suspended for a year, and I have to go on pilgrimage to the tomb of Saint Cyprian in Rome. On foot! If I get back in one piece, I have to perform an act of penance in front of as many members of the Society as can be bothered to turn up and help beat the crap out of me.

And if I don't do what I'm told, Gresh, as Grand Inquisitor, has a personal supply of dry timber and a box of matches, and Matthew won't be able to stop him.

'Do I really have to walk?'

Matthew actually laughs. 'I think the Society will just be pleased to see you go. Seriously, Frank, this could be good for you – no, don't pull faces – you need a little humility.' He sits down beside me. 'Do you even know what that means?'

'Humility consists in keeping myself within my own bounds, not reaching out to things above me, but submitting to my superior.' I learned that by heart when I was eight.

'Being a sorcerer, it isn't a licence to run amok, it's a

287

huge responsibility. The Society could rule the world, but instead we choose to serve . . .'

And he goes off into this long sermon about my duty to God and to the Society and all that stuff. We all know this isn't the first time Matthew's saved my bacon. And I can see that by using his veto to get me off the bonfire, he's given Gresh something to use against him. But to be honest, I sort of drift off a bit. I'm thinking about Cimerez: what did he mean? James Groce: did he really commit suicide? Marvo: have I totally narked her off? Kazia: will I ever see her again?

'. . . And I'll smooth things over while you're away.' Matthew doesn't seem to have noticed that I'm not listening. He probably knows he's wasting his breath anyway. 'The Society needs you – but don't forget that you need the Society too.'

He gets to his feet. I want to ask him what really happened in Kernave and about how he adopted Kazia and whether that's all there is to it . . . but this doesn't seem like a good time.

'Right,' he says, 'let's get you out of here. And one last thing, Frank – please don't do anything else stupid.'

CHAPTER TWENTY-TWO

Digging

I know I just said it, but I'll keep on saying it till we all get bored. There's something wrong with me.

The clock in the cathedral tower is striking three. Maybe somebody up there likes me after all, because it's a dry night, with clouds covering the moon. The cart is parked behind bushes on waste ground. I should be packing a rucksack for my hike to Rome, but here I am, underdressed and shivering as usual, following Charlie's resurrection men over the wall into the suicide plot, with two spades, a covered lantern and a crate of beer.

There are no markers – the whole point of a suicide plot is that the residents should be wiped from public memory – but there's just enough light from a narrow chink in the lantern to locate Groce: he's the freshly dug mound in the corner, under an ancient, grotesquely deformed yew tree. The lads seem to think it's a major find and worth a beer apiece.

Leo is this old bloke with a face that's sort of

crumpled in on itself, and long grey hair combed flat across his bald crown and glued into place. Martin's the masher: younger, red-faced, about five feet six tall and six feet wide. If you want a couple of rooms in your house knocked through, Martin's your man. Just make sure you've got someone standing the other side to stop him carrying on through the back wall and out into the garden.

They toss the empty bottles into the bushes and get stuck in with the spades while I pull five dead twigs off the yew tree and arrange them in a pentagram on the grass. It hasn't rained since Groce was planted, so the earth is loose and dry. Every time I look back, it's flying out.

'How much further?' I hiss, an hour and a couple more beers later.

'No more,' says a soft voice right behind me.

Even in the middle of the night, he's wearing his sunglasses. His flat-headed friend is beside him, looking mean.

'I am Vitas Siménas.'

This is interesting, in an alarming sort of way. He holds out his hand. It's huge, with dry, hard skin.

I manage some sort of smile. 'I think I know your daughter.'

Leo and Martin are still digging away with their backs to us. There's a hollow thud as a spade hits wood. 'Frank!' Leo calls. He looks round and sees

Flathead standing over the grave, holding a pistol.

'Keep digging, Leo.' I turn back to Siménas. 'You don't mind.'

He shrugs.

'I was reading about you and your wife.'

'He steal my daughter, your chief . . .'

'It was a legal adoption. I saw the papers.'

'I think Church take her, or she is dead.' Siménas sounds genuinely upset. 'Ten years I look for her . . .'

Leo lays his spade on the ground beside the grave. Flathead steps back and lets him climb out slowly.

'What's going on?' Leo asks, squinting as he opens a couple of beers.

'Dunno yet.' I uncover the lantern. Siménas follows me over to the graveside, where we peer down together.

The coffin is a crude affair. A rough wooden box built to hold together just long enough to get James Groce into the ground. Martin levers the lid off and clambers out after it.

The body lies there in a coarse shroud, smelling of quicklime and decay. There is a thin wooden stake protruding about six inches from the chest, to prevent him coming back as a vampire or something.

'I don't really get this suicide malarkey,' says Leo, passing Martin his beer. 'Dead's dead, far as I can see.'

'There are spells to make the dead rise again and foretell the future,' I say.

'But what does dead person know?' sighs Siménas.

We can't stand around all night getting morbid. I hop down into the grave. Standing with one foot on each side of the coffin, I pull out the stake, which is just going to be a nuisance, and toss it on to the grass. Flathead jumps back, crossing himself frantically and kicking my protective twigs away.

Trying to ignore the smell, I balance the lantern on one corner of the coffin and pull out a penknife. I sense Siménas still standing over me as I start cutting away the shroud from the face.

'Go ahead. I'm listening.'

'I want my daughter back.'

The cloth pulls away. Groce has the disillusioned expression of someone for whom death has lived up to all his worst expectations. For a moment I ask myself, what am I playing at? But I carry on cutting down the length of the shroud.

'Outside bishop's house, by river, I see him.' Siménas points down at Groce's body. 'Young woman too.'

'And a dog?'

While he puzzles over that, I brush a few insects away and lift Groce's hands. They're cold, obviously, and flabby – like fish that's been too long on the slab. But I haven't got enough light to read the gashes on his wrists.

'OK.' I shuffle backwards to the bottom of the coffin. 'Let's get him out.'

I look round, expecting to see Leo and Martin. Instead I get a spadeful of dirt in the face. As I try to scramble out of the grave, something cracks into the side of my head and I find myself face down in James Groce.

Let's just say it's disgusting.

I try to pull myself up to my hands and knees, but there's something cold and sharp pressing down on the back of my neck. As I realise it's the edge of a spade . . .

'Where is she?' Siménas hisses.

'Kazia? I don't know!' The pressure increases, forcing me down. 'She went home to the palace—'

'I look there!'

Oh yes, the burglary that wasn't a burglary.

I hear shouting. The pressure of the spade is released. More yelling, then several sharp bangs. The spade rattles against the coffin as Siménas lets it drop.

I make another attempt to raise myself, but all the breath is knocked out of me as someone jumps down on to my back. I'm not on James Groce any more; I'm *in* him, retching and gasping. The foul taste in my mouth could be my own bile; it could be him. I'm howling and screaming – I'm going to die down here, buried alive with a rotting corpse.

'Shut up, Frank!' Leo hisses in my ear as he scrambles off my back.

My arms are like jelly, but I manage to straighten them. I'm spitting out dirt and God knows what.

There's a scream. More shots. Running feet . . .

I peek over the side of the grave and see two silhouettes scrambling out over the cemetery wall. As I climb out, an armed jack vaults after them. A distant shot. The crunch of glass under my feet. I crouch and fumble gingerly around. I'm holding Siménas's broken sunglasses up to the faint glow of the cloud-shrouded moon when I spot a more immediate problem.

Everyone who's got it in for me is here tonight. The new arrival is the Greek god from the ASB – the one who's afraid of mice. The good news is that he doesn't seem to have his knife. And the bad news, of course, is that he's pointing a pistol at me.

The fat priest waddles up. He's knock-kneed, with huge thighs that sort of roll round each other. He makes the sign of the cross. 'Get thee hence, Satan! For it is written, thou shalt worship the Lord thy God, and him only shalt thou serve.'

OK, that didn't hurt but I figure the next bit will. I can see the Greek god's finger tightening on the trigger. I feel I should close my eyes for this, but I can't. I'm thinking, wow, this is it!

When I was at Saint Cyprian's, they promised us heaven and threatened us with hell. Light and happiness. Fire and pain. You're a kid, right? You buy this stuff. And you kind of put it away inside you so it's always there, even if you never really think about it till it's too late.

The Greek god is in no great hurry. Which way? Maybe no way.

This is such a waste of time. Run for it, Frank. You never know your luck. But all I can do is stare back at this maniac who's dead sure about hell and is about to send me off there . . .

When Martin steps out from behind the yew tree and crowns him with the back of a shovel. The priest turns and lumbers off at an astonishing speed.

No point in us hanging about, either. Leo passes up the body. We roll it over the wall and toss it on to the cart. No sign of Siménas. We throw a tarpaulin over Groce and make a dash for my place.

CHAPTER TWENTY-THREE
Too Clever By Half

Running along the narrow street behind the termite nest, there's this wall, about twelve feet high. And if you look carefully, in the right place, you'll see a couple of iron pegs hammered into the mortar between the stones to make footholds.

Getting Groce over the wall and into the corridor outside my studio is the easy bit. My door turns its nose up at the smell and it takes me ten minutes to talk it into opening. We park Groce in the space I've cleared on the bench. I give Leo and Martin half their money. They clamber out over the wall and rattle off into the dawn with the promise to come back tonight and get rid of him for me.

It's freezing in my studio; but with the state Groce is in, fires don't seem like a great idea. I knock back a couple of glasses of my personal energy brew; then crush rosemary and thyme leaves, roll them in a couple of tiny squares of muslin and poke them up my nostrils. I bring in all my lamps, and set about examining Groce's wrists.

Right, first of all, the slashes on both wrists run across the veins. Not a very effective way of killing yourself: if you really want to make a good job of it, the trick – useful tip, this – is to cut *down* the forearm, following the veins. But since most people don't know that, it proves nothing.

Second point: there is a single deep, clean cut all the way across the left wrist. But the right wrist is a total mess: almost a dozen short, shallow slashes, only a couple of which actually hit the veins. Think about it. You pick up the knife in one hand and slash your other wrist. The handle's all slippery with blood now and you've probably severed a few tendons, so you're not going to do a good job when you change hands . . .

And finally, when I bring one of the lamps close in, I find a couple of hesitation cuts on the left wrist. You get them with most knife suicides, wrist or throat: sort of nervous dry runs while the punter's trying to work up the courage to go for the big slash.

After an hour I throw a sheet over the body and sit down to sulk. No question about it: Groce killed himself.

So basically it's seven o'clock in the morning and I'm stuck here all day with Stinky James, until Leo and Martin come back to take him off my hands. If they come back at all.

I realise that half the trick of being a sorcerer is not

to think about what you're doing. Angels and demons. Marvo hit the nail on the head: suppose it's all true . . .

I don't want to think about that right now. Change the subject.

Am I in love with Kazia, or do I just fancy her something rotten? What's the difference? When I see her, my heart skips a beat. When I think about her, it's like someone's punched a hole clean through me. Maybe that's love and I just can't get my head around it, like it's too grand for an idiot like me. I don't do serious stuff. It only gets me into trouble.

I pull the sheet away from Groce's face.

What was he playing at? He was a priest, so he shouldn't have been playing around in the first place. But maybe he loved Alice, whatever that means.

I close my eyes and paint pictures in my head . . .

It's late – nearly midnight. Groce wakes up and sees Alice creeping out. I imagine him following her, down to the towpath behind the palace and through the gate into the garden . . .

Was it the power of love that knocked the security elemental out? That's not a serious question, by the way.

He follows her somewhere; I still don't know where, but it has to be around the palace because Wallace is waiting for her. And there's a pain in Groce's heart, so fierce that he can only fix it by sticking a knife through Wallace's heart.

I stare into Groce's dead face. 'Why didn't you kill Alice right there and then? Why'd you wait?' He just lies there with his eyes closed. He doesn't care any more. Sadly, I do.

Maybe he did try to kill her and she ran for it. So why didn't he go after her? Who helped him carry the body into the library?

'And why all the stuff with the head?' I say aloud.

Groce seems to have this faint smile on his lips now. He knows but he isn't telling.

OK, let's say he really loved Alice. He finds her with another man and does all this crazy stuff because he loves her. She hides, but he finds her and kills her because he loves her. Thinks he loves her, anyway.

Could I ever feel strongly enough about anybody to do something like that?

When I was a kid, things used to catch fire around me. Stuff in the house. The nursery where my mum used to leave me. After the pub where Dad used to hang out burned down, the penny dropped and they called in the Society. Then the Christmas after I started at Saint Cyprian's, I came home for the holiday and this time it wasn't the plum pudding that went up in flames. It was Dad.

So I guess there's all sorts of things you can do to people when you love them.

James Groce. Killed the best part of himself. Then finished the job by opening his wrists.

Frank Sampson. Too clever by half.

I stuff more herbs up my nose, purify a tiny pair of tweezers and lean over Groce's face. I pinch the lashes of his left eye and pull the lid back . . .

The outside door creaks. I blow out the lamps. Footsteps in the corridor.

'Frank?' Marvo, of course. 'You there?'

She knocks on the door. There's just enough light seeping through the window for me to see the wood realign itself, ready to attack.

'Frank!' She bangs on the door. I hear it snarl; and her footsteps as she jumps back.

'Frank, I know you're in there!'

Good for you.

'Frank, I'm gonna hit the door again. You can let it bite me if you want . . .'

I don't realise quite how angry I am; but the door does, and by the time I get it open the damage has been done and she's cringing against the wall opposite, clutching her arm.

What's the hell's happened to her? Her hair has turned white.

I drag her inside. There's blood all over the place and she's in shock, trembling so badly that she can barely stand up.

I haul her up to the fireplace and drop her into a chair. I relight a couple of lamps. The cuts don't need cleaning – the thing that bit her doesn't, strictly speaking, exist. But she's losing quite a lot of blood and I can't send her home like this. Quickly I throw the sheet back over Groce, before ducking back to help Marvo off with her duffel coat. I dig out the aloe, comfrey and exorcised water and sprinkle them on to a scrap of silk, then wrap it round her wrist.

'Am I hurting you?'

'What's the smell?'

'I farted.' Her eyes are already darting around the place. I have to get her out of here before she notices Groce. 'Sorry.'

'You look like hell.' She's staring up at me. Her voice softens. 'Do they look after you here?'

'They're not here to look after me. They're here to keep a lid on me. They feed me. They pray they're not in the way when the devil comes for me. You can't say fairer than that.'

I make a pass over her arm and mutter a few words. I unwrap the silk. She stares down at the unbroken skin for a moment then says, 'How did the hearing go?'

'Water off a duck's back.'

'Seriously!'

'It was OK. I've got to go on pilgrimage to Rome, that's all.'

'When?'

'No hurry. Any time today is fine.'

She looks up at me for a bit, then she says, 'Travel broadens the mind.'

'Actually, it hurts the feet. I'm supposed to walk. So what are you here for, anyway?'

'I wanted to explain.'

'Why you grassed me up, or why you put in for a transfer? There's nothing to explain.' I pull her to her feet. 'Goodbye.'

'Frank, wait – you gotta understand. I can't deal with this right now.'

'You managed to deal with a bottle of peroxide.' She had me going, but now I see she's bleached her hair, like Caxton and the rest of the CID. 'I thought you were on my side.'

'Frank, I *am* on your side.' She's gone red in the face.

'Doesn't look like it.'

'You don't make it easy.'

'The door's behind you.'

I let go of her arm, but she doesn't move. She looks like she's going to cry. She mumbles, 'What I said before – you know, about who told Caxton about Cimerez . . . Well, it wasn't all true. One of the dieners spotted something. Caxton had me in. Frank, she wasn't letting go of it . . .'

OK, so I know what it's like – I mean, you're just a kid and you've got Caxton shouting across her desk at you. But that's why you've got to stick together.

302

Marvo's doing her helpless look: big eyes, arms out. 'What was I s'posed to say?'

'You could've lied.'

'I'm crap at lying. I can't handle all this.' She's making this wide gesture round the studio, but she stops dead and stares. 'What's that?'

And before I can grab her again, she's ducked past me and dragged the sheet off Groce.

'Are you mad?' Her face has gone whiter than her hair. 'Trying to get yourself killed?'

'Yeah, but look at this.' I grab the tweezers and pull Groce's eyelid back. 'See there? That mark?'

It's a tiny black dot, no bigger than the head of a pin, on the inside of the eyelid.

'It's a mark of submission,' I say.

She lights a candle and brings it close. Finally she mutters, 'Never heard of it.'

'Well of course you haven't. I've never seen it before – they didn't teach it at Saint Cyprian's – but I read about it in this old grimoire I found.'

'What's a grimoire?'

'A book of magic. We don't make this crap up as we go along, you know. We get it out of books written by dead guys who made it up as *they* went along—'

'What I see is a ruptured blood vessel.'

'Well it's not. It's an attribute, like my licence. The way it works, the sorcerer sends a demon to talk to the victim and convince him of . . . you know, the utter futility of everything—'

'You need a demon to tell you that?'

'The mark, it's a secret token of submission to a state of diabolical despair that can't be healed by divine grace.' That's what it said in the grimoire, anyway. 'Basically, the demon talks the victim into a state of total depression. Then he tells him what to do. How to end it.'

'Got a magnifying glass?'

I hand it to her. She leans back, takes a deep breath and leans in to peer at the dot. Finally she steps back and exhales.

'So Groce murdered Alice then killed himself. But we *knew* that. Caxton closed the case.'

'She's a fool.'

'We knew that too.' She sighs. 'C'mon Frank, you've got something you don't like, so you just make up this story—'

'It's not a story. Someone *made* Groce do it. Same person who spooked the security elemental by the gate. Same person who stuck Wallace's head in the reliquary then messed up the contiguity with the body . . .'

'Can you do that?'

'According to Einstein, no: contiguity can't be destroyed by magical means. But I don't see how any of this could've happened without sorcery.'

Marvo hands me back the magnifying glass.

'Caxton knows it don't make any sense. But she's been told to wrap it up and she's pretty sure Groce *did* kill Wallace, and that's good enough. You're wasting your time.'

'But what did Cimerez mean, "This guy *has* no head"?'

I'll have to get that carved on my tombstone. Not that I'll get one, the way I'm carrying on. Just a small box of ashes on Ignacio Gresh's bedside table.

'Maybe he was taking the mickey,' Marvo suggests. 'Demons do that, right?'

'But I'm supposed to know when they're taking the mickey.'

'It's always about you, Frank, isn't it?'

'Just get out of here, OK?'

She throws the sheet at me. 'C'mon, you know who's behind all this.'

'Do I?'

'Christ, Frank, for a bright kid you're incredibly slow sometimes. The girl! I told you, she's not right.'

It takes me a moment to catch on. 'And I told you, girls don't get the Gift.'

'Sez who?'

'Sez all the books.'

'And you believe them?' She grabs her coat, thank God, and I'm just about to tell the door to open—

When she chucks the coat down again and says, 'So prove it.'

305

'Prove what?'

'That it's not her. You're right: there's gotta be sorcery. So prove it's not her. That John Dee crap up there' – she's pointing at the code on the blackboard – 'you said it was to raise the dead.' She walks over to the body. 'So raise Groce. Ask him what happened.'

'You gotta be kidding!'

She's standing beside the bench, pinching her nose between two fingers, staring down at Groce. 'Frank, I saw you call up a demon. I got no idea what's goin' on any more. You told me "nekker" was short for necromancer and that means bringing people back from the dead to predict the future, right? So obviously you *can* do it.'

This is suddenly moving far too fast for me. I'm feeling a bit light-headed. 'We did it at Saint Cyprian's . . .'

'So there you are.'

'Yeah, but actually we didn't. What they told us, people like Simon Magus and John Dee *claimed* to have done it, but they were lying. And if we tried it the Society would show us what it'd be like, being dead.'

'I won't tell anyone.'

'It's not up to you!' I yell. 'It's me who's gotta do it and it's not just whether the Society'll catch up with me, it's—'

Groce is just lying there. Marvo's candle has gone out, so his face is in shadow. He looks . . . less pissed off about being dead.

I drop the sheet over him. 'It's whether it's right.'

'Didn't stop you digging him up.'

'That was different.'

'But you're still saying it was a sorcerer twisted his arm.'

I nod. I feel like I'm in hell myself. Not our hell, all fire and brimstone and demons poking pitchforks up you. I mean the Greek version, Tartarus, where that bloke Sisyphus is condemned to push a boulder up a hill for all eternity, and each time he gets to the top it rolls back and squashes him and he has to start over . . .

'An' I'm telling you, Frank.' Marvo jabs her finger into my chest at every word: 'It was the girl.'

Which is where I lose it, big time. I scoop up her coat and chuck it at her. The door bangs open and as I push her past it the wolf's head jumps out from the wood, snapping and snarling at her.

She crashes into the corridor wall. But she hasn't finished with me yet.

'An' you said you'd find out who killed Sean. You promised.'

'I did no such thing.'

'Yes, you did. You're a shit, Frank. You tell people you'll do things an' then you don't.'

'I never promised anything. Anyway, what am I supposed to do?'

'Contiguity.'

'What with?' Why am I even talking about this?

'You need stuff to do contiguity. With Wallace, we had the head and body. You want me to dig Sean up and hack some bits off him? Coz I can do that if you like!'

'Don't be disgusting.'

'Then what?'

'You're useless!'

'That's right. I'm useless. That's what my dad said.' He was happily pocketing my money at the time. 'Look, will you just get out of here?'

'Not unless you promise to help me.'

'I can't help you.'

'You could try.' Her fingers are digging into my arm. 'Can you bring Sean back?'

And I find myself screaming, 'Well, let's bloody find out!' I drag her back into the studio and throw her into a chair. There's this dead scared look on her face, but I'm not interested in what she thinks any more because I'm over at the bench, pulling the sheet off Groce's body.

'OK,' I say. 'See if you still want Sean back when I'm done.'

CHAPTER TWENTY-FOUR
Necromancy

Right, this is weird. I mean, obviously it isn't going to work and I sure as hell hope it doesn't. But I've been playing around with Dee's incantation for months without really thinking about where I was going with it . . .

And here I am. I've got no idea what I'm trying to achieve. Do I really think I can bring Groce back from the other side, or wherever, and get some sense out of him? Or am I just trying to throw a scare into Marvo and get her off my back?

It's another of those occasions – I get them a lot, have you noticed? – where I'm hard at work and screaming at myself: what are you playing at, Frank?

Anyway, I start by laying it on heavy with the herbs and spices. As the pall of smoke thickens, I trace a series of circles on the tiles, and draw Dee's symbols round them. I stand there staring down at the result.

'What are you waiting for?' says Marvo.

'Do those look OK to you?'

'How should I know?'

I drag it out for another hour, kind of hoping she'll give up and go away. I can see it's doing her head in, and that's half the point. Finally I can't find anything else to fiddle with. I don't really want this to work, but I'm giving it my best stab.

'OK, let's move him in.'

Fifteen minutes later, Groce is lying naked on the floor at the centre of the circle, looking bored. Marvo has stopped throwing up and is standing in a small circle to his left, with a cloth over her nose and mouth, feeding herbs into a brazier.

I have decided not to tell her that mixed in with the herbs and spices are some bits of cat and the ground-up fragments of the tooth I took from Saint Oswald's skull. Useful things, relics.

I seal the outer circle with my knife then step into another small circle on Groce's right-hand side. I check that I can still see the blackboard through the thickening pall of smoke. I pull my wand out of my belt.

'Adonai, Tetragrammaton, Jehovah, Tetragrammaton . . .'

I run through the usual names to establish control of the magic space. The smoke has retreated to form a thick cloud billowing along the ceiling like a gathering storm. I take a deep breath and recite Dee's incantation from the blackboard.

As I reach the end, Groce's eyes open. He sits up.

'Oh dear God!' That's Marvo.

I'm standing there with my mouth open thinking, bloody hell, I've just brought somebody back from the dead, am I a clever boy OR WHAT?

Losing it – are you kidding? I mean, when's the last time *this* happened?

And suddenly I feel very, very sick indeed.

Imagine a clock where you've stripped all the cogs off the wheels. Groce has been dead for five days and all sorts of yucky stuff has been happening. He's sitting there like a rag doll that's been propped up. His legs sticking out like two white matchsticks. His hands flopped, palms up, on the floor beside his thighs. His head lolling on his shoulder. The hole in his chest where I pulled out the stake.

I've really overstepped the mark this time.

This long, fat centipede crawls out of his mouth. Herbs fly everywhere as Marvo screams and throws her hands over her face. If the object of the exercise was just to scare the shit out of her, I've succeeded beyond my wildest dreams. But since Groce is here, I suppose I'd better do something with him. Assuming it *is* him . . .

'James Groce.'

He can't control his head. It falls forward on to his chest and his eyes roll up until they vanish into the shadows beneath his brows.

'In the name of the Father most mighty—'

311

I need to cover my back, because I've no idea what I've got here. But whatever I'm doing, it's working: the floor around Groce is alive with insects and maggots – rats leaving the sinking ship. Each side of the body, they crawl towards me and Marvo . . .

She's just standing there gasping, her hands over her face.

'Don't move!' I hiss.

Unnecessary. She's too freaked to do anything. My skin is crawling. I shuffle back, to the far side of my circle.

The creepy-crawlies have reached the chalked perimeter of my circle. It's supposed to protect me, but do they know that? I'm shaking all over and about to turn and run for it when they swing round like troops on a parade ground and file round the outside. They reassemble as they pass me and wriggle out until they reach the outer circle.

They stop dead, then all turn to face inwards, towards Groce. A shimmering black circle.

Despite the cloth mask, Marvo has stuck one finger in her mouth and she's biting down hard on the knuckle.

'James Groce.' It's time to roll out the Usual Suspects. 'I command thee by order of the great God, Adonai, Tetragrammaton, Jehovah . . .'

It's like someone's blowing air into a balloon. Groce's neck straightens. His head lifts. His eyes fix glassily on me.

'Who are you?' His lips move mechanically, forming each syllable a split second before the words emerge from somewhere in the distance, beyond the studio walls. And I realise what he reminds me of: a puppet, moved by invisible strings.

So who's doing the pulling?

'My name is Frank Sampson. I'm the forensic sorcerer investigating your death and I want to know—'

His face crumples. 'What have you done to me?' He has managed to raise one hand. As he stares at the palm, a raised lump forms and cracks open. A small grey maggot falls to the floor and starts wriggling away across the tiles. It's too slow, though. The hand falls back, squashing it.

I can see blood staining the cloth around Marvo's mouth and running down the back of her hand. She whispers, 'Stop it, Frank. Stop it.'

But I can't. I've got this far. The stench is over-whelming. Groce's skin is grey, breaking out in raw fissures.

'You killed yourself. Do you remember?'

There's a long silence. It's like he's staring through me at something. It's so spooky that I turn to look over my shoulder, but there's just my studio with shelves of books and equipment and the picture of the pope with a disapproving expression on his mug.

I jump as Groce cuts loose.

Look, I've heard people swear. Usually at me. But what's pouring out of Groce is this obscene torrent of filth and hatred. This is one very angry dead bloke indeed. There's one name, constantly repeated:

Wallace.

And if I'm getting it straight, what he's screaming is that Wallace killed him.

I finally manage to get a word in. 'But it was you that killed Wallace.'

There's this obvious problem with Groce. When he stops screaming abuse and stares at me and his mouth falls open, I don't really know if he's just surprised or if he's reverting to being what he actually is.

Dead.

So I say, 'Do you understand what I'm saying?'

He's staring at Marvo. 'You're not Alice.'

She shakes her head.

Tears roll down his cheeks. 'He killed her.'

'No, you did. And Wallace—'

'—killed me.' He points to the hole in his chest. 'Knife.'

I don't see any point in putting him straight about the stake. This is getting silly.

'I saw a dog,' he says.

That's better.

'Windows.'

'Yes?'

He stares left and right, then raises his head,

314

like he's gazing up at something. 'Angels,' he says.

I realise that this is a dream. It's a comforting thought, since it means that all I have to do is wake up and none of it will have happened.

'Stairs,' says Groce. 'Down.' His hands drag across the floor, palms open, away from his thighs. He seems to be tracing a circle . . .

'That's enough, Frank,' says Marvo. And she's right. I raise my wand and take a deep breath.

'Adonai, Eloim, Ariel, Jehovah! I charge thee to return whence thou camest—'

Groce convulses, like whoever is holding his strings has given them an almighty wrench. He spins round and collapses.

For several seconds, nothing moves. I croak my way through the incantation. I can't hear Marvo. Groce is just lying there in a crumpled, broken heap.

There's a faint rustling that grows to a sound like the wind through corn. The insects are moving across the tiles, crawling and wriggling towards the centre of the circle. Through the mouth and ears, through the cuts and fissures, they disappear into Groce's body.

When everything's stopped moving, I turn to Marvo. 'Happy now?'

'What's wrong with you, Frank?'

I've fixed the bite marks in Marvo's finger, and we're sitting on the steps outside my studio. There's a cold

315

wind, but since I messed about with him, Groce is really living up to his name and the stench indoors is intolerable.

'I mean, that was barbaric.'

'You made me do it.'

'OK, so I pushed you, but I never thought—'

'That's enough!'

I've no idea what I raised in there. All I know is, I was in way over my head. And all I want is for Leo and Martin to come and take the body away so I can pretend none of this ever happened.

Across the vegetable garden, Brother Andrew is digging away dutifully in the midday sunshine. Overhead, a puttering Montgolfier drags a plume of steam behind it. I'm just wondering why I'm not on it, when Marvo says:

'What he said, about Wallace killing him . . . I mean, it's not like people can't come back from the dead. At least you've proved that.'

'Groce killed Wallace.'

'I didn't hear him confess.'

'What you heard in there, that wasn't Groce.' At least I hope it wasn't.

'So what was it?'

'I don't know. It was traumatised to hell and back – I don't think it even knew it was dead.'

'It knew about Wallace. All sorts of stuff.'

'There was something driving it. Hatred, revenge,

whatever. But that could have nothing to do with the murder.'

'It knew about the library, too.'

'Huh?'

'It said, "Angels". Don't you remember? Looked up, like at the library ceiling . . . ?'

Angels. Stairs down . . .

'You know your trouble,' I say quickly. 'You're too clever for your own good.'

'I'm telling you, it was the girl.'

'Don't be stupid.'

'Don't be blind!'

'Look, girls can't do sorcery. How many times have I got to tell you that. They never get the Gift—'

'Says who?'

'Says the Society. Say all the books . . .'

'An' you believe them? Frank, you're a pain in the neck but you got one thing going for you.'

'Just one?'

'Shut up and listen for once!' She waves her finger in my face. 'One thing: you don't swallow the crap people feed you. So why d'you swallow that?'

I've certainly got this unpleasant taste in my mouth.

'What d'you know about her? What's she doing at the palace?'

I'm still wondering if I should explain what I've found out about Kazia and her parents and how Matthew rescued her, when Marvo yells:

'Jesus Christ, Frank, wake up!'

'Huh?'

'I don't like her, yeah? But I don't want to see her dead and if you don't stop messing about and do something that's how she's gonna wind up.'

A bit after midnight I'm rubbing out the code on the blackboard when my door growls and I'm relieved to find Leo and Martin standing nervously in the corridor. They both stink of booze, so I guess they've drunk away the money I gave them.

Their arrival is the only good news in a very long day. I've still no idea what I raised. Was it really Groce; or was it some sort of diabolical joke?

I've spent eight hours alone with him, cleaning up the mess he left and trying not to think about it, and I'm just relieved to see the back of him. I pay Leo and Martin off, help them roll the corpse over the wall, and watch the cart disappear round the corner.

Maybe the end justifies the means. But the last thing Marvo said to me, as she watched me sew the sheet closed around Groce, was, 'Aren't there a few parts you want yourself?'

CHAPTER TWENTY-FIVE
Invisibility

Most books on sorcery have a chapter on how to make yourself invisible. According to the *Grand Grimoire*, you need a black cat, a mirror and a pot filled with water collected from a fountain at the stroke – ah, but which stroke? – of midnight. You put the cat in the pot, then boil it for twenty-four hours, take it out and throw it over your left shoulder with the words, 'Take what I give you, and no more'. Now comes the fun bit. You dismantle the cat and, looking in the mirror, stick the bones, one at a time, behind the teeth on the left side of your mouth until you see your reflection vanish. You say, 'Father, into your hands I commend my spirit', and keep the bone that did the trick for future use. The grimoire doesn't say what to do with the rest of the cat. Or whether it should be alive or dead when it goes into the pot.

Alternatively, you can draw symbols on a piece of paper with octopus ink, say a few invocations, make a couple of passes over it, and pin it to the front of your coat. It took this clever kid called Zebediah Wharton the best part of seven years to figure it out. His work only came to light posthumously when the Society found his notes in his lab. They never did find his body.

So how does it work? You know when you're walking up the road and you're so busy worrying about something that you pass people you know and you don't even notice them . . . Well, it's like that, only someone's made it happen. It's a form of misdirection, the technique that conjurers and pickpockets use to distract their victims.

An invisibility spell 'forbids' anyone to see the invisible object. The viewer fills in the gap either by patching in other parts of the visual field or by contriving to think about something else at the critical moment. Either way, it's exhausting for them – which of course helps the spell work.

The unsettling thing about actually being 'invisible' is that you can still see yourself. Fortunately, self-confidence is not a requirement.

'Angels.' That's what James Groce said. He looked upwards and said, 'Angels.'

It's just after half past two in the morning. I'm still not on my way to Rome. Instead, I'm at the main palace entrance, trying to sneak past the knock-kneed old porter and his crutch. A stone crunches under my foot. He stumbles round and stares suspiciously. I freeze. There's enough light to see his eyes glaze over as the spell kicks in. I stoop and manage to pick up a couple of pebbles without making any noise. I toss them against the wall behind him. He spins round and trips over the crutch, and by the time he's back on his feet and has pulled his tights up, I've scuttled off up the drive to the palace.

There's a small oil lamp burning in the entrance hall. When I peer up the stairs I can see another light flickering dimly on the second floor. Not a sound, apart from my own breathing.

There's all sorts of clever spells for generating light, but they take time and a certain amount of gear. However, two years ago a small electric torch was found at a crime scene. It subsequently disappeared from the jack shack and turned up unexpectedly in my studio. Getting batteries for it is a nightmare – they cost a fortune – so I use it as little as possible.

It takes me down the corridor and into the library, where I shine it up at Groce's angels – the cherubs prancing across the ceiling. When I turn the torch off, there's enough moonlight filtering through the curtains to see by. I lock the door and turn the contents of my satchel out on to the desk.

Item: one small compass.

Item: one copper disc on a copper chain. The disc is about four inches in diameter, engraved with the first pentacle of the moon. Not a thing of beauty, but it has the power to make the invisible visible. I put it round my neck.

Item: one copper wand, nineteen and a half inches long.

Item: one sachet of copper filings.

I feel sick, which is actually encouraging. I sit down in the chair behind the desk, where the body was found. I close my eyes. I listen. I smell. I feel. My chest rises and falls. My heart beats. I open my eyes.

Nothing.

I'm not psychic. I can't read minds or pick things up and tell you who they belong to. I don't even get insights, like Marvo; just wild guesses – usually wrong. I stare up again at the cherubs on the ceiling. They stare down at me, like they know a fool when they see one.

I get up from the chair, lift the rug and find nothing more sinister than floorboards. I walk the perimeter of the room. This is a waste of time. I'm too tired to think. My head hurts. My legs are shaking. A healer would say I was coming down with the grippe, but I recognise the symptoms of psychic resistance. I know there's something here. It knows I know and the spell that protects it is doing everything in its power to knock me over.

It's a battle of wills. My powers against those of sorcerer or sorcerers unknown.

The compass finds magnetic north for me. I close

my eyes and spread my arms and shuffle round – I practised this over and over at Saint Cyprian's – to face true north. Wallace stares disdainfully down at me from the portrait above the mantelpiece. The hell with him; he's dead anyway and he probably asked for it.

I bow. I manage not to spill any copper filings as I sprinkle them into the palm of my hand. I mutter the incantation and blow them across the room.

I turn round to face south. Bow. Mutter. Blow.
West.
East.

I stumble across to the fireplace and an infinite weariness descends upon me. I have to lean against the mantelpiece and beg my legs not to give way on me. My mind has gone blank. What am I doing here? It's a couple of seconds before I can remember what I'm supposed to say—

'Nitrae, Radou, Sunandam.'

I pull myself upright and put the tip of the wand against the wall, immediately below the portrait, and start tracing a wavering line along the wall, anti-clockwise – widdershins, if you want to be a smart aleck. I scrape along the backs of a shelf of books and turn the first corner.

One of the French windows bangs open. The curtains billow in the draught and wrap themselves around me. I try to twist my way out of them and succeed only in tangling myself even more tightly.

I panic. The drapery feels alive. It has forced my left arm down to my side and is grasping and pulling, trying to wrestle the wand out of my fingers. It has pulled the pentacle tight and wound the chain round my throat. It covers my nose, and is forcing itself into my mouth and tightening round my chest, squeezing the breath out of me.

My instinct is to fight it, but I know there's nothing to fight. I stop struggling. I make no effort to breathe. I let go and fall back into the drapery's hold. It clutches me, like a mother rocking a child. The world is dark and warm . . .

The floorboards are cold against my cheek. The curtains hang motionless.

'Looking for something?' Wallace is grinning down at me from the wall.

'Yeah, your murderer.' I realise I'm hallucinating, but I can't stop myself. 'Are you going to help me?'

'Help you do what? Make a fool of yourself? You don't need my help for that. Skinny little freak!'

'Arsehole!'

Sorry, I keep saying that. I roll away from the curtains and struggle to my feet. Where was I? Oh yes:

'Nitrae, Radou, Sunandam.'

More bookshelves. Another corner. The wall behind the desk. My legs are like rubber. The wand shakes uncontrollably in my hand.

I stop to catch my breath. The rows of books are

writing before my eyes, stretching and contracting like giant accordions. I can feel Wallace staring down at my back like a father watching a toddler mess about in a playpen.

I struggle on, supporting myself with my free hand, as far as the door. I'm close to throwing up. There's a noise like a steamhammer in my ears. I close my eyes to stop the room spinning. I can't breathe . . .

It takes an enormous effort of will to carry on. I realise that I'm wrong. I should be out looking for the girl I love. Instead I've made a complete fool of myself and narked everybody off. Marvo's bound to spill the beans about Groce and then I'm sunk.

One of the necessary attributes of a good sorcerer is that you keep going when any normal, responsible person would stop. The downside is that ninety-nine times out of a hundred you make a complete arse of yourself.

Like I have now. Big time.

Only I haven't. My spell bites, and I realise that although I looked all round the library the morning after Wallace was killed, there is one spot that I never actually managed to see. It's the corner to the right of the fireplace, left of the door. And I've found what I was looking for: a second door, invisible until this moment. It's narrow and comes to a pointed arch at the top, and it's covered with magical symbols. Some of them look centuries old – carved and scratched into the surface. Some are recent, drawn in what looks like blood. The tip of my wand scrapes a shower of dust from the dry, grey wood.

'Hey!' it growls. 'Do you mind?'

I can breathe now. The room has stopped spinning and I've wiped that smug grin off Wallace's face. The copper disc has done its work: I take it off and stick it in my pocket. I turn the ring handle slowly and silently, and feel the latch lift on the other side of the door. There's a flight of stone steps leading down through the darkness towards a hint of light.

I listen. Nothing.

I take my boots off and carry them as I creep silently down the steps. The tingle of magic through my socks gets steadily stronger until I find myself standing in an arched colonnade that runs all the way round a candlelit circular space at least twenty yards across. The outer wall has shelves, cupboards and several doors, all closed.

I put my boots down on the bottom step. The cellar floor is made of black tiles and although it's been washed I can still make out the remains of five concentric circles, the outermost about seven yards across; and of various letters and symbols scattered around them. At the centre is a triangle containing a circle large enough for one person to stand in.

Just beyond the outer circles – to the east, I guess –

a dozen or so scattered strips of what looks like goatskin. Before they were kicked loose, I figure they were pinned together to form a triangle. I can see a couple of the fastenings: bent iron nails traditionally taken from the coffin of a dead child.

There are a few unorthodox touches, but what we're looking at here are the remains of a Grand Honorian Circle. It's not something I use myself. It's mainly associated with a ritual described in the *Roman Grimoire* and used to summon up Lucifuge Rofocale, but it will stretch to any demon. It's simple and powerful, but hard to control, so the Society deprecates it. A lot of unlicensed sorcerers like it for its rapid response time: the quicker you get an illegal summoning over, the better!

Four silver candlesticks have been pushed to one side. Three still hold red candles, as thick as my wrist and burning steadily. Shattered fragments of the fourth have been swept into a pile with chalk dust, herbs, lumps of charcoal, several gold coins and more nails from the goatskin triangle.

I peer up into the dome, where gold stars twinkle in the candlelight. My God, I'd kill for a place like this! They should open it up to the public: a perfect example of a medieval sorcerer's lair.

I find a mop sticking out of a bucket of dirty brown water; an overturned brazier; a linen coat and paper crown thrown over a chair. I crouch beside a bundle on the floor and open the silk wrapping to reveal several knives and a ceremonial sword. One of the knives still has dark smears along the blade. I examine the sword: the blade is short – probably less than two feet – but razor sharp. Some attempt has been made to wipe it clean, but I can see the traces of written characters, and more dark brown smears.

Moving around in my socks, trying to avoid spatters of dried blood, I step on something sharp. I stoop and pick up a big, ugly, square ring. Gold, with a whopping great amethyst. I slip Henry Wallace's episcopal ring into my pocket.

Let me conjure you up a dirty old man who fancies one of the housemaids; only she doesn't fancy him. But he's got a card up his sleeve: a young secretary who can do a bit of illegal magic and summons up a demon to go and compel her to come to him.

The trouble with unlicensed sorcerers is, they don't get the training or the practice. So mistakes get made. The spell is supposed to put the maid's boyfriend into a deep sleep. But it doesn't. He follows her and the demon . . .

That's what Amber Trickle said she saw. Not a dog, a *demon* leading Alice Constant through the gate from the riverbank, past an elemental who just falls over, and into the palace where James Groce catches up with them and finds . . .

Well, all this stuff I can see lying around the place. And a naked bishop.

People start forgetting that they're grown-ups. Groce grabs a knife. Wallace's chest looks like a good place to park it. Alice, I assume, snaps out of the spell and runs for it, leaving Groce and Akinbiyi standing over a dead bishop. I bet it was Akinbiyi who had the bright idea of covering up the use of black magic and preserving his employer's reputation by making it look like a political assassination. They cut off Wallace's head and stick it in the reliquary. Totally barmy, but it works. It looks like the nutty wing of the Anti-Sorcery Brotherhood have dreamed up this grotesque gesture . . .

Until I come along and find no affinity between the head and body. OK, Ferdia comes along behind me and does find contiguity; but like I said he's post-peak and not very clever, so he's just getting the result he expected.

The guy who hits the nail right on the head is Cimerez. 'Fact is, Frank, this guy has no head.'

I get the joke now.

Conjuring a demon is a risky business. If you don't dismiss it properly and put it back where you got it from, it's like it's got this hook into your soul and it can just reel you in. Might take years, but it'll land you eventually. So you've got to cut the line . . .

This ceremonial sword I'm clutching, it's been consecrated. I've got a dozen just like it: I use them at the end of a ritual to sever the affinity with any Presence I've summoned – like I did with Cimerez. And I figure that if I hacked off a human head with it . . . well, despite Einstein's second law, the natural affinity between the head and body would be destroyed. They would be magically traumatised into forgetting each other. No contiguity. A body with no head.

I'm feeling good. Like I'm on top of this. Like it all makes sense.

Like my Gift is still holding.

Except I'm juggling my torch, my wand, several knives and a sword . . . and something's got to give. The sword rattles on the tiles. And as the echoes die away I hear something move.

I do magic, OK? Not tough guy stuff. I leave the sword lying where it fell, and duck behind one of the columns. A door creaks open. I peer round the back of the column and wait for Akinbiyi to step out.

It's all so obvious, once you've worked it out. I'm remembering the first day: how he came running after me and Marvo on our way down to the riverside gate; the look on his face when Charlie suggested sorcery. He's around the palace, doing stuff for Wallace all the time. OK, Kazia said he was twenty-one or something, so it's a bit of a stretch, but he's not too old to do a bit of informal sorcery for his boss . . .

But of course I'm wrong. It isn't Akinbiyi, is it? He's no more a sorcerer than Caxton is. The only person I'm fooling is myself – and I'm not making a very good job of that.

A silhouette appears. My heart stops dead as Kazia stumbles out into the chamber.

CHAPTER TWENTY-SIX
Visibility

S he looks like she's been to hell and back. Hollow cheeks, red-rimmed eyes. Her hair is greasy, standing up in peaks where she's slept on it. She's barefoot; shaking hands fumbling with the buttons of a frayed cardigan, which looks kind of vulnerable and cute over a crumpled blouse. She starts to yawn—

Then freezes with her mouth wide open, staring at the fallen sword.

She stoops to pick it up, glancing round nervously. As she catches sight of my boots at the bottom of the stairs, I step out behind her and say, 'What the hell are you doing down here?'

Nice work, Frank. She jumps a clear three feet in the air and lashes out with the sword. I jump back to avoid being decapitated like Wallace, fall over a candlestick and go flying. My head hits the floor . . .

And my headache's back. Also, my neck is hurting, just below the Adam's apple where the tip of the sword is pricking my skin. When I try to crawl away, it bites deeper. I feel a trickle of blood running down my throat.

'But it can't be you,' I stammer. 'You're a girl!'

She steps away. I put my fingers to my throat. Yep, I'm bleeding.

She's waiting to see what I do, knees slightly bent, the sword held in both hands, like a startlingly attractive Roman gladiator.

I'm not doing anything. I'm still fighting to get my head round this, because it's all wrong. We did it in first year: girls never receive the Gift.

Is there anyone I can believe?

'How long have you been down here?'

She has to think for a moment. 'Nearly four days.'

'Hiding from your father? I bumped into him.'

She lowers the sword. 'Did he hurt you?'

'I'm OK. You?'

She's as pale as death, with lines etched into her face like the design engraved in the silver pentacle hanging round her neck. As she moves, it dances on a thin chain, glinting in the candlelight.

Marvo was right all along. Damn her and her insights.

Let me conjure you up another picture – like the first one, but different in one very important respect. We're in this cellar, ten days ago. The Grand Honorian Circle is complete, with four red candles burning at the north, south, east and west. It isn't Akinbiyi, though; it's Kazia standing at the centre, facing east towards the goatskin triangle. She's wearing the usual paper crown, linen coat and slippers. She's got her wand in her hand, the knives tucked into her belt and the sword balanced across her toes.

She's not alone. In the flickering candlelight she can see Henry Wallace sitting beneath the colonnade, inside another circle. He is wearing his blue silk dressing gown, and tapping his fingers impatiently on the arms of his chair. Behind him, a door leads through to a small chamber with a freshly made bed.

Her voice rises and falls. The candles flicker and almost go out. She holds out the tip of her wand to the coals glowing in the brazier—

'I invoke and conjure thee, by Baralamensis, Baldachiensis, Paumachie, Apoloresedes and the most potent princes Genio and Liachide; I exorcise and command thee—'

It goes on for a long time. The downside of being an unlicensed sorcerer is that without formal training you can't get a fix on which bits are padding and can be safely skipped. I can cut out pages of this stuff and get through it in less than half the time it takes her.

Still, she gets there eventually.

'Do thou forthwith appear and show thyself unto me in a fair and human shape, without any deformity or horror. Come presently, come visibly, manifest that which I desire—'

And he does. In the goatskin triangle, but as a black dog who apparently understands English.

'Go to the house of James Groce, rector of the parish of Saint Ebbe's, and cast a deep sleep upon him. Then bring to this place Alice Constant . . .'

The dog turns and pads off up the stairs and out of sight. Wallace sighs and stretches in his chair. One hand slips inside his dressing gown. Kazia stands immobile in the circle. The candles flutter in the draught filtering down the stairs.

An hour passes.

Wallace has dozed off. Kazia is the first to sense a change, a thickening of the atmosphere in the chamber. There is the sound of claws scratching on stone. Wallace's eyes flicker open. He gets to his feet, securing the knot of his dressing gown. He smoothes back his hair as if there's some sort of consent involved here.

The dog is back. It stops and looks at Kazia, mouth open like it's grinning, its long forked tongue darting out of its mouth. It brays like a donkey.

And Alice Constant steps down from the staircase into the chamber. Her eyes are fixed. Her mouth hangs slightly open. Her hands are at her neck, holding her nightdress closed. She doesn't react when Wallace pulls them away. She's like a mechanical doll.

335

The dog pads back into the triangle. As Kazia shuffles round to face it, the sword still balanced across her toes, Wallace's dressing gown falls to the floor.

Does he think he looks sexy?

Rushing feet on the steps. James Groce flies into the room. He stops dead, staring at Alice and Wallace. He darts into the circle and grabs one of the knives from Kazia's belt.

Wallace is holding Alice by the shoulders and swings her round to shield himself. The candlelight glints along the blade. Wallace squeals and dodges, trying to keep Alice between him and trouble.

With his free hand, Groce pulls her out of the way. Wallace yelps as the blade slashes across his palm and suddenly the knife is in his chest. Groce stumbles back. Wallace is just standing there, staring down at the handle protruding from his ribcage. He tries to grasp it, but his hand won't obey him.

He looks at Kazia, but she's busy re-establishing the integrity of the circle. He manages one step towards her, then drops to his knees and crashes down on his side.

Kazia has a lot of balls in the air. A dead bishop. An angry rector. A housemaid in a trance. And an increasingly restless demon who needs getting rid of. She raises her wand—

Of course, once you look at it from the right angle, it

all makes sense. The cropped hair, everything. I've got a lot to kick myself for.

I don't think Kazia had anything to do with chopping off Wallace's head: she looked too surprised when she pulled the sheet off his body that first morning. Must've been Akinbiyi's bright idea to stick it in the reliquary and make it look like the ASB dunnit. Kazia's sword was the first weapon to hand. It never even occurred to Akinbiyi or Groce that a sorcerer's sword is consecrated . . .

Chop, chop! Wallace's head rolls away. And me and Ferdia have got a puzzle on our hands.

Kazia is just standing there now, watching me put my boots on. I remember looking into those big, beautiful eyes and getting a sense of a film across them, hiding whatever was going on behind them.

Now it's like staring at blue shutters. She's closed down tight.

I haven't the heart for this. She's played me for a sucker all the way. She didn't have to wave a wand or throw herbs around, she just stood there and smiled and watched me bewitch myself. A dark veil that made me blind to what was really going on.

Some people say, if you can just recognise that you're under a spell, you can step out of it. Not true. I'm sitting here spellbound on the bottom step, like a mouse staring into the eyes of a snake, unable to shake myself free.

Her eyes clear. She reaches for my hand. I pull it away, but she makes a jump and grabs it.

She's cold. And just as I'm thinking I can warm her, she says:

'Will you help me?'

OK, I wasn't expecting that. But now that I think about it, this is a girl in a lot of trouble. All her old man's interested in is business: if he can get her back to Lithuania he can make a fortune milking her Gift while it lasts. If she goes to the police, they won't even bother to try her as an accessory to murder. They'll just hand her over for the Society to dismantle her and barbecue the pieces.

'That story you told me in the kinema,' she says. 'About the unlicensed sorcerer you tried to help . . .'

I didn't tell her how that ended. How he wound up on a bonfire, screaming at me because he thought I'd ratted on him. My fault? No. But I've always felt like it was and I'll do whatever it takes to keep Kazia from winding up the same way. Plus maybe she'd be grateful to a boy who helped her get out of this hole. She's still got hold of my hand. I let her pull me to my feet.

'I need to get this straight,' I say. 'You did stuff like this all the time. Summoned up demons to make women come to Wallace—'

'He told me if I didn't, I was an unlicensed sorcerer . . .'

'Didn't you talk to Matthew?'

338

'I was ashamed.'

She starts to sob. I know what I ought to do. I ought to put my arms round her, but I'm not quite sure what I'd do after that. Probably the wrong thing.

'So you do the magic and Alice rolls up. Only Groce is right behind her and he kills Wallace. You dismiss the demon, right?'

She nods reluctantly.

'I figure Akinbiyi gets hold of your sword and cuts off Wallace's head. And that severs the contiguity—'

There's a sound behind me: footsteps on the stairs.

I'm expecting – who? Or what? Akinbiyi? Caxton? A demon? James Groce, bouncing back for a rematch?

It's just this little kid in a brown school uniform with a canvas satchel slung over his shoulder. He looks about nine and if you passed him in the street you wouldn't even give him a second glance. I'm thinking, who is this guy that she trusts enough to let him know where she's hiding? And I realise that of course he's not a real kid; she's built herself an elemental and he's already pulling a loaf of bread and a flask of water out of his satchel.

'What about me?' I ask. 'Why the hell didn't you talk to me?'

'I tried to tell you—'

'When?'

'But then I saw my father and I was scared.'

I've been trying to stay calm and not spook her, but I can feel myself starting to lose it. 'So you just hide out in here like a ferret down a hole and think – what? That some knight in shining armour is going to figure out where you are and ride in and rescue you? How stupid can you get?'

'I told you, I was ashamed.'

'Didn't you trust me?'

'Why should I? You work for the police.'

I laugh. 'Not any more. Everything's messed up. I exhumed Groce—'

And suddenly I realise how Marvo feels when one of her insights comes whizzing in out of nowhere, because the thought hits me like a train: it had to be Kazia who sent the demon to talk James Groce into killing himself and Alice!

'Frank, why?' She's staring intently into my face. Her hand is on my arm. I've got this feeling that she knows everything that's going through my head.

'I don't know, I thought – Christ, I don't know what I thought! But I brought him back to life.'

After a few seconds she asks, 'Did he tell you anything?'

'Enough. I'm here, aren't I?'

'I had to do it – don't you see? If the police found him and he told them what happened that night . . . It wasn't my fault, but you know what they'd do to me. And he did kill Henry.'

'But what about Alice?'

'That wasn't supposed to happen.'

I could say, 'Oh yeah?' But I don't. Apart from anything else, I realise that if I hadn't spooked Alice by doing that stupid trick with the mouse, maybe she wouldn't have run off and maybe she wouldn't have found herself in the way of Groce's knife.

Kazia is watching me carefully. 'So what are you going to do?' I can't help noticing that her grip has tightened again on the hilt of the sword. One swipe and I'm luncheon meat.

Everything is screaming at me: run for it, Frank!

But I can't.

You don't choose to be Gifted. It seems like fun at first, when you're setting things alight and bringing your mates out in spots. But then you notice that people are scared of you. They resent the fact that you can do these tricks and they can't. They're afraid you'll turn them into something slithery.

The only people you can really talk to are other sorcerers – and they all turn sniffy on you when you do stuff they can't. And every sorcerer I ever met is scared of talking about the one thing that's on your mind day and night: how long does this last . . . and then what?

There's that physical Hole in the middle of Doughnut City. And there's the mental hole where every sorcerer lives, cut off from the rest of the world. What do you think my studio's about?

In Kazia's shoes, would I have done any different? I

don't care what she's done. I'm not leaving her skulking down here like a cornered rat.

'I'll get you out of here.'

'She raises the sword. 'I'm not going with my father!'

'Did I say that? I don't know yet, but I'll think of something.'

It's not like anybody's looking for me right now. Caxton doesn't give a damn, and Matthew and the Society think I'm back at the termite nest, packing for the hike to Rome. But Kazia's old man's on her tail and it's just a matter of time before the jacks start looking for her.

'I'll get you out of Oxford, anyway.'

The train's no good: the Society keeps an eye on the station. But I figure I can organise a trip on a barge down to London, no questions asked.

'What about you?'

Me? I realise with a shock that I'm a hair's breadth from getting what I want. That can't be right . . .

'I'm coming with you, if you'll put down the sword.'

I've got no reason to stay in Oxford. My fan base is shrinking. It's only a matter of time before the Society cops on about Groce's resurrection and starts gathering wood for a fire, so the more distance the better.

I check my magic watch. 'I gotta do some stuff.'

'Will you scry me?'

'It's not safe. I'll come back tonight. Late, when it's quiet.'

The sword rattles on the tiles. Her hand brushes my cheek. Her lips are soft.

I'm not saying this isn't stupid or dangerous. But it could be fun.

CHAPTER TWENTY-SEVEN
Vade retro Satana!

Lots to do. I go over my studio again, making sure every trace of the procedure to reanimate Groce is gone. Finally I stop to catch my breath. I take Kazia's silver disc from around my neck: the last thing she gave me after several increasingly interesting kisses.

It's weird, kissing. I don't know what else to say about it. I mean, you eat and swallow through your mouth for all your life and suddenly there's this new game. I'm not saying I don't like it. Actually, I like it a lot. But it's weird, that's all.

Anyway, I recognise the design engraved into Kazia's talisman as one of the pentacles of Jupiter, which offers, among other things, protection against all earthly dangers.

But I'm thinking: there's still something not right about all this – like I haven't got the full story.

From the moment I first saw her, I've had this fantasy that maybe Kazia fancies me as much as I fancy her. OK, I'm delusional. I realise that the obvious reason she hung around with me was because I was useful: she could find stuff out from me that nobody else would tell her and I was too starry-eyed to see what she was playing at.

So if all the cards are on the table now, why's she still willing to run off with me? I know she's got her dad on her tail, but there's something else and I think I understand what it is . . .

I got seven years at Saint Cyprian's. A library full of grimoires. Herbs, spices and animal parts, all there for the asking. Masters and fellow-students just itching to jump in and show me what I was doing wrong.

Kazia grew up waiting for a knock on the door. She saw her mother fried. She got dragged off to a strange country by some bloke she didn't even know. Then she spent a dozen years doing creepy stuff for a dirty old man.

Sure, there's still something not right . . . but she needs a friend. I'm a sorcerer and I'm in trouble. That's common ground.

Anyway, I need all the protection I can get. I hang Kazia's pentacle back round my neck and try to scry Matthew. I'm not sure what I'm going to tell him – and I don't have to come up with anything. The duty officer at the Society isn't pleased to hear from me; he tells me that Matthew is out and nobody knows where to find him.

Somewhere along the line, I can't fight sleep off any

more. I dream that I'm standing at an open window and there's this bird, not so much fluttering as hovering. And not so much a bird as a fish: just the head, covered with pure white fur instead of feathers. It's floating there, watchful but not afraid, just a couple of inches from my hand . . .

I wake up and tidy some more. I try Matthew again, but he's still out.

It's dark outside and I can't wait for him. I grab all my money and a lump of gold. I pick up my case – then put it down again. I spend ten minutes staring at it, feeling guilty about Matthew. But it's too conspicuous for where I'm going. I pull out a few things I might need – sachets of spices, a flask of exorcised water, a couple of wands, two knives – wrap them in silk and stuff them into a backpack. I leave my scryer; it's not like I want to talk to anybody.

I throw a change of underwear and a toothbrush in on top. I say goodbye to my door and climb out over the wall.

I dug up Marvo's address ages ago, but it takes me a while to find the place, off a narrow street round the back of Littlemore. There's a rotting wooden gate, hanging by one hinge, and a narrow path, knee-deep in wet grass and overhung with dripping branches.

I stumble up to the house and stoop under a mass of ivy enveloping the entire front of the house. No lamps on inside. It takes several minutes knocking before that changes. The door opens.

Marvo's mum is older than I'd expected. She's wearing Marvo's red duffel coat over a nightdress and slippers. Grey hair all over the place. Glasses on a string round her neck. Oil lamp in one hand. Kitchen knife in the other.

When I tell her who I am she nods, as if that explains everything. 'Magdalena is still at work.'

'I'll wait for her.'

'If you want.'

And the old bat slams the door on me.

Ten minutes later I'm still sitting on the doorstep, wondering how long I can afford to hang around before I go to pick Kazia up, when the door opens again. Marvo's mum still has the oil lamp, but she's replaced the kitchen knife with a Saint Benedict amulet.

'All right.' I get an Irish accent. 'In there.'

I step into the front room and she closes the door on me, leaving me in darkness. I stuff my hat in my pocket and drop my backpack on the floor. More time passes. It feels colder inside the house than it did outside. I find a box of matches and light a lamp.

I look round at an old sofa and armchairs with the covers worn through. A battered piano with the ivory missing from a couple of the keys. The usual picture of the pope looking relieved that he doesn't have to live in a dump like this. A table with a dish of sweets, a spare pair of thick spectacles and a magnifying glass.

I peer at a photograph on top of the piano. A plump kid, maybe eight or nine, grinning back at me like he's pleased because he thinks I'm going to do what his big sister wants and find out who killed him. I run my fingertip down the black silk ribbon pasted over one corner of the image.

This is all rather sad and I'm just beginning to think I should get going, when hooves rattle on the road outside. I peer out through the ivy hanging over the window and see Marvo stepping down from a jack van. I hear the front door open. Her mum's voice:

'It's the freak.'

Whispering. The door to the room opens.

'What do you want?' says Marvo.

'I came to say goodbye.'

So I've nearly finished my story and Marvo is sitting there staring at me. She points at the pentacle round my neck. 'Did she give you that?'

Before I have to answer, the door opens and her mother says, 'Are you still here?'

'It's all right, Mum.'

The old bat doesn't take the hint. She just stands there rubbing the amulet between her thumb and index finger, muttering under her breath.

Marvo whispers to me, 'You said you couldn't have female sorcerers.'

'Well I was wrong.'

'I warned you . . .'

'You should've warned me louder.'

She turns to her mother. 'Did you read that story in the paper the other week? This guy in Brighton loses all his money at the races. He heads down to the harbour, jumps in this flashy yacht he's got, sails out a hundred yards, loads up a shotgun and puts a couple of holes through the hull.'

I'm wondering what this has to do with me. Marvo ploughs on:

'People on the beach, they hear the bang. Look up, see him sinking. Someone goes out in another boat and the mad bloke jumps out on deck, waving the shotgun and threatening to shoot them if they come any closer.'

I'm not really interested in this. 'Why couldn't he just blow his brains out in the first place and save everybody a lot of trouble?'

'Wrong question. The real question is, how d'you rescue someone who doesn't want to be rescued?' She folds her arms across her chest and massages her own shoulders. 'Are you cold?'

'Frozen. I gotta get going.'

'Sooner the better,' says the shadow in the doorway.

'Mum, will you get out?' Marvo turns back to me. 'Where will you go?'

'London first – easiest place to disappear.' I don't like to say what I've got in mind: it doesn't sound so hot, spoken out loud. 'I thought maybe we could get to Lithuania . . .'

'Frank, that's a stupid idea. Have you even got a passport?'

'There's ways.' I waggle my fingers. 'How bad can it be?'

'There's something she's not telling you.'

'I'm sure there is.' I pull out my hat and put it on. 'Maybe I should try Matthew again—'

'No, Frank.'

'Why not?'

'I dunno.'

So I'm waiting for her to explain, but she doesn't. 'What's going on?' I ask. 'Marvo?'

She has to think for a moment. 'It's like you're putting him in this impossible position.'

'I don't get it.'

'So don't worry about it.' She shrugs. 'Have you told me everything?'

'Sure.'

'Coz I'm on your side, whatever happens.'

'Why?'

There's a long silence, just her mother muttering to herself in Latin: '*Vade retro Satana! Nunquam suade mihi vana. Sunt mala quae libas. Ipse venena bibas.*'

Begone Satan! Never tempt me with your vanities.

What you offer me is evil. Drink the poison yourself.

I say, 'Reg Garston said—'

'Yeah?' And when I still don't say anything, 'Said what?'

I mumble, 'Something about you fancying me.'

'Well, he's a fool!'

'I suppose. Anyway, you can't – I mean, it'd be stupid!'

Yeah, I know – not the smartest thing to say. It sort of slipped out. Her mouth has fallen open and she's just staring at me like she's suddenly realised her mum's been right about me all along.

'I didn't mean that.'

But it's too late. She's on her feet and I'm trying to find some way to explain.

'I said I'd help her.'

'Then you'd better get on with it. Goodbye, Frank.'

She pushes her mother out into the hall ahead of her. I hear footsteps going up the stairs.

I stand there, looking round the room. What is it about people? Why do they always get hold of the wrong end of the stick? Sean is smiling back at me from his picture, like he's congratulating me on being so clever. Well, there's no point hanging around here now. I pick up my backpack, blow out the lamp and step into the hall.

'I never used the word "freak",' says a trembling voice.

I can just see her in the dim light seeping in through the glass of the front door, a dark shape huddled at the bottom of the stairs. She's got her arms wrapped around her knees and when she looks up at me I can see tears glistening on her cheeks.

'I'm sorry,' I say.

A floorboard creaks upstairs.

'Will you go, Frank? Please . . .'

That would certainly be the best thing to do. But I find myself standing over her, with no idea what to do next. Just the way she looks up at me, it makes me feel really bad. I turn away and shuffle off along the hall.

'Why's it so cold?'

I'm about to open the front door and I realise that I'm shivering. When I run my fingernail down the glass, it scrapes away a thin layer of frost.

Oh hell.

CHAPTER TWENTY-EIGHT

The Exterminating Angel

'Get your mum down here. Now!'

I dash towards the back of the house. The kitchen is huge, thank God. There's an open fire, and a Welsh dresser stacked with ugly, unmatched crockery. I grab dishes and cutlery from the rickety table in the middle of the floor; the crash of breaking china echoes through the house as I dump them in the sink. I turn the table over and start breaking off the legs and tossing them into the grate.

By the time Marvo drags her mum in, I've cleared the centre of the room and rolled back the mat, and I'm pulling stuff out of my backpack. Before the old bat can organise her outraged look, I scream, 'I need string, a hammer and a nail.'

'Now look here—'

'Don't argue, Mum.' Marvo turns to me. 'How long?'

'Fifteen minutes, max. And all the salt you've got. Do you grow any herbs?'

'Thyme, rosemary—'

'Garlic too. And money.'

'What?'

'All the cash you've got in the house. And anything made of silk.'

I'll give them this: they're fast. A couple of minutes later I've banged a nail into the floor at the centre of the room and tied the string to it. I take the packet of salt . . .

'God of gods and Lord of lords, bless and sanctify this salt.'

Using the string as a measure, I lay a trail of salt in a surprisingly regular double circle, about six feet across.

While Marvo argues with her mum, I step back and examine the battlefield.

The circles are complete, apart from a gap of a few inches. I've calculated the points of the compass and got four small candles burning. Marvo has found me a basin of milk and a bottle of brandy; I've got my own flask of exorcised water.

The frost is thick on the window. Flames flicker from a pan of burning twigs. I'm on my knees chalking symbols between the two circles. Mother and daughter are standing side by side, staring down at me.

'Rings!'

I wrench mine off. Marvo tosses hers across to me. I chuck them both into the sink.

'Have you got a copy of the *Dictionnaire infernal*?'

They look at each other. 'Sean had a copy,' says Mrs Marvell reluctantly. 'Do you want it?'

'No, just curious.'

After a second she catches on. When she opens the hall door, an icy blast of wind sends it slamming back against the wall. The candles flicker and almost go out. As they revive, I point towards the small pile of herbs at Marvo's feet.

'The thyme. I need a few sprigs tied together like a brush.'

I'm pulling more stuff out of my backpack. I knot a red silk scarf round my waist and pin a piece of paper to my shirt.

Something is hot against my chest: Kazia's pentacle. I've known it was her since the moment I scraped frost off the inside of the front door, but I've managed to be too panic-stricken to think about it.

Now the proof is dangling from its chain, glowing blue.

'I told you,' says Marvo, so quietly I can barely hear her. She doesn't look triumphant or anything. Just scared.

Despair is a tempting option, but I decide to stick with panic-stricken. 'Let's get on with it.'

It's too late to throw the pentacle away now: it's done its dirty work. Whatever Kazia has sent for me knows where to look. I stick the silver disc in my back

355

pocket and let it toast my bum. I turn to a bundle of clothes that Marvo brought down, and hold up a pair of stockings. 'Are these pure silk?'

She nods and I pull them on, ripping them, over my boots.

'Sorry.'

'Will this do?' Mrs Marvell reappears with a battered paperback book.

'In the circle.'

She looks at me and deliberately drops it on a chair. 'Suppose you tell me what's going on.'

'There's a demon coming for me.'

She grabs her daughter's hand and drags her towards the back door.

'Too late,' I say. The temperature is still dropping and ice is forming on the surface of the milk and water. I've no time for an argument. 'If you try to leave now it will destroy you.'

'Don't talk nonsense—'

She screams as a snake falls writhing and hissing from the ceiling and vanishes through the floor. I dodge another falling snake and push the pair of them into the circle. I pull a wand and two knives from my back-pack and hop in after her and Marvo. I look around. The charcoal is glowing. I've got the herbs and liquids, my lump of gold and the money. Marvo's mother is clutching a handbag; maybe she realises I can't protect her and she's going somewhere . . .

The book, the book! I leap out of the circle. My feet slip out from under me and I go flying – the entire floor has iced over. I throw myself at the chair, grab the *Dictionnaire* and toss it to Marvo. I pull a blanket off the floor and dive back into the circle.

I've enough salt left in the packet to close the gaps in the circles. I scuttle round, leaving a smear of garlic. I grab my black-handled knife and pour a few drops of exorcised water out along the blade.

I bang through the incantation and race round with the knife, sealing the circle. As I throw the blanket at Marvo's mother, she's flicking goggle-eyed through the illustrations in the *Dictionnaire infernal*: a gigantic fly; a donkey with a peacock's tail, standing up on its back legs; a creature with the heads of a man, a sheep, and a bull, legs like a rooster's, and a serpent's tail, riding a lion with dragon's wings and neck; a man with an owl's head and wings, riding on the back of a wolf . . .

I dip the thyme brush in the milk and sprinkle it towards each of the candles. I close my eyes . . .

What we've got here is, of course, a desperate lash-up. Everything's wrong: the hour, the place, the materials, the smells. I'd have felt better if I'd had the time and the gear to jump through all the hoops, but I'm just going to have to rely upon force of will to hold it all together.

And it feels . . . well, better than I'd have expected.

I open my eyes. Marvo is staring doubtfully at me. I look round . . .

'I had a pen . . .'

I can see it lying on the floor on the other side of the room, like it's trying to tempt me out. But it's too late now. The flickering candles cast no light and the only illumination comes from the sickly phosphorescence emitted by the thick frost covering every surface in the room.

I'm shivering uncontrollably. The old bat opens the blanket and tries to spread it over Marvo's shoulders.

'I need something to write with!'

The dimensions of the room have changed: it's as if the walls have shifted off into the distance. The snakes are falling thick and fast now, writhing and exploding in tiny bursts of flame as they hit the floor. A flock of black birds wheels to and fro, the wind from their wings fanning my face. A fire is burning in the grate and a baby lies there, writhing and screaming, its skin blistering in the flames.

'Eyebrow pencil?' Marvo pulls it out of the handbag.

'Why don't you do something?' her mum screeches.

'I *am* doing something.'

I'm drawing a symbol on a paper hat and jamming it on my head. I'm pulling a white silk blouse out of the pile of clothes and scrawling more symbols across the front . . .

'Hey, that cost a fortune!'

I'm throwing milk everywhere and sprinkling brandy into the brazier while I struggle into the blouse and mutter incantations. I toss a handful of herbs onto the charcoal and the smoke rises in a column to the ceiling, billows out horizontally, then flows downwards to form a translucent cylindrical wall within the space between the two circles.

I'm waiting for the Presence. Until I know what we're up against . . .

A small, indistinct shadow is forming, inside the room, yet infinitely far beyond its walls.

'Sit tight. Don't move. Whatever happens, stay in the circle.'

'Anything else?' says Marvo.

'Anything I tell you to do, do it – however stupid it sounds.'

'That one's easy, eh, Mum?' She nudges her mother in the ribs. A nervous smile flickers across her face. 'Is this going to work?'

Luckily I don't have time to answer that question: the shadow has grown and taken shape.

We have two eyes, golden and bright like a bird's. Sharp yellow teeth, fixed in a predatory grin. Goat's horns – well, that's traditional, I suppose. I'd expected wings, but I guess they'd only get in the way when the simple objective is to rip, impale, disembowel and dismember. I don't know about dragging us off to hell, but he's certainly here to mess us up and smear us over the walls. He has the tools for the job. He's clutching a three-bladed, serrated dagger in one hand, and an axe in the other. In case that isn't enough, he's got a scourge in his belt, with a dozen weighted chains ending in metal hooks.

He's a good seven feet tall and under-equipped in the clothing department. He halts just outside the circle, staring contemptuously down at us through the wall of smoke. He takes a swipe with the axe. There's a noise like a ship hitting a dockside and the entire house shakes. The blow leaves a deep red gouge in mid-air. Blood drips on to the floor.

Marvo's mum has pulled the blanket over her head, leaving just one hand sticking out, clutching her amulet. I'm searching frantically through the book. It's a cheap, incomplete edition – only half the size of the copy back in my studio. I hope this bastard is in here because I need to know who he is.

He walks slowly round the circle.

Got him! Alastor – the executioner. The exterminating angel.

This is what you get for trying to help somebody.

He stops dead. He transfers the axe to the same hand as the dagger and runs his free hand over the wall of smoke. One taloned finger moves to and fro, like he's trying to work it into an invisible flaw in the barrier. He pulls the scourge from his belt and raises it over his head. The hooks sweep down with a ghastly ripping sound, leaving trails of blood in mid air. Lumps of flesh sizzle on the frozen floor.

Now that I know who he is, I've an idea what might hold him. But I need to buy time until I can get the smells and symbols working. I grab a coin from the pile and toss it out to him. He opens his mouth and swallows it. I shake Marvo's shoulder.

'Chuck him one, any time he looks like he could get through.'

She makes a grab, scattering the coins. One rolls out of the circle and she's about to go after it. I pull back her arm a split second before Alastor's dagger stabs deep into the floor.

I need blood, and I haven't got any small creatures to butcher. I pick up my white-handled knife.

'Oh King Eternal! Deign to look upon thy most unworthy servant and upon this my sacrifice—'

Marvo gasps as I slice into my forearm. I let the blood run down into a small bowl, then use one finger to scrawl inside the circumference of the inner circle. Old friends – 'Adonai', 'Tetragrammaton' and 'Jehovah' – just visible on the floorboards.

While I'm checking that I've spelled everything right, Marvo wraps a silk scarf round my arm and ties the ends.

'Don't want you bleeding to death on us.'

Alastor is hacking away with his axe. At every blow

361

the air inside the circle compresses violently. It's like being bounced around in a giant drum. Marvo is shaking so much she can hardly grasp them, but she keeps tossing out coins. The demon stops dead with a curious smile on his face every time he swallows one. Then after a few seconds he goes back to work.

By some miracle I've managed to keep the brazier going. I sprinkle in more brandy and let a thin stream of herbs drop on to the steaming charcoal.

'Alpha, Omega, Elohim, Zabahot . . .

The protective wall of smoke thickens. Alastor stops to examine it thoughtfully, head on one side. Then he gives it everything he's got, axe in one hand, scourge in the other, pounding away—

'More money!' I yell.

'There's none left!'

'Burn the notes.'

She's staring at me. I grab a ten-pound note and drop it into the brazier. It explodes like a firework. Alastor reels back with a stupid grin on his face.

While she feeds money into the flames I crawl round the circumference of the circle with the bowl of blood, madly scrawling symbols inside the inner line. I'm gabbling the incantations.

'I will open the book, and the seven seals thereof. I have beheld Satan as a bolt falling from heaven. It is thou that hast given me the power to crush dragons, scorpions and all thine enemies . . .'

At every blow, blood and tissue fly. Strictly speaking they may not be real, but it's beginning to look pretty messy out there. He's not getting through, but he's got nothing better to do than keep hacking away with an axe that never gets blunt. Marvo's mum is staring out from under her blanket, white in the face and trembling like a leaf.

'Do something!' she yells.

'Like what? Appeal to his better nature?'

She chucks her amulet at him. He opens his mouth and swallows it.

'There must be something!' Marvo's faith in me is touching.

'I can't fight a demon—'

Two sounds in quick succession: a deafening thunderclap, then an almost inaudible metallic rattle. The stench of sulphur fills the room. A couple of feet behind Alastor, Mrs M's amulet glints on the floor.

'They're immortal beings,' I explain. 'By definition.'

'So what are you going to do?' Marvo asks.

'Give me a break, will you?'

'I'm scared!'

'You think I'm not?'

For some reason that seems to calm her down. 'What do you need to do?'

'Demons don't just roll up on your doorstep like Jehovah's Witnesses. Someone sends them, and the spell has to be sustained, so somewhere there's another magic circle with a sorcerer inside.'

'Told you – the girl!'

Marvo's mother is feeding the last few banknotes into the brazier. I dig Kazia's pentacle out of my pocket and turn it to the light so I can read the symbols etched into the silver. I look up: Alastor is gazing longingly at the pentacle with his golden eyes. He holds out one hand, palm up . . .

'Where did I put that eyebrow pencil?'

'Here!' Marvo watches me scrawl symbols across the pentacle. 'What's that for?'

'I've got to leave you here. Is that all right?'

'No.'

'He'll follow me. You'll be fine.' I think they will, anyway.

I realise what Marvo's afraid of: that I'm going to leave them to be sliced and diced while I save my own skin.

As I turn in the circle, Alastor follows me. He's actually weeping tears of blood as he gazes at the pentacle. The chains of his scourge drag across the floor, leaving trails through the frost; every now and then a hook catches the edge of one of the floorboards and pulls a thick splinter away.

'We're coming with you!'

'You can't come with me. Damn!' I can barely control my hands and I've messed up one of the symbols. I rub at it with my fingertip and succeed only in smearing it. 'How does this stuff come off?'

'Use your shirt.'

Why not? It can't make things any worse. I spit and scrub away furiously until the smear has vanished. I redraw the symbol and move on to the next.

'What's that supposed to do, anyway?'

'It's supposed to keep him from tearing me limb from limb.' I turn the pentacle to the light and point. 'That's the moon, right? It reflects light and if light is reflected it doesn't illuminate what's beyond. Diana – the huntress – she's the goddess of the moon—'

'That's gibberish!'

'Magical gibberish, though.'

'Why can't you take us?' Mrs Marvell whispers as the final banknote flares up and disappears into a twist of ash.

'Because you'd be in the way. You'll be safe in the circle.'

I take Marvo's hand. It's ice cold and I'm surprised how small it is. I can feel her trembling.

'It's me he's after. He's probably in pain.'

'He just looks incredibly pissed off to me.'

'That too. Kazia woke him up and forced this deal on him: if he rips my heart and lungs out and tears me into pieces no bigger than a postage stamp, she'll let him go back to bed. But if he can't nail me, he'll go back to her at dawn and she has to give him some of her own blood – like, to buy him off. Then she has to dismiss him and sever the affinity.'

'What affinity?'

'She called him up. As far as he's concerned, that's a relationship. A lot can go wrong, dismissing a demon. If she makes a mistake, she's his breakfast.'

'That's good.'

I hang the pentacle round my neck. 'I'm going to see if I can get her taken off the menu.'

I'm a lot more scared than I'm letting on. It's like stepping into a dragon's lair armed only with a note from my doctor. One of the sorcerer's most powerful weapons is his belief in his methods and materials. I struggle to work up any confidence in any of this.

Marvo's hand is on my arm. 'Frank, she doesn't want your help.'

'Doesn't mean I don't have to try. Unlicensed sorcerers . . . they don't get the training and they'll go calling up demons all over the place when there's better ways to do it.'

They're all staring at me: mother, daughter and demon.

'She's been invoking Presences all over the shop and unless you really know what you're doing, that does your head in. The malice gets inside you, makes you paranoid . . .'

Yeah, I have to try. I hold up the knife.

'I'm going to leave you this, to seal the circle behind me.'

Marvo looks at it doubtfully.

'You just run it all the way round and keep repeating, "In the name of the most high". Can you remember that?'

'In the name of the most high.'

'You'll have to be quick, but don't gabble. Ready?'

Of course they aren't. And when I turn round Alastor is barely a yard away, looking down at me expectantly. Maybe this isn't such a great idea.

Back to Mrs M. 'I need you to think about Sean.' Marvo frowns, but I glare at her. 'Did you really love him?'

'How can you ask that?'

'Do you miss him?'

And her eyes fill with tears. I hold Kazia's silver pentacle up to her cheek. When I take it away, the candlelight glistens in a tiny bead of moisture that trickles down the surface and spiders out along the drawn symbols, turning them to gold.

Gripping its tip between finger and thumb, I hold the pentacle up, towards Alastor. He blinks. I cut across the inner circle. He inspects his arsenal thoughtfully, sticks the axe back in his belt and swings the scourge so that the chains whistle through the air.

I cut the outer circle, then hand the knife to Marvo and step out.

What are demons exactly?

The Church says that some of the angels rebelled against God, who cast them out of heaven into the pit. That places the Society in a difficult position: if demons are rebel angels, what are we playing at, calling them in to detect contiguities and make women take their clothes off? How can sorcerers claim to be doing God's work when we're invoking creatures from hell?

The Society's official line is that we compel demons to act against their will, through the power of divine words (all that 'Adonai, Jehovah, Tetragrammaton' stuff). We keep ourselves pure and holy and – allegedly – save ourselves from damnation.

If you can swallow that, conjuring a demon becomes an exercise in religious observance. The hard-liners devote themselves to chastity, fasting and prayer. Not my style. Fact is, I don't know what demons are. I just know that certain actions have certain effects.

Well, I hope they do, and I'm betting my life on it. I raise the pentacle towards Alastor.

'Behold that which forbids rebellion to my will and doth ordain thee to return unto thy abode.'

He doth not return unto his abode, but at least he steps back. Behind me, I can hear the point of the knife scraping along the floor and Marvo's voice:

'In the name of the most high . . .'

I'm not shaking any more. I'm juddering. My hand

is sweating so much, I'm in danger of dropping the pentacle; and I don't trust myself enough to adjust my grip or change hands. I shuffle sideways towards the door. As Alastor follows I can see Marvo and her mum behind him, staring after me. I gesture at Marvo to keep chanting.

'You'll be all right,' I call as I squeeze backwards along the hall, holding the pentacle up like a very small shield. 'Just keep calm.' I fumble for the front-door handle. 'And don't leave the circle till I come back.'

The last thing I hear as I step outside is, 'An' if you don't come back?'

CHAPTER TWENTY-NINE
Fancy Dress

O ut on the main street it's ten o'clock and the pubs are just tipping out. What better cover for a teenage boy wearing a paper hat and a woman's blouse, with silk stockings over his shoes, and a seven-foot, naked demon armed to the razor-sharp teeth?

'We're going to a fancy dress party,' I announce as a cab pulls up.

There's a nasty moment when I get in and I'm afraid Alastor may decide to snack off the driver. I've still got Wallace's episcopal ring in my pocket. I toss it to Alastor. His eyes light up, his jaws open like the gates of hell and he bites down on it with a crunch that makes my teeth ache. He falls inside after me and collapses on to the seat opposite, his eyes rolling back in their sockets. The cab moves off.

What do you say to the demon who's been conjured up to pull you apart and drag you off to hell?

'Can I ask you something?'

No reply. He's just slumped there, dribbling. In a

way it was true, what I said to the driver. Demons, they're like guests at a themed fancy-dress party. They come as pirates, knights in armour, pantomime horses, whatever . . . And always insanely over the top.

If you conjure up a Presence to find lost treasure you'll get some bloody great hound with walrus tusks, phosphorescent slaver and a Welsh accent. Or a thirty-inch jack on a tricycle. Somebody down there's definitely got a sense of humour.

But if you want somebody – me, say – rubbed out, you get a thug like Alastor. The effect of the ring is wearing off and I'm holding the pentacle up in front of me where he can't miss it. He just sits there blinking, shaking his chains . . . and farting.

Demons fart a lot.

'You don't mind . . .?' I manage to open the window.

He gives no sign of caring, either way. He's got too much drooling to do.

'So tell me, is it true? All that stuff we did in theology when I was at seminary?' I'm rattling, obviously. 'Like, was there really a rebellion in heaven and you were all kicked out?'

No comment.

'I guess it's not much fun, hell.'

What they taught us was that demons dream of returning to heaven. Some of them think they can fight their way back in; the rest think if they wait long

371

enough and don't make too much of a nuisance of themselves, God will relent and let them slip in quietly through the tradesman's entrance.

'So if there's anything else I can do to cheer you up . . .'

Peering through the window I see that we're crossing Iffley Bridge. And when I turn back Alastor's done a costume change.

Into my dad.

I don't understand how this works, but I'm standing in the kitchen back when I was a kid, watching my dad check through the envelope of money. I stretch out my hand.

'Dad, it's my money.'

'Yeah, right.' He holds a couple of notes up, just beyond my grasp. He's laughing, 'Come on, it's yours if you can reach it!'

I know this is a trap and the worst thing I can do is actually get hold of them, but I'm jumping up and down, trying to grab the notes. My dad's sneering:

'Skinny little freak!'

The cab stops with a jolt.

There's just me and the pentacle, and Alastor with his medieval arsenal.

'I don't see no party,' says the driver as I climb out backwards.

I pull out a banknote. 'Hope we haven't got the

wrong night.' I turn to Alastor. 'Have you got a couple of quid for the tip?'

Along the riverside, the new security elemental on the palace gate just shrivels up at Alastor's approach. The palace is silent. In the library, the door leading down to the cellar is visible – to me, at least, since I know it's there now – and open. It shivers as Alastor approaches. I don't know if surprise will get me anywhere, but I go down backwards as silently as I can, one hand against the wall, the other holding up the pentacle. Alastor follows, watching me steadily like a diner in a restaurant eying the dessert trolley.

At the bottom I risk looking round. There is light in the room, thick and dark like honey. Between two columns I can see someone sitting on the floor, head on knees. And I know this is stupid, but there's this split second where my heart leaps and I think maybe it isn't Kazia . . .

But of course it is. She's wearing a paper crown and a silk robe, both splattered with far more symbols than she actually needs. She's hugging her sword and has her wand tucked into her belt. Her other implements are arranged neatly on a small, silk-draped stool beside a bucket, covered with a cloth. She is at the exact centre of a sloppily chalked Grand Circle. Her eyes are closed but I know she isn't asleep. She's just concentrating on holding together an unresolved event.

I step out into the colonnade. Four candles, two-thirds burned down. Two braziers, from which thin wisps of smoke still spiral up to merge into the cloud that fills the dome.

There are two smaller circles to the east and west, each with a human occupant and a covered bucket.

Akinbiyi is standing at the centre of the western circle, his head bowed dejectedly. He is wearing a white linen coat closed with a black silk scarf.

I can tell that the figure in the eastern circle is a man, but can't make out who he is. He's wearing white robes, with the cowl completely concealing his face.

Behind me, Alastor farts.

Akinbiyi jumps. Kazia looks up. Her face is blank. She takes a firm grasp of her sword and climbs to her feet.

The cowled figure in the eastern circle hasn't moved. Who is it? Not Ferdia: he stands different. This guy is hunched over like he's trying to keep his face hidden.

I've entered the chamber at its northern point, and I'm standing over a chalked triangle containing a single item: a chalice filled with a dark liquid. Blood – presumably Kazia's. The demon's reward if he's still thirsty after failing to deal with me.

'How did you get out?' Akinbiyi asks.

I hold up the pentacle.

He snaps at Kazia. 'You should have foreseen this!'

'How am I supposed to know?'

'You're supposed to consider every possibility!'

The third figure straightens up and pushes back his cowl. My heart goes cold: the hand he uses is missing the little finger.

The Boss says, 'Why couldn't you just do the pilgrimage, Frank? Why couldn't you do what you were told?'

CHAPTER THIRTY
Blood

It takes me a while to work out how I feel.

Am I surprised? Not really. Now that it's there, right in front of me, it's like it was obvious, almost from the start when Matthew first started asking questions about the investigation. All I needed was for someone to turn the final light on.

Am I angry? I should be – I probably will be. But right now I can't manage it.

So what am I?

Sunk.

My heart is racing. I feel like I'm going to throw up. The arm holding up the pentacle weighs a ton. Everyone's watching me, waiting for me to give up now.

I feel more tired than I've ever felt in my life. Matthew is the one person I always thought I could count on. Without him . . . I dunno, it all falls apart. And you know the worst bit? I feel like it's me that's let him down. If I'd only listened to people and not been such an arsehole, it wouldn't all have had to end like this.

I can leave now. Get back to my studio, grab a few things, make a run for it. I mean, what's left to stay for? I'm about to take a first step backwards . . .

When Matthew says, 'What symbols did you use?' He runs his fingers down his beard, and it's like he's cast a spell on me. I can't move. All I can do is stare at him.

'May I see?' My Master's voice.

He holds out his hand. My legs move of their own accord. I step towards him.

'Come on, Frank. Don't be shy.'

I feel the lights going out in my brain, one by one. Soon it'll be dark and I can relax and go to sleep and somebody else will take care of everything . . .

His smile is warm and encouraging. All those years at Saint Cyprian's, he was the one person who kept his faith in me.

'What I told you,' he says. 'About you being the best student I ever had. I wasn't lying.'

I feel helpless. Alastor's breath is warm and comforting on the back of my neck as I hold the pentacle out to Matthew.

'My eyes aren't what they used to be . . .'

It's been lies all along; but it's this particular lie that saves me. A tiny thought – that Matthew has undergone the Society's procedure and that his eyesight must, therefore, be every bit as good as it was when he was young – worms its way into my addled brain.

The lights start to come on again. I jump aside and shove the pentacle in Alastor's face.

Matthew has tensed for a leap; but, seeing that the moment has passed, he relaxes.

'All right, Frank; you hang on to it.' He smiles again. 'I remember teaching you that, up in the old Kelley Room.'

I remember, too. For every novice sorcerer there's that terrifying first moment when you step out of the circle, clutching a pentacle, and feel the foul breath of a demon on your face. One kid in my year crapped himself. Another fainted and the Boss had to jump out and rescue him. Only about a quarter of novices make it through. Most of the others are kicked out or run out screaming. Every year or so, one is carried out in a box. What's left of him.

'Anyway, you were obviously paying attention.'

'It's just a pity I'm such an arsehole.'

'We can all change.' His optimism amazes me.

'You should've let Gresh burn me.'

He gazes at me for what seems like ages. 'But you didn't deserve it. And as I told you, I'm your Master and I'm supposed to *stop* people burning you.' He smiles sadly. 'I wonder, is it too late to come to some sort of accommodation? I'm not sure that you're at any great advantage here.'

He's got a point. This has turned into another of my marathon shifts. My world is flickering in and out, and it's not just the candles. I don't even have to drop the pentacle. It's my will that allows silver, salt water and eyebrow pencil to keep Alastor at bay. If my concentration lapses . . .

Akinbiyi pipes up, right on cue: 'Now what?'

The Boss doesn't even bother to look round. 'Well, it's rather up to Frank. How long he decides to drag it out.'

'I need to go.'

'Go? Go where?'

'To the lavatory.'

'Use the receptacle provided. I told you it would be a long night.'

Akinbiyi turns away and kneels over the bucket. The sound of trickling liquid echoes round the space.

And I get it at last. Marvo was right: I'm kidding myself. I have this Sir Galahad idea that I can rescue Kazia. Nobody else shares this fantasy, least of all her. She's standing there, still staring blankly past me. Run off to Lithuania together? Yeah, right. She wants me dead every bit as much as Matthew does.

It's a strange, cold feeling. I mean, if you asked me to name the two people who really matter most to me . . . It'd be funny if it wasn't so stupid. So humiliating.

But I haven't got time to stand around feeling sorry for myself. Gotta concentrate on staying alive. Then I can go home and poke holes in myself and see if it makes me feel better.

I look round the room. The burning candles and braziers. The chalked circles. Everybody in their party costumes. The pentacle in my hand. It occurs to me that I'm tucked up safely in bed in my studio and this is all a dream. It's a familiar feeling; but it's never been a dream so far . . .

The life and soul of the party is Alastor. He feels comfortable with being psychopathically, all-consumingly, cosmically demonic. It's what he's for – what he does best. He'll happily pull me to pieces. He'll happily pull Kazia to pieces. And Matthew and Akinbiyi better not get in his way either.

Matthew acts like he's running the show, but it's Kazia who did all the dirty work. She summoned Alastor and sent him on his mission.

Any power that gets called up must be put back down again. In the unlikely event that I survive until dawn, all his malice will be turned back, against her. She has instruments and methods to deal with that danger. The chalice contains blood. Her blood. If he can't eat me, she'll appease him with a piece of herself.

But finally, whether he's nabbed me or not, she still has to perform a further ritual to put him safely back in his box.

That sword she's clutching, it's to sever the affinity. It symbolically cuts the link between her and the power

380

she invoked, preventing Alastor from returning in the future to consume her.

It's all played out through the symbols. So if you're losing and you want to stop the game dead . . .

You smash the pieces. First, a little misdirection. I turn to Akinbiyi. 'It was you that cut Wallace's head off, right? You knew what he got up to down here. You found him dead and Groce looking guilty and you figured you could prevent a scandal – make it look like a political assassination and pin it on the ASB. You remembered the anniversary of Saint Oswald's death was coming up. You and Groce carried Wallace up to the library and put the book in his hands. Then you took the head into the cathedral and stuck it in the reliquary . . .'

'Something like that,' Akinbiyi mumbles.

'You must've resented him like hell.'

He just stares at me.

'I mean, chopping his head off – I'd call that over-doing it. Say what you like, it must've been personal . . .'

'Your point being?' says Matthew.

'Just satisfying my curiosity. Anyway, while you're there, you grab a candlestick and use it to smash the library window, so it'll look like a break-in.'

I'm shuffling backwards round the outside of the circle, pretending to examine the symbols. Alastor is shadowing me, dragging his chains along the floor. I'd be lying if I said I was getting used to him.

Anyway, back to Akinbiyi.

'After the jacks have gone, you go to Matthew – Kazia lives in the palace coz the Society's a religious order so she can't stay at Saint Cyprian's. She does stunts for Wallace, but really she's working for Matthew, right?'

Nobody says I'm wrong.

'Anyway, you go to him and you say proudly, look what I done! And he freaks . . .'

'Like you,' says Matthew, 'I thought it was all . . . somewhat over-theatrical.' He shrugs. 'You make the best of a bad job.'

'And it all seemed to go so well. Until the head turns up and I start meddling—'

'That's one thing I taught you: to be thorough.'

Actually that pisses me off. The thoroughness, that's just me – one of the many admirable personality traits that have made me so popular around Doughnut City. It's got nothing to do with Matthew.

'And I get this bizarre result: no contiguity between Wallace's head and body.'

Matthew nods. 'It took me a while to work out what had happened.'

I realise that he genuinely believes he's in control of the situation here. That shakes me: I thought everybody could see that I was. Am I missing something?

Matthew smiles indulgently. 'What are you playing at, Frank? There's nobody coming to the rescue.'

'Who says?'

'You say.' He points at Kazia. 'If you call the police in, I'll make sure she goes to the stake.'

Kazia goes stiff. Her eyes and mouth open wide. She looks like she's been pushed off a cliff and she's scared to look down in case she sees how close she is to getting squashed.

Matthew's got this ugly smirk smeared across his face. 'She did kill Groce, you know.'

'Not directly.' Who are you kidding, Frank?

'She summoned the demon who talked him into murdering Alice, then writing the note and killing himself. It comes to the same thing.'

'But acting on your orders.'

'I'd take my chances.' He smiles. 'I know a lot of important people's weak points.'

I'm aware that Kazia is standing there staring at me. It's not love – not that I'd know what that looks like anyway. I could say it was bewilderment, maybe regret . . .

I could say a lot of things. I talk too much.

But all this chatter has got me where I want to be, at the southern point of the circle. Kazia is standing almost directly between me and the chalice of blood. Alastor is a couple of yards away, trailing after me but with one beady eye on her. She looks almost as exhausted as I feel. She's been stuck in the circle, holding the spell together, for hours.

She yawns. She bends to put the sword down, across her toes, and straightens up.

She stretches. Her eyes close . . .

The Boss shouts, 'Don't let him—'

Too late! I throw myself forward. My bum rubs out a section of the inner circle as I slide across the floor. The blade of the sword slices into my palm as I snatch it. I roll frantically out the other side of the circle into the triangle, stopping just short of knocking the chalice over.

I grab it.

'Stop him!' yells Matthew. But I've already thrown the blood at him.

What happens next? Something I hadn't expected.

Picture the blood, frozen in mid-air—

Kazia is desperately re-sealing her circle, gabbling incantations.

I'm curled up like a woodlouse inside the triangle, still clutching her sword and waving the pentacle in the air.

Alastor is legging it clockwise round the circle towards me, radiant with anticipation, axe held high.

Matthew has frozen with his hands up. But he needn't worry . . .

Because Akinbiyi is out of his circle. I think he was trying to grab me, but he missed and overshot, and as he turned to scamper back to safety he took the blood full in the face. It's dripping down his surcoat and he's suddenly the dish of the day!

Alastor keeps going past me. I see his feet leave scorch marks on the tiles, but I don't watch any more. It sounds bad enough. When I open my eyes, Akinbiyi has gone – to hell, if that's what you want to believe. There's nothing left of him anyway, just the blood from the chalice spattered across the floor and Alastor on his hands and knees, licking it up with a long green tongue.

Finally he looks up. And farts.

CHAPTER THIRTY-ONE
Begone!

Back in Littlemore, Marvo and her mum are still sitting in the circle, wrapped up in the blanket.

We spend half an hour arguing, which at least gives me time to fix the gash in my hand. Finally I make a couple of shapes with my fingers and Mrs M collapses in a heap.

I fish my ring out of the sink, grab my backpack and drag Marvo and her duffel coat across to the termite nest, over the back wall and into my corridor . . .

Where some bastard has petrified my door. Literally turned it to stone.

'Now what?' Marvo says.

I interlace my fingers and stretch my arms above my head, palms up, until the bones crack. 'Relax,' I say. 'Watch a master at work.'

If the Society can issue licences to practise sorcery, it can take them away. There's no judicial proceeding, no right of appeal. Just an owl at your window with a message in its beak; or, more likely, a couple of large men on your doorstep. I figure this is their work: an incentive to go on that hike to Rome.

I'm not putting up with that.

There are creatures that can survive being frozen in ice. Petrification is the Society's standard technique for immobilising door elementals, so I built mine to handle it.

The first thing it needs is human warmth. My body, pressed against it. My hands, stroking it. And the sound of my voice:

'It's all right, I'm here. Mezekiel, Ramoth. It's all right, it's all right . . .'

After ten minutes the surface is warm to the touch. After fifteen it has the texture of wood. After twenty it gives a weak yelp and its head emerges. I tickle it behind the ears and ruffle its fur. I tell it how clever it is and that it's my good boy . . .

When I look round, Marvo's leaning against the wall, grinning.

'What?'

'If you were only half as good with people.'

Whatever. We're inside . . . and the place has been wrecked. The good news is that although they got into my cabinet, they didn't find the broom cupboard where I keep my really dangerous stuff. Even so, there's papers and gear all over the shop; herbs, spices and concoctions scattered; glassware smashed and a smell of piss. Since I'm not supposed to be able to get back in here anyway, this is pure malice.

Let's start with the costumes: we'll both need full sets of robes. While I rummage through the pile of clothes beside the wardrobe I finish telling Marvo what she's missed.

'So who's still alive?' she finally asks.

'Apart from Akinbiyi, everybody.'

Exorcised water. Myrrh, cinnamon and sweet-flag in olive oil. Salt. Incense.

Marvo frowns. 'What's to stop Kazia just dismissing the demon?'

'Without her sword?' I pick up a ragged black book. 'Suicide.'

'Perhaps we should just turn everything over to Caxton.' Marvo watches suspiciously as I stuff all the gear into my bag.

I grab two silver discs and start scratching away at them. 'Matthew is the Superior General of the Society of Sorcerers. That makes him one of the most powerful men in the country. I'm a suspended member of the Society with a grudge.'

'And the girl? It's her you're really worried about.'

There's this thing in her voice. I get resentment, sadness, resignation . . . and I realise that preparing instruments and remembering incantations is child's play compared to figuring how people tick.

I don't want to hurt Marvo, but it's like she's dead set on being hurt. 'I'm sorry . . .'

'She tried to kill us.'

Money for a cab: this has turned into a very expensive night. 'What's she supposed to do? The way she sees it, it's her or me.'

'What do you want to happen to her?'

'I want to meet her before any of this started. Can you fix that for me?'

In the corridor Marvo says, 'So what *are* you going to do?'

'I can't just leave her there.'

'But if you let her go, what about your boss?' Her eyes widen. 'You're going to feed him to the demon—'

I shake my head. 'I don't know what it'd do with him.'

'You don't believe in hell—'

'I *won't* believe in hell. I could be wrong.' I open the outside door. 'I usually am.' I hand her one of the silver discs and a gold chain. 'Here, you'll want this. Just stick it round your neck.'

She turns the disc to the light and peers at the design: two concentric circles with symbols scattered around the place. 'Will this work?'

'With luck.'

I realise that I really meant to turn Alastor on Matthew, until Akinbiyi got in the way. But that was in the heat of the moment.

I'm cool now.

My pentacle – the one I got off Kazia – is still where I

left it, at the bottom of the stairs where it prevents Alastor from passing. At the centre of the underground chamber, the girl of my dreams is standing in her circle, turning on the spot to face him as he prowls round the outside, stopping now and then to hack away with his axe. The Boss just watches from the protection of his own circle.

As I pick up the pentacle and drop it round my neck, Alastor turns and rushes at me, then skids to a halt, screaming with rage and frustration and giving off clouds of foul-smelling smoke.

Marvo has her instructions. I cut the grand circle and push her into it. As I follow and reseal the boundary behind me, she hands Kazia the third pentacle.

The Boss doesn't take long to smell a rat. I'm burning white candles and incense. I've thrown salt around the place and sprinkled exorcised water over everyone inside the circle. Alastor has stepped back and is standing there scratching his head with the tip of his knife. This isn't my usual stuff, so I'm doing it from the book I brought, with Marvo leaning over my shoulder, reading the responses.

'From all sin . . .'

'Deliver us O Lord.'

'From the snares of the Devil . . .'

'Deliver us O Lord.'

The Boss pipes up. 'This isn't your usual style, Frank.'

I ignore him and plough on. We've a lot to get through. Psalms. Bible stories . . .

The Rite for Exorcism, as defined by the Roman Ritual of 1614.

'What are you trying to do? Wriggle out of losing your licence? It's playing with demons, Frank, and I'll see you burn for it.'

The demon himself is watching intently. You should never attribute psychological motives to supernatural beings, but he's beginning to look very uneasy. I'm sticking to the Ritual:

'I command you, unclean spirit, by the mysteries of the incarnation, passion, resurrection, and ascension of our Lord Jesus Christ, by the descent of the Holy Spirit, by the coming of our Lord for judgement, that you tell me by some sign the day and hour of your departure.'

And Alastor explodes in flames. Through the smoke, I can see my dad beating frantically with his hands, trying to put the fire out. He sees me . . .

'Frank—'

His hair is on fire. His skin is blistering. He's kicking and screaming . . .

'For God's sake, Frank!'

I don't think any of the others can see this charade; it's just Alastor messing with my head. I charge on through the ritual, wondering if the fact that I really don't believe any of it makes any difference. Marvo gives the responses; her voice is trembling, but she never loses her place.

Matthew is struggling to work out why I don't just give Kazia her sword back and let her dismiss the demon like any normal sorcerer. He keeps repeating, 'What exactly are you hoping to achieve?'

Amid the smoke, my dad is rolling on the floor, begging me to fetch the fire brigade, my mum, his mother . . .

Only Kazia is utterly silent. She just stands there, looking down at the floor.

We've got to the point at last.

'I cast you out, unclean spirit, along with every Satanic power of the enemy, every spectre from hell, and all your fell companions; in the name of our Lord Jesus Christ.'

Kazia steps back as I turn to face her. Marvo grabs her arm to keep her in the circle and holds her tight while I dip my fingertip in the oil and trace a series of crosses across Kazia's forehead—

'Begone and stay far from this creature of God. For it is He who commands you, He who flung you head-long from the heights of heaven into the depths of hell. It is He who commands you, He who once stilled the sea and the wind and the storm. Hearken, therefore, and tremble in fear—'

I can hear my dad screaming, 'Please, Frank. Please, Frank—'

'I adjure you, profligate dragon, in the name of the spotless Lamb, who has trodden down the asp and the basilisk, and overcome the lion and the dragon, to depart from this woman.'

Who wrote this stuff? Anyway . . .

'The Word made flesh commands you; the Virgin's Son commands you; Jesus of Nazareth commands you—

'Depart from her!'

I throw holy water around. My dad sizzles and smokes.

'Depart from her!'

Marvo joins in the chant.

'Depart from her!'

And just like that, my dad has gone. The flames have vanished; the smoke has dispersed. Alastor climbs unsteadily to his feet and stumbles around gathering his scattered armoury.

He mutters, 'That hurt, Frank.'

'Sorry. I didn't write it.'

'Bloody sadists.' He picks up his axe and sticks it in his belt. 'OK, I'm ready. Get on with it.'

He visibly braces himself. But I close the Ritual. I take off my paper hat and nod to Marvo to do the same. 'I'm finished.'

I cut the circle and step out. Don't forget, I've got the pentacle round my neck. I'm not a complete fool.

'Frank.' That's my Master's voice. 'You can't just leave him here.'

I beckon Marvo out after me. 'Why not?'

'Well, what about me?'

'You'll be company for him.'

Matthew has gone white. You have no idea how gratifying that feels. Like I'm finally in charge and if I so much as flick one finger, whole nations will tremble and fall at my feet. It feels great.

So great, that I'm sure I must have missed something.

Marvo isn't convinced either. 'What if he gets out?'

'Thanks for reminding me.'

I dig a piece of paper and a stick of charcoal out of my pocket. As I copy a series of symbols down each side of the wall beside the foot of the staircase, I hear Kazia's voice:

'What about me?'

'The exorcism severed the affinity, so he has no particular interest in you. You're protected.' I point to the pentacle round her neck. 'And once I've finished this, he can't leave the chamber.'

'And if someone wanders down here?' Matthew says.

'I'll maintain the concealment spell.'

'I'll starve.'

'I'll organise sandwiches.'

As Kazia steps tentatively out of the circle, Alastor

moves towards her. She flinches as he raises the scourge. But then his eyes fix on the pentacle. He stops dead. The scourge drops to his side, the chains rattling almost regretfully.

She ducks past him. She stops beside me.

And I realise I'm waiting for her to kiss me.

Coz I did save her, didn't I? I mean, I could've fed her to Alastor. I could've done a deal with Matthew and let the Inquisition have her. But I didn't and I figure that's worth at least a peck on the cheek.

And I think she did fancy me a bit. OK, a tiny bit. A very tiny bit.

And even if she was playing me for a fool, there was this other thing: I was a sorcerer.

I mean, imagine you're Kazia. You've got the Gift, but it's always been this secret thing that could get you killed. Matthew knows Wallace is making you do creepy stuff, but he does nothing to stop it . . .

Did either of them ever tell her she was clever or special?

I realise Kazia was always scared of me, right from that first morning in the Bishop's Palace when she leaned over the stairs and watched Marvo drag me in. But I figure she wanted to be friends with me too, because she realised she could only be herself – you know, the girl with the Gift – with another sorcerer who understood all the crap flying around.

So what about that kiss? I'm still waiting, but she's

got this blank, closed-down expression on her face again, like I'm a total stranger. She darts across to the staircase.

'Where are you going?' I ask.

'You think I'll tell you?'

Another reason to be thankful for the absence of mirrors down here. I wouldn't want to see my own face right now. I feel like I've been sat on by a horse.

'I'm sorry, Frank. I like you . . .'

She makes this weird gesture, like she's rubbing dirt off a table or something.

I'm desperate. I know Marvo and Matthew are listening, so I whisper, 'We could – you know, what we said before. Get out of here.'

'I didn't mean it.'

'But it's not impossible . . .'

'Oh Frank.' She takes my hand. This is progress, isn't it? 'I can't go home. They'd kill me.'

'They'll kill you here.'

'I know people. My father's here.'

'You can't trust him.'

'I understand him.' Her fingers brush across my cheek. 'I'm sorry, Frank, I don't understand you. I mean, you can't look after *yourself* . . . What can you do with me?'

'I'll think of something.'

'You won't get your licence back.'

'How do you know?'

396

'Working for Matthew . . .' I can't help following her gaze towards him. He's standing there in his circle, arms folded. I hate it when she calls him by his first name. 'I think I understand the Society better than you do.'

I've pulled my hand away.

'I did magic for him,' she says. 'That's all.'

Alastor sneers. 'That's what she says!'

But I don't believe him. I turn back to Kazia. 'And Wallace?'

'You do what you must do.' I get this final sad smile out of her. 'You will see now.'

And she turns and runs off, up the stairs. I shout after her:

'Wait!'

'Leave me alone!'

I race after her. I'm halfway up when a chair comes bouncing down and knocks me for six. By the time I pick myself up and get to the top, she's long gone.

I yell, 'Marvo!'

'What?'

'Can we just get out of here?'

CHAPTER THIRTY-TWO

Jump

Iclose my eyes and see Kazia stepping out of the
circle, her face blank like she doesn't even know me.
I don't like that, so I open them and Marvo's staring
across at me.

'You were right, Frank.'

'Right about what? I mean, I haven't been right
about anything since this whole stupid mess started.'

We picked up a cab outside the railway station, and
now we're heading past the Oxpens. Through the
window, I can see the ragged silhouette of the scaffolding round the cathedral spire, exactly like that first
morning. I didn't realise you could have so much fun in
just ten days.

'You were right to give her a chance.'

'You wouldn't be saying that if I'd got you and your
mum killed.'

Marvo smiles. 'Take more'n a demon to kill my mum.'

I've got used to her bleached hair. Trouble is, it
reminds me of Kazia and it's like Marvo's reading my

thoughts because she says, 'If she asked you . . . you know, to help her again—'

'Not that she would.'

'Yeah, but you'd do it, right?'

I nod.

'Must be love then. Nothing else could be that stupid!'

I can't think of anything to say.

'So what you gonna do now?' Marvo asks.

I shrug. 'Any ideas?'

'Talk to Caxton.'

I shake my head. 'The Society wants me to go to Rome. That's what I'm going to do.'

'You're kidding!'

'Any better ideas? Matthew isn't there to defend me any more. If I don't go . . . well, it's only a month to bonfire night.'

Marvo doesn't say anything for a while, just sits there with her face turned away, staring out of the window. At last she says, 'There must be someone else you can trust.'

'Just you and Charlie.'

'Charlie can't help you—'

'And *you'd* better not try. Just forget about me.'

She goes red and says, 'I don't think I can do that.'

OK, I'm slow but I finally get it. Reg Garston was right. But it's like Marvo's handed me this present, all beautifully wrapped up with a satin bow, and I know it cost her a pile of money and I feel grateful . . . and incredibly embarrassed and actually a bit pissed off, because I've got absolutely no idea what to do with it.

So I sit there and stare at it and don't even unwrap it, which is a crap thing to do.

'Then I'm sorry.' I don't know what else to say.

Yeah, I know it's unfair. I get to fancy Kazia, but I can't handle Marvo fancying me. Because I realise that Marvo really means it. And of course the whole point about Kazia was that in my heart of hearts I always knew she was winding me up, so it felt . . . well, kind of safe.

Apart from Alastor, obviously.

Anyway we ride on and after a bit Marvo shakes her head and says, 'You can't just leave him down there.'

'Huh?'

'Your boss . . .'

'I can't feed him to Alastor.'

'You can't afford to let him go.'

'So he'd better get used to the sandwiches.'

'The demon,' says Marvo. 'Won't he get bored or something?'

'No idea. There's nothing in any of the grimoires about a situation like this.' I smile. 'I'm breaking new ground.'

She pulls out her scryer. 'Let me call Caxton.'

I grab her arm before she can open the lid. There's this wrestling match, but I'm stronger than her.

'Did I hurt you?'

She shakes her head. 'You can't help her.'

'I can give her a head start. There's still stuff in my studio I gotta get rid of. And you and me, we've got to get your story straight . . .'

So we argue about that all the way back to her mum's place. We agree that none of last night happened and that she knows nothing about Groce's body disappearing from the suicide plot.

Finally she nods. 'That'll have to do.'

We're at her place. I check my magic watch. 'I'll say goodbye now.'

I see her hand move. It's going to be another of those cheek-patting moments and I really haven't got the strength for it any more. I lean back. I can see she's upset, but I can't help that.

'You were going to help me with Sean.'

'Now's not a good time.' There was never a good time. 'I'm sorry.'

She gives me this sad smile and gets out. As she pushes the front gate open, the surviving hinge finally gives up the struggle and the whole thing collapses. She kicks the rotten fragments savagely into the bushes and walks up to the house. She stops on the doorstop and shouts back at me:

'What about my mum?'

'She's just hypnotised. She'll wake up in an hour or two – won't remember a thing.'

The red duffel coat disappears into the house. The door closes. I bang on the roof of the cab.

The first train up to London is at 5.24. I'm back at the station with just enough time to buy a ticket and get noticed.

He's this great long streak of misery with a moustache. He's wearing a porter's peaked cap and jacket, but he hasn't lifted a suitcase in living memory. I know him because he used to show up at Saint Cyprian's when I was there. He's one of the Knights of Saint Cyprian's plainclothes goons. He hangs around the station, watching who comes and goes, and scries the Society if anything interesting happens.

He clocks me and the pilgrim's emblem I've pinned to the front of my woolly hat. I pretend I haven't noticed him. The train arrives. Yeah, I know I'm supposed to walk, but why should I be the only one to compromise?

I glance back as the train pulls out. The streak of misery is on his scryer.

We trundle past the Bishop's Palace and the cathedral, and bang over Boney's Bridge.

A bit further down the line, they've been working on the Black Bridge at Nuneham for months and the trains have to slow right down to cross it.

I'm ready, with the door open and steam and hot

cinders blowing in my face. I thought we'd be going slower. Don't think about it, Frank. Just jump.

There's a crash and all the breath is knocked out of me. I'm spinning and bouncing, and then I'm lying in the long grass at the bottom of the embankment, hoping that nobody's seen me. Nothing broken; just a few scrapes and bruises. I open my backpack and pull out the repair kit.

When everything's stopped hurting, I get to my feet, pull out a trowel and dig a small hole at the foot of a tree. I bury a small tin, its lid sealed with wax. I fill in the hole and conceal it. I toss the trowel into the river and start the long walk back along the bank to Doughnut City.

A hundred yards along, a flock of crows have come in to feed on the field beside the path. I run at them, yelling and screaming and waving my arms, and they scatter up into the sky.

Frank returns in Donald Hounam's
follow-up novel,
PARIAH

Read on for an extract . . .

Let's start with a chase and see how things go from there . . .

The guys doing the chasing, there's six of them. Knights of Saint Cyprian, the Society of Sorcerers' goon squad. They're fashionably attired in bronze helmets, with black capes over silver breastplates. The moon-light gleams dangerously on the swords they're waving.

The guy they're after? Me, natch.

The Knights are on horseback, so they're a lot faster than me. But I've got a head start and once I've jumped down the embankment from the main road and scut-tled into the woods, I've got the edge. I hear a crash and a yell. I look round and see one of them hanging from the branch of a tree while his horse disappears into the undergrowth.

More crashing and swearing as they all dismount and realise that the weight of all that metal means they can hardly move.

I stop to yell. 'Nah, nah, nah, nah, nah!'

An arrow hisses past my ear and thunks into the tree trunk beside me.

They never really made it out of the middle ages, the Knights. Everyone else has got guns and stuff; they're still arsing about with bows and arrows. Doesn't make them any less dangerous right now, though. I get running again, along a narrow track that twists down-hill through the trees.

More crashing noises behind me. I turn to look over

my shoulder and go flying over a tree root. As I hunt around for the small tin that I've dropped, I see that the Knights have dumped their helmets and armour but have decided to hang on to their swords.

Officially these guys are the Society's disciplinary branch, but that's just a polite way of saying they're thugs who get paid to smash things the Society can't be bothered to use magic on. They might have been Gifted as kids, but it never developed so, unlike me, they never made it as sorcerers. Also unlike me, they're fit and they're gaining on me.

I've found my tin and I'm on my feet, puffing and panting my way out of the woods. I dash across a street in front of a cab. The horse rears up. I duck a flailing hoof and dash down an alleyway between two houses. The Knights are about fifty yards behind. I can hear the bell ringing in the termite nest, just up ahead of me, and I'm working out my options . . .

Option A: I go round the back of the termite nest. But my legs are starting to shake now and there's a pain in my side and I doubt if I can make it over a twelve-foot wall before the Knights grab me.

Option B: I make for the front gate. The trouble is, the usual arseholes from the ASB – the Anti-Sorcery Brotherhood – will be waiting there for me. And the gate's probably shut and by the time I've rung the bell . . . well, see Option A.

But I've got a secret weapon. I mutter under my

breath and make shapes with my fingers, and when I open my hand there's a white mouse running round the palm in tiny circles. I blow on it—

Not a real mouse, by the way: I don't keep wildlife up my sleeves. Like I said, I'm a sorcerer, not a conjurer; it's just a simple elemental.

I lob it over my shoulder.

It doesn't do anything – doesn't even glow in the dark – just lands on the cobbles behind me and squeaks. I hear gasps and when I glance over my shoulder the Knights have screeched to a halt just short of it and are approaching it nervously, swords raised.

The mouse squeaks again and vanishes in a puff of green smoke, and by the time the Knights have recovered I'm out of the alley and across the street – right into the arms of the ASB.

Is there anybody out here who hasn't got it in for me?

What can I tell you? They're a brotherhood. And they're against sorcery. There's three of them, all in clerical robes. One to hold the lantern, one to clutch a long pole with a pointy metal cross on the end, and one to paint 'God will find you out' in big, drippy red letters on the wall opposite the monastery gate.

'It's him!' I've met the fat arse with the cross before, and we didn't exactly hit it off. 'The nekker!'

The can of paint comes flying through the air at me. I duck and it hits one of the Knights bang on the head. Shouldn't have ditched his helmet: he lets out a yelp of pain and charges past me, waving his sword. The three priests look at each other and take to their heels. As all the Knights chase after them, I hang out of the bell-pull beside the monastery gate and pray that someone will hear it over the din of the chapel bell.

The Knights have reconsidered their priorities and done a sharp turn. They're coming at me, swords gleaming ominously. I figure I've got about five seconds.

Four seconds later I've only got one of those seconds left and I'm beginning to worry that I've miscalculated badly . . . when the door opens.

Brother Thomas is my least favourite termite – Agrippine monks, by the way, a small order set up to look after sorcerers until Satan comes for them.

'Brother Tobias?' he gasps, fumbling for his spectacles. That's me, but for God's sake just stick to Frank.

I don't have to push him over; his eyes roll up in their sockets and he goes over backwards with a thump that shakes the city. I have that effect on a lot of people these days.

I jump over him and run past the lodge, across the cloister and into a dark corridor. Judging by the thud of heavy boots, the Knights are catching up again.

I skid round a blind corner – straight into a mob of termites, all filing out of the chapel clutching candles that flicker in the draught.

I've got this spell on me, sort of. Anyway, it kicks in big time: they're dropping like skittles before I can even bang into them. The candles flare up for a moment and I glimpse startled eyes, red from weeping. Something spills down my neck: hot wax or snot. A framed photograph smashes on the flagstones and I recognise the old Japanese bloke in the yellow and white robes as Pope Innocent XVII, who sadly can't be here in person tonight because he's busy dying in Rome.

I guess that's what the termites are all so upset about. But I don't have time to stop and offer my sympathies or a blow on my handkerchief. I trample my way through the pile of bodies and run on, appreciating the scuffling and yelling behind me as the Knights go falling over them.

I'm through a heavy door, flying down a flight of stone steps in one jump. My knees buckle under me and I nearly go sprawling. Under the circumstances, it seems wise to ignore the path, which winds all over the place, and take the direct route across the vegetable garden to my studio. I plough through the strawberry bed and crash through a row of bean poles. I take a flying leap over a lavender hedge and as I land my knees finally give up the struggle. I fall flat on my face. The tin rolls away and before I can grab it there's a whoop of triumph, right behind me.

I roll over on my back and this huge bloke, dripping red paint and with a face like a mutant potato, is looming over me, sword raised . . .